# Beetle Mania

Also by Paula Clamp

*Standing in a Hammock*

# Beetle Mania

## PAULA CLAMP

POOLBEG

This novel is entirely a work of fiction. The names,
characters and incidents portrayed in it are the work of the
author's imagination. Any resemblance to actual persons,
living or dead, events or localities is entirely coincidental.

Published 2003
by Poolbeg Press Ltd.
123 Grange Hill, Baldoyle,
Dublin 13, Ireland
Email: poolbeg@poolbeg.com

©Paula Clamp 2003

The moral right of the author has been asserted.

Copyright for typesetting, layout, design
© Poolbeg Group Services Ltd.

1 3 5 7 9 10 8 6 4 2

A catalogue record for this book is available from the British Library.

ISBN 1-84223-090-5

Typeset by Patricia Hope in Goudy 11/14.5
Printed by
Litografia Rosés S.A., Spain

www.poolbeg.com

## About the Author

Born in Nottinghamshire, England, Paula Clamp has lived in Northern Ireland since 1986. She is married with three young children. A theatre studies graduate from the University of Ulster, her plays have been performed in Belfast and Dublin. She has Masters degrees in Cultural Management and Anglo-Irish literature. She is a keen volleyball player and has played for Northern Ireland. *Beetle Mania* is her second novel.

# Acknowledgements

Special thanks to Paula and her team at Poolbeg and my editor Gaye. To the K Blundell Trust for their support. To the Tyrone Guthrie Centre at Annaghmakerrig for showing me how much I can achieve without three screaming weeins. To the three screaming weeins themselves: Jordan for her never-ending questions, Yana for making me wonder if there's an alien mother in outer space wondering where her earth-child came from – and Jay, who, as I was putting the finishing touches to this book, was setting off on his own journey by taking his first steps.

Thanks to my mate Linda for the invaluable insight into living with double D boobs and, literally, filling a gap in my own personal experience.

And finally, Gerry, for getting so involved in the book, that he feels compelled to tell everyone that he wrote it . . .

*For Jay*

## The Farrell Sisters, Present Day

# Chapter 1

Porn. Not exactly what Kitty O'Kane first had in mind when she and her husband decided on a romantic Saturday afternoon. But, what the hell, after fifteen years of marriage, maybe *Bed-knobs and Big Dicks* would do the trick.

"Pause it," suddenly interrupted Dermot, Kitty's husband.

She pressed the pause button, causing a close-up of Erik and Freda's naked rear-ends to flicker and gyrate ever so slightly.

"That's the camper van I was thinking we should get," said Dermot, panting slightly. "Look at that interior!"

Erik and Freda were cavorting in a rather stylish Wayfarer camper van. Kitty advanced the film frame by frame. The endless groans of '*Sehr gut!*' had been distracting, especially when there was a mini-fridge and built-in wardrobes to study. So, Kitty had already turned down the volume.

"Look at the size of that storage cupboard!" she contributed. As soon as the words left her lips, she was smacked full pelt

1

with the realisation of what they were discussing. Ouch, it hurt!

The enlightenment was purely one-sided.

"That's never a dishwasher in there!" Dermot exclaimed as Erik lifted Freda onto one of the kitchen work-surfaces. He rubbed his chin as he carefully studied the video. His week-old whiskers, which were grey speckled with bits of dirty-blond, began to itch. To Kitty, it wasn't that long ago that the whiskers had been dirty-blond speckled with bits of grey. He was naked except for the leopard-print boxer-shorts that Kitty had bought for him which were, slightly optimistically, two sizes too big.

Freda had changed positions and was now sitting astride Erik.

"Can you imagine how much stuff you could pack into those drawers?" Dermot now had a full-on shot of the kitchen area. The itching on his chin began to intensify. The whiskers on his face were the same length as the hair on his head, leaving only his forehead, the skin just below his eyes and his slightly Roman nose hair-free. In an attempt to economise over the last few months, Kitty had invested in a pair of hair-clippers and was responsible for the male-grooming function in the O'Kane household. She had only two hairstyles in her repertoire: a Number 1 all-over and a Number 1 with a very small spiky fringe. Her five-year-old daughter begged for the latter and Dermot got the former without asking. The all-over effect on her husband was that of an inflated pufferfish. But this was a small price to pay for saving five pounds every month. In addition, she charged two pounds for every man and boy in the neighbourhood. The money Kitty had charged the twins next door, first thing that morning, had paid for the blue movie and a packet of *Merry Maids* – half of which had been given to their daughter on the way to her sleepover. The loose change had then been ceremoniously added to the 'New Car' fund, which was an overflowing Bell's Whisky magnum hidden in the wardrobe.

Dermot chomped on the last of the toffees as he took the remote control from his wife and began to fast-forward through the boring bits – the bits that didn't show the full range of camper-van appliances. Oblivious to his wife's gaze, he enthusiastically scrutinised every detail.

Kitty dropped her head into her left palm and softly massaged the bridge of her nose with her fingers. She could feel its small indentation chiselled into an otherwise rather flat surface. Kitty and her two younger sisters all had the distinctive 'Farrell' nose, which was credited to their father, Roddy. The fact that Roddy had a wide but perfectly straight nose, until it was broken in a pub brawl when he was eighteen, was neither here nor there. The indentation was part of the package.

Kitty's father was expected later that afternoon, to take part in an unorthodox farewell party where he would play a key role. He was also expected to fulfil his promise to deliver a surprise package for his three daughters.

The living-room felt dark and cold. This was the largest room in the small terrace house and had two doors – one, the front door and the other leading to the kitchen. The warm rays of the early spring sun were held back by the tightly drawn, rich-velour curtains. Their heavy burgundy folds shielded the couple's X-rated movie from prying eyes and guarded the twenty-one-inch television set from the blinding sun which would otherwise threaten to bleach out Erik and Freda's nakedness behind a veil of dust-flecks.

Kitty slowly edged herself along the sofa, away from Dermot. The 'romantic afternoon' was her husband's idea. He said it would help take her mind off the big farewell. But it wasn't doing that. She now locked her arms across her chest. Combined with the 'Farrell' nose, Kitty and her sisters also shared a DD bra size. Naturally this characteristic couldn't be credited to their father and was bestowed *in memoriam* on their mother. She had haemorrhaged during childbirth and died shortly after presenting Roddy Farrell with his third daughter.

Kitty could now sense her own voluptuous 38DDs heave within her tightly laced basque, which Dermot had bought for her and was, optimistically, two sizes too small.

She felt anxious. She had to eat.

Even though Kitty's day had been troubled, as regards food she had been good up until now. Good in the sense that she'd eaten only the allowed quota of cabbage soup with one banana for breakfast and she had skipped dessert entirely. But now Kitty's heart sank. She reached for the coffee table in the centre of the small room. The slab of MDF had a cherry-wood veneer and four stout MDF legs. Dotted across the table was an assortment of mismatched bowls. These were Kitty's 'nibbling bowls' and pivotal to her campaign to lose weight. Whenever a hunger-pang threatened, the bowls provided comfort. The first bowl Kitty reached for contained a mountain of white muscat grapes. Each one had been individually washed and peeled. Kitty devoured each of their vulnerable, fleshy bodies in one bite. The largest bowl contained a low-fat chilli dip, surrounded by chunky slices of red and yellow peppers. The rules of the house stipulated that once dipped, the peppers could not then be bitten and re-dipped. Kitty didn't feel comfortable sharing her food or sharing the food of others. Even with her own daughter, she wouldn't share her fork or lick her ice-cream. Whenever Kitty wasn't looking, Dermot took great delight in raiding the fridge and guzzling the milk straight from the bottle. The mystery of how Kitty ever allowed herself to exchange bodily fluids with another person was a puzzle, even to her husband. The rest of the bowls contained thick chunks of scrubbed, raw vegetables. Having devoured all of the peeled grapes, Kitty began to chomp on a piece of carrot. Her stomach gurgled in protest.

Erik was now standing behind Freda, as she leant over the kitchen sink, with her face squashed against the window.

"Now that's what I call a good set of mixer-taps," Dermot said, mesmerised, "and is that . . . hang on a minute!" He rewound the videotape a couple of frames. "I thought so . . . a disposal unit!"

Kitty's focus was elsewhere. She was thinking of her father. She thought about the package he was bringing and how eager he was for all the Farrell sisters to be there. Kitty was also apprehensive about another matter: the letters she had been secretly sending to England. Was she ready to face her demons? Her husband was oblivious as to how she was feeling, but Kitty knew that this couldn't last.

Chewing on a celery-stick brought a moment of relief as

5

she was distracted by the sinewy pieces stuck between her teeth. The ebony wisps of her fringe refused to stay tucked behind her ears and fell across her burnt-caramel eyes. Along with the avalanche of emotions Kitty felt exposed to today, irritability could now be added.

"Imagine one of them parked outside, instead of that old thing!" Dermot had yet to take his eyes off the television screen. Squinting, he studied the video more closely. It was important that he knew which were standard fittings and which were optional extras when they visited the Camper Van Showroom tomorrow. Of course, Kitty knew they barely had the funds for a bumper, but why burst his bubble?

Dermot was itching to get there. The sooner he was there, the sooner he'd be back. He was frequently the butt of Kitty's sisters' jokes. Heather and Emer Farrell thought of their brother-in-law as the man who didn't travel too well – 'like a three-year-old on a rollercoaster, with a belly full of blancmange'. Dermot's final destination in life was always back home. If he went anywhere at all, it was only so he could come home again, as soon as possible. Whenever he did venture out, he would check his watch every ten minutes or so. He much preferred telling and re-telling the story of what he'd been up to, than the actual experience of it. For Dermot, these days, the act of reminiscence was always preferable to actual living.

Erik and Freda collapsed in an exhausted heap on the floor of the camper van. Freda looked at Erik with huge doe-eyes and the scene faded.

"I've enough notes for now. I could go and get some brochures and still be back within the hour, Kitty . . . Kitty!"

His wife was no longer sitting beside him on the sofa. For a brief moment he thought that he was all alone. The room was dotted with the heavy presence of imitation cherry-wood furniture, laden with the vanilla-cream Beleek pottery. The indentation remained on the sofa, where his wife had been sitting.

"Here, Kitty-Kitty!" Dermot chuckled to himself and then he saw the outline of her shape hidden behind the heavy curtains.

She was sobbing.

"I'm sorry, sweetheart! Here's me thinking about the van's mixer-taps, when this time was supposed to be for us – for romance. Come back on the sofa and see the size of this guy's –"

But Kitty interrupted Dermot by sobbing even louder. The outline of her head, shoulders and hips now rocked against the shroud of velour.

"Please, honey," pleaded Dermot, as he pulled the curtain back and let in a flood of sunlight.

Kitty ignored her husband and, still sobbing, stared out of the window, to the street outside. A couple of boys were kicking their football against the front wall and two men in their early twenties strolled past, pushing prams. All had Number 1 haircuts with short spiky fringes, as did the elderly man who then rushed past, dragged by his Border collie. Each of them appeared, or rather 'pretended' to appear, oblivious to the scantily dressed woman at the window.

Above the crumbling brick wall, Kitty could see the source of her deep despair. She could see the reason why she felt nothing but gloom and blackness. At four o'clock that afternoon, not only would the mystery parcel be hers, but she would also be saying farewell to the one constant presence in her life. Since she was a teenager, growing up with her two sisters and her father, there had been only one thing that had truly been close to Kitty's heart. She gazed out of the window, like she had done countless times before and, for the last time, whispered "Goodbye".

# Chapter 2

Tommy turned down the volume on the car CD player. He had something very important to say to Heather. If it wasn't the CD player, it was the television's remote control or even the extractor hood in the kitchen. Noise interference wasn't acceptable when he had an announcement to make. He then took his foot off the accelerator pedal, again reducing the noise level and allowing him more time to make his point, before they arrived at his girlfriend's sister's house. Heather's sister, Kitty, lived in a modest terrace house in the university area of Belfast. The property had been equally modestly priced when bought four years earlier, but now they were the only family left in a street of high-earning student bed-sits. Heather and Tommy were only a few minutes away on the Ormeau Road. They had only recently bought an apartment there together.

"You know, Heather, this farewell is long overdue. . ." Tommy was slowly building up his argument, for effect, "and there's to be no going back."

Heather sensed a degree of unfamiliar sensitivity in her boyfriend's tone. But she wasn't about to let down her guard. After all, he had helped her construct it over all these years. Tommy sensed this and changed tack.

"And do you want my honest opinion about what you're wearing?" Tommy added, without stopping for breath or waiting for a response. "It's not that I don't like it. I love it. But is it appropriate? You know, for such a big send-off. And with your old man there and all."

Heather had been waiting for this day for nearly ten years, when she had missed the opportunity to take matters into her own hands. So, for the occasion, she had chosen to wear tight black Lycra hipsters and a sunflower-yellow, acrylic T-shirt, with plunging neckline. For the last ten of Heather Farrell's thirty-two years, her dress-size had periodically fluctuated between a size 14 and 18, depending on whether she was in or out of love. The more unhappy in a relationship she became, the more she ate. This morning she was forced to put her size 16 black trousers back into the wardrobe and pull out her 18s. Her voluptuous 42 DD breasts were precariously balanced above the neckline of her T-shirt. 'The Lads' or more specifically 'Jackie and Bruce' as Tommy called them, were on parade. Named after Jackie Chan and Bruce Lee, 'two right hard nips', Heather's breasts were a great source of entertainment for her boyfriend. Heather herself was more concerned with why teenage waifs should have a monopoly on fashion. She began to try to explain this, but Tommy had turned the radio volume back up and had his foot gradually increasing the pressure on the accelerator pedal.

The windscreen on Tommy's granite BMW began to

mist over. Waves of smeared marks, where Heather had wiped the screen with her fingers the last time she had driven the car, began to appear. Her boyfriend tutted. Outside the car, the afternoon temperature had taken a sudden drop from its spring freshness to a hint of frost and a sprinkle of fine rain. Heather's head bounced on the headrest as Tommy swerved between lanes, in an attempt to dodge the slow-moving traffic. Fallen dyed-damson strands from Heather's tightly curled, shoulder-length hair, blemished the pristine beige upholstery. Indicating right off the main road, Tommy then reached over and turned down the stereo volume again.

"I love the way you look. You know that," offered Tommy.

Have you looked at yourself recently? thought Heather, but, "What's wrong with it?" was what she replied.

"Nothing's wrong, as such. It's just not, you know, appropriate." Tommy whispered 'appropriate' like it was a dirty word.

You miserable bastard, thought his girlfriend, before choosing, "You still haven't said exactly what's wrong with what I have on."

"Your father won't approve," Tommy blundered onwards.

Heather was silent.

"And your bra."

"What about my bra?"

"You know."

"What do I know?"

"It's a bit wee," Tommy pointed out, eventually. "That's all. It's nothing personal. You look lovely to me." He reached over and squeezed his girlfriend's right knee.

11

Tommy hadn't a hair out of place or a crease where it shouldn't be. Like Heather, he was thirty-two years old but, ever since she had known him, he always dressed like a man twenty years his senior. The neatly cut short-back-and-sides offset a crisp yellow cotton shirt with white collar, and fawn slacks, tightly belted rather too high for Heather's preference. They were pulled up so high that the outline of his wedding tackle was clearly visible and he drew attention to it by fidgeting in between gear-changes.

Heather had found his old-fashionedness quite charming when they first met nearly eight years before. He was punctual, always brought flowers and it was three months before he even hinted at taking their relationship to a 'physical level'. He had also written her poems, held her forehead when she was vomiting and said she was the most beautiful woman he'd ever seen.

"You look like an old slapper." Tommy had changed.

Heather still had some pride left. "Why do I?"

"Do you need me to tell you?" Tommy said matter-of-factly.

"Yes."

"Oh." The hesitancy in Tommy's voice betrayed his sudden realisation that he had reached rock bottom and was starting to dig. Ordinarily, Heather would not have been so stubborn. She was known for her sunny outlook and positive disposition. But then, this was no ordinary afternoon. Even Tommy appreciated that. The demister in the car had fully cleared the windscreen and the road ahead was a sea of winking tail-lights.

"I'm not saying you don't look nice. You do. You look lovely. Really. It's me. I'm just old-fashioned." When Tommy

12

opened his mouth, it seemed that it was only to change whichever foot was previously in there.

"Really. You don't say," Heather quickly interjected. "Will I go back and change? Is that what you want?"

"No, forget what I said. I didn't mean it." He forced a smile, but it didn't sit comfortably on his scrunched face. Once again he turned up the volume on the CD player and Celine Dion burst forth.

"You did mean it," fumed Heather, as Tommy obliviously drummed to the beat of the music on the steering wheel.

She looked down and all she could see in the shadow of her voluptuous chest were her small delicate hands, clenched tightly. The nails were long and manicured, emphasised by the recently painted, midnight-blue, translucent nail polish.

They were now only minutes away from the farewell party and Heather felt a sickness churning in her stomach. She had rehearsed her farewell speech time and time again. Would it be different from those of her sisters? She wasn't sure, but would theirs be as heartfelt?

The smattering of rain suddenly gave way to a torrential downpour and the pedestrians on both sides of the street ran for cover in shop doorways. The students used their folders and expensive-looking library books to shield their heads. A couple of elderly women improvised with plastic carrier-bags, in an attempt to protect their baby-blue perms. The traffic was at a standstill. Tommy's car was blockaded, immediately in front of the main gates leading to the looming 1850s brickwork that was Queen's University. The students were ignoring the red pedestrian light and sprinting haphazardly across the road, awkwardly dodging and weaving. But then, quickly, the mob of swerving individuals became a single mass of soaking bodies, forming a human barrier across the road.

And then one of them stopped. Right in the middle of the road, he stopped and lifted his face directly up into the full force of the rain. There was something strong and powerful about him. Heather thought and hoped that she recognised the man, but she wasn't sure.

"Daft eejit," leered Tommy. He seized a momentary break in the crowd as an opportunity to hurtle his car forwards and cut through the throng of drenched people. The man Heather had been drawn to melted away, back into the pack. On the CD player, a slow ballad drifted away, only to be replaced by another. As quickly as it had arrived, the heavy rain deserted the roads and inky puddles grew out of the oily tarmac. Tommy swerved the car around them so as not to drench a group of students waiting at a bus stop. As Celine Dion was about to explode into her final high note, she was rudely silenced –Tommy had something else to say.

"You know not to listen to me, Heather," he mumbled, trying to salvage some shreds from their argument. "I was only joking. You look terrific."

But the Heather he had known all those years and even the Heather he thought he knew as they had set out on their journey a few minutes ago had, like the rain, evaporated. Words were going to be said that afternoon that had taken a long time to rehearse and Heather had a few to practise right now.

"Well, sweetheart, I'm not joking when I say this," she

hissed as she squeezed Tommy's left knee. "When tonight is over, I don't ever want to see you again."

The BMW made an abrupt stop in Kitty and Dermot's driveway. This time, the radio, the engine and the two passengers were completely silent.

# Chapter 3

With her eyes tightly closed, Emer Farrell could be anywhere she wanted. She could feel the muscle contractions all over her body begin to ebb and the spasms relax. The duvet against her naked back and legs felt cool and soft. The tension in her shoulders melted away as the spasms of the orgasm dissolved and evaporated.

"Mummy, he won't let me play with his Action Man!" came a pitiful plea from outside her bedroom door. Emer opened her eyes. A flood of stencilled Japanese symbols, set against magnolia-painted walls flashed before her. She rolled over, onto her side. Emer was alone in the bed. As she had been for five years now.

"He's not sharing!" the same tiny voice pleaded again. Emer pulled up her Levi jeans and pulled down her white 'Morgan' T-shirt. She knew she was too old for both, but she didn't care. She hadn't lost three stone over the past six months for nothing. Her 36DD proportions stretched the bold, black lettering of *Morgan* on her chest, with the M and the N being grossly enlarged. Her hair was a wild explosion of short, ebony spirals, firing out in every direction but downwards.

She raced over to the locked bedroom door and bellowed, *"If you two don't stop it, I'll give you something to cry about!"* There was a moment of guilty silence. "The pair of you get dressed and get your things sorted out." Then she added with equal conviction, "Your daddy will be here any minute."

She returned to her bed, balanced a hand-mirror on her knees and began applying heavy charcoal eyeliner to the outside rim of her eyelids. The pencil was old and blunt. It was easier to use on the bottom lid and, when she smudged it with her finger, she was reasonably pleased with the result. A dab of Vaseline on top of her mulberry-pink lipstick and the effect was satisfactory.

"Gorgeous," she mimed to herself, revealing blobs of lipstick smeared on her front teeth.

The doorbell rang and she could hear the avalanche of tiny feet as they raced to the front door. She allowed herself one calming sigh and then hurried to meet their expected visitor.

The front door was already open and there stood a pair of muddy boots, leading up to a grubby pair of jeans, a tired-looking, navy-blue sweatshirt, a dirty neck and eventually a luminous shock of red hair. Tightly twisting a Chinese burn on the man's left wrist was James, Emer's eldest son, aged twelve. As he attempted to dodge the man's right fist, all that could be seen of him was his halo of bright red hair – a mirror-image of the visitor. Wedged tightly against the man's right leg was Luca, Emer's second son, aged five. His ebony curls and chocolate-brown eyes radiated joy and absolute excitement. For a brief moment Emer was pleased to see her visitor. But the moment passed, quickly.

"No late-night movies, no McDonald's and, William, don't forget to get them to brush their teeth," chanted Emer.

"Give us a break. I've only just got here and you're already having a go," replied William, with both his feet now pinned to the doorway. He noted the rosy glow on Emer's cheeks, but didn't comment.

"And keep them off the diggers," she said, barely stopping to catch her breath. She was known for her limited capacity to listen and was always busy planning what she was going to say next. "And keep them away from nails, hammers and anything pointy," she added.

Emer, at thirty-six and the middle daughter, still lived in the family hometown of Portstewart, on the Antrim coast – a small, 'nice place to retire to' kind of town. William was the site-foreman on a new housing development, just a few miles away in Coleraine, a larger inland town. Portstewart, Coleraine and Portrush (a busy seaside town four miles up the coast) marked out an area known locally as *The Golden Triangle*. William lived in a caravan on the Coleraine building site and the free rent was a perk of his site-foreman position. For Emer's boys, the site was an Aladdin's cave. The team of bricklayers, joiners and plasterers included the children as their own and when they weren't fetching nails and bits of wood, the boys were making tea and collecting the wages. But for their mother, who could make a drama even out of the smallest detail in life, William's home was her worst nightmare.

"And have them back here in one piece by twelve tomorrow," she continued abruptly.

William just gave her a knowing smile – knowing that it would irritate her. It worked.

"What's that smirk supposed to mean?" she asked.

"Nothing."

"Well, stop it then."

Emer and William had lived together for eight years. They had never married, and William had moved out of the flat and into the caravan five years ago. Outsiders and distant acquaintances may have guessed at the reason for the separation. Anyone seeing William and the two boys for the first time would immediately doubt the parentage of the younger boy, Luca, especially since there could be no denying who the eldest son belonged to. But to those close to the family, the family themselves and even William, there was never any doubt.

William peeled both boys away from him, and with one over each shoulder and their overnight bags draped around his neck, his body now fully engulfed the door frame. Emer stretched across and gave both boys a warm, long kiss. William pursed his lips and then smiled when she purposefully avoided him.

"You're doing it again," complained Emer.

"Doing what?"

"You know what."

With both boys still on his shoulders, William made his way down the stairs and out towards his muddy-white Hiace van, with 'also available in white' smudged in the dirt. The rain was bouncing off its roof, forming circular craters of mud and sand.

Emer and her boys still lived in the two-bedroom flat above a dry-cleaner's on the Portstewart promenade. What the property lacked in space was more than compensated for with views, as the living-room window looked directly across the main road and out onto the Atlantic Ocean. As children, the Farrell girls grew up with an ocean view and as an adult, Emer could settle nowhere unless first thing in the morning she could taste the sea-salt on her lips.

"Keep them away from scaffolding . . . and the old fella who smells and tells them dirty jokes," Emer continued even as the boys, waving vigorously, William and the van pulled out of from the kerb and were on their way.

Back inside the house and with the door closed behind her, there was silence. Action Men, train sets and glass jars containing ants and spiders were strewn around the floor. The heavy-duty woollen carpet, originally champagne and now weak-tea-coloured, was covered in a fine dust of sand – a price Emer reluctantly paid for living just a few yards from the beach.

But today she was in no mood for her usual twice-daily vacuuming. She knew that the farewell party was inevitable and felt deep regret and sadness. She brushed her bare toes across the carpet and tiny sand-grains popped up and danced. From nowhere in particular, she was overcome with a sudden sense of foreboding, as if this would be the last time she would be standing here. Scanning the battered and well-loved toys, Emer felt that she wouldn't see them again. The sense of loss was overpowering. But she couldn't understand where it came from or where it was leading.

Emer's kitchen and living-room were open plan and on the cork notice-board, pinned above the kitchen table, she found the bus timetable. Her father had been supposed to give her a lift up to Belfast that afternoon but he had telephoned first thing that morning to say that something important had come up and he would meet her there. He had sounded flustered and irritable over the telephone, but Emer knew best not to probe further. The Farrell sisters did not ask questions. So she was going to have to make her own way and public transport was her only option. She pulled a powder-pink woollen sweater over her T-shirt and then a chunky, ruby-red anorak, tightening the hood. Within a minute she was down the stairs and across the road to the bus shelter. The shelter was on the ocean side of the road and vulnerable to the crashing of the waves on one side and the torrential rain on the other. Emer huddled in the corner. She was more than familiar with the elements and quite enjoyed the battle against them. Even more so now as she found herself wishing that a mighty wave would come and take her back out to the sea with it.

Looking directly through the Perspex shelter out towards the raging ocean she caught a memory of herself, her sisters and their father huddled around a coal fire. It was the middle of winter, the last one that they'd all be together. They lived in a small detached house on O'Hara Drive, which was only a fifteen-minute stroll down the promenade and along the Nun's Walk from where Emer lived now. The house was one of only a handful built in the 30s, facing directly over boulders of basalt and out to the Atlantic. The storm outside was howling and the wind gushing down the chimney kept forcing the smoke from the fire back down and into the living-room. Their father was fighting a constant battle to keep the smoke out and the fire lit. Then, suddenly, above the crashing sound of wind and rain, there came an almighty thump at the front window, shaking the glass. They were amazed that the window hadn't been shattered and when they went outside to inspect the damage they discovered that a large sea bass must have been hurled out of the ocean by the storm and thrown against their window. The fish-and-chip dinner that night had been delicious.

"I haven't got all day. Where to, love?" the bus driver said, breaking the spell.

"The train station – please," Emer replied in a trance.

"Return, is it?"

"No, one way."

# Chapter 4

Over the past five years, the Farrell sisters had only really all got together for births, deaths and marriages, of which there had been few. But the gulf between them now was even bigger than the distance of time. Kitty busied herself in the kitchen, making cottage cheese and apple sandwiches with organic, wholemeal bread. She would have preferred juniper ham with Dijon mustard, but her budget wouldn't stretch that far this week. In her frenzy, she hardly noticed an ironed-straight thread of ebony hair escape from her pigtail. The hair fell, adding an extra texture to the lumpy cheese, while Kitty focused on wiping and rewiping the work-surfaces with her antibacterial cloth. Following the 'romantic afternoon' she had changed into a gold cotton sweater and a pair of tiger-print leggings. The outline of her upper body was intentionally swamped, but two floury marks blemished her jumper where she constantly battled to stop it from clinging to her chest.

Heather remained in the living-room, pretending to

scrutinise the CD collection. Her thoughts still simmered after her disagreement with Tommy and her usual sunny disposition was clouded.

Emer had been the last to arrive and immediately plonked herself on the kitchen chair beside Kitty and launched into a full description of every turn and bump in her journey. When the taxi had arrived from the bus station, Emer had got out even before it stopped and Kitty had hardly got the door open before Emer unleashed a cascade of 'gorgeous this' and 'wonderful that' relating to every soft furnishing, laminate flooring or stencilling that Kitty had.

While Kitty peeled and cored apples, Emer concluded the account of her travels and moved on to detail the intricacies of her domestic life. "Do you iron your towels, Kitty?"

"No . . . I don't know . . . I've never noticed."

Emer accidentally took a sip out of Kitty's teacup, mistaking it for her own. Her eldest sister was forced to make a fresh cup for herself.

"I used to." Emer launched herself into a favourite subject. "Well, the top layer anyway. I found the heat would then iron out the rest of it. But then I discovered rolling. Fabulous!" Emer wrongly sensed that Kitty was impressed, so she continued with, "I noticed it in the towel section of Debenhams the last time I was up in Belfast. Roll your towels as soon as they're dry and not only does that keep the creases out, but you know what? You can get a lot more of them into your small cupboards."

Emer was an expert at using unimportant trivia to mask the truth. Her performance now was first class. Kitty, as the eldest sister in the family, was usually difficult to fool, but even she thought Emer was taking the whole farewell thing in her stride.

This afternoon, it appeared that the unrestrained sociability would be left to Tommy and Dermot, who greeted each other like long lost brothers.

"You know, Tommy, it's been too long." Dermot had still to let go of Tommy's hand.

"You're right. But you know, don't you, if you ever need anything?" Tommy was equally reluctant to give up the security of the handshake.

"I know," enthused Dermot.

"I mean anything now, Dermot. Anything at all."

"I know, mate."

"Anything at all. Just say," repeated Tommy.

"Well, I could do with a few hundred quid!" joked Dermot.

"What's your name again?" replied Tommy as the two men eventually let go of each other's hands.

Emer and Kitty came back into the living-room. Emer carried a pot of piping hot tea and Kitty two large plates of nicely presented sandwiches, cut into tiny triangles.

"Jesus, Kitty, you'd need binoculars to see these sandwiches! Where's the crusts?" asked Dermot in total amazement. "Kitty, where's the crusts?"

"Leave her alone!" Emer came to her sister's defence.

"No, seriously," Dermot added. "I've never seen sandwiches without crusts before."

"Here, do you not want it?" Kitty briskly went to take the plate away from her husband.

"Aye, I do. Give us another one." And Dermot snatched a handful and perched himself on the arm of the sofa.

The sound of swallowing and slurping filled the silent void, only splintered by a 'What the fuck?' as Dermot discovered Kitty's hair entwined in his sandwich.

Tommy had perched himself on the arm of the sofa opposite Dermot. This gave him a position as far away as possible from Heather, who still crouched on the floor beside the CD collection and stereo. Kitty sat on an armchair with a plate balanced on each knee and Emer sat on her own in the centre of the sofa. She had allowed herself two of the small sandwiches and now occupied herself with the rest of the low-fat nibbles in the bowls on the coffee table. She sensed that it was going to be up to her to break the tension.

"Dad said he would meet us here at around four. What time is it now?"

Tommy answered first. "Ten to."

The invisible tension suddenly became visible, even to Emer. Both Kitty and Heather stopped chewing and stared at each other.

Undeterred, Emer continued, "And before I forget, does anyone know where the best place is to dry your washing this time of year? My stuff's just not drying the way it used to."

Dermot and Tommy saw this as a cue to go upstairs and play *Tomb Raider* on Dermot's computer.

Before anyone could miss them, there was a knock on the front door.

"That'll be him," said Emer, almost under her breath.

Rather than go straight and open the door, Kitty walked over to the window and looked out. For the first time since she'd arrived, Heather stood up. She sauntered over to join her eldest sister. Emer then followed.

They each looked at the figure in the doorway and then one by one looked away from him to check down the footpath and out onto the road. Seeing the figure had brought very different, contrasting emotions and feelings to each of the three sisters. This visitor was unexpected – well, at least by two of them. It wasn't their father.

But Kitty, Emer and Heather were united in how they felt now looking down the path, over the short wall and onto the street. He sat there with the rain bouncing off his curved roof and pouring efficiently into the ridge at the roof edge, before dripping down onto the wet tarmac. Patches of umber rust thirstily soaked up the moisture and blobs of poorly welded metal glistened. The navy bumper, golden bonnet and Windolene-pink door-panels, barely held themselves together under the pressure of the increasing storm. This was 'Merlin', a thirty-two-year-old Volkswagen Beetle. He had been a member of the Farrell family for twenty years – a constant in times of joy and those of sorrow. He had shared secrets and heartache, love and passion. Today the Farrell sisters were together saying a final farewell to Merlin. But, unbeknown to them all, as individuals they were going to face truths and bitterness that had taken twenty years to grow and breed.

Someone was going to have to answer the door.

*Kitty, 1982*

# Chapter 5

Discovered in a farmer's barn up the country, with a litter of cats in the boot and nettles growing in the engine bay, the twelve-year-old Volkswagen Beetle was a sorry sight. But over several months Roddy Farrell had secretly repaired, welded, oiled and polished until today, his eldest daughter's eighteenth birthday.

Now, with Kitty driving, Emer beside her and Heather in the back seat, the Farrell sisters were celebrating the birthday by 'doing the prom'. Every summer Sunday, the Portstewart promenade would be plagued with cars patrolling at five miles per hour, up and down, up and down and up and down the promenade again. The power of the Atlantic Ocean, a translucent blue in the summer sunlight, faded into insignificance for them against the parade of motor vehicles. The cars were mostly Saxos, Corsas and Fiestas. The 'Hot Hatch' look-alikes were polished to the nines. Every teenager from a ten-mile radius who was fortunate enough to get his or her hands on a set of car keys was there.

Proudly, Kitty caught sight of her reflection in a shop window. When her father had hinted earlier in the year that a car might be on the cards for her birthday, she had only one request. Well, demand really. It had to be gold. And now looking at the reflection she could see the sumptuous, sensual curves of its body and glistening chrome foot-treads and headlights. Set against the transient white surf, the car's rich tones and deep sheen were exaggerated further. The fact that the car was midnight-blue didn't matter any more. And in the window she also could see her own and her sister, Emer's, sparkling freshness and voluptuousness. They were stunning. Both had shocks of tight, curly hair, the colour of charcoal, and honey-tanned faces, the result of spending summer evenings out in the ocean air. Emer was slighter and her physique still child-like compared to that of her elder sister. But she was still beautiful. Kitty, however, had a confidence and seductiveness that was breathtaking. The girls were dressed in an explosion of frills and ribbons, with strings of pearls and diamante necklaces. The girls' heroes, Human League, were blaring out of the portable radio, which Emer hugged possessively to her chest.

The youngest sister, Heather, had a much more restrained dress sense. Her junior bra was evident through her crisp, white cotton blouse, but as yet she had very little to fill it with.

As she drove, Kitty let the steering wheel of her new car slide through her fingers and she caressed the curved indentations. She had little opportunity to shift through the gears as the pace of the strolling traffic dictated first gear. Kitty and Heather now had the windows of the car down fully and hollered and bantered with male pedestrians as they passed. The girls established a routine of poking fun at those from the farms and flirting with those from Coleraine Inst., the local boys' grammar school.

After turning the car at the roundabout at the top of the promenade and driving back down again, the banter began to become tiresome. That was until Kitty noticed a group of four spotty youths swaggering towards them on the passenger side of the road. The boy in front was wearing leather trousers connected with chains and straps, ankle boots, a red frilly shirt and scraps of ribbons plaited in his shoulder-length, dirty-blond hair.

"Hey, Adam Ant, does your ma know you're out like that?" hollered Kitty.

"No, that's Adam Maggot – his baby brother," quipped Emer.

"And does your da know you're cheeky bitches?" responded Dermot O'Kane in good humour. "Who did you shag to get the new wheels, Kitty Farrell?"

"Not you, that's for sure," Kitty shouted back as she leaned across her sister.

"That's because I wouldn't pay!" Dermot continued, encouraged by his young companions.

Kitty grabbed one of her large breasts with her right hand and seductively whispered, "You couldn't afford it."

At eighteen and sixteen respectively, Kitty and Emer Farrell were a vivacious, but dangerous cocktail of surging hormones and a convent education. In stark contrast, Heather made herself small in the back seat, hiding her blushing face behind a curtain of spirally hair.

Still in good humour, Dermot O'Kane started to chase the Beetle, but his friends pulled him back. Nonchalantly,

Heather rolled up the window and Kitty turned back to face the slow convoy ahead. On the left, a light ocean spray managed to catch a few seated tourists off guard. On the right, a myriad of small, locally owned shops were enjoying the busy Sunday trade. Women's fashion shops, with headless mannequins dressed in crochet dresses, competed with sweetshop displays of fluorescent jars on dusty shelves.

"I reckon that O'Kane one fancies you, Kitty," Heather teased.

"Vomit. He's so dense light bends around him." Kitty laughed. "His balls haven't dropped yet. Give us a smoke!"

Emer lit up a cigarette and the two sisters passed it between them. They sucked on the cigarette, amateurishly, with more spittle than tobacco being inhaled. Driving in the opposite direction, half a dozen of Kitty's school-friends came crawling past in a Mini Clubman.

A chorus of, "Happy Birthday, Kitty! Love the car! Great colour!" escaped from the Mini, which was bulging at the seams.

"And it's got a 1600 air-cooled engine, Empey wheels and a lowered suspension!" blurted Heather from the back seat. Kitty and Emer both looked round and gave their younger sister 'the look'. 'The look' translated, in short, to 'just sit there and be quiet – don't forget you're lucky to be here at all'.

The girls in the mini were also slightly bewildered by Heather's interruption. "Right . . . still, it's a great colour. We're off to Morelli's for an ice cream. Are you coming?"

Kitty agreed and parked her car in the only space available – the pavement.

The Farrell girls were all secretly relieved to leave the

car, which in the heat of the August sun had become a furnace.

Just before abandoning the vehicle for the pleasures of a Morelli's Belgian chocolate ice cream, however, Kitty gave it a casual kiss on the bonnet. Kitty hadn't grasped just how much money and work had gone into this birthday gift. Their father was raising three daughters on a bricklayer's wages. His own car was a beat-up Fiat and he hadn't bought anything new for himself for the past few years. Roddy had hoped that with a student life at Queen's University starting in eight weeks, this gift would be particularly precious to Kitty. She was going to be the first in the family to leave home.

"What will I call him?" Kitty asked her sisters as they dodged the strolling cars and skipped over to the ice cream parlour. The heckles and wolf whistles from the passing cars were deafening, making Heather feel very uncomfortable. Kitty didn't appear to hear them. "The Beetle needs a name."

"He's definitely a bloke," Kitty continued flippantly. "What's he remind you of?"

"Well, he's sexy . . . powerful. And got a big end!"

Heather strolled a few paces behind her sisters, studying and taking it all in – silently.

"Merlin," Kitty announced, confidently. "I'm going to call him Merlin."

Heather and Emer were not impressed by the choice but, as the glass door to the parlour flung back from Kitty's hand and almost hit them in the face, their disappointment was quickly forgotten and the name 'Merlin' accepted.

Joining a manic crush at the counter to be served, the

sisters each bought a double-scoop of ice cream. They then joined Kitty's school-friends and now the group of nine giggling girls occupied a bench designed for three at the most. Kitty began to sample all of the ice creams, before deciding that the lick of Heather's Turkish Delight was her preference and her younger sister was forced to make do with Kitty's discarded choice.

With ice creams tightly clenched in their hands, the girls sniggered and joked every time a new customer entered the shop. The customers were mostly young boys, buying a one-scoop tub between three, or retired couples opting for the deluxe nut-sundaes and then tutting when the convent girls didn't give up their seat.

"Jesus, Mary and Joseph!" a gangly girl, who was sitting nearest the door gasped. "Look, it's Sheehan!"

A tall, broadly built man in his late twenties entered the shop, hand in hand with a woman about the same age. His long, light-brown pigtail and large moustache contributed to the general Status Quo look. He had a short leather jacket draped over his right shoulder. This was Mr Sheehan – the Physical Education teacher at the Dominican Convent School. As one of only three male teachers in the school, with the other two being Maths and Chemistry teachers, both in their early sixties and with broken veins on their noses, Mr Sheehan had little competition. Hence, he was easily the most popular teacher in the school.

Mr Sheehan hadn't seen the girls and was busily recommending flavours to his female companion.

"*Hey, sir, show us your press-ups!*" the girl nearest the door shouted.

Mr Sheehan dropped his head, obviously disappointed to

be spotted out in civilian life by some of his former pupils. He reluctantly turned round to face them. Staring motionlessly, his eyes were now focused on one spot. And the subject of his gaze stared back, just as intensely. It was Kitty. Nobody else noticed, as the girls' attention spans were short and for a moment they busily gobbled the remainder of their ice creams. Everybody, except Heather. The twelve-year-old saw it all.

Once the ice creams were fully devoured and their fingers licked, the group of girls returned their attention to the unsuspecting teacher. Their confidence was buoyed by being part of a pack and also by the knowledge that, as of last month, they were no longer sixth-formers. They were grown-ups.

*"Sir, show us your pecs!"* another girl hollered.

Mr Sheehan's concentration was abruptly broken.

"Look, girls. I'm not your teacher any more." The colour had returned to his cheeks. "You don't have to call me 'sir', or even 'Mr Sheehan' – that's my da, for heaven's sake! Just call me Jack." He had a deep, gravelly voice, as a direct result of trying to make himself heard each day above a hundred giggly girls out on the playing fields. Once he'd replied to the girls, he took his leather jacket off his shoulder and put it on. As he turned around to leave, silver, sequinned letters, all individually and lovingly sewn into the soft leather, spelt out the word 'Merlin'.

# Chapter 6

"The handbrake's in the way!"

"Pull it off then."

"But we'll roll down the hill!"

"Well, let's get in the back."

"No."

"Why not?"

"Because you'll take advantage."

"And what am I doing now? Flying a kite?"

Jack was tiring of Kitty's false naivety. Somehow, Kitty Farrell had got it into her head that intimate foreplay in the front seats was, somehow, more acceptable than in the back. This had followed an hour-long, blazing argument about Jack's companion at the ice-cream parlour earlier that afternoon. But Kitty had been won over. Jack had eventually persuaded her that the woman was little more than a ruse, so that no one would discover the illicit relationship between teacher and former pupil.

The hot air from the heated argument, combined with the ensuing passion of the making-up, resulted in Merlin's windows being fully steamed up. The couple had driven out to Dunluce Castle at around ten o'clock in the evening and the Beetle was the only car remaining in the carpark. A buttermilk moon dived in and out of filigree clouds. The decaying castle, slowly being sucked into the sea, was thought by Jack to be an appropriate place to give his teenage girlfriend a special birthday present.

"Come on, Kitty! Let's get in the back," Jack persisted. "Don't you like your birthday present after all?"

A sterling silver bracelet, studded with green amber nuggets, was a generous present and Kitty was delighted. But even though her sexual experiences to date meant that her virginity was a mere technicality, she wasn't convinced that silver, instead of her preferred gold, was a fair trade.

"Surely you're not trying to buy sex with me?" Kitty said, dressing her words in a coy smile.

"Aye, I am."

"Well, don't be so bloody obvious about it!"

Jack, squashed into the passenger seat beside his girlfriend, turned his body fully round and leant across Kitty. He pinned her by the shoulders to her seat.

"You are the most gorgeous girl on the entire planet. Your eyes are like pools of . . . lovely stuff and your lips are like red . . . roses. That's it, like red roses. Now, Kitty, give us a shag!"

With his poem complete, Jack then tried to kiss Kitty on her neck. But she pulled away.

"Since you put it so nicely . . . get off!" Kitty hissed as she shoved him away. She knew he was wearing her down, gradually, but she didn't want him to think she was just anybody's. Not yet anyway.

Jack moved back over to his seat and crossed his legs, tightly.

Outside, the moon peeked out from behind a solitary cloud. Its rays were bright enough to illuminate the south wall of the castle and down the cliff edge, to the crashing waves below. The cartoon sky was then given a touch of realism as a dull band of charcoal cloud blotted out the moon entirely and all was a matt finish of greys and blacks.

"Look what you're doing to me, Kitty! I've got blue balls. I may never be able to have children," Jack said, struggling with a different tactic. "If you can't do it for me, do it for all those unborn babies!"

Kitty and Jack had been seeing each other for three months now. They had flirted with each other right through lower-sixth form and then into the first two terms of upper-sixth. But their relationship took on a 'special' significance when he offered Kitty private tennis lessons. None of the nuns' suspicions were aroused by their very non-sporty pupil suddenly choosing double physical education. Kitty had even bought a second-hand tennis skirt, plus a pair of towelling pants, in order to maintain the charade. At the start of their relationship, Jack's immaturity and straightforward humour had refreshed Kitty. She had been confident that she knew exactly where she stood with him. But now she realised that she had become far more emotionally attached than she had initially intended.

Kitty flattened down the white frills on her blouse. They had been slightly ruffled by Jack's exploring, eager hands.

"And you say holding hands was as far as you and that woman got to?"

"Aye," Jack impatiently answered as he twiddled with a

rubber button on the dashboard and a tiny pair of window-wipers began to sway from left to right. He then stretched his arms out – as much as he could within the tight confines of the Beetle. He tucked them behind his head and rested himself against the pale blue upholstery, trimmed with navy leather. The hairs from his long ponytail spread out like a fish-tail.

"Was it the same kind of hand-holding we did in the school showers?" Kitty persevered. "Or would it be more like what we did in the squash courts?"

Quickly it became noticeable that Jack's ardour was beginning to shrink. Kitty had achieved success. But now she was disappointed.

Jack used the side of his right clenched fist to imprint the shape of a baby's foot in the steam on the car window. With his index finger, he dotted five tiny toes. He then turned to stare at Kitty. A broad, sensual smile exploded from under his dark, thick moustache. The delicacy of the tiny footprint, alongside the warmth of his bright and open face, melted away the icy final threads of Kitty's objections.

"Kitty, if you don't want to, it really doesn't matter," he whispered with convincing sincerity. "We'll wait until you're ready."

It wasn't until Kitty felt the tension in her shoulders and stomach dissolve that she realised that she'd had it at all.

Jack continued with his verbal assault.

"We've all the time in the world." He leant across and gave Kitty a gentle kiss on the lips. The couple's breath highlighted the tiny footprint even more.

Kitty lost her virginity on the night of her eighteenth birthday, in the back seat of her Volkswagen. But what she found in return would affect her for the rest of her life.

# Chapter 7

*"No, I'm not pregnant!"* Kitty bellowed at her inquisitive youngest sister as, six weeks later, she was packing her bags for university. She wasn't pregnant, but her youngest sister was persistent in trying to find out why Kitty had been behaving so oddly recently.

Tattered posters of Duran Duran were plastered over with newer ones of Madness on the eaves of the small bedroom. Kitty had secured her own 'personal space' when she had her first period as an eleven-year-old. She decided it was a small price to pay for her father's obvious embarrassment at the time. Damp patches were causing the powder-pink floral wallpaper to peel and beyond the three-foot circle of dry heat from the electric fire, the rest of the room was cold. Kitty's window had an uninterrupted view of the ocean. Outside was calm, in dramatic contrast to the violent storm the night before. Kitty could still feel the gurgling in her stomach as the sea bass, that had unwittingly crashed against their window and become supper, stirred and churned. The sky was still dark and the sea a battleship-grey. The calmness was unnerving. It was the beginning of October and the threat of the harsh winter months infected the raw edges of the tranquillity without.

"Get your skinny arse off my records!" Kitty barked at Heather, as she continued to pack, absorbed by what was going on inside, rather than out.

Heather slowly stretched herself down from the bed like a cat and sat hugging her knees close to the one bar of the electric fire.

"I know there's something going on between you and that teacher we saw in Morelli's," Heather taunted, confident in the unusual position of having the upper hand with her eldest sister.

"Well, you're wrong!" said an increasingly flustered Kitty as she tried to cram a saucepan and three chipped plates into her suitcase. "Now, make yourself useful and fuck off."

"You love him, so you do!"

"Go away!"

Heather began to rock her spindly body. Even through her woollen, cerise pullover, the points of her elbows and shoulders could be seen jutting out. The circular caps of her knees, wrapped in opaque white tights, denoted the thickest part of her legs. Heather's thighs were much the same width as her calves.

"You love him!" Heather rocked again, "Kitty loves her teacher!" As the speed of her rocking increased, she added to the beat, "And he loves you back!"

Kitty threw a giant heart-shaped cushion and scored a direct hit at the side of her young sister's head. The victim tumbled over in a heap. The heart had been a Valentine's gift a few years back. It had no value. A jumbled mess of long arms and legs ran out of the bedroom, shouting "Daddy, Daddy!" as it went.

Kitty sat on the suitcase and attempted to fasten the stubborn buckles. Jumping up and down only seemed to contribute to their inflexibility. So, Kitty stopped and took a moment to look around her bedroom. After today it wouldn't be hers any longer. Emer was already packing her own stuff, ready to move in and Kitty could hear her sister's frustrated attempts to scrape blobs of hardened Blu-tack off the walls next door. From now on, any visits home for Kitty would mean sharing a cast-iron double bed with Heather.

So this was it. Kitty had most of her belongings jammed into the backseat of Merlin already and the boot was mostly full of books. She was heading to study English Literature at Queen's University in Belfast and her books meant the world to her. Her father had never really shown much interest in them until now when he said they were good for adding weight to her car and improving road holding. He insisted that was where she stored her books throughout her stay in Belfast. Three years did seem, to Kitty, to be a little extreme. But she didn't argue back. Unusually though, she did argue back when he offered to drive her to Belfast. Kitty 'wanted to go alone', she said. This was her future and she didn't want her past travelling with her.

Again Kitty scanned the room, tracing memories and picturing herself growing and maturing and drifting away. The frilly, cotton blouse that she had worn only six weeks earlier was already discarded and crumpled in the far corner. She was now dressed in a black and white checked dress. The checks were pulled tight against her chest, flattening

41

her breasts by squeezing them under her arms. At the extremes, the outfit was completed at the bottom by white leather ankle-boots and at the top by her hair, painstakingly ironed completely straight. A dusting of talcum powder left her cheeks milky white and charcoal eyeliner etched Cleopatra eyes. A talcum-power residue remained on her fingertips and a faint 'Miss Haversham' dusting followed whenever Kitty moved.

The sound of Emer scraping the Blu-tack stopped and was replaced by their father opening and closing Merlin's bonnet, as he added even more books to balance the car.

Heather's shrill 'Daddy, Daddy!', had quickly evaporated. Kitty wasn't concerned that Heather would spill her false conclusions to their father. The girls never told tales about each other to anyone, especially him.

"So this is it," Kitty repeated to herself, attempting a dramatic exit. She wanted to cry, but she couldn't. She wanted a soliloquy, but that wouldn't come either. Her leaving was inevitable and all she could do was repeat 'so this is it'. The stillness of the world outside, now for the first time today, was reflected in the silence of her own room.

"So this is it." Her words neither broke nor filled the silence.

Draped over the bed was her handmade, patchwork quilt cover which she had decided to leave. Begun in her first-year needlework class and eventually only completed six months before, the multi-coloured blanket was created from shreds of old clothes belonging to all three of the Farrell sisters. The fabrics were mostly faded, since by the time they were available as scraps, the three sisters, to various degrees, had enjoyed their use. The centre of the quilt, stitched when Kitty was only eleven, was mostly pale-pink and violet cotton floral prints. Around this inner circle, beige and cream stripes and swirls of lemon began to appear. The outer circles were a mishmash of blocks of bold colour: red silks, black velvet and blue denim.

The quilt wouldn't be going with Kitty. She would leave it on her bed for Emer.

"So this is it." And with Kitty's last forced sigh, the buckles on the suitcase gave up their struggle and were securely closed.

"*Are you ready?*" Roddy Farrell hollered up the stairs. The intonation of his voice was exactly the same as the thousand or so times he'd shouted up the stairs after one or other of his daughters. "The car's ready for you!" he added.

Kitty listened intently for evidence of emotion. There was none. The silence that followed was as empty as the words.

But the lull was only temporary as the bedroom door burst open and before she had fully entered the room, Emer launched into conversation.

"Did you leave me any of that perfume? Is there room in that there cupboard for records? Or, maybe, just tapes? Maybe, both? Where's the best place for knickers? Oh no, there's never going to be enough room for all my stuff! Put those boxes over in that corner."

Emer pointed to Heather, who had returned and had been commandeered to assist with the big 'move'. Kitty looked over at her twelve-year-old sister and rolled her eyes. Heather shrugged her shoulders and the two sisters smiled in their moment of shared understanding.

Oblivious, Emer leapt up onto the single bed and began testing the springs.

"You know, it's not that bad. Considering."

"Considering what?" Kitty asked, as she pulled the heavy suitcase off the bed and towards the door.

"Considering the amount of use those springs have taken."

Heather then joined Emer on the bed, adding squeaking sounds to emphasise Emer's point.

With Emer now bouncing furiously and Heather 'squeaky-squeaking', Kitty couldn't help but begin to laugh. She joined in the rhythm by banging her knuckle on the side of the suitcase and providing stifled groans.

"Are you ready?" Roddy Farrell's sterile enquiry silenced the girls instantly.

As the girls just stared at each other, Kitty was forced to question herself. 'Was she ready?' She hadn't been ready last week, when she had got her test results back from the doctor. Jack had waited outside in the carpark, refusing to believe that the results would have implications for him also. When Kitty returned to the car, she had discovered Jack hiding, huddled into a tiny ball in the back seat.

"You can come out now. I've got the results."

Kitty had to talk to the rear-view mirror, as Jack had yet to emerge from his hiding-place.

"And they're positive."

He still did not move and Kitty suspected that he might have stopped breathing. That was until he popped his head up between the two front seats and managed a pathetic half-smile.

"I'm sorry, Kitty. It's all my fault. Is there anything I can do? I'll do it. Just tell me. Please just tell me."

"Are you ready, Kitty?" The dull interjection from Roddy

Farrell burst through to the present. Kitty winked at her sisters and closed the bedroom door behind her, before dragging the suitcase down the stairs and out the front door. She knew they would be looking for her through the bedroom window, but she was determined not to look up.

Her father had left space in the boot for the suitcase and had disappeared back inside the house for a cloth to wipe the headlights. The dull grey of the sky was reflected in the gloss on Merlin's roof. His blue coat was now almost a murky black in the fading light. Kitty heaved the suitcase into the boot and as she pulled the lid down hard, she momentarily imagined Jack's sullen face peering back at her from his hidden lair as he wedged his cheeks between the two front seats.

"Please, just tell me. I'll do anything."

In a couple of hours, Kitty was going to be all alone, starting a new life in Belfast. Her first tutorial was at ten o'clock in the morning and she had an appointment at the clinic in the Royal Hospital on Tuesday the following day. She could hear her father walking back out of the front door and out towards her. She could also hear enthusiastic taps on the window of her bedroom, but Kitty chose to look away from her home and its surface of weather-eaten, Ballycastle Dry Dash and stare out towards the ocean. For years she had longed to look out and someday see the surface of the Atlantic broken by the mighty plunge of a humpback whale. But not today, as the glass-like surface continued uninterrupted out to the black horizon.

She closed her eyes and again heard the memory of Jack's words:

"Please, Kitty. I'll do anything to make it up to you."

45

And then a sardonic smile burst from her lips with the recollection of her answer.

"There is something you can do, Jack."

"Just name it. I love you, Kitty!"

"Make an appointment with the doctor yourself."

Despite accepting blame for Kitty's affliction, Jack Sheehan had somehow persuaded himself that this would not affect him – after all, he didn't have any of the symptoms. As always, he was untouchable.

"Do I have to?" he whispered through the tiny gap in Merlin's front seats.

"Not if you don't want to," Kitty remembered answering sharply. "You could just wait a year or two, until the gonorrhoea makes your knob drop off. You'll not give it to anyone else then, you bollocks!"

46

# Chapter 8

In the doctor's carpark, Kitty's feelings for her former PE teacher had taken a step back and her obsession with cleanliness and germs had taken a giant leap forward. Even now, as Kitty filled Merlin's petrol tank at the Shell station on the Ormeau Road, she used a flannel to clean the pump handle, before and after she used it.

Kitty had now been living in Belfast for four weeks.

Once she had replaced the petrol cap, she then walked over to the passenger side of her car to retrieve her patent-leather handbag. Sitting in Merlin were Gerry, Ken and Nigel – three chemistry students from Malaysia. She had befriended all three within her first week in the halls of residence and they had rapidly become a major feature of her new student life. Empathising with Kitty's sense of dislocation and of being somewhat of an outsider, they had easily welcomed her into their otherwise private fraternity. Their obsession with her chest-size was incidental. Kitty accepted the privileged invitation and now with her course of antibiotics completed, she was ready for her first alcohol deluge. It was October 31$^{st}$ and the Freshers' Hallowe'en Ball was being held in the Students' Union.

Kitty grabbed her bag from between the stilettos of *Star Trek's* 'Lieutenant Uhura'. Gerry had remarkably clean-shaven and shapely legs. The admiral-red minidress also emphasised very feminine contours and a tiny waist. In the back seat, Ken, alias Gandalf, sat fiddling with the individually crafted strands of his woollen beard, which tickled and pulled at his ears. His flowing hessian-sack cloak also irritated him, but he was unable to scratch himself satisfactorily because of the eight-foot staff he held across his chest and out through the front passenger window. The staff cut straight across Nigel, the TV set. Dressed in a grey pin-striped suit, with his hair slicked back, in an attempt to recreate the image of a newsreader, Nigel had a cardboard box on his head, decorated with an assortment of toothpaste lids for buttons, a plastic flower and picture-frame glued to the top.

With a five-pound note salvaged from the bottom of her bag, Kitty made her way to the payment desk in the filling station. There wasn't a hint of flirtation from the teenage cashier and Kitty shuffled back to her car feeling slightly disappointed.

Two minutes later, Kitty and her new Malaysian friends were joyfully jostling to get a drink at the bar.

Two hours later, Kitty and her new Malaysian friends were pathetically nursing half-empty pint glasses. Ken had been the first to become annoyed.

"Hey, it's Santa!"

"Ho-ho-ho!"

48

Drunken witches insisted on yanking hard on the unfortunate Ken's precious beard. And he was in no hurry to abandon what had taken him hours to make, even with the blood trickling from his weary ears. He sat grumbling 'heathens' as his *Lord of the Rings* costume continued to be misinterpreted. Kitty's 'Nobody will know who you are' and 'Who's interested in that fairy-tale nonsense anyway?' was irritatingly more accurate than he had anticipated.

Nigel wasn't faring any better, as people kept twiddling his knobs.

"What's on the other station?"

"What happens if I do this?"

"The picture's all fuzzy!"

And then Gerry's Afro started to steam with the heat, causing his chocolate-brown face paint to streak and smudge over everything he touched. Hence his last visit to the gents' resulted in grubby fingerprints where he had lifted up the front of his dress. He was also tiring of the incessant 'beam me ups' and 'Lieutenant Ya-Whore-Yee'. All three disgruntled students sat huddled next to the only empty space in the hall, right next to the speakers. They were miserable and Kitty attached herself to the end of the miserable line-up, consumed by her own disappointment that, in two hours, nobody had attempted to chat her up. She decided to stop drinking after half a pint of cider and was now suffering from a pineapple-juice-induced furry tongue.

So far, student life hadn't been what Kitty had expected. Her experience with Jack Sheehan had knocked the wind out of her sails and she felt that she was drifting along in a rubber ring, with her backside sticking out of the bottom –

exposed and massive. Looking down at her royal-blue cotton suit, she had to admit to herself that her hips had definitely got wider since she'd left home. What could she blame for this?

Kitty and her friends had given up on trying to pretend they were enjoying themselves and just as they made their way to the exit, four Frankenstein's Monsters suddenly blocked their way. The men's necks were as wide as barrels and their objective was to part Ken from his staff. Kitty swung her handbag dramatically, only connecting it with her own stomach as it swung back at her. But when Ken, Gerry and Nigel each held out their arms in a karate-style pose, the monsters swiftly became mice and scampered off.

Before further trouble, Kitty nudged her friends out of the hall and back into Merlin. The only upside to Kitty's evening was that she hadn't been drinking alcohol and they didn't have to join the frantic battle to hail down a taxi.

"How long have you guys been doing karate?" Kitty asked, impressed, as they eventually drove away from the sprawl of drunken bodies and headed down the University Road.

"We haven't," Ken replied with his fingers still tightly clenched around his stick.

"Haven't you seen *Karate Kid?*" Then he added with a perfect Belfast accent, "Wax on, wax off."

Five minutes into their journey back to the halls of residence and a gush of thick black smoke bellowed out of Merlin's exhaust and the engine shut off completely. The car crawled to a standstill. Kitty closed her eyes and whispered to herself, "What now?"

Lieutenant Uhura, Gandalf, the TV set and Kitty walked the rest of the way home.

Two days later the garage discovered an earwig had committed suicide inside Merlin's fuel-filter and his decomposing body had caused the engine to fail. 'The beetle trapped inside the Beetle' story became an urban legend around the campus and brought Kitty her five minutes of fame. Her infamy was still ahead of her.

Kitty didn't see as much of her Malaysian friends after the Hallowe'en Ball. The senior security guard there had spotted the 'karate' incident and offered them jobs most Friday and Saturday nights. In their three years as bouncers, their karate skills were, fortunately, never called upon.

The day Kitty got Merlin back from the garage, she rang home to give her father the mechanic's diagnosis.

"And you were on your way back from where?" Roddy Farrell shouted to compensate for the seventy miles between Portstewart and Belfast.

"A Hallowe'en Ball."

"And what did you go as?" asked Roddy, adding with what Kitty perceived to be forced enthusiasm, "I bet you looked terrific."

"I went as Margaret Thatcher." Kitty's voice trailed off in sudden realisation as to why she might have been considered a turn-off. She glanced down momentarily and caught sight of her thighs pouring over the edge of the paint-splattered bucket chair. But her interest in the telephone conversation was rekindled when she asked, "Has anyone been asking about me? Anyone from school?"

"Some fella Dermot-something-or-other told Heather he'd got a job up in Belfast and was looking to get hold of you."

"Is that it?"

"Yes."

"Nobody else?"

"No."

There was silence.

"Do you want me to come up and visit?" Roddy shouted.

"No." Kitty was abrupt. "I'll see you all at Christmas. Sure, it won't be long."

"OK. We might all get to meet Emer's new fella then. She's keeping him very secret. Saving him until you get home, I bet . . . she misses you."

Kitty really wasn't interested in her sixteen-year-old sister's love life. Her own had been blighted with VD and antibiotics. She pulled the telephone handset away from her ear and idly studied the notice-board above the payphone in the hall. Did she want to ring the Samaritans? Kitty's daydreaming meant that she didn't fully hear the conclusion to her father's story when he added,

"He's interested in sports – this boyfriend of Emer's." Roddy was unruffled by his eldest daughter's obvious silent indifference. "Jack something or other. Sounds like a sensible sort of fella."

# Chapter 9

There was a bomb scare. With her Christmas presents for home piled high in her shopping basket and her turn next at the checkout, Kitty Farrell was reluctant to budge.

"Go on, serve me," she pleaded. Adding, "It'll only be a hoax."

The customer behind her nodded encouragingly. She also thought she had a chance to be served, as did the third and fourth customers, clutching desperately on to over-full shopping baskets. But the cashier, all gold and fake tan and glad of the opportunity of a break, turned the key to her till and joined the slow procession of evacuees.

"I hardly call that customer care! Where's the manager?" Kitty felt empowered by her shopping comrades but, when she turned for support, she found that she was all alone. Along with the other disgruntled shoppers, she was herded across the road from the department store. An 'us and them' scenario emerged with the staff and the customers forming two factions – one bitterly annoyed and the other slightly relieved. Security guards found comfort in pairs, with their authoritative air enhanced by the constant crackle from their walkie-talkies.

Kitty was still feeling confident. Her frizzy hair suited the new 'big-hair' style and her fake camel-hair jacket managed to emphasise her voluptuous chest, while hiding other less flattering features. Black stiletto boots also lengthened her legs and gave her height. And even the bitter cold could not dilute the youthful glow of her complexion. She swaggered up to the guards nearest to her.

"Any chance I could get my car, lads?"

"Sorry, love. Carpark's closed."

"For how long? Is it a real bomb?"

"Can't say at the moment, love."

"It's bound to be a hoax. Let me go and get my car! I'll only be a minute. Not even a minute. A few seconds. Pretty please?"

Kitty sensed that her flirting was creating the desired effect. And to clinch it, her final touch was a heavily mascara'd wink.

An hour later, she was still waiting outside, accompanied by the miserable thought that what she had used to get her own way with schoolboys, in a small seaside town on the Antrim coast, just didn't quite hit the mark in Belfast.

The general agreement amongst Kitty's fellow-shoppers was that the scare was an IRA hoax and if the security guards didn't let them back in the store, there would be a shoppers' revolt. They had rights after all. Some felt the right to buy tinsel and Christmas cards, at half-price, was paramount. Two days before Christmas and most of the Queen's students had already headed home. South Belfast housewives, shrouded in a haze of cashmere and pearls, now surrounded Kitty,

Kitty could no longer feel her toes. The jacket kept her torso warm, but the rest of her body was turning blue. Her student grant and her taste didn't quite run to quality clothing. But as long as she looked sexy, even when frozen half to death, then she was satisfied. She had needed until last night to catch up on the three assignments that she was behind with and the quiet of the halls during the Christmas holidays had at least encouraged her to complete one of them. 'Twentieth-Century American Literature' and the 'Irish Big House Novel' deadlines could be renegotiated in the New Year. Kitty's father had telephoned her the previous night, accusing his daughter of not wanting to come home. Kitty had denied this. She lied easily for her eighteen years.

Outside the department store, the Christmas spirit had now turned nasty and the hushed babble of subdued dissent an hour earlier was now a flood of audible, "Shoot the lot of them!" and "Bloody inconvenience!". Their Volvos and BMWs were still in the cordoned-off carpark and the option of getting home via the bus stop at the far end of the street was not up for consideration.

Kitty, by contrast, was the sort who would use public transport. But she was also reluctant to abandon her car – 'a hostage of the Troubles'. As each long minute passed, she hoped it would be the last. Her short life to date had kept her pretty much sheltered from politics but now, forcibly separated from her car, she felt like a true victim.

'The store's still being searched. . .but the carpark's now been cleared," announced a grave-looking security guard, proud of his shiny lapels and '*love*' and '*hate*' tattoos on his knuckles.

Kitty was already way behind her schedule to be back home in Portstewart by six o'clock that evening. She joined the frantic race to the carpark and, having initially forgotten where she'd parked, she eventually spotted the curved blue roof in the far corner. She searched through her jacket's cavernous pockets and sifted through damp tissues and bent hairgrips for car keys. But, as she did so, she discovered that she had, in fact, left Merlin's door unlocked. Once inside, there was little space with the huge steering wheel crushing against the bulk of the jacket. She searched again in her pockets for the keys and this time unearthed a half-empty packet of salted peanuts. She'd recently read that nuts contained high levels of antioxidants. Kitty didn't know exactly what that meant, but it sounded important. After her recent visits to the health centre, she was determined to stay as healthy as possible. Stuck to the packet was a yellow Post-it, with the message '*Phone Dermot*' in her own handwriting. She'd written this over four weeks earlier and had yet to bother returning any of the numerous calls he'd made to her. With the peanuts quickly devoured, the Post-it went the same way as the empty packet – scrunched up and shoved back in her pocket.

Eventually, after further searching, Kitty could feel the weight of the car keys, attached to the even heavier pewter key-ring in the shape of the letter 'K', inside the lining of her jacket. They had fallen through a hole in the pocket. Dexterity and patience were required to salvage them and Kitty had neither. The other shoppers had all driven off and Kitty's car was the last remaining. She was now two hours behind schedule and would be going home empty-handed. She could sense her blood pressure rising as she thought of the inconvenience that she had been put to. Eventually she retrieved the keys at the expense of the lining being further torn and tufts of camel hair jammed under her fingernails.

"Got you, you buggers!"

"About bloody time!" whispered a nervous voice from the back of the car. "Drive on and nothing will happen to you!"

Kitty Farrell froze. Instantly, sweat moistened the Bakelite steering wheel, where her hands gripped tightly. Her knuckles were white.

"Jesus! Jesus! What do you want? I haven't got anything," Kitty splurted out as if she'd just discovered language.

"I don't want to frighten you. I'm not going to hurt you. I promise," the voice continued in a nervous hush. "Just drive out past the security guards and the army patrol at the end of the road and I'll be on my way."

Kitty quickly glanced through her rear-view mirror and then back again directly in front. The back seat was piled high with bags of clothes, books and folders. One of the bags had burst open and clothes were scattered everywhere. Her brief glance through the mirror only revealed what looked to be an old man's grey overcoat, hunched underneath her belongings. She dare not look again.

"Please, if it's the car you want, take it. I won't say anything to anybody. I won't. I really won't . . ." Kitty rambled on, until abruptly stopped by the voice.

"Just drive like you usually do and I'll be gone in a few minutes." The voice was male, but not deep. An anxious tremor filtered through the whisper.

Kitty felt that she had never been inside a car before:

suddenly the accelerator became the brake, the clutch the accelerator and the gear-stick and handbrake just lumps of moulded plastic. After two panic-induced stalls, she eventually staggered Merlin to the exit barrier. The pay station was unmanned and the barrier open. Kitty just about managed to drive through in first gear, with her handbrake still on, and out of the carpark towards the main road.

"Turn left," the voice suggested, rather than ordered, "and change gear before the engine explodes."

The painful sound of grating cogs informed the voice that the driver had complied.

The road was completely empty. At the far end, two grey Saracen armoured cars blocked the street, stopping traffic from entering the area until the department store had been fully cleared. There was space in the middle of the two Saracens for Kitty's small car, but this was blocked by a soldier, standing with his legs shoulder-width apart and a self-loading rifle held firm against his chest.

"There's a soldier on the road. What will I do?" Kitty blurted. Her body was completely soaked in sweat. Her thighs were stuck together and a red rash crawled up her neck. Her foot was now more firmly pushed against the accelerator pedal.

"Don't run him down, for God's sake!" The panic was infectious. "Slow down and smile!"

Kitty smiled like she'd just come from the dentist. By the time she was only a hundred metres in front of the soldier, the smile had become exaggerated to the point of grotesque. When the blue Beetle was a few metres away, the soldier eagerly stepped to one side and let the peculiar-looking driver pass through.

Now the road ahead of Kitty starkly contrasted with the ghost-town tranquillity of the road leading up to the blockade. The heaving Christmas traffic choked the city centre roads. Bumper to bumper, the disrupted Christmas shoppers angrily cursed in steamed-up cars and crowded buses.

"Are we through yet?" said the voice.

"Yes."

"Why are you going so slowly?"

"You can get out now."

"But why are we barely moving?" The impatient voice struggled to maintain the whisper.

"There's a traffic jam."

"Bollocks!" The voice broke through the shackles of restrain and its full depth and resonance was finally audible. "OK, keep calm and we'll be all right."

Kitty jammed her foot hard against the brake pedal. Turning round, she yanked at the largest of her clothes-bags and pulled it away from the grey coat. The smaller bags tumbled away and the outline of the man's back was fully visible. His face, however, was still turned away.

Kitty grabbed hold of the man's hair and yanked his head up.

"You bastard! I know who you are!"

# Chapter 10

*"Dermot O'Kane, what the hell are you up to?"* Kitty bawled ferociously.

"Shush! Turn around. Don't let anyone see me," the eighteen-year-old pleaded, while still huddled and his face shielded with his arms.

"You scared the holly bejesus out of me!"

"Please, Kitty. I'm in serious trouble."

"Too bloody right!"

"Please don't let the soldiers see me!" The grey coat shuddered.

"There's nothing the army can do to you that any way compares to what I'm capable of doing. You . . . you . . . wee shit!"

Tufts of long dull-blond hair had come away in her hand. She pulled hard on the overcoat – it was old and too big and smelled musty. She could see a fuzzy beard on his cheek, as he turned to face her.

Dermot's cheeks were wet. As his hazel eyes refocused on

60

Kitty's face, a solitary tear escaped before being abruptly cleared away with his left hand. Along with the disappearance of the independent tear, Kitty felt her anger subside.

"What are you up to?" she asked more calmly.

"If I tell you, I'll have to kill you," Dermot joked back. And then added more seriously, "Please, Kitty, it is better for you that you don't know."

The expression 'grace under pressure' came to Kitty. That was until a huge dollop of snot dropped off Dermot's nose and splattered on her well-read copy of *Wuthering Heights*. Her anger returned.

"Tell me!"

"You know I can't."

"How do you know what I know?"

"I dunno." Still cowering in the back seat, Dermot looked overwhelmed by Kitty's interrogation.

"So why did you say that?" Kitty badgered on.

"Say what?"

"That I know you can't tell me."

"Just."

"Just what?"

Dermot gave up and shrugged his shoulders. A car horn behind them blurted a frustrated staccato. Looking directly forward, Kitty realised the car in front of her had moved forward. She drove on a few metres until the gap was filled and Merlin was yet again flush to the bumper of the car ahead. The horn behind was satisfied, for the time being. Turning back around to challenge her hijacker, Kitty found herself drifting in and out of pity and then anger. As her mood battled with this conflict, a third emotion took liberty to sneak through – physical attraction. The element of danger was very seductive to the convent-educated, eighteen-year-old girl.

"You can stay there until I get out of all this traffic, but then you're on your own. Right?"

"Kitty, you're an angel! You really are a godsend! I've always said you were . . ."

"Don't push your luck, Dermot."

"Right you be."

Merlin nudged his way forward, metre-by-metre, and then gradually the steps forward became leaps of ten metres or so. Once they had passed three sets of traffic-lights, the traffic flowed more freely and Kitty and her reluctant passenger had almost cleared the city centre. Then, as Kitty managed third gear for the first time, she noticed an army jeep parked ahead, half on the road and half on the pavement. With the increased speed, Dermot confidently began to rise and straighten his stiffened spine.

"*Get down!*" Kitty shouted.

"Why?"

"There's another army jeep ahead!"

Standing by the front of the Saracen was a young soldier, looking not much older than Kitty and Dermot. Under different circumstances, Kitty would have found his uniform, broad shoulders and emerald green eyes an attractive combination. In fact, even under these circumstances, she found herself checking her lipstick in the mirror. Now that she was directly alongside the jeep, the young soldier waved his arms at her vigorously.

"He's waving at me. What'll I do?" Kitty's adolescent fantasy was shattered.

"Don't stop!"

"What?"

"Keep going. Don't look at him. You haven't seen him."

"Yes, I have."

"Drive past. Don't speed up or slow down. Take the next turn off. Please, Kitty!"

Kitty followed Dermot's directions.

"Did he follow you?"

Kitty scanned all around her, but the street was empty.

"No, but I don't know where I'm going."

Dermot peeked his head up, just high enough to see through the front window. The hair on the right had matted to the side of his head with the sweat, and his eyes were wide.

"Take the next right," he said confidently, "and then the next left."

"Do you know where we are?"

"No. I've been in Belfast less time than you."

She couldn't quite work out if Dermot was joking or not. But as they made the turn left, she looked through her rear-view window and discovered the army jeep following them. Dermot read the fear in Kitty's eyes and looked behind him also. There was no doubt this time as to whether Dermot was joking or not.

"Fuck!"

"What'll I do?"

"Go right!"

Dermot ducked back down again, plucking directions out of thin air.

"Are they still following?"

"No," Kitty answered swiftly.

"Thank God."

"But they are now. They're back again . . . and they're speeding up."

Within seconds, Merlin's windows had fully steamed up. A faint imprint of a baby's foot was evident in the steam. Even though Kitty managed to clear her front view with her hand, the rear window was a white veil.

"I can't see where he's gone."

And then through the opaque glass, two flashing lights burst forth.

"Shit! They're flashing their lights now." Her words hung in the air, fighting for space with the sound of Dermot's short shallow breaths.

Kitty was forced to clear her window a second time, leaving her right hand and cuff soaking wet.

"Dermot, tell me what to do!"

The sound of the breathing stopped and Kitty momentarily feared for Dermot's health. And then, with total calm and poise, he replied, "Pull over and wind down your window."

# Chapter 11

The grey Saracen slowly overtook the parked Volkswagen Beetle and stopped just in front. At the same languid pace, the soldier got out and swaggered in Merlin's direction. The chill winter air bounced off his broad frame and found victims to blast elsewhere. His rifle was held tightly against his chest, bedded in its own imprint created in the uniform. Merlin's reflection was visible in the sheen of his black boots and the nearer he came to the car, the less black and the more blue the reflection became. The soldier's heavy helmet sliced across his eyes, leaving full inky pupils to take in all that was around him. His face was expressionless, his body language severe. Merlin's driver-side window opened tentatively, in bursts of a few inches, almost in time with the soldier's heavy steps. He eventually stood beside the car, leaning on the roof, with his gun knocking against the paintwork as he breathed. Only at the point when the window was fully unwound did he laconically bend down and thrust his face through the opening.

"Lovely motor."

"Excuse me?" Kitty replied dumbfounded.

"A 1970, is it? I had one just the same back home. I flagged you down earlier, but you mustn't have seen me. I just wanted to tell you that they're great little cars."

At first, Kitty found the soldier's Northern English accent harsh, but as he continued to remark on Merlin's engine size and Ferdinand Porsche design, his voice had a sing-song quality only matched by his broad handsome smile. After a few minutes of car detail, Kitty also became conscious that the soldier was not only admiring the car, but also its owner. Every now and again she caught him looking down from her face to her figure. He blushed when he realised he'd been rumbled, which only endeared him further to Kitty.

"They say that a car's a phallic symbol," he said, and added, winking mischievously, "but believe me, just because I used to drive one of these, it doesn't mean anything."

"Aye, but look what you're driving now." Kitty teased, nodding to the six-wheeled Saracen, complete with turret and Browning machine gun.

The soldier didn't look much older than Kitty. She had never been this close to the army before and her preconceptions didn't quite match the reality. This soldier's youthful vulnerability hung as heavy on his soul as his uniform did on his body.

"Do you live here? You don't have a Belfast accent," he continued to charm.

"Neither do you!" Kitty dodged and avoided with what she thought was appropriate coyness. But when he looked lost for words, she added, "I'm from Portstewart. I'm studying here. And what about yourself? Where's home?"

"Home for me is cuddled up to a beautiful girl. One who has gorgeous brown eyes and an air-cooled engine. Do you know any?"

Kitty suspected that she was hearing chat-up lines that had been given more than one outing. But her suspicions mattered little when matched against compliments from a handsome stranger.

"No. But if I find any, I'll let you know."

"Well, I'd better give you a contact number at the barracks then. Just in case, that is."

The soldier took a pencil and a blank piece of paper from his top pocket. He scribbled a note and then handed it to Kitty, whispering "Please call me!" as he did.

He then turned away and, with the same easy gait, strolled back to the jeep. The minute he closed the door, the vehicle sped off and away from sight.

"Please call me!" Dermot mimicked from the backseat, sounding like an extra from *Emmerdale Farm*.

Kitty ignored her uninvited passenger and, turning the car around, drove off in the opposite direction to the soldiers. As she shoved the torn-off piece of paper into her pocket, she also touched the scrunched yellow Post-it with Dermot's telephone number on it. Beside that, she could also feel a neatly folded piece of card, which she knew had Jack Sheehan's contact number on. While she had been away at university, she hadn't unfolded this card once, but she knew there was still unfinished business there. The three telephone numbers became one jumbled lump in her pocket.

"Gorgeous brown eyes and drives a cool car!" Dermot

67

continued to imitate as he now, for the first time, sat bolt upright in the back seat. Kitty's clothes from the busted bin-bag decorated him like a Christmas tree. "Where did he get it from? That's the Brits for you – haven't a clue how to talk to a woman . . ." Dermot peeled one of Kitty's bras off his shoulder, "Jesus, Kitty, that's one hell of an over-shoulder-boulder-holder."

Kitty decided not to get dragged into her passenger's ranting and focused on the road ahead. Dermot fell silent and when Kitty looked back through her rear-view mirror, she discovered her bra had mysteriously disappeared.

Making eye contact with the driver again through the mirror, Dermot took this as an invitation to press on.

"Mind you, he seemed to be pressing your buttons all right, Kitty Farrell."

Kitty had only recently passed her driving test, but her aptitude with the emergency brake was demonstrated now, to perfection. Dermot lunged forward, slamming his shoulders hard against the two front seats, while dull-blond tresses filled the void between them with only his nose peeking out.

"Dermot O'Kane, I'm going nowhere until you tell me exactly what you're up to."

Thirty minutes later, Dermot and Kitty were sitting opposite each other in a roadside café, five miles before Ballymena. Dermot had responded to Kitty's ultimatum by saying he would tell her everything if she drove him as far as Coleraine. Again Kitty found herself seduced by the excitement, which was further intensified when Dermot agreed to provide the full story over a meal on the way.

They were both thankful for the heat from the café's

open fire. The second-hand camel-hair jacket and fifth-hand, grey mac embraced on the coatrack by the door. Kitty caught sight of herself in the mirror above the fire. Her relentless backcombing and heavy use of hairspray earlier that morning had done her proud. Her hair hadn't moved an inch all day. By contrast, Dermot looked dishevelled and weatherbeaten. But they shared a fierce hunger and attacked their meals even as the waitress was setting them on the table. Dermot's explanation could wait until their rumbling stomachs were silenced. As they ate, they complained.

"My chicken's still frozen in the middle. How's yours?" Dermot enquired, piling the food into his mouth.

"The menu said, 'Italian bread plumped with chargrilled vegetables and lashings of Mozzarella'."

"Cheese on toast?"

"On a good day maybe. It's rotten."

"And the chips are hard in the middle."

"Mine too."

"Everything OK with your meal?" their waitress butted in as she returned to the table carrying a jug of water.

"Yes, lovely," Kitty replied.

"Really nice," contributed Dermot.

The waitress disappeared through the swing-doors leading to the kitchen. As they swung open, the sound of a radio could be heard. The local news announcement gave details of a bomb-disposal officer who had been involved in an incident earlier in a city centre department store. The doors swung back closed. Seconds later the waitress reappeared carrying fresh ashtrays and "he lost both hands" leaked out from the radio before the doors closed back again.

The meal was devoured in minutes and as Dermot made his excuses and went to the toilet, Kitty took the liberty of ordering two double-chocolate fudge cakes, with extra helpings of vanilla ice cream. She was still hungry and couldn't wait. By the time she had finished her own dessert and Dermot still hadn't returned. Kitty was tempted to eat his as well and then hide the empty plates and just re-order desserts when he came back. Guilt held her back.

Kitty checked her watch. It was nine o'clock in the evening and she'd been expected at home hours ago. She considered telephoning her father, but quickly decided not to. Instead, she shuffled white and brown sugar sachets around. The waitress returned to the table and Kitty hurriedly pushed the sachets into a pile in the middle.

"Excuse me. I've a note for you." The waitress handed over one of the café's take-away menus. She hovered over Kitty's shoulder, before being forced to respond to a customer's impatient finger-tapping a few tables along. At first, Kitty couldn't see any message, until she discovered a spider-like sentence running along the edge of the menu, which read, '*Sorry, Kitty,*' followed by a series of scribbled out words. Kitty quickly realised that Dermot had abandoned her. She was all alone with only her resentment and a bill for five pounds and twenty-five pence to keep her company.

She paid the bill by cheque, and was further delayed when the waitress returned asking her to sign it.

She then made her way to collect her jacket. Dermot's was also still hanging on the rack beside her own. Lifeless, colourless and structureless, Dermot's coat looked even more abandoned than she was. It was worthless. But Kitty lifted his too, confident that he wouldn't be returning.

The evening had got much chillier and Kitty was relieved when Merlin started with the first turn of the ignition. Before changing into first gear, Kitty checked the back seat, something she would now do for the rest of her life. There was no one there. All was as it had been that morning. All except for the muddy grey coat perched on the passenger seat beside her. Without thought, she reached over and put her hand in the left pocket.

"Oh, my God!"

# Chapter 12

'Meeny, miney, mo!' The three telephone numbers had been burning a hole in Kitty's jacket pocket all over the Christmas holidays. She'd only stayed in Portstewart until Boxing Day and had escaped back to Belfast at the earliest opportunity. Having to share a bedroom with Heather took her patience to the edge and listening to Emer's relentless hints about her new, mystery boyfriend made her topple over it.

Now, well into the second university term, the pieces of paper nestling in her pocket still remained unopened. Sitting at the desk in her room, surrounded by unopened volumes of literary criticism, she placed the pieces of paper in front of her. They glowered back at her from a blank note-pad. She'd finally decided that whichever telephone number came out first would dictate the direction her love life would take. Kitty mixed the papers up and, with her eyes closed, pulled out the first – Jack Sheehan.

Kitty still had grave misgivings about re-igniting this

relationship but she was also, as ever, flattered by his interest in her. There were unresolved issues there and fate had dictated that now was the time to address this.

With her short pile of two-pence pieces, Kitty ran down to the telephone in the hall. It had taken her weeks to come to a decision and now she wanted a result in seconds.

*Ring-ring . . . ring-ring . . . ring-ring . . .*"Hello, Dominican Convent School."

"The PE Department, please."

"One minute."

She waited.

"Hello . . . hello?"

Kitty hung up.

Just as the second 'hello' was out and the too-familiar sound of Jack Sheehan's gravelly voice boomed out, Kitty changed her mind.

Back at her desk, she closed her eyes again and this time selected 'Dermot O'Kane'. His coat and the contents of its pockets were jammed into a cardboard box under Kitty's bed. Dermot too was unfinished business and she hadn't fully decided what direction to take. He had the potential to offer what Jack had once done – an element of risk. He really wasn't that bad as a second choice and, after all, the decision wasn't hers – it belonged to fate. Kitty briskly walked back down to the telephone.

*"Ring-ring . . ."*

A harsh, male voice abruptly answered. "Yes . . . hello?"

"Hello. Is Dermot there?"

"Who's this?"

"Just a friend. Is he there?"

"No," the man snapped, before appearing to have a

sudden change of heart and adding softly, "But if you see him, would you mind giving him a message?"

"Sure."

"Tell him if he comes back here again, there'll be a bullet waiting for him, with his name on it."

Kitty hung up a second time.

The third and last telephone number on her desk looked very lonely. The final choice was a British soldier. Kitty dawdled back down from her bedroom to the telephone. She scanned the notice-board as she slotted in her final two-pence piece. Someone really was determined that she should ring the Samaritans. The unfolded piece of paper had the soldier's name in block capitals, followed by the telephone number. Kitty decided that she would simply phone and leave a message. The rest was in the hands of the gods.

"Good afternoon, Palace Barracks."

"Hello. Could I please leave a message for Matt Edwards?"

"Matt! Matt! Phone for you."

Oh, no! Kitty hadn't expected him to be there. This had all gone terribly wrong. She didn't feel nearly as brave as she did ten minutes ago. Fate was playing a cruel game with her. Should she hang up again?

The following evening Kitty met her British soldier for a quiet drink in the Wellington Bar on Botanic Avenue. Out of his uniform, he was even more handsome than she remembered. His crew-cut hair was the colour of black tar and his green eyes were speckled with turquoise and deep blue. On his chin there were a few marks, evidence of teenage acne. But his scars only appeared to add character to what would, otherwise, have been too pretty a complexion. His drainpipe jeans and white T-shirt announced 'soldier in civvies' a mile away and she was relieved they had chosen a neutral location for their first date.

Kitty's own Ska style was lasting much longer than any of her other recent fashion fads and over the last few weeks she'd added a black and white polyester mini skirt, with matching slashed-neck blouse, to her wardrobe. She'd discovered an excellent second-hand bookshop in the city and ten *Penguin Classics* equated to the value of one *Miss Selfridge* sweater. Kitty had also discovered the value of the video-suite in the University Library. One viewing of the BBC's *The Tempest* took only two and a half-hours, compared to a full week of reading the text. Kitty's clothes, therefore, for her Friday-night date had cost a *Collins Dictionary*, the full set of Shakespeare's *Greatest Works*, plus a pristine copy of *Ulysses*.

Matt took Kitty's coat in a gentlemanly fashion as she sat down, before scrunching it up and throwing it on the floor beside them.

"I'd almost given up on you," he admitted later.

"Sure, isn't waiting for something often more exciting than actually getting it?" Kitty teased as she sipped her cider and blackcurrant, while holding her glass with an affected crooked finger.

"Not in this case. You look fabulous. I'm the envy of every bloke here."

Bullshit or not, Kitty didn't care.

"Are there any more of you at home?" Matt smiled and shifted his seat until it was closer.

"Two sisters . . . too young for you."

"What about your mum? She'll do me."

"She's dead."

The smile on Matt's face, for the first time since they'd met, deserted him. Without the wrinkles and creases of his grin, Kitty could see how truly handsome he was.

"Oh, Kitty. I'm really sorry."

"Don't worry. Honestly. She's been gone a long time now."

"So who raised you guys?"

"My father."

"But the rest of your extended family helped out, right?"

"Not really." Kitty took another, much bigger gulp of her cider, before elaborating. "He wasn't born here. My father's adoptive parents were Irish, hence the Farrell name. But they went to live in England in the 40's. It seems they adopted my father about that time and he took on their name. He then met my mother when he was a teenager. She was also an only child and they moved back here when he got a six-month work contract to help build the university in Coleraine. He's a bricklayer. I was only wee at the time. And we never went back. With both sets of grandparents long dead and buried, there's just us."

"That's remarkable – a bloke raising three girls on his own."

"Aye," said Kitty, adding with a slight hint of sarcasm, "My father is definitely remarkable." Then she rushed on with, "Some first date this is turning out to be. What happened to lines like, 'What's your favourite colour?' and 'Do you like Depeche Mode?'"

"Do you like Depeche Mode?"

Kitty and Matt drifted easily into mild banter. Kitty

found herself floating beyond her usual 'first-date' coyness and into – well, just being herself.

After the bar called 'last orders' for the second time, Matt walked Kitty the mile or so back to the halls of residence. They stood for a further thirty minutes, idly chatting and childishly taunting each other.

"Kitty Farrell, I think you're going to be the ruin of me."

"And what's that supposed to mean?"

"You've already wrenched open my heart. What are you going to do with the rest of me?"

Bullshit is indeed a glorious thing, Kitty thought, as she reached up onto her tiptoes and kissed him. The tender kiss became full-blown snogging in a matter of seconds and lasted that way for a full hour. The young soldier made no indication of advancing his intentions further and, following Kitty's recent sexual encounters, she was content to wallow in the innocence of their embrace. Matt held her tightly around the waist – like the black and white movies, Kitty initially thought to herself. But, as he discovered her ears, her eyes and her throat with his lips, this was definitely not the movie that she was thinking of.

Following a natural break in their intimacy, they said their goodbyes – several times. Eventually, Matt resisted his own inclinations and walked away. They hadn't arranged a second date, but neither seemed in any doubt that a second would follow.

"What would your father think of you going out with a Brit?" Matt whispered back as he continued to walk away.

"Are we going out?"

"Well, we're 'going' and we're 'out'."

Matt didn't wait for Kitty's answer before turning off the

path at the corner and disappearing behind a dense blanket of conifers and cedars.

What would her father think – his precious, Catholic first-born dating a British soldier? Kitty drew the conclusion that her father would be furious. And the community she grew up with, she reckoned, would probably disown her. What would Jack Sheehan and Dermot O'Kane make of it?

Back in her room, Kitty checked through her timetable and picked out five scheduled lectures that she could avoid this week, at no great loss. This would free up ten daytime hours, combined with all her evenings, for Kitty to focus on her one objective: to lure, seduce and eventually marry Matt Edwards.

*Emer, 1985*

# Chapter 13

The car keys dangled, tantalisingly, only a few inches from her fingertips. If she could stretch just that little bit further, she wouldn't have to walk on the creaky floorboards that would definitely disturb her father's afternoon nap. Emer Farrell decompressed her joints and ligaments, until she managed to find another two inches (which she didn't know she had).

Roddy Farrell was lying on the living-room sofa, facing away from her. Above him, hanging on the wall, was a gallery of crooked framed photographs, taken by him of his daughters. A recent chest infection, which he was susceptible to because of his outdoor work, had left him wheezy and, as he lay softly snoring, Emer knew it would be four o'clock before he awoke. Which was time enough. Heather, as usual, would be away to Mass and then out for a walk. She wouldn't be back until late

After two years of paying his eldest daughter's outstanding road-tax and insurance bills, Roddy had taken the train up to Belfast and returned four hours later behind the wheel of Merlin. Kitty hadn't even put up a fight and had appeared relieved to part with the car.

Now Merlin's safekeeping was in the hands of Roddy's second daughter, Emer. And that was on one condition: Emer had to pass her driving test. She'd had two attempts already. In the first, she didn't even get to sit behind the steering wheel, since she failed to read the number-plate of the car parked ahead of her. It turned out to be a very expensive eye-test. By her second driving-test, Emer had acquired a pair of red-plastic, wide-rimmed glasses and that test lasted a little longer. It was ten minutes before she drove through two rows of cars, parked either side of her, clipping every one of their wing mirrors with her own. So, naturally, Emer was keen to get as much driving practice in the car as possible. But her father was often too tired at the weekends to be any use to her as an instructor. So, whenever she could, Emer would sneak out and get a few extra lessons with her boyfriend.

The keys slipped off the hook, just above the dozing head of her father, with a delicate clink. Roddy didn't stir from his traditional Sunday afternoon doze.

Outside the house, Jack Sheehan was cowering behind the Volkswagen Beetle. When his girlfriend threw the car keys at him, he swiftly jumped into the car and drove the two of them along O'Hara Drive and out onto the main road.

"Jesus, I feel like I spend my life ducking and diving from your family," Jack moaned with a pitiful whimper.

"Here we go again!"

"What?"

"You moan. Then I say, 'OK, let's tell my father and my sisters' and then you say, 'Maybe not' and I say, 'Why not' and then you say, 'Because they'll tell the school and I'll get the sack'. And then I say, 'But I've nearly finished school' and you say, 'Doesn't matter. I'm thirty and you're just eighteen and I'll still get the sack'. OK, I've just saved you all that trouble. Now get on and let me have a go at a three-point turn."

Emer had come a long way in the last few years. In particular, her no-nonsense approach had blossomed without the shadow of her eldest sister. Emer was also enjoying the mystery of her lover. She enjoyed the smugness of feeling that she had something her eldest sister had never had, a grown-up boyfriend. Jack had never told her otherwise.

"Better still, let's drive over to Moore's," she continued, "and I'll nip in and have a look at their sale. Their stuff's gorgeous. I'm sure to have to practise parking or something when I get there."

Emer had also become an expert shopper. Not that she had much to spend, other than a portion of the family allowance, given to her by her father every fortnight. But limited means meant that she had become an expert at sourcing the best value. She'd walk from one side of the town to the other, if it meant saving a few pence, or availing of a five per cent extra offer.

"But that'll mean having to duck down again and . . ." Jack was silenced by one of Emer's 'looks'.

Emer had spent nearly a year hiding under coats and books in Jack's Nissan Micra and she wallowed in seeing her boyfriend having to do the same – and even more so, since the Beetle was much more of a distinctive car and therefore concealment in cramped, uncomfortable conditions was essential.

It took Emer four attempts before she finally parked on a quiet side street. As she hurried across the road in the direction of the department store, she checked behind her to inspect if Jack was appropriately hidden. He was. She also noticed how ragged Merlin had become. Even in the bright sunshine of this spring afternoon, his crystal-blue shell had lost its lustre. Splodges of rust had started to appear on the wing tips and the once pristine chrome bumpers looked lifeless.

When Emer returned to the car fifteen minutes later, the back bumper had given up and was hanging off.

As she drove home, Emer squeezed in three emergency stops and two reverse parkings – which Jack concluded with his own two 'Our Fathers' and four 'Hail Marys'.

The rest of the journey was taken up with Emer's minute detailing of every hem-length, button design and discount price that Moore's had to offer.

"Are you listening?" Emer wasn't convinced.

"What are you planning to do, Emer?"

"I'll save up and go back in the summer sales."

"Not that. With your life. What are you planning to do with that?"

Emer had never in her eighteen years thought beyond the nitty-gritty detail of everyday living. She'd made all the discoveries she wanted, for now: she'd finally discovered a hair-care product that didn't frizz her curls, she'd discovered Wrangler jeans that made her size ten figure look like an eight and she'd discovered that a 34DD bust size always got you noticed when the soldiers stopped and searched the bus on the way to Belfast.

As Jack continued to blankly stare out of the window, Emer realised that her boyfriend's questions were not directed at her at all. At the traffic-lights, she reached over and gently placed her left hand on Jack's leg.

"You have a great job. All the kids love you. The parents love you and even the nuns are mad about you." Emer squeezed his leg, looking for a reaction. "And you've got a terrific girlfriend, who's even more mad about you than all the rest put together."

But neither the words nor the touch generated a response. "Look, Jack, I can meet you at the usual place, while Dad and Heather are watching *Songs of Praise*. We can do some more 'talking' then?"

Even the promise of sex didn't break his trance.

With still half an hour to go before Roddy Farrell could be expected to wake up, Emer decided to take the coast road home, via Portrush, and complete *The Golden Triangle*. The faded markings of the starting grid for the Northwest 200 were barely visible. The annual motorbike road race was institutionalised in the Farrell family calendar. They scoffed egg and onion sandwiches on the grassy banks, and watched as the 500cc bikes careered deafeningly around the course, in the anticipation of a dramatic accident on the corners.

When they reached O'Hara Drive, Jack gave Emer a quick peck on the cheek and then disappeared behind the billowing smoke gushing from his ten-year-old Micra, which had been discreetly parked further down the street.

Roddy was still sleeping. Her youngest sister, who hadn't been to Mass at all due to alleged period pains, idly sat reading a book and nursing a hot-water bottle on the wicker chair by the front window.

Having replaced the car keys in their rightful place, Emer returned to the front step and sat down. She took off her glasses, which she had forgotten she was wearing, as they usually were never worn outside of the car. She thought back to the past few months and how the relationship between herself and Jack had changed somehow. These recent memories had a heavy fog over them. Jack was different.

There was a freshness to the ocean today. It looked almost transparent. Emer watched for white foam as waves broke in the distance, longing for the vision of a humpback whale to break the surface. When this didn't happen, just as it had never happened before, Emer then transferred her thoughts back to happier memories. She thought of last summer and the tail-end of the school holidays. As per the norm, Jack and herself had met up somewhere secluded and driven away from Portstewart. Jack lived twenty miles away in Limavady and their dates usually occurred straight after school. In the school holidays, however, they got to see much more of each other. The memory she chose now was of Mussenden Temple. Even now, as Emer sat on the cold front step, she could still feel the sun's rays on that sweltering evening. They lay, with the tips of their bare toes touching, on the honey-stone step that surrounded the ancient temple. Every few minutes the sun would escape from behind a cloud and bathe them in heat.

"Stop, here it comes again."

When the sun came out, Jack and Emer would stop talking, just close their eyes and bathe their faces in its rays.

In between silent minutes of radiation, when the sun disappeared again, Jack told Emer stories about how the temple had been built by the Bishop of Londonderry as a place of worship for his daughter. They were enjoying and celebrating the last of the summer, topping themselves up before the grey, wintry days ahead. Even when the setting sun had been gulped up by the Atlantic, they remained with their faces looking up at the sky and their backs against the stone. Jack had given Emer his leather jacket as a pillow and the sequined 'Merlin' tickled her neck. They were both dressed in cut-off denim shorts and casual T-shirts. Emer's hair, loose, added a marbling effect to the stone. Each had an assortment of tanned bands across their bare arms and legs, where the sun had periodically burnt them over the holidays.

"Tell me again," Jack pleaded.

"Which one?"

"The one about the whites and the coloureds."

"OK. Well, if you mix your whites and coloureds, you're in big trouble. Keep your whites until you've a load. And what I've learnt is always check the pockets. You're best to do your smalls separately too – keeps them fresh-looking . . ."

And as Emer went on to catalogue every conceivable washing permutation, Jack closed his eyes again and gave a wry smile up to the sky.

"But, Emer, what about jumpers?"

Emer was given licence to continue to define the most suitable washing powders and the best drying methods for woollens and polyester mixes.

"Don't stop yet," Jack begged, as Emer took a moment to gather her thoughts.

She continued with a study of drying clothes outside, versus inside, by the open fire. And every time she paused, Jack would kick her foot with his and start her going again.

"Jack, what do you see in a silly teenage girl, with her head full of unimportant rubbish?"

"Everything."

"Wouldn't you prefer someone more sophisticated? Someone with an interest in the bigger picture?"

"I see the bigger picture at home and at school every day. And the answer's no."

"Then is it just to have sex with a schoolgirl?" Emer joked, flicking her bare foot against his.

For the first time since they had started dating six months earlier, Emer saw Jack angry. He was enraged. Standing bolt upright, he towered over Emer.

"Have I ever asked you to do anything that you didn't want to do? Have I?"

"No, of course not," Emer replied immediately.

"Did I pressurise you? Did I rush you? Do I ever force you?" The veins on his neck throbbed and his bottom lip clenched his heavy moustache tightly.

"No, never. I was only joking . . ." But Emer didn't get to finish.

"We were seeing each for four months before I even touched your tits. And that was because you insisted on not wearing a bra that time and it was raining." The fond memory broke Jack's trail of thought and, as he paused, he saw that under the weight of his rage, Emer had begun to cry. He instantly leant over his young girlfriend and lifted her to her feet.

"I guess I just want to be with you," he said softly. "Not a care in the world. Being with you I can be silly. I can be a stupid teenager again. I'm sorry, Emer. Even if I don't show it at times, I really do love you."

As Emer now sat on the step looking for the back of that elusive whale, the 'I love you' ran laps inside her head. That summer's evening had been the first time Emer had ever heard those words addressed to her. Not even her father had managed them, in that particular order. She also remembered how she had held Jack's face within her hands and kissed him.

To Jack Sheehan's pleasant astonishment, she also unearthed a rather professional approach to giving oral sex. And from then on, the request 'Can I have a Mussenden Temple, please' had a whole new meaning.

Emer smiled and, taking one more glance out to the Atlantic as she stood up from the step, she headed back inside the house, to discover her father finally stirring.

The next morning Emer discovered that Jack Sheehan had been killed.

# Chapter 14

The chapel was bunged. The seats, aisles and the carpark in front of the chapel, under the shadow of the convent, were swamped with family, colleagues, pupils, ex-pupils and their families, neighbours, and a few curious American tourists. Realising the strength of local sympathy, the deceased's family had decided to hold the service in St Mary's Star of the Sea, Portstewart, before transferring the body to the Sheehan family plot in Limavady. Emer and Heather had managed to secure a space on a bench at the very back, directly in front of a statue of Mary and Child. Roddy Farrell waited outside. The coffin was engulfed with white lilies and orchids. An elderly woman beside Emer commented that 'they were beautifully arranged'. In different circumstances, Emer would have responded 'Yes, fabulous', but not today.

After leaving Emer, that day of her shopping trip to Moore's, it appears that Jack had himself driven over to the Northwest 200 course. Having stopped his car at the faded start markings, he had subsequently raced his Micra at full speed, until he reached its first bend. At sixty miles an hour, the car had skidded and ploughed down the bank to the rocks below. At the wake, the coffin had been closed.

"Dear, you don't look well," the old woman added, as the priest began his service.

Emer looked across to discover the woman had a leg missing, a bandage around her right hand and cataracts.

The silence of the congregation was only broken by the occasional tearful whimper from the immediate family seated at the front. The front bench mainly comprised elderly relatives, with one young boy about Heather's age and a woman. From their appearances, Emer guessed they were Jack's brother and sister. The nuns in the second row sniffled with restraint into white lace handkerchiefs.

There were two priests for the funeral service, the local one and one from Jack's family parish. It was obvious from the Limavady priest's recollections that he didn't really know Jack. He spoke about the deceased interest in 'archaeology' and 'landscape painting'. Judging from the immediate family members' nods and 'ayes', Emer guessed that Jack's family didn't know that much about him either.

The onset of drizzly rain didn't hinder the mourners outside who huddled together under a canopy of golfing umbrellas and newspapers. Emer knew that her father didn't like getting his head wet and would have been the first to find shelter. In anticipation of a large turnout, a loudspeaker had been set up and the service was transmitted outside the chapel through an ethereal reverberation.

The priest concluded his personal tribute with 'Jack was loved by many and he will be missed by many'. The readings followed and family members took it in turns to read extracts from the Bible. The first was a stately-looking man in his early sixties, who enunciated and projected with the skill of years of amateur drama training. In particular, he got enthusiastic about his s's at the beginning of sentences and t's at the end. Next up was the boy who Emer had guessed to be Jack's young brother. He was a gently spoken boy and in a whisper he introduced himself as Michael and talked about his love for his 'big brother', who he 'looked up to'. He had exactly the same features as his older brother, if slightly less developed and more refined – even down to the light-brown hair-colouring, just about short enough to be acceptable in school.

Halfway through his reading from the letters of St Paul to the Corinthians, the young boy's voice became so inaudible that the priest had to read along with him. The powerful sound of the priest's resonant tones, compounded with the hushed echo of the young brother, sent a Mexican wave of female sobs out from the chapel's altar as far as the mourners outside.

Fourteen-year-old Heather joined the vocal wave of grief. Emer didn't. A week of crying had left her exhausted. The old woman had been right: Emer did look awful. Her youthful, translucent pallor was grey and drawn. Under her eyes were smudges as black as her mother's mourning suit which she was wearing – she had found it boxed in the attic. Emer had been too young to grieve for her mother, but somehow the outfit had significance today.

Along with her Wrangler jeans, at eighteen Emer had discovered loss. What answer would she give Jack, if he had asked her now what was she planning to do with her life? And in keeping with their relationship, her grief was kept hidden and amplified further as a result. Her father had assumed that she was coming down with something and given her hot-lemon Beecham's Powders for it.

Emer knew that she wouldn't be able to pretend as easily to her eldest sister and was relieved when Heather offered to telephone and let Kitty know what had happened to her ex-teacher. Heather hadn't relayed the conversation back to Emer, only to say that Kitty had decided she wouldn't be coming back for the Easter holidays after all.

With Michael Sheehan's reading complete, the priest escorted him back to his seat, where he collapsed into the arms of an elderly relative. The next and final speaker was the woman on the other side of him. She was much more composed and radiated a confidence that Emer had also recognised in Jack. They were strikingly similar in manner and gait. The woman was carrying Jack's jacket and the sequined word 'Merlin' in various shades of gold flickered in the light from the altar candles. Now Emer struggled to contain her tears. She hadn't thought it possible that she had any left, but as the woman spoke of Jack's love of his school and of the staff and the pupils, Emer tried to stifle her tears by holding her hand across her nose and mouth. Heather was too absorbed in counting off Hail Marys on her rosary beads to take any notice of her sister's dilemma.

"And this jacket is all we have left." The woman spoke with gravitas and composure, as she held Jack's jacket up for the entire congregation to see. "Merlin, the magician . . . Jack's lucky mascot . . . couldn't do his magic and save him this time."

Even a few men in the congregation wanted to weep at this point and the chapel became a jumbled mess of both suppressed and expressed grief.

Emer knew that her hand was the only thing protecting her from a full-blown, hysterical sob.

"But this jacket says a lot more about the man who wore it," the woman continued in the same tone and level of emotion as before, "because hidden away in the pockets, Jack kept trinkets and important personal mementoes dear to his heart . . ."

The woman could no longer maintain her composure and, before completing her speech, was also escorted in tears back to her seat.

Holy Communion followed, given by the local priest, which considering the numbers there took nearly forty-five minutes to complete.

Heather, who had recently become the family 'Holy-Joe', was the first in the queue to take communion. Emer remained seated.

"The body of Christ," said the priest, first looking at Heather and then across the congregation to Emer for a brief second.

"Amen," replied Heather.

The eager, elderly lady with the one leg nudged Heather out the way.

With the funeral service complete, behind the coffin carried on the shoulders of six men, the congregation trickled out of the chapel. Emer told Heather that she would follow shortly, as she wanted to stay on her own for a few moments. Heather queued at the chapel door with the other mourners, waiting to leave.

"Hello, Father. It's Heather," Heather confidently announced as she tugged on the priest's gown as she left.

"Yes, of course. Helen. How's your daddy doing?"

Roddy Farrell was well known in the village.

"It's Heather, Father. He's good, Father."

"Is he taking care of that chest of his, Helen?"

Still inside, only Emer and the woman remained, each too consumed by their personal loss to notice the other. After half an hour, the sound of the last few cars driving away broke Emer's concentration. She knew that her father and sister would be left waiting for her, but still she was not ready to leave. When her local priest re-entered the chapel, he did not see her, but went to comfort the woman still seated on the front bench. Sitting besides the woman, he mumbled a few comforting words, before guiding her by the arm to the door. The woman was unsure on her feet and would have stumbled without the priest's assistance. The priest and the woman walked back down the aisle at the same, measured pace as that of a newly married couple. Just as they were about to leave, they both caught sight of Emer.

"Can I help you?" whispered the priest.

"Thank you. But no, Father, I'm just leaving," Emer replied, finally standing.

"Aren't you one of the Farrell girls?" the priest asked as he held out his other arm for Emer.

"Yes, Father. Emer."

Emer showed no reaction when the priest then introduced the woman beside him as the deceased's widow. She had drawn that conclusion herself, the moment the woman had to be helped down during her speech. The discovery had left Emer numb but, deep down, she realised that she wasn't surprised to hear that her lover had been married. But she was surprised when Mrs Jack Sheehan didn't shake her tentative, outstretched hand by way of a greeting but instead stared directly at her and said:

"I know all about Emer Farrell and her sister Kitty. I have things belonging to you both, found in my late husband's jacket." She paused, took a deep breath and then added, "And, if you don't mind, Father, I won't be shaking hands."

The sound of the chapel door crashing closed and the sight of her young sister, Heather, only a few feet away, signified to Emer Farrell that her father had been there moments earlier and, having overheard enough, had departed.

The Volkswagen Beetle found a temporary home in a neighbour's garage, shrouded in a grey plastic cover and with house-bricks propped against its wheels. Roddy Farrell insisted that Emer transfer from the convent school to the local Further Education College in order to finish her 'A' levels. At the same time Heather was ordered to transfer to St Joseph's, a co-ed secondary school in Coleraine. The sisters complied with little fuss. The priest was pacified with a 'my daughters will repent before entering the chapel again' speech by Roddy Farrell the day after the funeral. As for his eldest daughter, Roddy wrote her a short note a few days later, which Heather managed to secretly prise from its envelope before she posted it.

*Kitty,*

*By now, I'm sure you will have heard the ugly news. I expected so much more from you, my eldest daughter. You were always a role model for your sisters and I believe that Emer's part in all this was only possible because of the example you set. I will always love you and love the memory of when you first said my name. But you can no longer be part of this family. What you and that teacher have done to us and to his poor wife is unforgivable. The disappointment I feel is so deep, I feel physical pain in my heart when I think of you.*

*Please show me at least one final trace of respect and do not contact me, or your sisters, again.*

*I hope the thought you give to your future will be much more than that given to your past.*

*Roddy Farrell.*
*25th March 1985*

Heather resealed the envelope and posted it, as were her father's instructions.

After the funeral incident, Emer and Kitty had, for their own reasons, stopped talking to each other anyway. Heather, therefore, became the only member of the Farrell family left with open communication. With her eldest sister, 'open' meant clandestine telephone calls via the payphone in the local VG.

The plastic cover protected Merlin from slight changes in temperature, but failed to provide adequate protection against more dramatic, climatic changes. Cracks began to appear in the paintwork and blistering broke out around the headlights. An oil-seal, that had begun to leak when it was being regularly driven, also eroded and expanded further and dripped into a rainbow pool on the concrete garage floor.

Merlin remained stagnant and shielded this way from the outside world, for the next two years.

*Heather, 1987*

# Chapter 15

Heather Farrell passed her driving test at the first attempt, six weeks after her seventeenth birthday. Emer had failed for the fifth time the week earlier. Their father had predicted both results and in anticipation had finally removed the seventeen-year-old Volkswagen Beetle out of storage. The car now belonged to Heather. There hadn't been much money around for any major repairs, but enough to repair the oil-seal, replace the brake-pads and get it taxed and insured.

Driving Merlin for the first time and for the first time being in a car by herself, Heather rejoiced in the totally new experience of liberation.

Over the last few years, Heather had felt like the family were strangling her. Roddy Farrell treated her as his last bet on a successful and fulfilled daughter, applying the pressures on her education and her social development. Kitty used her as a secret go-between, relaying news and updates about the family over the telephone, while maintaining her charade that she really wasn't all that interested. And Emer manipulated Heather as a platform to vent her anger and frustration, when her moods swung haphazardly between deep troughs and high peaks. Heather had become a puppet. Feeling alienated from the chapel, Heather had also lost her one inspiration, her faith. She had become privately cynical and last year had given away her rosary beads and Bible at a school fundraising fete.

Now, as she carefully steered Merlin around the bends on the road, Heather sensed that she had been finally given an opportunity to regain control of her young life. She wanted to step out from the umbrella of gloom that at times engulfed her. Perhaps 1987 would turn out to be her year.

The route to St Joseph's High School looked and felt so different, compared to her usual method of travelling by the school bus. Lower down in her small car, every lump and bump in the road ricocheted through her bones. The lush sheen of the holly, tethered against the dry, bare branches of the sycamores, created the division between tarmac and white fields. The early morning frost added crispness to all around her, on an otherwise bleak and dull April morning. Heather could no longer see into the first-floor windows of the grey, pebbledash farmhouses that dotted the road.

As she drove, Heather tilted the rear-view mirror, so that she could check if her hair was tidy. She was disappointed to see her face fill the mirror entirely. Heather was no longer the svelte nymph of her pre-pubescent youth. She would describe herself as 'round' – round face, round body, round hands and feet. What her self-conscious self-analysis failed to see were the provocative curves, the honey-toned sheen of her complexion and her vibrant youth. A droopy curtain of long, frizzy, shapeless hair, masked so much.

Quickly, she tilted the mirror back, until she could only see the road behind and nothing else.

When she arrived at the school carpark, Heather's classmates leapt upon her car, twiddling the tiny controls on the dashboard and turning the indicators on and off. When the bell sounded for the first nine o'clock class, Heather and her car were brutally forgotten. They were now abandoned to the past, as her classmates, bored already, moved on in search of the next new thing. Heather double-checked that the hand-brake was secure and the gear-stick in neutral, before following her classmates indoors.

Each of the tables in the 'A' level mathematics class was large enough for four pupils, but mostly were taken up with three students and the end seat was left spare. The boys sat on one side of the room, the girls the other. Heather was the only one at her table. She could have sat on the end of the tables in front, or behind, but she didn't like the idea of being at the end. And they in turn didn't feel the need to move over to her table. So Heather had got used to sitting on her own, deciding that it afforded her better concentration and focus.

She was the last to enter the classroom and, as she did, she found the girls laughing at some subject or other. Heather forced herself to laugh along with them. She was rarely interested in what they had to say or could understand exactly what they found so funny, but she had gradually learnt that if she wanted to stay included, she had to perform. Heather's home life had given her the skills to become quite a performer all round.

With their schoolbooks open, the teacher began by running through the answers to the previous week's homework. Mrs Hagan was famous in the school for her mispronunciation of 'logarithms' and her pure-white, lacy bra that peeked out when she bent over to make corrections to their homework.

Heather had, as per usual, scored full marks and amused herself by reading the next chapter in the textbook. She also, as per usual, took the opportunity to inspect Cillian Harte seated two tables in front. Cillian and Heather competed to be the class swots. Usually Cillian had the upper hand, because he also managed to maintain an air of popularity and coolness, which Heather didn't. He was also a brilliant artist. They both managed to irritate each other on a regular basis. Today, Heather's adversary was dressed in an over-sized cream woollen sweater and army surplus trousers with tears along the knees and back pockets. His desert boots were slightly turned up at the front. With his head dipped forward as he scribbled on his exercise book, Cillian's greasy, shoulder-length hair flopped down and Heather could see the soft fluff of reddish, new whiskers along his jaw-line. Mrs Hagan left the class to find new chalk in the staff-room and the class launched into debate as to how many times their teacher had already mispronounced words today. Cillian looked up from his studies and turned his head in Heather's direction. She quickly looked back at her book and flicked through the pages casually.

"I make it three 'loogorithums'."

"I've written here four, plus one 'parrelel'."

The boys and the girls compared notes, passing them across the tables which formed the divide between the sexes.

"Farrell, how many did you get? Or can't you count that far?" Cillian jibed at Heather through a confident smirk.

"At least the nine-times table doesn't give *me* cold sweats," Heather replied without lifting her head up from her book. "Do you know you're depriving a village somewhere of an idiot?"

Cillian was silenced, for the time being, as Mrs Hagan returned without any chalk.

The suspected liaison between their mathematics teacher and the new student placement took up most of the conversation in the break. Through lunch-time and by the final break of the day, it was generally decided that the teachers in question would be getting married and all the classmates would be guests at the wedding. Heather had little to contribute to the debate, but laughed and joked along at the appropriate times.

As they said their final farewells at the end of the day and made plans for the weekend, the classmates parted company with Heather and her car, shouting cheerfully, "See you Monday!".

Without the constraint of having to get the school-bus home and then spend the evening reading in her bedroom, Heather had other plans for the next few hours. Leaving the school carpark, she turned left into Coleraine town centre, rather than right in the direction of home. A blustery wind had built up and Merlin rocked slightly with each fresh blast. En route to her final destination, she stopped at the petrol station and, with a pocket full of loose change, she entered the telephone box pulling the door tightly closed behind her.

Discarded chewing-gum stuck to her shoes and she could

100

smell the heady scent of stale tobacco as she lifted the receiver.

"Hello."

"Kitty, it's me. Can you hear me all right?"

It was Heather's turn to telephone her eldest sister. The act was usually hidden by the excuse of going to the VG to pick up a copy of the *Coleraine Chronicle* for her father.

A few years previously, Kitty had moved out of halls and into a rented house on the Ravenhill Road in Belfast. Amongst other things, the house didn't have a telephone. The sisters, therefore, took it in turns to phone each other at arranged times and Heather knew the telephone box in which her sister would be waiting for the call was often very noisy. The whirring of army helicopters on surveillance had hindered many of their calls up to now.

"Yes, Heather, it's surprisingly quiet here this evening. Well, tell me, did the old man give you the keys? Is he yours?" Kitty's voice was full of excitement and joy.

"Aye, he's all mine. Drives like a bomb – literally. I think it may go off at any moment."

"I remember too well. You can hardly hear yourself think in him. Is my little tube with the plastic rose still stuck to the back window?"

"No. Dad must have thrown it out."

"How is he?"

The wind rattled the telephone-box glass and Heather had to block her ear with her finger so that she could hear her sister better.

"Usual!" Heather shouted. "Work-home-work. They're talking about giving him indoor work for a while."

"I don't really care, you know." Kitty paused. Her voice was flatter. "How's his chest?"

"It's been playing him up, but a bit of indoor work will do him good. What about your new job?"

Kitty Farrell hadn't been back to Portstewart for the last three years. All that Heather really knew of her sister's life was that she'd astonished her class, and the faculty, by last summer graduating with a first-class degree in English Literature. Kitty had since then been taking a year off and doing casual bar-work in Belfast.

"Yes, starts in a couple of weeks. It's a similar sort of bar to the one I'm in at the moment. But this one's in Kingston – right smack on the Thames and only a twenty-five-minute train journey from central London." With the lightness returning to her voice, Kitty joked, "Since you nabbed mine, it's a good job that I won't be needing a car after all!"

She never volunteered details of her private life during these brief calls and Heather didn't want to know. Always the quiet, observant one, the one easily forgotten, Heather had been the only family member to have known what was going on with both Kitty and Emer. She had brutally learnt that knowledge is not always an advantage and had subsequently focussed her learning on schoolbooks, and not on life.

"Emer still shows no intention of heading off to university. She's got herself on a reflexology course now."

"Who cares?" Kitty paused. "Maybe she'll finish this one. The aromatherapy and hairdressing ones didn't last too long, did they? Is she seeing anyone?"

The telephone door swung open with a gust of wind and Heather yanked it closed again.

"I don't know. I don't think so."

Heather genuinely didn't know, or rather she chose not to know.

"And, Heather, are you still taking the vitamin supplements I told you about?"

"Aye."

"And the herbal tea?"

"Aye."

The youngest Farrell sister was out of change and the telephone pips interrupted Kitty's parting request.

"Next week I'll be able to give you my new number in Kingston. Promise me you'll ring, Heather. There's someone I want you to –"

The telephone line was dead.

Heather made it to the swimming-pool just in time for the five o'clock session. On her seventeenth birthday she had promised herself that when she got the freedom of the new car, she was going to get in shape. The Jane Fonda exercise videotapes just weren't doing it for her. The last time, in fact, that Heather had visited the Coleraine Leisure Centre was when she was twelve and she could fit into a fluorescent pink bikini, trimmed with a sea-shell-patterned little skirt and with a eight-year-old label-size in the back. Now she squeezed into a plain, black, size fourteen swimsuit, with foam shell-inserts for added chest support and a thick halter-neck strap. The changing cubicle was a degree warmer than the freezing wintry conditions outside. Heather hurriedly and awkwardly changed, as she kept her bath towel pulled tight around her until she was decently dressed in her swimsuit – she was in a private cubicle. She completed the route along the icy white floor-tiles from the changing room to the pool in seconds and only when her body was submerged up to her shoulders, did she, for the first time, relax and breathe out.

The pool was like a huge bath. The temperature had been raised for a mother-and-toddler group earlier that afternoon, and it had retained the heat. Heather just lay on her back and floated. Only her face, her breasts and the small, round curve of her stomach broke the surface. She could hear the muffled deep tones as the water lapped against the chrome steps and muffled voices of swimmers around her. She felt serene.

"Farrell! Farrell!"

Heather gulped a litre of chlorinated water as she thrust her head up.

"You'll never make the Olympics, training like that." Cillian Harte was beaming through saturated straggly hair.

"I will if floating becomes a competitive sport." With seven-eighths of her body hidden under the water, Heather surprised herself by how confident she felt in dealing with her irksome adversary. "Now don't annoy me and buzz off."

"Ah, come on. I'll have you a race."

"No."

"Why not?"

"Because I'll win, as usual, and you'll cry, as usual."

Heather had never met Cillian out of the school environment. It was strange seeing him like this. She compared it to seeing a member of the Orange Order at Mass or her father having a laugh. Cillian didn't have his usual entourage of school cronies and she had to admit, he suited his naked bits – the ones that she could see, that is. But he still annoyed her and she was determined to let him know that he still annoyed her. She was determined to get rid of him.

"Well, Farrell, if you won't race, what about a fish supper afterwards?"

"OK."

After half an hour of Heather watching Cillian show off his back-stroke, diving and spitting water-fountains, they swam back over to the steps in the far left corner of the pool.

When the coast was clear and Cillian had disappeared into the male changing rooms, Heather took her turn to leave the pool. She and Cillian were going to have a meal together: she and Cillian, she and Cillian. What did this mean, if anything? As Heather climbed the steps, she caught sight of the droplets of water trickling off her arms. Her sallow skin looked rich and healthy compared to the pasty swimmers around her. She could also feel her hair dripping on her shoulders and down her back, wet and luxurious.

Heather hauled herself out of the pool and up the steps. As she did so the halter-neck strap snapped and two voluptuous breasts poured out. As Heather furiously scrambled to retrieve her costume and her dignity, she also discovered that the water clinging to her legs had made the hairs on them appear long and thick, and above all, highly noticeable. She dare not begin to think what her bikini-line looked like. Her breasts were poured back into their sling and glued there with a Barbara Windsor style clench, with her hands on each breast.

Luckily, for Heather's sake, the other swimmers had been too busy with their technique to notice her embarrassment. That is, all except one. Cillian Harte stood some distance away with his mouth open and the swimming goggles he'd returned to find shaking in his hand.

# Chapter 16

"Ouch, not so hard."

"It's supposed to be sore."

"I don't think so."

"It is."

"Not"

"'Tis."

"No."

"Is."

Just the sound of 'n' and 'i' followed as Emer yanked hard on Heather's little toe. Heather wasn't convinced that Emer knew what she was doing after only one term of reflexology lessons.

After her swim, nearly two months ago now, Heather hadn't stayed for chips. But she devoured four packets of Tayto smoky bacon crisps, three Galaxys and a tube of Smarties when she got home that night. That was, after she walked the half-mile home, in the lashing wind and rain, because Merlin's windscreen wipers refused to wipe. The next few months had proven very uncomfortable for both Heather and her unsuspected voyeur. Neither Heather, nor Cillian, mentioned the incident. And after a while they returned to their usual pattern of criticism and competition. Cillian showed no signs of suggesting a chip supper again and a few weeks before it had become common knowledge around the lower sixth form that he was dating the school head girl, Siofra Bones.

Emer didn't have any aromatherapy oils and had begun massaging her younger sister's feet with cooking oil. They were also out of fresh towels and, as she worked on the left, she wrapped the right foot in a tea towel, stained with blackcurrant over an image of Mother Teresa's face.

Roddy Farrell was out front, tinkering with Merlin's engine. In the eight weeks since Heather had the car, he had twice been called from work to collect her when it wouldn't start and once he'd been pulled away from a union meeting because Merlin mysteriously ran out of petrol en route to Heather's school.

"Give over, will you, Emer! My little toe doesn't bend that far."

"It does now."

Emer's touch was not delicate and when she moved onto Heather's heel, her young sister shrieked and jerked her foot away.

"That's only sore, Heather, because you've got a problem there."

"What kind of problem?"

"Well, that fleshy part there on the side of your heel . . ." Emer pointed to her own, ". . . is connected to your ovaries."

"But what about all the other bits that have been sore?"

"You should be concerned about your bowel, kidneys, intestines and your lower back. Either that, or you're just a big wuss. Give us your foot over again."

Emer was in an unusually good mood, for her. Since Jack's death she hadn't seemed content, or at ease with herself. She appeared to Heather to have lost all interest in the very simple things that used to give her great pleasure. Emer hadn't been shopping in quite a while and her old clothes had begun to hang lifelessly, as she was gradually losing weight from everywhere she couldn't afford to.

The friction from Emer's enthusiastic rubbing generated heat on Heather's foot and the smell of cooking-oil wafted through the living-room.

The foot massage was intended as a treat, before Heather got herself ready for the end of term 'bash'. St Joseph's had booked Kelly's Disco, three miles down the road in Portrush. The school's Parents' and Teachers' Association had also invited the sixth-form classes from St Patrick's High School in Dungiven and two Protestant grammar schools from Coleraine, as a cross-community initiative.

Emer's 'general feeling of wellbeing' treatment needed work and Heather found she could hardly walk for half an hour afterwards. Roddy shouted through the open front door that he was ready to give Emer a lift to college and as she left with a sponge cut-out of a giant foot, she donated her parting, sage advice;

"You look fabulous. But don't do anything I wouldn't do."

Heather, therefore, felt quite at liberty to do whatever she wanted – which included raiding her sister's make-up bag and jewellery box. She picked out some gold lipstick, copper blusher and a bunch of silver bangles. The tears in her jeans weren't quite wide enough, so having cut them further, she then rubbed the edges to help them fray. Black Doc Martens boots and a baggy, black T-shirt completed the look. The Smiths being miserable in the background contributed the appropriate musical atmosphere as she dressed. Heather then spent a good hour, first straightening her hair with a hair-iron and then backcombing it all back up again and spraying it with sticky, cheap hairspray. Emer's make-up contributions, combined with her own heavy black eyeliner, provided the finishing touch. As she made her final adjustments in the bathroom mirror, Heather could see for the first time beyond her 'round' self-image and could appreciate her voluptuous curves, leading to a slim waist and long shapely legs. And above all else, she had a beautiful, radiant face.

Some of the girls in Heather's class were meeting up beforehand in one of their houses, partly to compare outfits and partly to discuss flirting tactics. Protestants or not, there were going to be new boys to conquer tonight. Heather had happened to be in the girls' toilets when the final details for meeting up had been arranged and she had been invited too. Being included was definitely a contributing factor to Heather's newly found confidence.

But Heather didn't get as far as the girl's house. Merlin's engine overheated and after chugging along at ten miles an hour for fifteen minutes, he eventually gave in altogether. By the time he cooled back down and started again, there was only time for her to drive straight to the disco.

Inside, she immediately spotted and latched onto the group of girls she had been supposed to meet. They expressed interest in her predicament for a few minutes before continuing the discussion that had obviously been started in the girl's house earlier. Heather laughed along with them.

At ten o'clock, the dance floor was heaving with a mixture of restraint and total abandon, depending on which school you came from. The no-alcohol ban was also being visibly flouted and no amount of supervision from the exasperated volunteer stewards could constrain the Babycham bottles in the girls' toilets or the mugs of cider in the boys'. Heather hadn't told her father that the school was looking for supervisory assistants, just in case he volunteered.

The group of eight girls commandeered a velvet sofa near the bar and with the coming and going to the dance floor, there were usually two or three left seated, including Heather, who was always there.

"You're letting your standards slip, Farrell. A 'B' in statistics?"

Heather hoped Cillian Harte wasn't talking about her vitals.

"My A-minus beats that one," he continued as he leant behind her, dangling his arms over the back of the sofa. His hair was washed, for a change, and the fragrance of *Head and Shoulders* breezed past as he tossed his head when he spoke.

"Aren't you just a great wee fella? You know, you're a gross ignoramus – which is 144 times worse than an ordinary one."

"Now, now, Farrell. You'll have me thinking you're jealous."

"Jealous of what?"

Cillian didn't have a chance to answer before Siofra Bones, in a haze of red, shiny plastic and silver glitter, dragged him away to the dance floor. Cillian was an awkward dancer and Heather was enjoying watching him, like a pinball, bounce and knock into all around him, including his girlfriend. But Heather didn't like it quite so much, when as soon as the slow music began, Siofra reached over to him and spent the whole of Lionel Ritchie's *Hello* with her tongue down his throat.

"Are you Heather Farrell?"

While Heather had been absorbed in the dance floor, she hadn't noticed that she had company. Sitting beside her was the all-Ireland equivalent to the all-American Boy, only paler and with less dental work.

"Who wants to know?"

"Me."

"And who's me?"

"Mike. Would you like to dance?"

"Is this a bet?"

"No, why should it be?"

Heather gave her handsome stranger the benefit of the doubt and let him lead her by the hand to the dance floor. She could sense all her school-friends staring at her, including Cillian. Mike held her close, not too close, but just enough for her to feel his right hand at the base of her back, while his left interlaced with her fingers. At over six foot in height, he dwarfed Heather. And as he dipped his face down to meet hers, his warm friendly smile spread from his mouth to hers. She could hardly believe what was happening to her. Mike had light-brown hair, cut short and neat, and wore chinos with an ironed crease down the centre. Heather could not believe that she would be his type of girl.

On the last beat of the Lionel's '*I love you*', Mike softly lifted the hair away from Heather's face and whispered in her ear:

"You are the most beautiful girl I have ever met."

Heather bolted off the dance floor and ran sobbing outside. Mike ran after her and only managed to forcibly stop her as she reached Merlin, parked alone at the back fire-exit. Heather pulled her arms away, but he continued to restrain her as through her sobs she shouted at him, "You've had your fun! You've won the bet – now leave me alone!"

"I swear on my life, I didn't ask you to dance for a bet! I swear, Heather!" He could feel her struggle relax. "If you want me to go I will, but please just stay and talk to me for a while." He could sense that she hadn't been completely won over, but there was a definite chink in her armour. "OK, Heather, I'll talk and you listen."

Still imprisoned within his arms, Heather spent the next half-hour listening to him telling her about his school, his friends and his passion for rugby. He told her stories of his childhood and made her laugh by admitting to a secret passion for the smell of firelighters, Mary Ingels out of *Little House on the Prairie* and Pot Noodles, in that order.

The full moon, outshining the brightest stars, broke through cloud and cast the young couple's shadow, and the Beetle's, right across the carpark. Heather turned away, so that Mike wouldn't now see her splotchy, tear-soaked face. Mike, Heather and Merlin occupied the entire parking space at the rear of the disco and only the sound of Heather's infectious laughter competed with the dull thud of disco music to fill the sultry summer air.

"You are beautiful, believe me," Mike whispered, still holding her arms, as he tilted his head to kiss Heather's neck. But before he got there, she turned her face round and redirected the kiss to her lips. The tiny bristles of his teenage whiskers tickled her face and then her neck, as he explored every contour. His eyes were closed. Heather's were open as she watched every move and studied every new sensation. She wanted him to touch her, but he kept her held tightly by the arms. The tightness of the restraint magnified all that she was feeling and experiencing for the first time. He was gentle and delicate and all that Heather did not expect. She responded accordingly. That was until he gently moved his right leg until it was between both of hers and, uncontrollably, Heather found herself rubbing her groin, first against it, and then slightly up and down. At this one involuntary action, Mike abruptly let go of her arms and pressed her against the front of Merlin. The curve of the bonnet arched and stretched out her back. Staring now directly into his eyes, Heather sensed a bewildering combination of innocence and also maturity and seriousness. For a moment there was sadness in his eyes and, as it looked like he was going to pull away from her, Heather undid the button on her jeans. When he slipped them down, along with her panties, she felt completely vulnerable, as the warm air completely sensualised her nakedness. Mike then unzipped his own trousers and Heather slowly placed her hand onto his erect penis. The feeling was like nothing she could have, or would have, prepared for. The feeling of control and of knowing that she had caused this reaction was erotic and empowering at the same time.

As he lifted her legs apart and entered her, Heather felt a moment's brief pain, followed by a wave of pleasure.

Heather, indeed, felt beautiful.

The second after Mike ejaculated, he pulled out and still breathing hard, he whispered into Heather's ear:

"Now that means all the Farrell sisters have been fucked by a Sheehan!"

As he spoke the words, it was obvious that he was crying.

"Hello, Mr Farrell?"

"Yes, speaking."

"I'm ringing about your daughter."

"Which one? What's wrong?"

"Heather. She's all right. But I think someone had better come and collect her."

"Who's this?"

"I'm one of Heather's school-friends – Cillian – Cillian Harte."

"Is she hurt?"

"No, no. We're all still at Kelly's, but I don't think she's fit to drive."

"Has she been drinking? Is that it?"

"No."

"Well, what's the problem then?"

"She's locked herself in her car."

"And why doesn't she get out?"

"Please, Mr Farrell. Perhaps your wife should come."

"Why do you say that?"

"Because your daughter is in floods of tears, Mr Farrell, and the only sense I've managed to get out of her has been 'I want my mother'."

# Chapter 17

Heather and Merlin drove into Kingston upon Thames two weeks later. All she had with her was one small suitcase and her father's gift of an annual membership to the Automobile Association.

Surprisingly it was Roddy Farrell's idea that his youngest daughter should go and spend time with Kitty. He didn't like the idea of her being away for all of the school summer holidays, no more than he liked having to place his trust in Kitty as her guardian. But after a fortnight of hiding herself away in her room, speaking to no one, Roddy knew that Heather needed something that he, as her father, couldn't give. Emer had tried to console her sister, but got bored after a few days. Heather was giving little away and painfully kept secret the connection between all the Farrell sisters and their deception at the hands of a Sheehan.

Even as the travel and accommodation arrangements were being made, Roddy still had no direct contact with Kitty, and Heather passed on his messages down the telephone. His pride would not afford anything more.

The night ferry crossing had been rough, but the motorways calm. The welded patches that Roddy had managed to inflict on Merlin before the journey had been remarkably resilient. Heather arrived into Kingston the following lunch-time, having only had to call the AA once, a few miles outside of Carlisle.

Kitty had given her the directions to The Jolly Man and Heather found it easily. This once quaint English pub, nestling directly on the banks of the Thames, was bustling with Saturday lunch-time trade. A trickle of Pringle and Lacrosse sweaters sat drinking pints of tepid real ale on the tables outside, as they admired their boats moored at the bottom of four steep steps. The pub had been given the makeover treatment and its old beams and original features had been replaced by new beams and fake original features. But, inside, Heather found it airy and cheerful, with floor-to-ceiling windows facing out onto the river. The smell of bangers and mash, and shepherd's pie mingled with ale and tobacco.

"Have you any ID? You don't look eighteen to me!"

"Just a triple vodka and I'll be on my way."

"Coming up!" Kitty laughed as she poured her younger sister a Coke from a bottle. "It's last orders in an hour. I'll be done then. Go and grab that table in the corner. I'll get one of the girls in the kitchen to bring you over a bite of lunch."

As Heather took her time dipping hunks of wholemeal bread into wild-mushroom soup, she studied Kitty busy at work. Along the bar were dotted a number of middle-aged men on their own, each nursing a pint of Guinness. Every time Kitty passed them, their eyes lit up and their heads popped up. They reminded Heather of the fun-fair game where plastic worm-heads would pop up randomly and the aim of the game was to whack them with a big hammer.

Each customer would try and engage Kitty in conversation and, as she shot them down every time, they chuckled into their pints. The meaner she was to them, the keener they were.

"Here, Kitty-Kitty!"

"What now?"

"Have you a match?"

"Aye, your face and my arse."

Kitty glided, as if on wheels, down to the far end of the bar and began pouring a slow pint of Guinness, as her next waiting customer tapped impatiently on the granite bar.

"Hey, you big bollocks! Do you want this done right or what?"

The tapping stopped immediately.

In the three years since Heather had seen her eldest sister, Kitty had blossomed. Aged twenty-three, she radiated confidence and youth, self-belief and guts. Her figure was much fuller than Heather remembered and totally dominated by two huge, pert breasts, bound in a low-cut, tiger-print T-shirt. They were magnificent. How they defied gravity had become a regular after-hours talking-point in the pub. Which Kitty often instigated. Heather was also intrigued as to how Kitty had also managed to tame her long, ebony locks into a neat, French plait.

Kitty slowly topped up the Guinness that she had been pouring and had let settle for a few minutes. This gave her an opportunity to inspect her sister who had now moved on from her soup and was stuck into a steamy beef casserole. Heather had transformed since Kitty had last seen her:

transformed into a seventeen-year-old going on forty, she thought. No amount of searching could find the skinny, carefree, innocent that Heather once was. The butterfly had transmogrified into a caterpillar. Where had she gone? Her clothes, hair and even expression belonged to another generation and another era. Kitty couldn't place her in any time. The tight, suffocating bun which controlled her frizzy hair belonged to the fifties, her ankle-length floral dress the seventies and the rest somewhere in the future.

Five minutes later, Kitty was given permission by the bar manager to finish her shift early. She was too valuable an employee not to accommodate.

Kitty and Heather sat on the steps leading to the river, with giant slices of baked lemon cheesecake on their laps.

They chatted frivolously for ten minutes about Kingston, about the river, about nothing.

"You're not going to tell me what's wrong, are you?"

"No."

"Heather, you can tell me anything."

"No. Not yet. Please, Kitty. I just want to put it all behind me. Please let's not talk about home or anything to do with it."

"I'll let you off for now. But just for now, mind!"

Kitty then filled Heather in on the arrangements. The bar manager had given Heather a job in the kitchen – mainly preparing vegetables and cleaning pans. She would also be on the same shift-pattern as Kitty – eight in the morning until ten, midday until three in the afternoon and finally seven in the evening until midnight. They also would both get Tuesdays off. Heather could share Kitty's room above the pub and the deal included as much pub-grub as she could manage. Heather had never had a job before and she was ecstatic.

"Now, it's tough going," Kitty warned.

"I don't mind."

"Your feet will be hanging off you after the first week."

"Great."

"You'll have to watch out for some of the punters."

"No problem."

"And standing up all day gives you varicose veins."

"OK."

"And piles."

"Oh."

Kitty helped Heather get her suitcase out of Merlin's boot.

"He looks like I feel." Kitty hugged the bonnet and, as she stood up again, tiny flecks of rust attached themselves to her T-shirt. "But it's great to see him again all the same."

"Well, Kitty, he belongs to both of us now."

A new era had begun where Merlin now belonged to two of the Farrell sisters at the same time.

Kitty had cleared two drawers for Heather's use. The room was simple – a double bed with crisp white linen, a mahogany chest of drawers and matching bedside table, a natural hessian carpet and a mahogany rocking-chair with brown leather seat. Heather was struck by two dominating features in the room – the first, a huge sash window facing directly onto the river. The window was over the flat roof above the pub's entrance and guessing from the towel and magazines on it, Kitty used this as a balcony. The second feature was a gigantic Perspex picture frame, containing a colourful collage of photographs. A few, of Kitty as a child,

119

she recognised and there were some of Heather also. There were no images of either her father or Emer. But dominating the entire mosaic was one recurring image of a striking, handsome man, mostly with his arms around Kitty. But in the one Heather particularly focused on he was wearing a British army uniform.

Kitty read her sister's reaction and responded first.

"Aye, that's my boyfriend, Matt."

"Aye, but . . ." Heather struggled to find the words.

"I know, who'd ever think I'd get a fella as good-looking as him."

"All I can see are his lapels and shiny boots! For heaven's sake, Kitty, he's a Brit!"

"So?"

"Well, for your sake, it's a good job you only met him over here!"

Kitty didn't correct her.

"Where's he based?" Heather asked, inspecting his uniform more closely.

"He was transferred last month to Germany."

"Transferred from where?"

"He is handsome though, isn't he?" Kitty raced on. "He has a week's leave next month, so you'll get to meet him then."

Heather was too transfixed by the image of the man to notice how Kitty hid her near-blunder. Having to meet a Brit, in the flesh, distracted her from her questioning.

"I'd better not tell our Emer and Dad about this new fella of yours. A Brit's a Brit back home, handsome or not." And finally taking her gaze away from the photographs, she added, "They do miss you, you know."

Kitty put away the last of Heather's formless dresses, ramming the warped drawer shut with the side of her knee.

Heather began her first shift in the pub at seven that evening. Kitty introduced her to the cornucopia of bar-staff representing the Commonwealth and beyond. Kitty advised Heather not to get too friendly as all were backpacking students and once they'd earned enough for their next journey and ripped off a few hundred pounds from the till, they'd be off.

"As long as the brewery still make their money, they don't care," Kitty added for all to hear.

The bar manager, Jim, joined them an hour later and showed Heather around the kitchen, where she remained for the rest of her shift. By coincidence or not, Jim was an exact mirror-image of the jolly man on the pub sign outside, down to his red nose and broken veins in his cheeks.

"Give it a few days, petal, and you'll think you were born here. The cook will be with you in the morning and your main job in the evenings is to get all the stuff ready for her then. Peeling, scrubbing, slicing – that sort of thing. Any questions? No, grand."

Heather's induction, health and safety training, and employee welcome were thus complete. When the manager was gone, Kitty popped in for half an hour and guided her though the main tasks, before she was called away to change an ale barrel in the cellar.

Heather quickly realised that Kitty ran The Jolly Man. The manager propped up the end of the bar, chatting to the steady stream of customers and offering complimentary drinks and cigars. Eventually, by close of business, he was carried unconscious to his room by two of the Australian staff.

Besides a two-hour nap on the ferry, Heather realised she had been awake for the past twenty-four hours.

She lay beside Kitty in the double bed, exhausted. Her hands were raw from peeling potatoes and scraping carrots, her feet ached, her back ached. The sisters lay, silently trapped in the present, fearful of the past and unsure of what the future held.

"I didn't know he was married, you know, Heather."

"So, why didn't you tell Dad that?"

"Should I have had to?"

Without further words, both sisters cuddled each other, fitting together like spoons, and drifted to sleep.

# Chapter 18

"Wake up and smell the coffee!"

"Wake up and smell your socks!"

"I'm wearing your socks."

"Well, wake-up and smell my socks."

"It's the 80's, Heather, not the 70's. That colour's mingin'."

Kitty and Heather were spending their day off rummaging through colour-charts. Between them, over the last month, they'd saved enough in wages and tips for a half-decent respray for Merlin. Kitty was still drawn to gold, but Heather had her heart set on what her sister teased was 'Windolene Pink'. Heather's persistence was partly due to the fact it matched, exactly, the new miniskirt she had bought in Camden Market, size twelve. Being constantly surrounded by food had had a positive effect on Heather and while the rest of the staff tucked into the leftover cottage pies and beef wellingtons, she usually opted for a boiled egg. But the bulk of her weight loss was down to Heather Farrell being the happiest she had been in a long time.

Kitty, however, was taking some persuading on the choice of colour.

They were sunbathing on the flat roof outside Kitty's bedroom window, disturbed only by the gaggle of brent-geese, the ripple of the river and the occasional 'Get your tits out!' from the brewery draymen. It was the middle of August and the midday sun was blistering the tiles on the roof. In order to protect their feet from getting burnt as they popped in and out of the room, the two sisters had combined skimpy polka-dot bikinis from Kookai with black socks from Woolworth.

"There's no way Merlin can be pink," Kitty persisted. "It'll offend his masculinity."

"We're talking paint here, not castration," Heather argued, as she turned on her back and undid the fastener on her bikini. She reached over and grabbed a glass of ice-cold lemonade, removing Kitty's straw and replacing it with her own. She had learnt a lot about Kitty's hygiene habits since she'd been here.

Kitty continued to flick through the colour charts, but only received a flat 'no' to every alternative colour and hue she selected.

"Don't let me forget to phone Dad tonight," Heather said – only to remind herself, because she knew Kitty would never dream of reminding her. "He was livid when I forgot last time. You know, you should talk to our Emer at least. She is your sister too."

"Jack must have told her about me and him. But she still went ahead with their little affair. What kind of sister is that?"

Heather had no answer, because she genuinely knew no

answer. Her brief, two-minute conversations with Emer over the last few weeks concentrated on her eventual, successful eighth driving test. Emer had no message for her eldest sister.

"Was the funeral awful?" Kitty asked Heather.

This was the first time, even with their countless, secret, telephone conversations, that Kitty had ever mentioned the death of her ex-boyfriend to Heather.

"Aye."

Kitty's silence said more about how she was feeling than words. Heather considered describing to her who was there and what was said, but the image of Michael Sheehan, the young innocent struggling with his grief, before he turned into a monster, was too vivid.

"Did anyone ever find out what kind of shit Jack was keeping, tucked away in the lining of that jacket of his? I never gave him anything personal, that's for sure."

"I dunno. Nobody hung about after the service, as you can imagine."

Kitty had imagined, over and over as she had imagined the accident, the coffin, his arms around her one last time, his arms around Emer.

As Kitty struggled with her thoughts, the sound of two groaning voices came from underneath the fire-exit at the side of the pub. The vivacious smile returned to her face.

"Who's that?" murmured Heather.

"I don't know who. But I know what – a pair of dirty brutes," Kitty whispered back. "They're always at it. Must be students or something." For once, she was appreciative of the horny couple's distracting whimpers. "What's wrong with gold, Heather?" she continued.

*"Shift over."*

*"We did it this way last time."*

*"But my bum's freezing!"*

"No, Kitty, it's a colour for grannies."

"It's not. It's sophisticated."

*"Give it to me!"*

"Who wants to be sophisticated? I'm seventeen. It has to be pink or nothing."

*"Yes, yes . . . yes!"*

Kitty and Heather giggled as more, deeper groans, ran alongside the sound of the creaking iron staircase, as the amorous couple changed position.

*"Oh, my God!"*

*"What? Did I bite you?"*

The tempo of the groaning shifted as short, panting bursts were followed by long, slow sighs. Kitty and Heather stuffed the corners of the towels they were lying on into their mouths, in an attempt to muffle their sniggers.

*"Quick, say something dirty!"*

*"No, I'm embarrassed."*

*"Hurry up!"*

*"Like what?"*

*"Anything. Go on!"*

*"I can't!"*

*"Quick!"*

*"OK, OK – come on, big boy. Give it to me!"*

Gagging on the towels, Kitty and Heather were struggling to contain their laughter and once they heard 'give it to me' one more time, they couldn't help but burst into hysterics. Every time they tried to stop, one would look at the other and it would start all over again. After ten minutes of sore laughter, both sisters rubbed their aching ribs.

"Is this a private joke, or can we all join in?"

Blocking the sun and casting a long dark shadow over the two sisters, Matt Edwards, bronzed, muscular and handsome, towered above them.

"Matt! You didn't see the couple shagging on your way in?"

"No, but I heard a few scrambling sounds on the fire-exit and the hasty departure of two fluorescent orange jackets. Seemed to be in a bit of a hurry to get back to their yacht moored down there. It couldn't be them – they were in their seventies at least." He scanned in disbelief as the yacht pulled away, before adding, "Anyway, what happened to 'Honey, I'm pleased to see you?'"

"Honey, I'm pleased to see you," Kitty giggled as she stood up and gave her boyfriend a long, smouldering kiss.

"And this must be the second most gorgeous girl in the world. Hi, Heather, I'm Matt."

Matt reached out his hand and, as Heather accepted his greeting, she instantly liked him. He had the greenest eyes she had ever seen and they rightfully dominated his kind face. She had never thought she could have accepted a compliment from a stranger again. But this time, like before, she couldn't help herself.

Matt, Heather and Kitty soaked up the last of the afternoon sun. Matt playfully teased both sisters in equal quantities. Kitty loved the way he didn't leave her young sister out and Heather loved the way, when he thought no one was looking, he affectionately touched or cuddled her older sister.

The hot afternoon had melted into a sultry evening and then a balmy night, seamlessly. Matt lay between the two sisters, pointing out the star constellations and spotting roaming satellites. He casually chatted about his navigation training and his love of the army.

By the end of the night, and, as Kitty had hoped, Heather's perceptions of a British soldier – well, of this British soldier – were transformed.

Heather volunteered to spend the night in the office next door and finally said her goodnights just after midnight. As Heather squeezed herself back through the open bedroom window to get her night things, Kitty called after her.

"What about letting Matt have the deciding call on whether it's gold or pink? He can make the choice between the two."

Matt smiled and gave a knowing, sexy wink to Kitty, and then to Heather.

# Chapter 19

Matt chose 'Windolene Pink'. The next day, while the two sisters completed their morning shift, Matt took Merlin to the car body shop. For a few hundred pounds the rust was sanded down and gashes and cracks packed with filler, before being finished with a quick blow over. But regardless of the quality of the finish, Matt, Heather and even Kitty fell in love with the colour when they went to collect Merlin the following afternoon after work.

"He's like a giant marshmallow," enthused Matt as he ran his fingers along the roof.

"I want to eat him," added Heather.

"I want to have his babies," said Kitty.

The rest of Matt's leave was spent on driving trips. In between shifts in the pub, they got lost in the maze in Hampton Court, nearly sank in a hired boat along the Thames and got ripped off several times in the flea markets. Heather was impressed by how close Matt and Kitty had become in such an apparently short courtship and as neither mentioned their past, she continued to think that way.

Neither Kitty nor Matt would accept Heather's offers to bow out and let them have time to themselves. Even on the Friday night, the last night before Matt had to return to barracks, Kitty arranged for herself and Heather to swap shifts with the two Australians, and a table was booked in a Chinese restaurant in Soho.

As Heather didn't drink, she offered to drive. She had one week left of her freedom, before she had to return home and back to her final 'A' level year, so she was determined to have a good time.

They had decided to dress up for the occasion and in a shirt, tie and jacket on the top half and his ever-faithful, drainpipe jeans on the bottom, Matt half-made it. Kitty was totally flamboyant in a leopard-print blouse, with square shoulder-pads and tight black Lycra trousers. Her breasts were even more astonishing than ever. Heather opted for a cerise velvet minidress, with a high neck and an even higher hem-length.

Once at the restaurant, the waiter seated them nearest the front door. Kitty assured her fellow diners that this seating choice was because they made a stylish contribution to the general ambience of the place. Shortly after ordering, Heather left the table to visit the ladies' toilet and Kitty asked her to confirm her hypothesis by reporting back on the occupants of the table nearest the toilet door. Heather passed an elderly couple, with matching orange fluorescent jackets, right smack in front of the ladies' door on her way in.

When Heather returned to the table, a few minutes later, she caught the tail-end of what appeared to be a very heated conversation between Kitty and her boyfriend.

"Not now, OK?"

"Well, when?"

"Every time I'm about to go away again, it's the same old story. Leave it for now."

"Leave it till when, Matt?"

"Shush!" Matt whispered, as Heather could no longer, comfortably, hover unseen behind them.

She was greeted by beaming smiles, as if all was as it had been before she left.

"Was I right? Were the mingers near the loos?" Kitty asked Heather, just as their meals arrived.

Heather and Matt shared honey chilli chicken with fried rice, while Kitty kept her own portion of prawns in black-bean sauce to herself. Neither Matt nor Kitty betrayed any shred of tension and the meal fell quickly back into the relaxed, comfortable mood that had been evident throughout the last week.

"So, our Heather, will you be glad to go back home again?" enquired Matt as he fought with her over the limp, token lettuce leaf, stuck to the bowl.

"Yes . . . yes and no . . . more no than yes. Well, no actually," Heather eventually replied, knocking Matt's fork away with her own.

"I love a woman with a decisive mind."

"I miss my dad and sister nagging me, but that's about it."

"Why don't you stay here for that? I'm sure Kitty could do enough nagging to make up for both of them," Matt joked, but then more seriously changed direction to his girlfriend. "You don't mention your old fella. You'd think you were embarrassed about him or something."

Kitty didn't answer.

"It can't be because he's a brickie," Matt continued.

Kitty half-smiled and half-grimaced. But as he playfully nudged her elbow, she was instantly melted away with his familiar, enigmatic charm.

While they waited for desserts, it was Matt's turn to visit the toilets. With him gone, Kitty leant across the table to Heather.

"I do love him." She nodded in Matt's direction. "The way things were at home and the whole Jack thing, I was a complete mess. If it hadn't been for Matt, I don't know what I would have done. You do like him, don't you?"

"Who couldn't?"

"For the first time in ages, I'm just enjoying the present and hopefully my future will run its own course. As long as Matt's in it, that is."

"What about your degree?" Heather asked, feeling the need to be the caretaker all of a sudden.

"This bar work is just a stop-gap, don't you worry. When Matt applied for a transfer and was accepted, I thought it would be wiser to base myself over here. Don't say anything, but his birthday's coming up in the next couple of months and, as it's a Leap Year, I'm going to propose." Kitty beamed from ear to ear.

Heather thought first of the shortness of their courtship and secondly, of how such a marriage would be accepted, if at all, at home. But these two obstacles were nothing against what she could see, for herself, was true love.

Matt returned and reassured his girlfriend that he'd washed his hands.

The orange sorbets were devoured with terrific gusto and were polished off with bottles of Tiger beer and a Coke for

Heather. Kitty exhibited incredible bladder control and it wasn't until they had paid the bill and were leaving that she took her turn to visit the toilets.

Matt and Heather waited for her inside Merlin, parked directly in front of the restaurant. The road was busy with fast-moving heavy traffic. With each passing van or bus, the Beetle lightly rocked.

"Heather, your sister will miss you when you're gone."

There was a gentleness and kindness in Matt's voice that Heather had warmed to over the past week. She could place its tone and resonance somewhere else, but for now she couldn't make the connection.

"I'll miss her too," Heather replied.

"You've been terrific company for her while I was away. As you well know, that pub work can be pretty torturous."

"Tell me about it. I've got calluses to prove it."

Heather stretched out her hand and Matt held it to inspect the damage. A double-decker bus drove past and Merlin shuddered violently to one side. Matt then pulled Heather's hand towards his mouth and licked the tip of her little finger.

'Now, *that means all the Farrell sisters have been fucked by a Sheehan,*' flashed across Heather's mind. That was what was so familiar, so seductively familiar about Matt. He reminded her so much of Michael Sheehan and she had been too blinded by her sister's and her own happiness, to see it.

She snatched her hand away. "Stop it!"

"I'm sorry. I couldn't help it."

"Yes, you could."

"OK, I could. But I didn't want to."

The fact that the man her sister adored and was planning to propose to had made a seductive gesture to her, or more the fact that she had wanted it to happen, tore at her bitterly.

Heather and Merlin drove back to Stranraer the next day and then took the next available space on the early morning crossing over to Northern Ireland.

Heather had rambled on at Kitty about getting some extra preparation done for the start of term and of missing her dad – so much so that in the end Kitty was glad, for her sister's sake, to see her go.

That morning, Kitty had to push Merlin to get him going. Heather lifted her foot off the clutch and the car chugged to start. Fearful of stopping moving, in case Merlin broke down again, Heather drove away from The Jolly Man to the sound of a rattling engine and, above that, Kitty shouting after her:

"Wish me luck!"

## Emer, 1988

# Chapter 20

Bad luck struck Heather four more times over the next seven months and by the fifth time that the AA were called out to repair her car, Heather decided that she and Merlin were jinxed.

Itching to get her hands behind the wheel, Emer Farrell was more than happy to accept the Volkswagen Beetle as hers. She chose to celebrate the gift by offering to drive Heather to the St Patrick's Day parade in Donegal Town.

"God forgive me! What have I done?" Heather screeched at her sister, as she clenched both her hands around the tiny handle above the glove compartment.

"You've given the car to someone who'll appreciate him," Emer nonchalantly replied, with only one of her hands loosely caressing the steering wheel as she drove.

"Well, for heaven's sake, remember the fact that the Free Staters drive on the same side of the road as us . . . left! The other left!" Heather barked back.

The hour's journey left Heather unsettled and she wasn't convinced that her sister had got a driving licence by orthodox, legal, means. The landscape outside reflected an ambiguous combination of crystal-blue sky up above and muddy, soggy ground below. The sheep and their spring lambs lay soaked in the tough-looking grass, with the steam rising from their backs. To Emer, the rural terrain was tinted with bronzes and rich reds. To Heather, who wasn't wearing sunglasses today, all was barren and bland. The sky was empty except for the occasional rogue Bohemian cloud and the tracks of a jet, stark and harsh and then fading to the shape of tyre-tracks in mud.

The border crossing was signified by the increase in potholes on the road and the rattle of Merlin's chassis in response. As a result, conversation was brief and loud.

"Watch the bump!" Heather had yet to take her hands from the handle.

"Which one?"

"The one in your head, if you don't slow down." Heather was regretting every minute of the journey. "You're going way too fast. We're in the country, you know – sharp bends and all that."

"Oh." Emer replied casually, not really listening and busily planning what shops she was going to visit.

But having now driven past Letterkenny, Heather didn't have to argue with her sister to slow down any more, because a tractor did it for her.

"Buckin' rednecks!" shouted Heather, in the same vehement vein as earlier, but this time redirected from her sister towards the two farmers inside the tractor cabin and the six children balanced on the rack at the rear.

"It'll turn off soon," Emer responded, with her head in the clouds – if there had been any.

The huge tractor wheels ploughed through the puddles on the road, spraying Merlin in the process.

An hour later and another half-a-dozen tractors were now ahead of them. Emer had spent all that time weaving in and out as she tried to sneak a glimpse of the road ahead. But she hadn't overtaken once and, as a result, had given up. As had Heather's stomach, as she struggled to control motion sickness.

"Just our luck," muttered Heather, in between sick-scented burps. "Where are the buggers off to anyway?"

When Heather and Emer eventually reached Donegal Town, it quickly became apparent that the 'buggers' were the main feature of the St Patrick's Day parade. Decked with green, white and gold ribbons, a steady procession – tractor, tractor, tractor, harvester, tractor – weaved its way through the town. The town was now packed and Emer was pleased with herself for finding a parking place, on an empty field just a few minutes' walk away from the town centre. She had parked the car, and was out of it, before Heather even had a chance to unfasten her seat belt.

As they squeezed through the parade spectators, Emer was now starting to feel guilty for telling them at work that she had a sore head. As per her usual form, she hadn't completed her reflexology course – the verrucas and corns on the feet of the volunteers in term two had put her right off. Under pressure from her father and pressure of now having to find the funds to run a car, she had secured a receptionist position with a beauty salon in Portrush. The days were long and the work boring, if it hadn't been for the departing disappointed faces of those seeking miracle results – or better still, guessing which of the arriving customers were in for a Tortilla Chip or a Mohican bikini wax.

Now in the centre of the town, Emer and her sister had perched themselves on a wall outside a busy pub. Heather, having turned eighteen the previous month, lifted her 'spirits', in both senses of the word, by nipping in and out of the pub for gin and tonics for herself. Each visit to the pub would ensure an opportunity for her to laugh out heartily at the tail-end of some joke or story being recounted at the bar which, of course, she never fully understood.

The farming vehicles were starting to get bigger and more heavily laden with whole families, including pets. The drivers enthusiastically waved out to family and friends in the crowd and got the occasional drunk heckle in return.

"I told you we should have gone to Dublin," Heather moaned as she returned from the bar carrying her G&T and a bitter lemon for her sister.

"No, you didn't," Emer muttered back.

"I would have, if I'd known we'd spend the day looking at what happens when brothers marry their sisters."

Emer was tired of her younger sister's incessant grumbling and made an excuse to get them some pub grub from the bar. She had to squeeze through a sea of green woollens and thin cagools, to get to the food counter and, as she waited to be served, she tore a beer mat into tiny pieces. Three men beside her were almost at blows over a conversation about farming subsidies and the price of red diesel. Emer's thoughts were on why Cadbury's Dairy Milk tasted so much nicer over the border.

"Can I get you a drink?" enquired one of the men, who had said his piece on the debate and now sought fairer company.

Preferably from someone with just the one head, thought Emer, before politely replying, "Thank you, but no, thank you. My boyfriend's getting me one. Nice of you to ask though. Gorgeous day. Really beautiful."

Emer had difficulty in just saying 'no'. Since Jack Sheehan's death three years ago, she'd had the occasional short-term romance, but had quickly tired of them. In comparison to Jack, everyone she met soon became boring. Recently she'd even started to tire of the simple day-to-day things that she once found so satisfying. Retail therapy helped, but Emer knew that something was missing from her life. She was twenty-two and she was bored with men.

Carrying two large plates of champ, chunky pork sausages and rich green cabbage, Emer returned to her sister, who was still propped up on the wall outside. They sat on the cold, damp stone and as Heather tucked into the meal with vigour, Emer picked and poked. Their eating techniques exactly reflected Heather's now 16 dress-size appetite and her sister's size 10.

"Have you finished with that?" enquired Heather, before ramming her fork into Emer's untouched sausages.

With their appetites satisfied, Heather quickly hit parade-fatigue and Emer, in turn, soon was weary of her sister's long face. When the muck-spreaders were next in line, the Farrell sisters took it as a cue to leave and pushed against the flow of the crowd, back towards their car. Emer struggled to spot Merlin. The field was no longer empty and the pink curve of the Beetle's roof was just about visible to Heather, above a sea of classic vintage vehicles. Morris Minors, Bentleys, Triumph Stags and E-type Jags crammed the field. When the girls finally managed to reach their own car, they discovered that not only was he now boxed in, but he also had a white badge stuck to his windscreen, with the number 18 printed on it.

"Excuse me, what's this?" Emer asked one of the picnic-hamper and tartan-rug-carrying people who surrounded the cars.

"You must be number 18 in the rally."

"What rally?"

The classic car rally began in the field, where all the cars had been told to assemble, before being marshalled into the parade. There was nowhere for Emer to turn the car and under protest, Merlin and his slightly bemused passengers became number 18, out of over a hundred classic and vintage cars, taking part in the St Patrick's Day Parade. Emer got quite into the spirit of things and developed a rather regal and presidential wave as she pretended to recognise people in the crowd. Heather, by contrast, hunched her shoulders and tried to disappear behind the dashboard.

Heather dozed off on the way home. Even the sharp turns and high speeds over ramps couldn't compete with the inebriated stupor she'd fallen into. Emer looked down at her sister's bobbing, sleeping head, as it rocked from side to side. With Kitty out of Emer's life, Heather was the only sister she had left in it now. But suddenly, for the first time, she realised that she didn't know her at all. The annoying little urchin who stole her things and used her make-up, had changed without Emer noticing. The signs had been there, like when she first went off to stay with Kitty seven months previously and also when she came back again a month later. Heather had been changing and re-forming all along and Emer had missed it all. Emer had been elsewhere.

Even physically, Emer had to admit to herself now, they bore little resemblance to each other. The shared, rich skin tone of their youth, was now a dull grey on Heather's cheeks. Whereas Emer celebrated her tight curls and let her long locks fall free about her face, Heather's were restrained and contained behind a thick, beaded Alice-band and a tight plait. Emer's clothes were tailored and smart, Heather's old-fashioned and flouncy. Emer's attention to detail left her immaculate and polished, Heather's attention to nothing left her looking uncared for and . . . unloved. That was it, Emer realised – her baby sister looked unloved.

As she drove, Emer felt her thoughts being dragged into a complex mire of what a dysfunctional family the Farrells had become. But she pulled herself back. Stay on the surface of things, she chanted to herself. It was safe there. Where could she get some new shoes with ankle straps and how could she make repairs to the patchwork bedspread Kitty had given her all those years ago? Yes, the detail of life was enough. But was it enough to dampen the unfulfilled feeling she herself now had bubbling to the surface? What changes could she make to her life and what role model could she become for her sister?

It was now early evening and bright yellow gorse appeared to greedily absorb the last of the daylight, and bare trees, shrouded in green moss, appeared to be settling down for the night. As Emer got nearer to home, the poorly stitched patchwork of fields abruptly changed into small houses and chain-link fences around redbrick police stations.

For the first time since she'd left the house that morning, Emer took off the tinted lenses that clipped onto her red glasses and threw them into the glove compartment. The sun had been completely swallowed up by Bisnevenagh Mountain and the familiar urban landscape of home and all that she knew stretched before her.

On the evening of St Patrick's Day 1988, Emer Farrell made her first 'bigger picture' decision. She decided that she was now tired of champ. Emer was about to taste something far more adventurous – far more exotic.

# Chapter 21

The first was a Brazilian – the man, that is and not the skimpy bikini wax. Emer's strategy to transform her life was based around the one talent that she truly felt she had a natural gift for: sex. After all, Jack Sheehan, who had initially been the teacher, had soon become the pupil when it came to imagination and versatility. Emer felt that there was nothing she couldn't get with the aid of a condom and a can of UHT spray cream. And she then realised that what she was after was right under her nose within the University of Ulster campus, just five miles down the road, on the outskirts of Coleraine. The fact that her father had come over to Northern Ireland, in the first place, to build the campus's foundations, only added to the excitement of her master plan. The project was based on one highly flawed hypothesis – all foreign students were wealthy, good at sex and would offer an escape to a better place.

The university, until now, had been far removed from Emer's daily existence. The locals in Portstewart very much kept their distance from the student population who rented rooms there. They took their money in the shops and let accommodation, and that was all. But now, as the students studied, Emer studied them. She studied where they shopped, where they played sport and more than anything, where they socialised. Emer built up quite a portfolio of local pubs and in her personal notebook she drew a map of *The Golden Triangle* and marked where the various nationalities preferred to unwind. One of her favourites had become The Anchor Bar at the far end of the Prom in Portstewart, but her most successful conquests to date had been achieved at the various society fund-raising functions dotted around the three towns.

The Conservation Society's Ball in the Londonderry Arms in Portrush was where she met her first conquest, the Brazilian. *'Lots of noise'* was how she noted the experience in her notebook. This one experience would be the basis for her gross generalisation of all Brazilian men from now on. Sex with a French student followed the Swimming Club's 'Blind Date' evening in the Student Union. Emer picked Number One because of his accent and then dismissed all French lovers as *'wet and windy'*. *'Dry and sandy'* was her next description of the very polite East German, whom she captivated at the Mountaineering Club's beach barbecue. The location, of course, contributed to the 'sandy'. But Emer's most challenging conquest in the two months since she'd embarked on her mission had been the Jehovah Witness marathon volleyball match. She had only played for thirty minutes before being politely 'rested' as her profanities, every time the ball whacked off her arms, was upsetting some of the other players. The Glaswegian player with a rucksack full of *Watchtowers* had slipped into Emer's 'foreign category' by a mere stretch of Irish Sea. He had been full of remorse and promised to pray for her soul, along with his own, immediately afterwards (well, after a second time, doggy-style). The notepad simply registered '*!!!!!*' next to Scotland.

Emer was averaging about three new sexual conquests per month. Since Heather had dropped into Sunday dinner conversation that Kitty was getting married the following summer, Emer's conquest rate had increased to four in the last three weeks alone.

Emer's rationale behind her master plan was that ultimately she was searching for a relationship that would better her current circumstances. If, in the process, she ended up just having sex with one or two, or ten or eleven, then that would be put down to primary research. At the start of each evening, as she picked out her outfit and her underwear, she battled with the internal struggle between her convent-educated past and her modern, promiscuous present. The present won each time and the past was featuring less and less.

Tonight, Emer had set herself a particularly difficult challenge. The nationalities she had sampled to date had been, on the whole, a disappointment. And more than that, they had been easily come by. So this evening, she was setting her target higher.

Emer's usual partners in crime were the trainee beauticians from the salon. But her regular consorts had either recently got boyfriends, or had tired of Emer's games. So, in the past few days, Emer had targeted the brand new trainee, Wee-Sarah. At six foot tall in bare feet, Wee-Sarah had unfortunately not grown out of the nickname given to her as a premature baby. Emer had tried to persuade Heather to keep her company, thinking a night out would give her a break from revising for her 'A' Levels, but Heather, as always, was wise to her sister's antics and declined. So, Wee-Sarah it was who, after rigorous persuasion, had agreed to meet Emer outside Traks Nite-Club in Portrush that Wednesday night.

"Wee-Sarah, you're late. You look gorgeous," Emer enthused in relief that she had arrived.

Wee-Sarah had obviously been practising some of the beauty treatments on herself at home. Tiny red dots on streaky, orange legs, revealed a waxing and fake tanning experiment. But Emer was inwardly pleased. The other girls from the beauty parlour, all tanned, blonde and shiny, had on occasion stolen her thunder – and her conquests. But tonight, she was quietly confident. Emer's crushed red-velvet minidress with matching sling-backs dramatically contrasted with her dark looks and emphasised every gentle curve of her slim physique. A square neckline modestly hid, and at the same time drew the eye in expectation to her more than ample chest and the red plastic glasses had been replaced with contact lenses. Emer had conquered the Farrell sisters' battle with their curls by recently cutting hers to an inch all over and what she lost in hair she only gained in the emphasis to her chocolate eyes and full lips.

Now inside the disco, Wee-Sarah and Emer selected a high-profile position against a plasterboard Roman pillar right beside the dance floor. Emer pretended to listen to her companion's lengthy accounts of the tragedies of her first working week, but when she spotted a handsome student staring at her from the bar, she laughed hysterically, as if her colleague had just told her a fabulous joke. Wee-Sarah was quickly starting to think that perhaps the receptionist she was out with was as bright as Alaska in December.

Around them, well-pressed checked shirts and beige corduroys swayed to Simple Minds and The Smiths. Emer knew not to expect the usual student types at this particular fundraising event and was now hoping Wee-Sarah's and her own 'holiday rep' fashion statement wasn't too off-putting.

"This one customer from Bushmills had hair running almost all the way down to her knees," Wee-Sarah continued, undeterred by Emer's lack of interest and unaware of her arched shoulders slowly bending further and further downwards as she bowed to Emer's level. "We didn't have waxing strips long enough. And, my God, they were so thick . . ."

Emer winced.

"Her pubes were so thick, I had to yank at a few with the tweezers," Wee-Sarah added, dramatically miming the action as she pulled with two hands and raised her left leg as if she was holding the woman down while she tugged.

"Too much information, even for me!" Emer shouted in response. "Here, make yourself useful and go and get us a drink."

"What do you want?"

"Whatever's going. Don't be expecting a big choice."

Wee-Sarah looked confused before asking, "Aren't you coming with me? I can't leave you on your own."

"Why not?"

"It's not proper. Not . . ." 'Lady-like' was what Wee-Sarah was thinking, but something stopped her from continuing and she sloped off towards the bar on her very unladylike size nines.

The second Emer was on her own, the disco lights changed to ultra-violet and an ocean of dandruff specks bobbed up and down before her. There were none of the usual girls dancing around handbags and boys propped up at the bar – there were boys dancing with girls, girls with girls and even boys with boys, with total gay abandon. Emer leant against the pillar and rested her head, while making sure her breasts were elevated to their maximum potential. Vulnerable and sexy were two poses that, by her now twenty-two years, she'd learnt to combine to perfection. She wasn't annoyed that nobody seemed to notice her as she was enjoying studying the beaded details on the girls' cardigans and the assortment of brightly coloured Alice-bands and ribbons. "Gorgeous," she said to herself, and even under her breath added the usual dragged-out emphasis on the 'gor', followed by an abrupt 'geous'.

"I asked for two vodka and oranges and the boyo behind the bar laughed and gave me two cans of Fanta. What kind of do is this?" Wee-Sarah moaned as she returned with her tiny handbag in her giant left hand and in her other, two tin cans and two pint glasses.

"Let's just say, it's not your normal crowd," Emer sniggered before being distracted. "That's a fabulous handbag. Where did you get it?"

"My mum got it me for my last birthday."

Emer stopped admiring and ceased smiling.

"Don't worry, Emer, we're bound to get chatted up soon," wrongly interpreted Wee-Sarah, as an orange bubble refused to stay down and she burped loudly.

The tempo of the music was suddenly brought down a level. Instead of the expected mass exodus, followed by a few awkward couples shuffling from side to side, the existing dancers stayed where they were, casually forming relaxed pairings and occasional huddles of three or more.

From out of the centre of the huddle, a broad, redheaded man appeared and confidently strolled right up to the two women.

As he was about to speak, Wee-Sarah abruptly interjected, "Look, before you waste anybody's time, you're too small for me and my friend is only interested in foreigners."

Emer was half-thankful for her colleague's bluntness and half-disappointed because this man instantly set the butterflies flapping away merrily in her stomach. He smiled the widest, warmest smile, that instantly reminded Emer of Jack Sheehan, before leaning towards her and whispering in a thick Alabama accent:

"Would you like to dance?"

"No," Emer replied as Wee-Sarah nodded in approval of her decision, "but, we can go for a walk if you like?"

"But . . . but . . . you can't!" Wee-Sarah protested as she shoved her miniature handbag under her arm. She knew the agreed rules: whichever one of them met a man first, the other had to simply look after themselves. But Wee-Sarah hadn't banked on it being her. "You can't leave me with all these – all these shirt-lifters!"

As Emer left the disco, she could have corrected her colleague's incorrect assessment and admitted that the disco was organised by Born Again Christians, but she was far too pleased with herself to bother.

It was only outside on the now empty street that Emer could fully hear the richness of her new friend's American accent.

"I don't mind if your friend wants to come along. Will she be all right?"

As she listened, Emer could instantly taste gumbo and Alabama Fudge Cake. She hadn't travelled much further than Dublin and didn't have an extensive vision of the Southern States of America.

"Don't worry. She'll be fine."

"I supposed she'd used to it – you being snatched up all the time. Not that I'm saying you're always going off with guys."

Emer picked the straw threads of the compliment out from the thatch of potential insult.

"Well, I at least usually know the names of the hundred or so blokes who walk with me."

"Apart from Bumbling Idiot, you can also call me William Todd."

"I'm Emer Farrell. How do you do?"

Now Emer was marginally disappointed: 'William' was a name for a Protestant from Ballymena. But the disappointment was erased as the American removed his navy and jade cotton shirt, revealing a taut white T-shirt, before wrapping his warm shirt around her bare arms.

"It's gotten a little bit chilly," William whispered.

Not where Emer was standing.

"But then you're used to much hotter weather back home," she batted the gentle conversation back as she ran her fingertips along the soft stitching on the shirt's cuffs and then explored the detail of the buttons. For once, she didn't feel like hurtling full steam ahead with her usual conversation, drenched in minute detail and minute significance.

There was no discussion about the direction they should take and the couple instinctively strolled away from the flashing neon lights of the disco and out along Eglinton Street in the direction of the beach.

Emer discovered a tiny, loose thread dangling from one of the cuff buttons. She was reassured to think that William wasn't like the other pristine Born Again Christians, but then she shouldn't forget that it was the challenge she was looking for.

They strolled past the locked barrier gate leading to the train station. A dying bee lay squirming on its back on the pavement. William stepped over it, careful not to injure the poor creature further. As William looked ahead, Emer squashed it with one sideways stamp of her foot, immediately putting an end to its suffering.

"Have you been over from the States long?" Emer enquired as, without words, they agreed to rest on a green wooden bench, blistered and graffiti-ridden.

"Long enough to know that Northern Irish girls are the most beautiful in the world."

"And why do you think that is?"

"Obviously, because right here is the epicentre of the planet. I've discovered that if you take the exact centre of all the latitude and longitude measurements, then the maths suggest that right here is dead centre. And that's where all the beauty is drawn to – centrifugal force."

"What – Northern Ireland?" Emer replied, caught up with the banter and half-believing all that he said.

Listening to his anecdotes, flavoured with his American drawl, made her feel ignorant, provincial and dull.

William shrugged his shoulders. "More specific than that."

"Not County Antrim? What – Portstewart?"

"Right here, Emer. This very bench," he whispered again with seductive charm.

Emer dipped her head and lifted her eyes to the night sky, with a hundred and ten per cent demure effort and effect. The smell of a half-eaten bag of curry chips wafted out of the bin beside the bench and they both stood up and continued to walk.

Emer looked ahead steadfastly as they ambled along, but from her peripheral vision she sensed the blur of her companion, a few inches taller than her, with thick arms and legs. She could hear the jeans on his thighs rub as he walked and guessed this was the muscle of the university rugby hero, or the international cyclist. His shock of deep red hair and emerald eyes were no doubt a legacy of Celtic kings and queens. Emer knew her clothing brands and the flash of LaCoste and Abercombie informed her that this was no ordinary student. William had class and he had money.

As he spoke, while they continued their walk, Emer was mesmerised by an accent drifting from thick and syrupy tones to a light and familiar resonance.

They were now on the edge of The Strand – a mile of desolate, uninterrupted white beach, sheltered by rolling sand dunes and shards of grass. A light evening rain had begun and pockmarks speckled the sand. The slowly breaking surf was the only noise beyond the sound of Emer inhaling, as her negligible stomach was sucked in even further and her chest stuck out for maximum effect. The crushed velvet of her dress forcibly resisted. Emer took her sling-backs off and with one shoe in each hand tiptoed to the edge of the water. William didn't follow her, forcing her to question whether Born Again Christians were, perhaps, a challenge too far. After all, she'd played her major seduction cards including: demure expressions, vulnerability, her 32DD's and now, barefoot and wet.

Even in the height of the summer, the Atlantic was still ice-cold and Emer gave up paddling when she could no longer feel her toes. She walked back over to William and the two now stood side by side, staring out at the ocean. Emer imagined that he was also looking for a whale, but she suspected he was more likely searching for Moses parting the waves. Her hands, still clasping her shoes, hung by her side, as she contemplated the least embarrassing exit strategy. She stopped holding her stomach muscles in. Then, at the point of total resignation and as she was about to scratch her left bare foot with her right, she felt the back of William's hand gently brush against her own. It was such an innocent gesture. A second later, it was the fingers touching and then the fingers interlocking. And still he said nothing, as she felt him gently clench and unclench his wide, strong fingers, as he explored every contour and every crease of her own hands.

With this one, pure and simple gesture, Emer, for the first time since Jack's death, felt complete. She was estranged from her eldest sister, her youngest sister confided in no one and her father, well, he was as he had always been. Emer got a minimum wage for minimum effort and drove a car held together with Blu-tack and string. Aged twenty-two, she felt that she had no direction and no future to look forward to. But somehow, by some chance, one plan had succeeded. Emer had widened her experiences and her opportunities and set herself the one challenge in her life that she could complete.

As the hand she was holding finally gripped her own and she felt a total, all-consuming shudder thoughout her body, Emer Farrell pledged her spirit and she knew later, her body, to the Born Again Christian from Alabama.

Without self-consciousness or pre-planning, Emer looked up directly into William's wide and innocent green eyes and whispered, "I've known you for one hour and yet I feel like I've known you for ever."

And interlocking his fingers in between Emer's, William softly replied, "I've known you for one hour and yet I feel I will know you for ever." Delivered in the thickest, strongest Ballymena accent and finished off with a "Hey".

## Chapter 22

It turned out that William Todd wasn't a Born Again Christian from Alabama, United States of America. He was a Free Presbyterian from Ballymena, ten miles down the road.

"Didn't the name William give the game away?" Heather asked her sister as the two young women were wedged into their seat by a rickety, slightly rusting, aluminium bar.

"It did and it didn't. I don't know. I just forgot about it. He was just so good-looking and kind and good-looking and. . ." But Emer was forced into silence by the plunge of the rollercoaster down its first sweep.

It was a week since the Born Again Christian disco and Emer had suggested a day-trip for her younger sister and herself, to celebrate the end of Heather's 'A' Level examinations. Understandably, Heather was slightly disappointed when a visit to Barry's amusements in Portrush, four miles from Portstewart, was offered. The wooden rollercoaster felt far from safe and every creak and groan was audible as the cart now chugged while it laboriously climbed again.

"I would have . . . loved to see his face . . . when . . . you gave him his marching orders," Heather said as the carriage jolted. From Emer's expression, Heather quickly realised that no marching orders had been given. Both girls' faces, however, changed to pure terror as the rollercoaster dipped and soared into an embankment, before noisily twisting into a second steep bend.

Teenage boys lined up with their mouths open and eyes wide as the two finest pairs of breasts they had ever seen wobbled and bashed into each other with every sweep and dive. For once, the Farrell girls' caramel-coloured cheeks were pure white and drained of blood. They teetered out of the carriage and, with legs of jelly, collapsed against a railing.

"That was brill!"

"Aye, will we go again?"

Emer and Heather had two more rides on the rollercoaster, before stopping for a 99 for Heather and a Diet Coke for Emer. In between slurps out of the can, Emer studied the local fashions and enthused "Gorgeous!" every ten seconds. Heather focused on her ice cream and studied her sister.

"But, Emer, he's a Born Again Liar!"

"Technically not. He didn't actually tell me he was a Born Again. I just assumed it. He was given tickets to the disco by some fella he was working for."

"So, he's not a student either?" enquired Heather, while licking chocolate flakes from around her mouth.

'Technically . . . no."

"He is a . . . ?"

"Bricklayer."

The ice cream dripped down Heather's hand without her noticing it and fell onto her now very old and very scuffed Doc Martens boots.

"He knows Dad. Well, knows of him." Emer visibly squirmed as she spoke.

"It gets better and better."

"Look, it's nothing serious. I said I'd go out with him for four days . . . and so I did and I only gave him another four days because I felt sorry for him. But that's it after tomorrow. I'm not going to waste myself on some no-hoper." And that was that.

The seagulls hovered and darted around the sisters' legs, all wings, beaks and feet, expecting offerings, but neither Emer nor Heather were offering. As the last of her ice-cream cone was swallowed, Emer dragged Heather away from the railings and over to the Waltzer. The teenage boys, hovering like the gulls, followed and perched themselves around the edge of the ride.

But before Emer and Heather had time to pay for their turn, the music started abruptly and all they could see of the fairground-hand was a whirl of floppy chestnut hair as he began to spin their carriage, vigorously and without respite. Emer whooped and hollered as the carriage rotated, but Heather was silent, crushed by her sister against the side. Combined with the incessant music, flashing lights and whirr of the twisting carriage, vanilla ice cream with a dab of undigested chocolate flake was vomited over a ten-foot radius. The spray miraculously missed Emer, but saturated her wretched sister and the unfortunate line-up of their teenage admirers.

Emer returned to Merlin, parked outside of Barry's, on

Kerr Street. She had a spare clean jumper in the boot for Heather to change into. While Emer offered to fetch it, the very apologetic fairground-hand had taken Heather to the staff toilets to clean up. It appeared Heather knew the boy from school – Cillian something or other – and this, along with painting gaudy murals on some of the rides, was his summer job. Emer dismissed him in the mental appendix to her notebook, as *'grubby hair, nice smile, makes you vomit'*.

Heather found Merlin easily. She'd parked him four feet from the kerb and as a result, a passing car had clipped his wing mirror. She also noticed that he was dipped at the front and it was only when she was right beside her car that she noticed William Todd leaning against the bonnet – one foot still on the ground and one day away from getting the boot. She knew that he worked until noon on Saturdays and he'd obviously been on his way back from a job when he must have spotted her car. The expensive designer clothes were replaced with cut-off jeans, frayed and grubby, and a *Frankie Says Relax* T-shirt, with a pink tint as a result of a boil-wash with a red sock. Emer knew her washing cycles. His legs were tanned and muscular and at first very sexy, before Emer caught a glimpse of a pure white line where he'd been wearing longer socks.

"Hi," William cheerfully said, bouncing off the bonnet, allowing Merlin to groan with relief. "Fancy going for a drink?"

The Ballymena accent jarred with Emer and she winced inwardly and outwardly.

"What, right now?" Emer answered abruptly. Jack Sheehan would never have dressed like this. "I'm with our Heather. She's waiting on me. Back there . . . in Barry's."

Emer felt like an awkward teenager. She'd never seen William in the daylight and the light of the day only seemed to magnify all that happened between them in the night.

"She can come too." William was persistent.

"But she's covered in puke."

"Look, if you don't want to, Emer, you just have to say."

"Honest, she is." Emer was slightly insulted that William thought if she wanted an excuse that was the best she could come up with. She nervously pulled at a few of her tight, short curls and then tucked them back in with the others. Unusually for Emer, she was lost for words and she filled the silence by jangling her car keys. There was one key and the rest were an assortment of key-rings: a pewter 'K' (Kitty's), a picture frame, still with the image of somebody else's family in it as bought in the shop (Heather's) and tiny troll with fluorescent pink hair (Emer's). Where he had been seated, William had left dusty bits of plaster and mortar on Merlin's bonnet. The blemishes kept distracting the vehicle's owner.

Emer knew she had to end this relationship now, before it ever got started. Emer had set her sights on the university campus in the hope of finding a life with a foreign student, and the thought now of finding a bricklayer, within the very bricks that her father had laid over twenty years earlier, made her feel nauseous.

"Get your tits out for the lads!" heckled the teenage admirers, who had unearthed new-found bravery in the back of an Ulsterbus, driving past at thirty miles an hour.

"Are they shouting at me?" William joked and then crossed his arms across his chest in feigned embarrassment. But Emer immediately caught his eye looking at her own chest and now, with genuine embarrassment, both instantly recalled Merlin's backseat only last night, when Emer introduced William to the full programme of her multi-talented DD's. The conflict between the intimacy of their nights together and the physical and emotional distance between them now, confused and exasperated Emer. She couldn't go on with it. There was no future.

"I have to get back to our Heather. I'll give you a call."

"Oh, it's like that, is it?"

"Aye."

Emer forgot about the jumper for her sister and turned to walk away, with as much dramatic poise as she could muster.

"Is it because I'm a Prod?" William shouted after her, but she didn't answer. "What if I found Jesus?" No answer again. "What if I found Jesus in Texas?"

Emer was now across on the far side of the road, behind her a flashing halo of amber and bright yellow lights from Barry's amusements. Her shoe slightly clipped the curb, but she maintained her posture and kept her shoulders back.

"What if I just loved you, Emer Farrell?" William, now forced to shout, bellowed through the gaps in the traffic.

Emer stopped and turned around.

*Emer, 1989*

# Chapter 23

"So, Miss Farrell, what faults would you say you had?" the interviewer asked, without looking up from her notepad.

"I'm too hardworking – too much of a perfectionist. I like everything to be just so. I take work home with me and I find it hard to turn off when I get home because I'm so passionate about the work I do –"

"OK, OK," the interviewer interrupted, finding it hard to keep her shorthand at the pace that Emer answered the questions. Emer guessed the interviewer was in her late forties, with heavily bleached cropped hair, dry and wiry, and more gums than teeth when she smiled. She was the owner of the beautician's and had introduced herself to Emer, who immediately forgot her name. Either side of the interviewer sat two girls about Emer's age, immaculate and identical, like Robert Palmer's backing group in "The Addiction to Love" video. Without a note-pad for a prop, the two girls just stared blankly at Emer, without expression and, in Emer's opinion, without interest.

"If those are your weaknesses, what are your strengths?" the interviewer asked, visibly preparing herself for a lengthy answer.

The interview room was one of the treatment rooms in the rather too graphically named Pores for Thought. A blur of rag-rolling and stencilling, interlaced with a blend of bird-song and "Bat out of Hell" played on Pan pipes. This beauty salon in Coleraine was the most established and sought after in *The Golden Triangle*. Many a manicured nail was broken in the scramble for a beauty apprenticeship there. This was a golden opportunity for Emer to progress from being a bored receptionist.

"I'm hardworking. A perfectionist. I like everything to be just so. I take work home with me and I find it hard to turn off when I get home because I'm so passionate about the work I do —"

Emer stopped herself just at the point of *déjà vu* and surrendered her best 'I'm here to please' smile. She'd spent the entire morning waxing, plucking and preening to give her optimum, high-maintenance impression. Heather had loaned her the least old-fashioned, but smart, navy jacket and skirt she had. Emer had put on weight lately and, as well as being too tight, she felt her own clothes were more Rimmel than Estée Lauder. Emer's youngest sister was waiting for her outside the salon, in Merlin, just in case Emer tried to chicken out at the last minute. It was January 1989 and Heather was now about to embark on her second term at the University of Ulster at Coleraine, where she was doing theatre studies. Between the two sisters, over a New Year's Day burnt chicken and mushy sprouts cooking fiasco, they had pledged to set four resolutions for each other, after deciding it was impossible to stick to their own. Emer's list, drafted by Heather, was wedged into her suit's top pocket and as the interviewer asked for a moment to gather her thoughts, Emer ran the top three resolutions through her mind: *1. Stop frittering your time away and get yourself at least on the bottom rung of a career ladder. 2. Buy and read* The Sunday Times *every week. 3. Try and listen to what people are saying before answering back.* Well, she was applying for a new job and she had a half-read copy of yesterday's *Times* stuffed in the pocket on Merlin's door. The interviewer returned to her questioning.

"And what experience do you have in –"

"I was halfway through my City and Guilds . . ." Oops! Emer stopped, realising she hadn't quite heard the interviewer's question properly. Well, the third resolution was to 'try'. "I'm sorry, what was the question?"

Emer hadn't been to many interviews before and found it hard to judge if it was going well or not. Between them, Heather and her father had both pressurised her into applying, but now that she was here, she was surprised at just how much she wanted the job for herself. She was approaching her twenty-third birthday and for the first time in her life, she had ambition for something other than sex. She wanted to be independent and she wanted a secure future. Right now, this job meant everything to her.

As the interviewer scribbled some more notes, Emer kept her arms crossed in front of her, with her breasts balanced on top. Occasionally she put the flat of her hand against her short hair, flattening any wayward curls. The interviewer's backing group remained motionless, even as Emer squeezed out a further 'I'm here to please' smile to each of them.

The interviewer then lifted her notes and flicked through them, obviously searching for something important. When she couldn't find the answer in her pile of notes, she opened several files from the treatment table behind her. They were speckled with aromatherapy oils and hair.

"I don't see anywhere details of what school you went to, Emer."

Emer, against both her sister and her father's advice, had decided to avoid giving the name of her secondary school.

"Dominican College, Portstewart. Renowned for its excellent exam results, discipline and –"

"I see," interrupted the interviewer, by now familiar with Emer's tendency to waffle. "You do know that the majority of our customers and all our staff here would be from a Protestant background and –"

"Some of my best friends are Protestants," Emer found herself pleading, before being struck by the stupidity of what she was saying. She felt awkward and vulnerable and then awkwardness and vulnerability led her into anger. "But if you're going to be a bigot, you know where you can stuff your job!"

"And as I was about to say," the interviewer calmly interjected, "I would like to redress that balance. Pores for Thought is an equal opportunity employer."

Back outside in the parked car, with Heather beside her, Emer rocked her head against the steering wheel in frustration. She was in floods of tears.

"I did everything you said I shouldn't do. I'm such an eejit. I was so embarrassed. I had everything going against me, me included."

"Did they just say no, there and then?" Heather asked as she rifled through the glove compartment looking for a tissue amongst the make-up and wire coils that had fallen off Merlin and hadn't been replaced.

"She said she'd call me."

"That's not a 'no'."

Emer lifted her head from the steering wheel and raised one eyebrow at Heather.

"OK, so what if it is a 'no'?" said Heather. "This was the first trainee job you applied for. What's the odds on getting the first one anyway?"

"But, just look, Heather. Who in their right mind's going to employ me?"

"They were obviously just prejudiced. They couldn't see what you had to offer." Heather the youngest, and always the wisest and most selfless of the Farrell sisters, fought desperately to bring Emer back from the brink of despair. The sobs had fully steamed up the Beetle's windows and the two sisters shivered in the winter chill. "We'll try somewhere else, maybe a bit further afield."

"It's no use." Emer rested her head now against the steering wheel and let tears and mucus drip to the floor. The carpet had long since been worn away and the tarmac road was visible through small gashes in the floor pan.

"You can't give up before you've started, Emer. Treat this as a learning experience. When you've calmed down a bit, you'll see that you probably didn't do too badly. Did you remember to listen?"

No answer.

"Did you keep your answers short and to the point?"

Again, no answer.

"Did you give them your best 'I'm here to please smile'?" Heather was grasping at straws.

"Yes, yes. And what bloody use was it?"

"It's a start, Emer."

"I've too much going against me." Emer wiped her nose on her sleeve. "Even *I* wouldn't give me a job."

"So, you rant on a little."

"And?"

"And you've no hands-on experience." Heather didn't like the way the conversation was going, but couldn't see a way out.

"And?"

"No qualifications."

"And?"

"And, I'm sure as hell not going to say being a Catholic goes against you."

"Heather, don't be so naïve. It's sweet, but dense. There's one or two other bigger obstacles in my way, don't you think?"

A knock came on the now completely steamed-up driver's side window. Emer rolled it down to as far as it could go, which only left a four-inch gap. Just about managing to peek through, came the heavily made-up nose and eyes of the interviewer.

"I just saw your car still outside and thought it would save me the bother of telephoning you. Emer, could you start on Monday?"

Emer was dumbstruck and needed a dig in the ribs from Heather, before she could reply.

"Yes . . . Monday . . . yes."

"OK, then."

As the interviewer's nose disappeared and she turned to return to the salon, Emer opened Merlin's door wide and shouted after her.

"I don't get it! Why are you giving me the job? I was awful in there."

The interviewer turned back and strolled over to the car. She knelt down and with her left hand wiped a tear away from Emer's cheek.

"Because, like you, I needed a break once." She then used the same hand and placed it on Emer's very obvious, five-month-pregnant stomach. "And I didn't get it."

# Chapter 24

Without a doubt, this was the most unattractive Emer had
ever felt. Getting her breath back, she sat on a rock on
Portstewart strand, wearing Heather's Aran sweater, her
father's deerstalker hat and a pair of William Todd's old,
bottle-green, track-suit bottoms. He had persuaded her to
get some fresh air and exercise and while he sat reading the
*Coleraine Chronicle* in Merlin, parked on the beach, Emer
did laps.

As she sat scanning the dimples on her thighs through
the cheap cotton of her trousers, Emer thought back to
yesterday's surprise farewell party at Pores for Thought. She
was about to go on maternity leave and the other staff had
pretended that there was a late appointment with her for a
pedicure. She had been training in-house for three months
now, but until she started her night class after the baby was
born, hands and feet were the nearest she was allowed to the
customers. As Emer had tutted at the rudeness of some of
the clients' time-keeping, the other beauticians had come

into her treatment room and plied her with Iced Diamonds and Snowballs. And while Emer pigged out with buns on the inside, on the outside she was cleansed, toned, manicured, and massaged. Barbara, who had turned out to be both the interviewer and the salon's owner, took responsibility for the waxing.

"Now, Emer, are you sure you want this done?"

"Just think of me lying in that hospital. Don't you want me to look my best?"

"Up there maybe," Barbara put her hand on Emer's face, "but if it was me, I wouldn't give a flying monkey about anywhere else, thank you very much."

"Think of the reputation of Pores for Thought. I don't want those nurses thinking we don't practise what we preach."

"Or the doctors," one of the backing group kindly interceded.

"If any of the nurses – or the doctors – find themselves checking out the volume of your pubic hair, well, good luck to them," Barbara said as she applied a thick dollop of hot, syrupy wax to Emer's groin.

Emer was thankful that the size of her bump meant it was impossible for her to see what was going on down below. She had stopped weighing herself when she got to four stone over her normal weight. She consoled herself that she was carrying a stone of baby and three stone of fluid.

The sound of Emer's involuntary screech, when it came to the underarm wax, woke the baby but Emer was the only one aware that her unborn child was hiccuping away merrily. She smiled to herself. That was until the baby somersaulted and her belly-button popped out.

"That's gross," a young beautician responded, as she squeezed enthusiastically at Emer's nose in the hope of finding a stray blackhead.

"If you think that's gross . . ." One of the older beauticians was about to share her second-hand knowledge of placentas and meconium.

"Stop. All I care about right now is the cost of nappies and wipes and I've managed to source some cheap, shop-own brands." Emer was pleased with herself.

"Aye, but are they as good?" The older beautician had two godchildren and had begun to annoy Emer by having the upper hand on shopping for babies.

"It's poops and pee that go into them, so what's the odds?" said Emer.

"The odds are pretty high that if you buy cheap nappies, you'll end up paying the price," said the other woman with an air of shopping seniority that Emer did not appreciate.

Emer had managed a full month of the New Year before she eventually gave up *The Sunday Times* and replaced it with *Good Housekeeping* and as yet she hadn't come across a 'buying for baby' feature. But she now remembered point three of her New Year's Resolutions and listened grudgingly to the beautician's opinion – and only butted in the once. Anyway, she still had her career, against all the odds, and that surely more than counterbalanced the second and third resolutions.

The beauticians giggled and preened and Emer giggled and beamed back.

"I wonder what the wee soul will look like," the youngest beautician thought aloud as she finished Emer off with an Indian head massage.

Her short contribution to the conversation brought deadly silence – just at the point when the background music changed to trickling water and a lone blackbird. Emer had heard this question a hundred times already – from her father, Heather, Wee-Sarah whom she still met for the occasional Diet Coke and even William, all with their own reasons for asking, but all receiving the same icy glare.

By nine that evening, Emer's pampering was complete and her unborn baby nestled under her ribcage to sleep. As she was leaving the salon, Barbara secretly placed an envelope into her hand.

"What's that?"

"Just a little good-luck bonus."

"But, Barbara, you've done so much for me already. Keeping the job open for me is just fantastic. Really, please don't –"

"For once, I'm not going to listen to you. You've furniture for that new flat of yours to get and if I waste my money on one more face-lift, I'll literally be talking out of my backside!"

Emer had gone out that morning and knowing exactly where to go and what to get, spent the £500 given to her on a Hooverpoint washing-machine and a tumble-drier. With the few pounds left over, she bought herself a maternity bra from Marks and Spencer, causing quite a stir as their first ever FF customer.

As she now sat on the rock, her double F's heaved as she gulped in the spring sea air. Her breasts were no longer hers or even William's, to his great disappointment. They belonged to the baby. Reaching to the sides, as it was impossible for her to reach forward, she pulled off her wellington boots and her one navy and one black sock and dipped her toes into a shallow pool at the sheltered side of the rock. Her toes were olive and plump, her pedicured toenails crimson red. Years of wearing ill-fitting but highly fashionable shoes had forced her little toes into hiding. Her two big toes overcompensated by being bulbous and wide. There was absolutely nothing Emer could find attractive about herself right now. And as she slowly watched her feet shrivel in the icy seawater, she saw her own reflection shrivel with the gentle ripple of the pool.

"Say cheese!"

Emer looked up and saw William standing a few feet away, glaring through his cheap Instamatic camera. He insisted on cataloguing every stage of the unborn child's development and had so far assembled a wide collection of shots of Emer having morning sickness, Emer going for a scan, Emer wearing her first maternity clothes – and he had got a corker this morning of Emer's shocked face as she read FF on the label of her maternity bra.

"If you point that bloody thing at me one more time – I'll – I'll sit on you and then you'll know all about it!" Emer covered her face with her outstretched hand.

"That's just your hormones talking," William said, still peering through the lens. "I read that the last few weeks can make you very irritable and easily annoyed."

"Really?" Emer struggled to remain composed. "Is there anything else you read that you would like to share?"

"It'll be at least three years before you get your figure back."

"Fuck away off!"

"No, only joking, Emer. It's only twelve months."

Emer had quickly tired of William's habit of exaggerating bad news, in his feeble attempt to lessen the impact of the truth. He had tried it by initially doubling the price of the flat they were interested in – in a warped hope of lessening the impact of the true price (which was already stretching their meagre salaries to the limit). Or the fact that his employers weren't going to give him any paternity leave and then announcing he was 'only joking' and was getting two days.

Emer had nurtured a method of counter-attacking this irritating habit.

"Oh, well, then maybe that'll give us time to get a wedding organised," she wryly smiled.

William stopped glaring through the lens and peered over the top, hopefully.

"No, only joking!" She laughed as she lifted her feet out of the pool and let them drip-dry.

From the moment she had thrust her positive pregnancy test in William's face, shouting 'Look what you've done!', he had been angling to marry her. She had, at first, confused him entirely by saying 'mixed marriages don't work'. The truth was that while she had continued her ad-hoc relationship with William, she had also been having casual sex with foreign students. The true parentage of her unborn child was anyone's guess and she buried this burden deep into the back of her consciousness. Too big a thought and a problem for her to tackle right now. But, somewhere, in the shreds of respect she had for William, Emer decided that she could not dupe him into marriage. Anyway, she didn't want to spoil her chances of someone better and more exciting coming along.

William had eventually yielded to Emer's proposal that they buy a flat together and give it a trial run before the birth of 'their' child. Situated along the Portstewart promenade, the two-bedroom flat was right above a dry-cleaner's, with views from the living-room window directly across the main road and out into the Atlantic Ocean. Two weeks in and with four weeks to go before the baby was due, Emer still felt like she was giving William a pardon for good behaviour and he, in turn, still felt like he was on parole.

William lifted a clump of wet sand and threw it at Emer's now blotchy legs.

"That's a rotten thing to say! Some day, Emer Farrell, you're going to beg me to marry you and do you know what I'll say?"

"What?" Emer half-answered, only half-interested.

"I'll say 'yes'."

William turned around and headed back to Merlin. He was dressed in his Sunday best of La Coste and Pringle. He had tried to persuade Emer to go to church with him that morning, if only to please his family. As usual, she had resisted. The spring sunshine bounced off his deep-red hair, and his strong, broad back cast a wide shadow on the sand. No matter how much William annoyed her, she could not deny his physical attractiveness. But everything else about him was wrong. He was nowhere near her dream and wide off the mark when it came to comparisons with Jack Sheehan.

William Todd had also, somehow, managed to build a friendship with Emer's father, overcoming obstacles such as being a Protestant and getting Emer pregnant. And now, they not only worked on the same building site but, on occasion, they were known to share their packed lunches. When Emer came home from her late-night shift, she often caught William and her father gossiping like old women. Emer concluded that they were conspiring as to what groom and father-of-the-bride outfits to buy, before announcing, 'We want to wear shiny, grey suits . . . no, only joking, pink cummerbunds and brown slacks will do'.

In rare moments of charity, Emer decided that, with her now having moved out, Heather hardly there any more and Kitty still ostracised from the family, perhaps her father had found the son he'd never had. But these moments were indeed rare and made her head hurt.

Emer dusted sand off her feet and legs with her socks and then put both the socks and the wellington boots back on. She slowly dawdled back to the Beetle. Merlin had been part of the Farrell family for nearly seven years now and apart from the cheap respray Kitty and Heather had saved for, he had had no maintenance other than the occasional splash of oil or tweak of a stray wire. The Windolene Pink was now camouflaged in rusty brown splodges, where autumn leaves and bird-droppings had been left to corrode. The chrome detail along the centre of the bonnet was held together with rust, and a gluey, yellow patch denoted where the circular VW badge had been vandalised and forcibly removed. Scratches along the wings, like silvery stretch-marks, had been scored on by a jealous vandal with his own Fiesta key. But Merlin was a miracle of engineering and resilience.

William had impatiently started the engine and it angrily and noisily chugged away, baying for Emer to return. Neither William nor Emer spoke as she squeezed herself in behind the steering wheel and beside William, who continued to stare blankly out of the window and out to sea. When she sat down, the car visibly dipped to the driver's side and audibly groaned in response. As she herself looked blankly out to sea, she thought of the final resolution that Heather had written for her over three months ago: '4. Be happy.' Emer lifted off the handbrake and put her foot down on the accelerator pedal. An avalanche of fine sand shot up from the back wheels. She tried again and as the engine raced and tried to force itself forward, it could not move. Merlin was stuck. They were stuck.

*Heather, 1989*

# Chapter 25

When the seat belt wouldn't fit around Emer Farrell's stomach any more, William Todd persuaded her to hand Merlin over to her youngest sister. He hadn't been convinced of the car's safety and considering its current state of disrepair, this was an excellent opportunity to persuade her to finally accept the Nissan Micra he'd bought her for Valentine's Day. William felt that Emer's acquiescence was a reconciliatory step and a signal that she was now starting to listen to him. Emer, on the other hand, had her own reasons to part with the car.

"Sure, you take it now. It'll be better than getting the bus to the university every day,"

Emer enthused to Heather, while, for the tenth time, she checked and re-checked the contents of her hospital bag. She was now six days past her expected date of delivery and with William forced to go back to work, Heather had taken a few days off from her first-year studies to take care of her sister.

"I don't know," said Heather. "Jesus, you could surf on one of them!" She laughed, holding up a maternity sanitary towel. "When's the MOT due?"

"Aren't these Babygros gorgeous? Look at the detail of the little matching cap . . . MOT's due tomorrow . . . and what about these teeny-weeny socks . . ." Emer rambled on.

Emer's motivation to part with the car, as Heather suspected, ran deeper than veiled concern for her sister's transport arrangements. Emer didn't want the hassle or the cost of ensuring that Merlin was roadworthy.

With mixed feelings, Heather became Merlin's reluctant owner for the second time.

The next day, with William still back at work, Roddy Farrell took a day's leave to take care of his heavily pregnant daughter, while Heather drove Merlin to the Vehicle Testing Centre in Coleraine.

The last time Heather had driven the Beetle had been on the painful and emotional journey from Kingston upon Thames over a year ago. And now as she drove, her feelings and thoughts jumped along in time to the splatters and chugs of the old car's engine. Over the past year she had kept in telephone contact with Kitty, but conversations were always short and to the point. Kitty was preoccupied with the plans for her wedding later that year and when she wasn't gushing about how wonderful Matt Edwards was, she enthused about her new responsibility as manager of The Jolly Man. The conversations were always one-sided and neither Kitty nor Heather appeared to mind.

Over the telephone, Heather knew that Kitty probably still perceived her young sister to be the same as she was when she had driven away abruptly over a year ago. What Kitty didn't see was the introvert nineteen-year-old, always willing to please – as long as that wasn't to please herself. Within twelve months she had ballooned from a size twelve to a size sixteen. As she drove today, her ever-faithful black Doc Martens were carefully pushed down on the pedals, her black saggy leggings were stuck to the blue vinyl seat and her navy, gent's T-shirt stretched across her 40 DD's which were squashed against the steering wheel. Her long, ebony curls were pulled tight into a plait and her dark skin was dusted down with cheap face powder.

Heather tempered her dislike for Merlin and the jinx she had felt between them, by recognising that she and the car now had a lot in common – which included being wrecks at nineteen.

"Please drive your car up to the ramp," a crisp, boiler-suited man with a clipboard ordered.

Having arrived at the test centre, all of Heather's knowledge of the car and of driving drifted away with the fumes from the exhaust. First, she went off the ramp and then too far over and then stopped three feet too short. Eventually, on her fifth attempt, she got Merlin's wheels on the top of the ramp and the inspector gave her a rather exasperated thumbs-up signal. Driving over the gaping ravine that was the pit for the chassis inspection brought Heather and the inspector both out in a cold sweat.

"Headlights . . . no, headlights . . . no, not indicators . . ."

Heather felt that this was the first time she had ever set foot in the Beetle and every switch, knob and pedal was unfamiliar. She closed her eyes and hoped that everything would go away.

"Drive the Beetle on, please," said a loudspeaker at her window.

Heather drove on twenty feet, then stopped the car at the ramps for the final brake test.

"I'm sorry to say that your car has not passed its Vehicle Inspection."

Heather didn't care – she just wanted to get out of there as fast as she could.

"And I'm afraid to say that I have to record the car as not safe to be out on the road . . ." The clipboard clipped and the boiler-suit rustled. "And I can't, under law, allow you to drive the car away. Would you like to use the office telephone and contact a vehicle recovery service?"

Four of the inspectors pushed Heather and Merlin out of the garage. Even through the heavy coating of face powder, a full, bright-red flush of embarrassment burst through as Heather sat in the test centre carpark, staring at the grey pebbledash wall in front of her. "Come on, Cillian. Isn't this a cue for you?" she asked.

But not this time. Cillian Harte was studying Fine Art at Manchester University and, the last she had heard of him, he was seeing a ballet dancer from King's Lynn. This time there was no one she knew to witness her embarrassment, but she blushed all the same.

A short taxi ride later, with Merlin abandoned overnight to the sniggers in the test centre, Heather was back to take her turn at minding her elder sister. When she arrived, Emer was sitting all alone at the bottom of the steps leading up to her flat, with her hospital bag at her feet.

"What's happened? Have you gone into labour?" Heather panicked, immediately forgetting the rehearsed

180

speech she had planned along the lines of 'you know where you can stick that heap of a car?'.

"If only. If this baby won't make its own way, then I'm going to get the wee bugger pulled out." Emer was as determined as her ankles were bloated. "I rang the hospital and they're going to induce me at six in the morning. I've got to go in tonight for different sorts of checks and stuff."

"So, where's Dad gone?"

"We couldn't get William on that number he left us, so Dad's gone to fetch him and they'll meet us at the hospital. You can take me in Merlin."

Emer looked as disappointed and dejected as her young sister when Heather gave her sensitive and censored account of the past hour. Emer's eyes plumped round and moist as she pathetically stifled her tears.

"I just knew I shouldn't have let William go off to work. Just look at me – can't keep a man in and can't get a baby out," she confessed with her guard down.

Heather was used to feeling like her sisters' guardian, but for the first time in her life, her own insecurities about her physique were echoed by Emer's heavy, bloated and extremely vulnerable appearance.

Emer mistook the empathy for sympathy.

"Don't you dare pity me, Heather! Things may look bad at the moment – pretty horrendous actually – but I'll bounce back. Wait and see! Everything is going to be fantastic. Brilliant in fact. Now go down to the dry cleaner's and ask them if you can call Andy's Taxis."

Heather hesitated.

"Go on!"

When Heather returned from making the telephone

call, the expectant Emer was still waiting expectantly on the stairs. Her eyes looked like they had been rubbed sore and her nose was pink, but she greeted Heather with a beaming, chin-doubling smile and asked, "How are *your* New Year's Resolutions going by the way?"

Emer had difficulty sitting in the back of the taxi and rocked from side to side in an attempt to shift the weight bearing down on each buttock. The seat belt made a deep slash between her breasts, exaggerating their size from absolutely huge to freakishly awesome. Heather attempted to hold her sister's hand a few times, but Emer was having none of it.

"Now, I'll only be away a couple of days. You can bunk in my place if you like." Emer's right cheek was now numb, so she leant on the left. "William will be busy annoying me in the hospital and you'll get a break from Dad annoying you. I've a few nice nibbles from Marksies in the fridge, which you can have, but don't think of using the washing-machine without checking with either the manual or me, first."

"And what if you're in labour when I need to do a boil wash or something?" Heather smiled.

Emer genuinely thought long and hard before answering. "Phone the delivery suite and one of the nurses will get word to me."

Within a few hours of Emer's life being transformed, forever, she could still only function on a superficial level. The magnitude of her predicament was buried deep down. This was beyond the understanding of Heather, who now sat chasing her sister's hand around the back seat, with her own stomach in knots and her pelvic-floor muscles clenched tight.

Eventually, Heather trapped Emer's puffy hand, with its silver eternity ring that cut into the flesh of her finger.

"For over nine months now you've been pregnant." Heather wasn't going to let go of the struggling hand.

"And, your point?"

"And now, Emer, there's a baby about to enter this world."

"The education you get at those universities these days is terrific."

"Be serious for a minute." Heather was sombre and selected her words carefully. "You've spent all those months focusing on being pregnant, on the mechanics of it all, on the dilemma between Pampers versus Huggies. But now you're about to have a baby . . . a baby!" Heather's own wonderment and anxiety was combined with genuine concern for her sister's state of mind. And then at the point when she felt that she was getting through, she spoilt it by adding, "And what will the wee soul look like?"

Before Emer could answer, the taxi pulled up at the hospital and, as *pro forma*, Emer was out of the car before the driver had reached a complete stop. William was waiting for her at the door, a mass of floury plaster and dust. He immediately hugged her with all his might and she hugged him back, with part of hers. Heather was going to pay the taxi-driver when Emer held her back.

"Sure, you head on, Heather. Nothing will be happening tonight but tests. Pop round in the morning."

"Are you sure?"

"Absolutely."

The sisters were unaccustomed to physical expressions of affection and kissed each other on the cheek awkwardly.

183

Their backs were stiff and their arms fixed and firm. But their chocolate oval eyes, complete mirrors of each other's, twinkled in a fleeting moment of true sisterly love.

"Good luck! Break a leg!" Heather shouted after her sister.

"Break my water more like!" Emer shouted back as she linked her arm into William's and began leading him into the hospital.

Heather then discovered that Emer had left her hospital bag on the back-seat floor of the taxi and, grabbing it, ran after her sister and William.

"Aren't you forgetting something?"

William took the bag from her, spattering it with mortar. Emer rolled her eyes and tried to dust the contamination away, but the rubbing only made it worse and she gave up when her unborn baby decided to suddenly thrust its head deep against her bladder, making a visit to the toilet imperative.

"Never mind. It'll wash," Emer resolved as she went in search of the nearest ladies'.

"Aye, but on which cycle?" William nervously asked Heather.

# Chapter 26

Heather Farrell's drama workshop was divided between those who were breakfast cereals and those who were milk. She had snapped, crackled and popped for half an hour and was running out of improvised ideas. Applying Stanislavski's acting techniques when cast as a bowl of Rice Krispies was causing her concern.

Emer had been in hospital thirty-six hours already and there was still no sign of Junior making an appearance. Heather had decided she couldn't afford any further time off from her studies and had returned to the university on the basis of hourly telephone calls to the hospital. But as she went all limp and soggy after being doused in very enthusiastic milk, she couldn't help but think there was a more important place she should be right now. The theatre studies course had attracted both extrovert egotists and introverts like Heather. It so happened that in today's workshop all the introverts chose to be cereals and the would-be John Gielguds were the milk – some semi-skimmed and others very definitely full-cream.

"Heather, how do you feel right now? What is your motivation?" the barefooted and comfortably dressed, hobbit-like lecturer asked, as Heather internalised being eaten and turned into a huge fart.

In between her acting workshop and a lecture on Sean O'Casey, Heather managed two more telephone calls to the hospital and a boiled-egg curry in the refectory. All of her old schoolmates had either gone to universities in Scotland or England, or were taking year-out trips to the States. Heather wasn't quite sure why she had stayed so close to home. Her university friends, therefore, were mostly new.

Heather was now in the second term of her first academic year. Somehow, in her first term she had successfully avoided enrolment to the countless clubs and societies on offer. She had gone to the 'Freshers' Bazaar' in the first week, where the various clubs tried to round up the fledgling undergraduates, but the fact that her sister Emer appeared to be known by quite a few of them had put her off. So now her weekdays were divided between Method Acting or sitting in the refectory chatting with a bun or a cake, or whatever inanimate objects her fellow students were acting today.

Heather made a second trip for more curry and returned halfway through a conversation between the rest of her class.

"Are we going to get a degree for this?"

"I know – can you imagine the physics students going up to get their degrees – all worn out and haggard like – and then we prance up and do a monologue!"

"To be or not to be – Shredded Wheat!" contributed one of the students, who with straggly, straw-coloured hair and round shoulders looked rather too much like a Weetabix for comfort. He sniggered and the group laughed along in the conspiratorial 'we know something you don't' group. Heather laughed too – the loudest in fact.

The tutorial after lunch focused on *The Red Book of Gestalt*. Heather was tasked with having a conversation with herself and flitting between two chairs. She was actually surprised at how interesting she was and found she had lots to talk about, even when all the other students had got bored and were secretly whispering to each other.

As soon as the class was over, Heather ran out to the lobby and telephoned the hospital. There were still no developments.

The final workshop for the day was an audition for the end-of-year production of Bertolt Brecht's *The Caucasian Chalk Circle*. Heather, like most of the other breakfast cereal types, had opted for behind-the-scene duties. The role of Assistant Deputy Stage Manager sounded grand, but translated into Heather being required to discreetly move pieces of set and props in between the scenes. This suited Heather, as she got to legitimately wear her beat-out Doc Martens and baggy, black clothes. The downside, however, was that all backstage crew had to have minor acting parts. The minor and the major female roles were all being assessed by the same audition piece, which involved crossing an imaginary bridge, carrying an imaginary baby. Alphabetically, Heather was fourth in line. The first student took nearly five minutes to make her crossing, against incredible, imaginary monsoon conditions. The second managed to muster all the skills of a very suspect street mime-artist, even to the point of running into a pretend wall. The third crossed a bridge held together with thread and tissue, as every imaginary plank crumbled under her feet and every rope-handle she tried to save herself with, snapped, forcing her to drop inch by inch to the crevasse below.

By now, even Heather – up next – wasn't convinced of the bridge's safety. Before she could begin, she decided she needed a crutch – a prop to hide behind. She chose to fold her sweater into a tiny bundle, wrapping it around her arm. This was the baby. With her hand inside, forming a fist, she imagined a tiny heart beating as she slowly clenched and unclenched her fingers. The movement was so slow that no one, other than herself, was aware of the beat that signified life within. Heather carefully scrutinised the distance from her side of the room to the far side, where her bridge ended and where the tutor marked scores out of twenty in his notebook.

At first, the rest of the class tittered, before receiving a serious rebuke from the tutor. The room was now completely silent. Heather tried to envisage the bridge and her crossing it, but initially all she could think of was her lumpy self, waddling across. That was until she looked down at her sweater, with her fist still inside, nestled next to her breast. This was her baby, totally helpless and utterly dependent on her. Suddenly she didn't feel self-conscious, but just energised by the task of getting her baby across and to safety. Her focus was complete. She tentatively used the tip of her toes to test the first few planks. They were secure. With the baby still clenched as tight as possible, she then used her left hand to reach along the rope support. This was strong too. Heather continued balancing caution and control, until she reached halfway across the bridge and then with only her baby in her thoughts, she briskly and surely stepped across the rest of the bridge, reaching the far side with genuine relief and mental exhaustion. The baby had been clenched so tightly that all down the right side of her body was soaked in sweat. She immediately thought of Emer.

Heather, along with the other Kellogg's varieties, were cast as numerous wedding guests and mourners. The mime-artist got Grusha, the female lead.

Merlin was still abandoned in the naughty corner of the Vehicle Testing Centre, so once the auditions were over and she had telephoned the hospital for the fifth time that day, Heather made her way to the bus-stop. Her plan was to head back to Portstewart and Emer and William's flat. But as she thought of lying down on the tulle chenille sofa, still with the plastic cover on, she had a change of heart. She took the 4.35pm bus in the opposite direction, straight into the town centre and the hospital. She had decided she would rather be in the waiting-room of the hospital than in either her own house or her sister's new home.

"I'm looking for my sister, Emer Farrell," Heather asked one of the midwives, whose green waspy belt at her waist and tight collar around her neck reminded Heather of a Christmas cracker.

"Emer, aye, she was still in the induction ward until an hour ago, but she's been taken to the delivery suite."

"Is everything OK?"

"Finally we were able to break her waters and since then, well, things have started to happen pretty quickly."

'Waters', 'break'. Heather felt quite ill. "So who's with her?"

"Her partner, William." The midwife whispered the 'partner' part of her answer.

"Is my dad around?" Heather whispered the 'dad' part of her question.

"He was here most of the day, but had to go to work. I think he said he'd be back around six. You can stay in the waiting-room just over there," the midwife pointed, forcing the belt to slide up, "and we'll keep you up to date."

The hands of the clock on the wall ticked slowly, as Heather and two heavily pregnant mums-to-be sat nervously in the room. One was wearing a short nightdress with Winnie the Pooh stitched to the front, the other a tartan dressing-gown which rose up at the front, revealing a flash of off-grey large knickers when she uncrossed her legs. Both openly were sucking the life out of their cigarettes.

Heather looked again at the clock and the hands hadn't moved at all. Back out in the corridor, she discovered a drinks machine and selected a milky coffee with sugar. She reluctantly took the black tea, no sugar, dispensed to her and returned to the waiting-room. To her great relief the two mums-to-be had left, leaving a haze of smoke and an overflowing crisp packet that had been used as an ashtray. The hands had moved on by five minutes. She read one poster promoting folic acid and another denouncing soft cheese and eggs. She then managed half a magazine article, which graphically detailed a movie-star couple's declaration of undying love. The magazine was over a year old and she lost interest when she remembered the celebrities were now divorced and both had undying love for someone else. She thought back to the New Year's Resolutions Emer had set for her, five months previously: *1. Lay off the crisps. 2. Lay off trying to please everyone. 3. Lay off Doc Martens boots for the rest of eternity. 4. Get laid.* Heather was quite proud of herself for failing so absolutely to achieve any of these. With only a few minutes gone by, she then opted to rehearse her one line from *The Caucasian Chalk Circle*: *"There's hardly a pear on our trees this year"*. But she wasn't convinced she had the emphasis in the right place. She stood up so that she could add resonance. *"There's hardly a tree on our pears this year.* Bollocks." Once more, with feeling, *"There's hardly a pear on our trees this year!"*

"Could be the green-fly," beamed a very proud and somehow even taller William Todd, as he stood in the doorway to the waiting-room.

Heather rushed over and grabbed William by the sleeves of his sweater. "Any news?"

"Go and see for yourself. Third room on the left."

As Heather rushed out through the door, she left William behind her, running random laps around the waiting-room and using the chairs as hurdles.

Heather held her breath as she pushed the door to the delivery room open. There were gas tanks, monitors, drips and beanbags scattered around the room, all evidence of mayhem only minutes earlier. But now all was serene and calm and in the centre was a starched, pure-white sheet, hiding who knows what underneath, but at the top of which was the exhausted, smiling face of her sister, clenching a bundle of blankets that slowly raised and dipped with the beating life within.

# Chapter 27

"James, wee fella, say hello to your Auntie Heather," whispered Emer softly, as she cleared away the blanket from the baby's face.

Auntie Heather burst into tears, "James . . . James . . . he's a boy . . . he's a boy," she managed in between blubbers.

And then, in emotional unison, Emer interrupted with, "Isn't he just perfect . . . my son . . . my wee son . . . all mine!"

William entered the delivery room carrying a huge bouquet of slightly wilted, white lilies in the one hand and a giant silvery balloon with 'It's a Boy' written across it, in the other. He nearly dropped both when Heather raced over and hugged him, before she then rushed back to her sister and wrapped her arms around her and the baby she was nursing.

"Would you like to hold him?" Emer asked, breaking herself free.

"Are you sure?" Heather couldn't stop smirking.

"Just make sure you keep your arm under his head." Emer repositioned her sister's hand for her. "That's it. You're a natural."

"A natural baby-sitter," William added as he struggled to tie the balloon to the end of the bed, his eyes transfixed by the tiny bundle.

As Heather held James, the question of who the baby would look like was answered instantly and succinctly, when the soft cotton blanket fell away from the baby's head and a shock of damp, vibrant, red hair escaped. His tiny body was motionless in his swaddled blanket, but he managed to stretch his neck out as he snuggled himself down for warmth. His skin was pink.

"Isn't he gorgeous?" Emer whispered to Heather, knowing she had discovered the true definition of the word she had in the past idly thrown away.

"He's wonderful," Heather agreed, finally able to contain her tears. "And how was it?"

"No problem. Hardly felt a thing." William laughed, with his thumb now tied in the balloon's string knot, as he had yet to take his eyes away from his son.

"Well, Heather," Emer ignored William's remark, "you know, the way they say that you don't remember a thing about the pain, as soon as the baby is born – bollocks! Excuse my French, wee fella, but I thought he was never going to come out. At one point I would have gladly have had him shoved back in and left there."

"But he came out naturally, Emer, eventually? You didn't get a caesarean, did you?"

"No, it was natural all right. A natural mix of gas and air, pethidine, an epidural and forceps. I can't feel a thing from the waist down, which I reckon's not such a bad thing considering the size of the wee soul."

"What does he weigh?" Heather knew this was one of the first things you were supposed to ask, after sex and name.

"9lb 15oz."

This meant absolutely nothing to Heather "Is that big then?"

"Big? He's only a cream-egg away from being a ten-pounder!"

Heather hoped that James wasn't always going to be an 'only a something away' for the rest of his life. "And where did you get the name 'James'?"

"We had an agreement. If the baby looked like William, then he would get to pick the name." Emer rolled her eyes, before adding, "If it looked like me, then I'd choose."

Heather had been, grudgingly, all too aware of the prior concerns over whom the baby would look like. Yet again, she had been forced to share one of her sisters' secrets and this time it had been Emer's promiscuity. With guilt, she dare not look at William. So, with self-imposed blinkers, she stared down at the baby still sleeping in her arms. And instantly, her anxiety was soothed and calmed.

"Emer, you have another visitor!" The midwife returned carrying a tray with tea and toast made in heaven by angels. "Will I say to come back when we've cleaned you up a bit and you've had a rest?"

Emer was eager to get her father's visit out of the way, especially as he was one of the keenest interrogators as to who the baby would look like. "No, it's fine. I'm OK."

The nurse left the suite and, immediately after, the

rubber-flap door opened onto the visitor, who wasn't Roddy Farrell.

A swirl of *Dynasty* shoulder-pads and lip-gloss preceded a very nervous, "Wee fella, say hello to your Aunt Kitty!"

# Chapter 28

"Kitty, what on earth are you doing here?" Heather spoke for everyone – well, except for William, who'd never met Kitty before.

"What kind of welcome is that?" Kitty tentatively answered in a very peculiar hybrid accent.

Heather had heard Kitty's voice over the telephone and had picked up on how easily she had lost her North Antrim accent. But face-to-face, she now saw for herself how differently Kitty shaped her mouth, as she held onto her 's's for as long as possible and pouted on her 'w's and 'y's.

"Have you lost your manners, Heather Farrell?" Kitty continued from the doorway.

"Have you lost your senses?" Heather, conscious of being the family go-between, could find no alternative role for herself. "Dad will go buck-mad if he sees you. When did you get here? Are you staying long?"

"Father can take a running jump," Kitty answered.

Both Heather and Emer raised their eyebrows at the formality of 'Father'.

Kitty continued, "I'm here to see the baby, if that's OK, Emer, and then I'll be gone again."

Emer was too overcome with the emotion of childbirth to say anything and just nodded approval to Heather, who was still holding the baby. William remained motionless, confused and with his thumb still tied. Kitty now had the confidence to enter the room. Heather placed the newborn baby directly into her eldest sister's outstretched arms. There was an atmosphere of the arrival of the Wicked Fairy, forgotten to be invited to Sleeping Beauty's christening.

James slotted into a perfectly formed bend in Kitty's arm, as if he was the completing piece in a child's jigsaw puzzle. She carried him gently over to the window where the early evening sunlight flickered through dimpled glass. His eyes instantly opened for the first time. Heather was expecting a fire-flame to burst out of Kitty's head at any minute, as the Wicked Fairy pronounced her curse on the poor soul.

"He's smiling at me!" Kitty enthused with wonderment.

"It's wind," Emer rained on the parade.

Heather awkwardly moved over to the doorway. With Kitty still at the window, Emer rigid and unable to move in the bed and Heather now at the door, a perfect triangle was formed between the three sisters. Outside of the triangle was William. A small leak had appeared in his balloon, it seemed, which was causing the helium to sift out and the balloon to fall.

"I don't want to appear rude, but did you say 'Auntie Kitty'?" William directed his question to the strange woman nursing his hour-old son. The woman was shrouded in expensive perfume and weekly visits to the hairstylist's. She was slightly heavy around the hips, but this was largely hidden behind an appropriately coutured, designer trouser suit.

Kitty's existence was still a taboo subject in the Farrell household and Roddy had removed any evidence of her from the house. Emer hadn't felt at liberty to go into any detail about her past life and William hadn't felt emotionally intimate enough to enquire.

Kitty was far too distracted to hear William's question and she continued to hungrily absorb what she knew to be limited time with her nephew.

"Am I talking to myself? Do I exist?" William asked, with his irritation evident as he yanked his thumb free.

Without taking her eyes away from her son, Emer answered, "That's Kitty – our eldest sister." Emer had felt emotionally, as well as physically, numb on the unexpected arrival of her sister but now, as the epidural wore off, she felt upstaged and angry. "She's just out of Armagh Prison – serving five years for fraud. A bit of a family skeleton in the cupboard. We don't like to talk about it."

"Emer!" Heather barked abruptly.

"Don't worry, Heather." Kitty calmly placed the baby back in his mother's arms. "Now's not the time or the place. I won't outstay my . . ." She hesitated and held back the word 'welcome'. "Whatever you think of me, Emer, I do wish you and the baby all the best in the world." At that, she left the room.

As Heather chased after her, behind her she could hear William asking again, "Do I exist?"

"Kitty! Kitty!" Heather grabbed her sister's arm in the corridor and yanked her around. "She didn't mean any of that. Come back, please!"

"It's obvious that I'm just erased from your lives." Kitty had lost her acquired accent. "I really don't exist!"

"Of course you do and now that you're back we can fix things again," Heather pleaded.

"I'm not back, Heather. I never went away. Just because you're not here in person should never, ever, mean you're forgotten. Just let me go!" Kitty pulled her arm away. "I have to get back to Kingston. There's nothing else for me here."

"You've got it all planned then?" Heather stood back. Suddenly, she felt aggrieved for her own situation. This was an unusual sensation for her.

"Like clockwork." Kitty's hybrid accent had returned. "None of you need me. That's obvious."

"I need you," Heather said matter-of-factly.

Kitty had been so consumed by the drama of her own return and of facing Emer, that only now, at this instance, did she acknowledge her youngest sister's role in the chaos that surrounded their young lives. What Kitty hadn't planned for was seeing Heather look as she looked now, glaring back at her. Her young sister's bloom had faded. Where had it gone? Had it been casually and neglectfully lost, or worse, stolen?

Kitty and Heather bought two Diet Cokes from a vending machine and found a grassy patch to sit on by the entrance to the hospital. It had recently been cut, bringing instant memories to both sisters of school playing fields.

"So, who was your man?" Kitty asked with her long legs crossed.

"Emer's boyfriend, William."

"I never would have thought Emer would end up with a ginger-nut. Surely he's not her type?" As she spoke, Kitty poked her tongue in and out of the ring-pull from the can. "He must think I'm a total bitch. But there was just so much going on in there, I didn't even notice him until I was storming out. Couldn't quite turn round at the last minute and say 'Nice to meet you!'." The ring-pull was now slotted onto her wedding finger and as she admired it, she added, "Kind of spoil my exit."

"Now you're talking to the right person when it comes to entrances and exits." Heather burped her response masterfully.

"How is the course going?" Kitty asked casually, hiding her anticipation that this was an opportunity to find out more about her young sister.

"Don't book your frock for the Oscars just yet," Heather replied, straining the last few carbonated burps out. "But I don't get it. How did you know that the baby had arrived?" She had diverted the conversation back to more comfortable territory: someone else.

"One of the nurses in the maternity unit knew me from school. We ring each other every so often. She phoned me on Monday to say our Emer was brought in for an induction. This morning was the first flight I could get." Kitty winced as she cut her little finger where the ring-pull had broken. "Luckily for me, the baby seemed to be in no rush. He must have had some idea what was waiting for him on the other side."

"Aye, it's hard to believe – our Emer and a baby."

"Hard?" Kitty licked away the tiny trace of blood from her cut. "Bloody impossible. But what about you, Heather, the only sane one in the family? What have you been at?"

"What have I been at? What about you more like . . ."

Heather gulped the last of her drink. "The wedding? Is it still on?"

"Of course it's still on." Kitty was swept off guard. "Why shouldn't it be?" She again transformed her accent from North Antrim to North London. "August the ninth, as planned. And as planned, Matt and myself will be flying off to New York to get hitched." One pause for breath, before adding, "A week there shopping and shagging and we'll be back for a big knees-up in The Jolly Man on the seventeenth. You are coming over, aren't you?"

"Wouldn't miss it." Heather flicked a fly away from her empty can and watched it lie stunned on the concrete pathway beside her.

"And then I'm moving into the base with Matt. Just temporarily." Another breath and then Kitty rambled on with, "There's talk that Matt has officer potential, you know. So we're expecting a big move in the next few months."

"Sounds like you've got it all planned, Kitty." The fly didn't regain consciousness.

"Like clockwork."

Silence followed, affording Kitty breathing time and Heather an uninterrupted opportunity to successfully swat the second and third visitors to her empty can.

"How is Dad?" Kitty, harbouring injured feelings which she herself couldn't fathom, had decided if Heather didn't want to talk about herself, then so be it.

"Same."

"How's Merlin?"

"Don't ask."

But Kitty had asked and inadvertently discovered the

one subject area that both sisters felt comfortable with. Heather went on to regale Kitty with her adventures at the Vehicle Testing Centre, adding her own colour and exaggeration to embellish the story. She stretched out her legs in the short grass, letting the stretched mounds in her leggings, where her knees had been, sit proudly. Kitty followed suit by stretching out her legs, layered firstly with duty-free French moisturiser, then mink-coloured pop-socks and finally Gloria Vanderbilt trousers.

"And he's still in the carpark now?" Kitty asked, looking almost tearful.

"As far as I know, or care," Heather replied, looking very much relieved.

"Can I have him back?"

"You what?"

"Can I?" Kitty pleaded. "I've a spare bit of cash right now. The bar-manager job pays well, plus all the extras that come with being in charge. I can afford to do him up a bit. Do him justice." Kitty was back to charging ahead. "He shouldn't be left like that."

"I don't know." Heather dipped her head forward and her reckless frizz of hair fell, hiding her face completely.

"Well, if you don't want to, Heather, I understand. . ."

"Yes, yes, take him, please, God, take him!" Her head shot up again and the frizz took a few seconds to follow suit.

"Well, that's that sorted." Kitty was calm again.

"Aye."

"Aye."

Now that Merlin's future was secure, for the next while anyway, both sisters momentarily relaxed, taking respite from what had hitherto been a volatile half-hour. Now that they had reached relative calm, they enjoyed the shared silence. The wet of the newly cut grass began to be absorbed through to their skin.

"Will you go back in later and talk to our Emer?" Heather bravely, or naively, re-lit the fuse.

"Don't start that again."

"It's all just a misunderstanding that's been allowed to go on and fester."

"Do you know what has festered with me, Heather?" The dampness was forgotten. "She must have known how much Jack Sheehan meant to me and she still went ahead and saw him behind my – behind all of our backs. I wasn't even invited to the funeral. She even had that all to herself." Kitty didn't have to delve too far into her memory banks to pull out her accusations.

"Look, I was there too and believe me, you wouldn't have wanted to be there." Heather crossed her arms across her chest in a matronly fashion and spoke with the authority of an elder sister, or of a mother to her daughter.

"That's where you're wrong, Heather," Kitty stuttered, paused and then barged on with, "and then she was quite happy to let the old man shut me out from your lives. I expected it from him, but not her. It was all too easy for her, with me out of the way. That told me exactly what she thought of me. She was jealous and with me out of the way, there was no competition."

Kitty was too self-absorbed to judge the potential insult to her youngest sister, but luckily Heather was too lacking in self-confidence to ever view herself as 'competition'. All Heather could think was that Jack Sheehan was to blame for all of this. The Sheehans, Jack and Michael, still cursed

Heather's living and sleeping hours. When Kitty had asked her 'What have you been at?', Heather could have told her about the frequent nightmares she still had of the night outside Kelly's Disco and of the fear of ever trusting a compliment or a smile again – or of her mistrust of men and her mistrust of herself. Was she cheap and vulgar and is that what Matt Edwards had thought when seductively he licked the tip of her little finger? Was it all her fault? And above all, could she admit that she secretly wanted it to happen? Heather rubbed her temples and blocked out her black thoughts – Kitty's and Emer's problems were far more pressing right now.

"Please go back inside," Heather begged her sister.

"No, Heather, I'm being picked up and taken back to Belfast tonight. There's a flight back to England first thing in the morning. The last thing Emer and I need right now is a blazing row and if Dad appears on the scene . . . well, none of us needs that." Kitty stood up and dusted the matted tufts of grass from her trouser suit. "I'll arrange to get Merlin towed over to me next week."

Heather stood up and didn't notice the grass cuttings clinging to her clothes.

On Kitty's initiative, the sisters hugged and kissed cheeks – continental style. Well, Kitty did the kissing, while Heather floundered and brushed her lips against her sister's heavily lacquered hair, or her ear. Both were unsure as to whether one, two or three kisses were *de rigueur*, so they settled on two and a half.

"Now, the party's the 17th of August – don't forget." Kitty had herself forgotten all about her initial concern for her sister.

"I won't."

"And take care of yourself. No saying 'McDonald's' or whatever on the stage."

"Macbeth."

"OK, then, Heather, no Macbeths."

"Good luck in New York."

"What do I need luck for? I'm a Farrell."

She threw the ring-pull over to her sister, like a bride's bouquet, and ran off down the knoll, gathering speed as she went. She then peered into a few parked cars, as if looking for someone, before turning the corner around the hospital and disappearing.

Heather sat back down. *'There's hardly a pear on our trees this year,'* she chanted to herself, hugging her knees and giving in completely to hot tears that spiked her eyes. She had never felt so alone. In spite of the family squabbles and battles, everyone was moving on with their lives: Kitty was getting married and living a glamorous life that Heather could only dream of and Emer now had independence and responsibility for a brand-new life. What did Heather Farrell have in all of this? *'There's hardly a pear on our trees this year,'* she chanted to herself again.

She scrubbed her eyes with her sleeves. After five minutes she stood back up and strolled back over to the sliding doors that were the entrance to the hospital. But the doors opened automatically before she got there. Walking in the opposite direction towards her and heading outside was Matt Edwards.

The intense turquoise of his eyes immediately radiated joy, warmth and sensuality. And as he recognised his fiancée's youngest sister, a broad open smile spread from ear

205

to ear. His hair was even blacker than she remembered and his features more striking.

"Are you looking for Kitty?" Heather forced herself to ask.

"No, you," Matt answered.

*Kitty, 1989*

# Chapter 29

The next day, Kitty Farrell was seated in the checking-in area for the flight from Belfast's Aldegrove Airport to Heathrow. She was alone. She had been surprised and slightly put out when Matt Edwards had dropped the bombshell that he wouldn't be travelling back to England with her. Something about old mates he wanted to look up and he was going to stay in and around Coleraine for a few days. 'An impromptu stag weekend' was how he had phrased it. This was rephrased to 'selfish bollocks' by Kitty before she was eventually persuaded by Matt's closing argument: 'These few days are for me. The rest of my life is for you.'

The flight and check-in was already an hour delayed and the fake-tan sample she had discovered in her copy of *Marie Claire* and used on her hands, had now had time to develop into orange streaks. They stopped completely at her wrists.

"*Passengers are reminded not to leave luggage unattended at any time,*" was announced over the tannoy, in a plummy,

South Belfast accent. *"Due to the delay of the in-bound aircraft, flight BA143 to Heathrow will be delayed for approximately one hour."*

Kitty was getting restless. She didn't like flying – too many germs circulating around the air-conditioning. She also hadn't appreciated the frisking by the over-zealous female security guard, or the search through her suitcase, sifting through tampons and yesterday's dirty underwear. It brought home to her exactly what 'normality' in Northern Ireland meant.

She threw the magazine into the waste bin beside her. She felt that she could have written far more interesting problems for the agony aunts and was convinced that what she was wearing was months ahead of the fashion features. Scanning the airport for the 'C' and 'D' list celebrities that she would often find when flying from airports in England, she was disappointed with a Gloria Hunniford look-alike and John Hume. She decided to stretch her legs and take a walk to the viewing gallery. The chevron-shaped room had windows from floor to ceiling on one side and wooden benches on the other. Sticky fingerprints on the glass scaled all the way up as children of all ages, mesmerised, watched the coming and going of the aircraft. At the top of the windows a few grown men added their imprints too. Kitty found an empty spot on a bench alongside the other women, and rested from what stretching she had done in the short walk. At the windows, the general mild excitement at the landing or take-off of the domestic aeroplanes was broken occasionally by mild hysteria whenever a military aircraft made an appearance. Kitty was more preoccupied with her view of the luggage-handlers as they threw the baggage into the cargo hold and especially their heavy-handed technique with boxes clearly marked '*Fragile*' and '*This way up*'. What had started as a mild summery day had, by lunch-time, become blustery and Kitty studied the handlers as the wind filled their shirts and played games with their caps.

Standing up, she brushed out the creases that were forming in her designer jeans and sat back down again. A toddler toddled past carrying a dripping ice-lolly in one hand and a carton of juice in the other. At one point the child was a mere inch from coming into contact with Kitty – close enough to bring her out in a cold sweat.

She wished Matt were here to keep her company. She knew she could rely on him to entertain her and keep her spirits up. Well, usually. The past twenty-four hours had been tough for Kitty and right now all she wanted was to be hugged and softly told 'there, there'.

"How are they hanging, Kitty Farrell?" A navy pinstriped suit with black loafers at the bottom and a crisp white shirt and starched collar at the top, blocked Kitty's view of the runway.

"Very well. Long time no see," Kitty answered without a clue who she was talking to.

"You don't remember me, do you?"

Kitty arched her neck to see the face that was in silhouette against the large glass window. Short, neatly cropped hair framed an otherwise plain, nondescript face.

"Of course I do."

"OK, who am I then?"

"You're that fella I used to know. Sorry, I'm useless with names."

"Do you want a clue?" the silhouette asked cheerfully.

Now this is childish, thought Kitty. And she really didn't care anyway. "Yes."

The man lifted his jacket over his head and then bent down as close to Kitty as he could reasonably get and whispered: "About bloody time! Drive on and nothing will happen to you!"

With her fist clenched and full might, Kitty Farrell whacked Dermot O'Kane about the head and shoulders half a dozen times. He managed to duck out of most, but the odd one slipped through and knocked him squarely on the jaw and temple.

"You bloody great eejit! Fucking . . . fucked up . . . fucker!" Kitty was warming up nicely, causing the watching plane-spotters to miss the landing of a Westland Helicopter behind them.

Dermot obviously felt that his punishment was due and didn't try to stop the abusive cascade. He took his punishment like a man – eventually dead centre on the bridge of his nose. The punch immediately released an avalanche of blood which dissipated Kitty's pent-up anger.

Dermot looked a sorry sight outside Burger King, splattered in dried blood and with rolled-up tissues stuck in each nostril. Kitty brought a tray with two Bean-burger Meals and a wad of napkins over to him. She'd recently given up processed fast-food meat.

"So you don't remember me then?" Dermot joked as he tried to bite into his burger without one of the bungs in his nose falling out. "And what's happened to your accent?"

"Don't push your luck." Kitty scowled at him. "This is the second and last free meal you're ever getting out of me. You're only getting this because you bleed so well."

"You see, I do have my good points." Dermot smiled with bits of tomato stuck to his teeth.

"Go on, I could do with a laugh – tell me what makes that plural."

"I've a habit of bumping into you, Kitty, for one."

"Twice in seven years is hardly a habit. And the last time we met was hardly 'bumping' into one another." Kitty could feel her fist clench again, this time at the sesame bap's expense. "Don't you think you at least owe me some kind of explanation?"

"Kitty, Kitty, you're always in such a hurry. Relax. Enjoy your burger – it's – it's – an old sock?" Dermot only now looked at what he was eating. "What have you been up to?" His cheerfulness returned. "The last I heard on the grapevine was you'd got a First at college and were off to bigger and better things."

"That's right. I'm in management now. I'm in charge of a very successful bar." She paused and then added, "And bistro, in Kingston upon Thames – The Jolly Man." Kitty casually attempted to flick strands of her poker-straight hair from around her face. But the lacquer refused to budge. She was also dying to undo the top button on her designer jeans, not designed for burger and chips. "And I'm getting married in a couple of months and I'm madly in love."

"Congratulations. He's a lucky man." Dermot pushed his half-eaten meal to one side. "He must be some fella to have snaffled you."

"He is. Some fella, that is, not a lucky man . . . Well, he is lucky, of course – but not lucky because he's marrying me, if you know what I mean. But he'd do anything for me."

"Is he with you now?"

"*Due to the late arrival of the in-bound aircraft, the BA143 to Heathrow will be delayed for a further sixty minutes.*" The announcer was greeted with loud groans from around the lobby, but not from Kitty and Dermot. "*If passengers for this flight make their way to the Customer Services Desk, refreshment vouchers are now being distributed. We apologise for the delay.*"

With a bean-burger and a portion of extra-large fries gurgling in her stomach, Kitty was persuaded by Dermot to spend her vouchers in the arrivals lounge bar. He informed her en route that he was at the airport to meet someone on the delayed in-bound flight, so he was as 'stranded' as she was.

Fifteen minutes later, perched on stools at a table near the bar, Dermot had a creamy, Guinness-foam moustache along with his bunged-up nostrils. Kitty had managed a double Bacardi and Coke, plus a packet of peanuts, before he had time to reach the bottom of his half-pint.

"So, are you ever going to tell me what you were up to hijacking my car?" The alcohol had thawed Kitty's spirits slightly.

"Kitty, that was a long time ago and I've moved on a long way since then. As I'm sure you have." He straightened his tie and re-fastened a jacket button.

"I know one thing about you, Dermot O'Kane." Kitty's air of superiority soared.

"What?"

"Something to do with that package I found in the pocket of that dirty mac of yours."

"Oh, that!" Dermot was relieved. "Have you still got it?"

"What, the mac?" Kitty smiled for the first time they had met.

"No," blushed Dermot.

"I've still got both actually and you can have them both back if you answer a few questions." Now she grinned.

"OK." His grey eyes twinkled. "I will, but only if you answer ones back in return."

"OK."

"OK, Kitty, you start then."

"Who are you meeting off that plane today?"

"I can't say."

"Wrong answer." Kitty's scowl returned.

"Ask me another."

"No, you can't pick and choose what you're going to answer. The game doesn't work like that."

"But, Kitty, this isn't a game for me."

Dermot left his seat and went back to the bar. As Kitty's eyes followed his departing back, she could still visualise the spotty, handmade, New Romantic of the boy, inside the smart, shop-bought, old romantic of the man. He returned with another half-pint of Guinness for himself and a double Bacardi and Coke for her.

"How's the family, Kitty?" Dermot asked while using his finger to draw a smiley face in the head of the stout.

"Now you can't change the subject that easily," Kitty sharply replied.

"No, genuinely, how are they doing? I haven't been back to Portstewart for ages and I've lost touch with all that's going on. How's your Emer and the younger one?"

"Heather."

"Aye, Heather." The smiley face only marginally faded as he took a big gulp of stout. "How are they getting on?"

What the hell, Kitty thought as she took an even bigger

slug of her drink and then undid her jeans-button. "Heather's at Coleraine now, studying acting or something or other."

"Get away! Wee Heather at Uni? Jaisus!"

"I know."

"And your Emer?"

"Had a baby yesterday."

"Jaysus!"

"No, James actually, but same initial." Kitty's next two gulps of her drink almost emptied the glass. Her self-tanned hands were now tangerine, but she didn't really care.

"I didn't even know she was married." Dermot suddenly looked fifteen rather than twenty-five.

"She isn't."

"Oh." Now he was five.

"Aye."

"So who's the fella, Kitty? Is he one of our crowd?"

And what crowd would that have been, was Kitty's first thought but something about Dermot's innocent expression held her back. An expression she never saw in Matt. "I dunno who he is." She added matter-of-factly, "It's no big deal, but me and our Emer don't talk. It's a long story. And before you ask what my dad thinks of it all – I don't talk to him any more either." She strayed randomly, "Well, he doesn't talk to me – it's an agreement. There was a man involved and that's all I'm going to say."

"This fella you're marrying?" Dermot's swung full round on his stool until he was face to face with Kitty.

"No. Someone else. He's dead now." Still matter-of-factly.

"Jaysus!"

214

"Don't wear it out. And don't look so shocked. You're the one who hijacks cars and meets mysterious people at airports."

"That's true." He remained staring directly into Kitty's caramel eyes.

"So, Dermot, who are you meeting?"

"I told you. I can't say." He turned away. "Please, Kitty, don't ask me. What about this husband-to-be of yours? What does he do? Don't tell me he's had four wives already or he's a transvestite – no, better still, he's a Brit?" Dermot laughed.

Kitty didn't.

Summarised so succinctly between the announcements for the 1.45pm arrival from Glasgow and the 1.50pm from East Midlands, Kitty suddenly realised the depth of the Farrell family's disfunction. There wasn't even an echo remaining of the three sisters driving along Portstewart Promenade seven years ago. All three, like Merlin, had been so shiny and proud and new. If it hadn't been for the prospect of her wedding, Kitty didn't know what she would do with her future and with herself. How could she tell Dermot that?

"*The inbound flight from Heathrow has arrived. Could all passengers flying on BA143 please make their way for boarding to gate number nine.*" There were cheers following the announcement from all around the bar, except from Kitty and Dermot.

"I'm sorry, Kitty, but I have to head on." Again, Dermot was facing her directly, but this time there weren't any confused furrows in his brow or innocence in his wide grey eyes. There was something more intense, more mature in his expression. "Yet again, you have made a lasting impression on me, Kitty Farrell.' He pulled out the nose-bungs and stuffed them in his pocket. He then fastened the other three buttons on his jacket, hiding the bloody stains. "Next time we meet, I hope it is in better circumstances."

"For you or for me?"

"For both of us."

Sitting so closely, Dermot had only a few inches to lean in order to kiss Kitty on the lips. The kiss was uninvited, soft and steeped in sensuality. But for Kitty, who had closed her eyes, it was far too brief and she opened her eyes to see Dermot's back heading to the door.

If Kitty had been angry before with Dermot, now she was enraged. Who did he think he was? And what on earth was he talking about? She was getting married in August – why should he think that her circumstances were anything other than good? She looked into the bottom of Dermot's empty glass and the smiling face still remained. As she swallowed the last of her Bacardi, her rage drifted to indignity and hurt. With the final gulp of melted ice, she realised what a fool she had been. Dermot O'Kane knew everything about her and what did she know about him? Absolutely nothing more than she knew before. Kitty grabbed her Ankler suitcase and ran out of the bar in the direction of baggage reclaim. She was rushing against the crowd, as reconciled families hugged and children ran over to brief-cased fathers, laden with last-minute-bought toys and sweets.

'Where is the little bastard?' Kitty thought as she scanned frantically, peering over the tops of heads and between gaps in trolleys. Like a 1930's peep-show movie, she eventually saw flickers of Dermot through the sways of a young couple's passionate embrace and bobbing heads of lost passengers. The first image and Dermot's hand was outstretched to greet a hand reaching towards him. Kitty couldn't see much of the person Dermot was meeting, other than the bronzed hand and a gold Rolex watch. The next image, Dermot was lifting a tan brief-case. The third image, Dermot was leaving the airport, still carrying the brief-case and all alone.

# Chapter 30

*Kitty Farrell and Matt Edwards*
*invite . . . . . . . . . . . . . . .*
*To their big bash on the return from their wedding in New York*
*on the 17 August 1989 at 7.30pm*
*in The Jolly Man, Thames Street, Kingston upon Thames*

Kitty scored out 'big bash' and replaced it with 'bit of a do' and then finally opted for 'hooley'. She could wait until Matt was next back on leave to decide, but that wouldn't be for another four days and with only two weeks to go, Kitty was reluctant to waste any more time. It'll have to do, she said to herself as she handed the details over to the printer. She was slightly concerned by the amount of 'it'll have to do's' she had used in the wedding arrangements over the past month. She was pleased, however, with the front image on the invitation: she had found a Confirmation photograph of herself when she was eleven and one of Matt as a pageboy at around the same age. Sticking the two photographs together produced a lovely miniature version of the bride and groom-to-be. Matt's photograph was in full-colour and Kitty's in black and white, but she decided that 'it'll have to do'.

The next stop on her list were the mechanics. 'The Admiral', owner of the garage and so-called because he also owned a small fishing boat, had been working on Merlin for three weeks now and there was still no sign of a completion with the repairs. His son, 'The Captain', had agreed to meet Kitty today to go through her snag list. As she approached the garage, Kitty could hear a lot of colourful language and frantic hammering. The nearer the got, the heavier the smell of diesel, sweat and empty lobster pots which hung in clusters around the garage walls. When the mechanics eventually saw her approach, all went silent and very, very polite.

"Don't be alarmed." The Captain stepped forward. "He looks worse than he is." Kitty initially wasn't sure if the reference was to her car or his father clattered in oil and eating cold baked beans at the back. That was until she saw Merlin in the far corner. He looked like he had been hung, drawn and quartered. Only the chassis remained and loose parts and debris were randomly distributed around the pitiful-looking corpse.

"What have you done to my car?" Kitty wailed.

For the next ten minutes The Captain listed numerous mechanical improvements, gearbox modifications and suspension adjustments. All that Kitty heard was '*blah, blah, blah!*'.

"What have you done to my car?" she tried again.

"Everything is in hand." The mechanic tried a different approach.

"Well, when can I have him back . . . in one piece?"

"Now you're asking."

"Yes, I am." Kitty could feel her chest wobble as she stifled her anger. "When?"

"Depends." The Captain then began to repeat exactly what Kitty had just listened to.

"Put it this way," Kitty interrupted. "I'm not paying you guys a penny until he's finished."

"It'll be ready Thursday!" The Admiral shouted from the back, concluding business and his lunch-break.

For the rest of the week, Kitty spent her spare time, between shifts, either fetching parts from the specialist dealers, picking colours or chasing up the interior upholsterers. She also found herself doing the occasional double-shift, just to cover the escalating out-of-control renovation costs.

It was now Thursday afternoon and Kitty's shift had been quiet. The miserable wet weather had kept the cruisers and the tourists away. Kitty was by herself and, as she emptied the dishwasher, she kept glancing out across the lounge and through the far window, for a glimpse of Merlin with his expensive makeover. She knew the chances of him being delivered on the date agreed were slight and only the cheque in her back pocket kept her hopes up. It was ten past three and there were only two regulars still finishing their pints, sitting at the far ends of the bar. Kitty could see their glasses wobble each time she bent forward to lift the shiny pint-mugs back onto the shelf.

"You've missed one, Kitty," the customer on her left whistled through his slipping dentures.

"Yeah, you have," the one on the right added, smiling widely to reveal he still had his own teeth, just.

"Look, boys – show's over. Now feck away off home. Pub's closed," Kitty bantered, before she gave them one last thrill and removed a stubborn lipstick-mark off a glass by rubbing it vigorously against one of her 38 DD's.

Charlie and Bill sniggered and shuffled out of the side door, leaving their coats behind for their prompt return at the evening opening time.

Kitty peeked through the door as they left, but still no car.

She wiped away the spills on the mahogany bar-top with a beer mat and just as she was about to give up waiting and head back upstairs to her room, the telephone behind the bar rang. She was more than ready, with her own verbal ammunition to tackle The Admiral and his Captain's excuses.

"Hello, The Jolly Man." Kitty's tone was abrupt.

"Hello, Jolly Man. It's the Jolly Horny Man here."

"Matt, those bastards still haven't turned up with Merlin yet." Kitty was relieved to unleash some of her anger on her unsuspecting boyfriend.

"Have faith." Matt, as usual, sounded calm and in good humour. "Use the Force."

By contrast, Kitty was still in foul form. "I need the bloody air-force to sort those pair out! What are you ringing for anyway?"

"Can't I just ring for a chat?"

"No."

"OK." Matt sighed. "Something's come up and I won't get over until next week."

"Jesus, Matt, what about all this wedding stuff we've got to get organised?"

"I know, I'm sorry. Is there anything I can do?"

"Aye, get on a train and get over here!" Kitty couldn't

believe her mood could get any worse. "Why can't you come?"

There was silence.

"Matt?"

"I have to head back over to Ireland for a few days." He took a break before adding, "Those mates I met up with last month – they've something special organised for me."

"You are joking?" Kitty thought of scanning the bar for Candid Camera.

"I'm sorry, Kitty, but they wouldn't take 'no' for an answer."

"But we're getting married next week!" She wanted to cry, for effect alone, but the tears wouldn't come out. How dare he? "How do you fancy a 'no' in front of the registrar?"

"I'll just go over for a couple of days and spend the rest of the leave with you. How's that?"

"Matt, I'm all on my own here. I've no family to help me out."

"I know."

There was a tone to Matt's voice that was unfamiliar to Kitty. She suddenly felt very uncomfortable and unsure. She had every reason to be completely livid and yet she wasn't.

She backed down. "How many days over there?"

"Three at the most." His cheerfulness returned. "I love you, Kitty Farrell."

"I should hope so. By the way – big bash, bit of a do or just hooley?"

"Piss-up. See you soon. Remember – use the Force. Bye!"

"Bye . . ." But before she could end with 'I love you too', through the lounge window she saw the glimmering, pearlescent, sumptuous curves that were Merlin. Kitty had her own way and Merlin was gold at last.

# Chapter 31

"And how's the baby doing?"

"Great."

"I bet he's a wee dote. Does he look like me yet?"

"No."

"Does he have any of the Farrell features?" Yet again, Kitty attempted to prise more than one-word answers out of her younger sister, who was at the other end of the telephone. She had initially telephoned to tell Heather about Merlin's overhaul, but her younger sister appeared remarkably indifferent.

"He's got a wee bit of the nose." Heather sounded hesitant, slightly awkward. "But the rest is pure pink and ginger. I think he's managed to skip a generation."

"Good for him." Kitty couldn't quite fathom why Heather should feel embarrassed at such good news. Maybe there was more to it. She tried a different tack. "I suppose Emer sends her love."

"Kitty!" Heather scoffed.

"Well, no harm in asking. How is the wee tart anyway?"

"Emer's either sleeping or feeding." But since Kitty didn't respond immediately, Heather added reluctantly, "Not much in between."

"Well, surely the bazonkas have come into their own now. There has to be some practical use for Double F's."

Unbeknown to each other, both women simultaneously looked down at their own ample breasts and breathed a sigh of relief that theirs weren't any bigger.

"Not according to Emer. James wants nothing to do with them." Heather sounded more forthcoming, but still her mood was flat.

"Maybe the wee fella's overawed," Kitty said, laughing.

"Maybe."

"Any other craic, Heather?"

"Dad's in good form. His chest doesn't give him so much gyp in the summer."

Now Kitty was getting somewhere, but her father's wellbeing definitely wasn't an area she wanted to go into. "Matt's over there at the moment. You haven't bumped into him, have you?"

"No, why should I?" Heather's flatness was punctuated by an abrupt sharpness.

"Just," Kitty answered, herself now irritable. She felt that every time she tried to get inside the head of her little sister, something happened to block her. Yet again, she found herself defensive and unwittingly self-absorbed. She added tersely, "Portstewart's a pretty small place."

"Sure, I'm busy with rehearsals – I haven't seen anyone," Heather quickly interjected, before rudely concluding with, "Have to fly! You know, lines to learn, spears to carry."

"Have you your flight booked yet for the 17th?" Kitty was adamant that the conversation would not end there.

"Not yet."

"God, Heather! You'd better get a move on, there's less than two weeks to the party."

"OK. Must go. See you soon."

Kitty and Heather's telephone conversations over the years had been forced to become very cloak-and-dagger; either from a public telephone box or when their father was still at work. But even so, today Kitty couldn't help but sense that there were additional factors influencing her sister's current nervousness.

Kitty replaced the telephone handset and returned to the bar, ready for the onset of Saturday-night trade. She had tried recently to drum up a bit of extra business by providing live entertainment and 'happy hour' promotions. Tonight had a French theme, with the bar-staff grudgingly dressed like Parisians, an accordion player called Mary-Kate and house red wine at half price. As manager, Kitty decided that the fancy-dress outfit for the staff was not appropriate for her and she opted for a navy dress-coat, heavily shoulder-padded and ten inches up from her knee. Large gold buttons with an anchor design held the garment together and the top two buttons were left undone. At this morning's usual Saturday hairdressing appointment, she had bravely opted for a fringe and, with a dab of wet-look gel, was inwardly pleased with the spiky result. The bar-staff, shuffling past her in their berets and with strings of onions around their necks, were less complimentary.

The promotion had attracted a very different crowd to their usual Saturday nights and Benjamin and Trafford had usurped Charlie and Bill's chairs. Kitty had aspirations to transform The Jolly Man into a yuppie bar and she was beginning to feel that her ideas were paying off. The Jolly Rich Man was the direction she favoured.

By ten o'clock the bar was six deep and Kitty and the other evening staff were having difficulty in keeping track of who was next in line. Coin-tappers on the bar, finger-waggers and whistling customers were cleverly avoided. Exceptionally rude customers got their change given to them in a pool of beer on the bar, or an extra few quid added to their total bill.

"Hey, I was next!"

"No, you weren't. I've been here for yonks!"

"I didn't have a moustache when I started waiting."

"When I came in, this bar was still a tree, with leaves growing out of it."

With the new clientele, the heckles to attract attention hadn't changed that much.

Kitty's feet were aching. She'd been on her stiletto heels for three hours now without a break and it didn't look like she would get one now until well after closing time.

As she carried two ginger-ales over to Tim and Pete at the door, Kitty took the opportunity to get a breather from the chaos behind the bar. Tim and Pete were the regular weekend bouncers. They were difficult to tell apart: both had necks as wide as their heads and thighs that met. 'Pim and Tete' was how Kitty referred to them, but not to their faces.

"How's it going, lads?" Kitty handed over the drinks, seductively brushing fingers with them as she did.

"Cheers, darling! We've had the usual few assholes," Tim

answered, before Pete joined him in a chorus of, "but nothing we can't handle!"

"I'm sure," Kitty coyly teased.

"Feel that and tell me it does nothing for you." Tim, or was it Pete, flexed his bicep, filling the sleeve of his second-hand dinner jacket.

"Very good." Kitty caressed the arm delicately, half-fearful it would burst. She had become very fond of her bouncers, partly because of the sense of security they brought, but also since she'd discovered that Tim wrote verses for greetings cards.

A shout from behind the bar, saying there was a telephone call for her, gave Kitty a second excuse to prolong her break.

"Hello, The Jolly Man." She was slightly out of breath having had to push her way through clambering customers and fight off an unlicensed rose-seller.

"Hello, Jolly Man, The Jolly Roger here! It sounds like it's jumpin' in there?" Matt's bright spirit instantly flooded the telephone line.

"No, just me and a few friends over for a drink. When are you getting back?"

With the noise from the bar, Kitty couldn't hear Matt's reply. "What did you say?"

"Two more days and I'll be back to give you a good seeing-to!" Matt shouted back, following with a lascivious cackle.

"You wish!" Kitty's feet didn't ache any more. "How's it going over there?"

"Oh, you know, just catching up on lost times. I bumped into your Heather." Matt was still bubbly and relaxed.

Kitty wasn't. "You did?"

"Yes, she said to say 'hello'." Matt had picked up on Kitty's cool response and in turn sounded more edgy.

"When was that?" Again Kitty didn't hear his reply. "When?"

"Yesterday. Look, I can hear you're busy. I'll ring when I get into Kingston. Can you pick me up at the train station in Merlin? I can't wait to see him all spruced up."

Hurried farewells fought against the sound of a rushed member of staff dropping a glass.

Safely behind the bar, Kitty saw the crowd swell to double in their escape from the slightly out-of-tune accordion player. The staff were stretched to the limit, with all pumps on the go and Pimms and Vodka optics running dry. Kitty was far too busy to be able to give any serious thought as to why Heather had not said that she had seen Matt.

When Kitty eventually rang the bell for last orders for the second time, they were completely out of mixers, kegs had been left unchanged and there wasn't a clean glass to be had anywhere. Amidst the jumbled sweaty mass that was her staff, the smell of overflowing drip-trays and full ashtrays, Kitty felt satisfied that she had achieved what she set out to do. Her monthly sales figures were bound to reflect the up-turn in trade. This could only signify to the head-office that Kitty was ready for a more senior position and as she fished out a cigar stub from the bottom of a beer mug, she hoped preferably away from the hands-on grind.

But the night wasn't over yet. She still had the worst job of the evening to do and that was to get the tail-enders to drink up and move on. As she herded up the last few strays, she casually scoffed at their pitiful compliments and even bribes, in their attempts to persuade her to offer after-hours drinking. They quickly gave up and moved on to nightclubs in the town. But a group of four men in the corner of the bar, next to the window, had blankly ignored Kitty's requests on the half-a-dozen times or so she had already asked them to 'drink up'.

"Come on, lads. Have you no homes to go to?" Kitty used her usual approach.

"We would, if we had a pretty girl like you waiting for us," answered the youngest of the men, about Kitty's age, in a very strong Dublin accent. The words were nothing Kitty hadn't heard a hundred times before, but there was something in the tone that was unsettling, intimidating. Kitty immediately looked around for Pim and Tete. They were nowhere to be seen. Only then she realised that, in fact, they were never anywhere to be seen when it came to tricky customers.

"What's a nice Irish girl like you doing in a place like this anyway?"

Again the snide tone of the younger of the men and the way he blatantly looked her up and down made Kitty feel totally vulnerable. She crossed her arms across her chest to give herself an air of authority and to hide her womanly assets.

"Now, please." Kitty remained calm and professional on the outside, while inside she felt like an amateur whose bluff had been called. "Last orders were twenty minutes ago and we've all got an early start in the morning."

The young man leisurely leant backwards, balancing on two legs of the chair. "These three gentleman and myself have been travelling all day. All we want to do is sit here, in the peace and quiet and finish our pints. Now, there's no harm in that, is there?" He spoke slowly and deliberately, like a father teaching a lesson to a child, before adding, "Now run along and don't bother us."

His companions tittered and continued to drink their pints. Kitty could hear the banter of the remaining two bar-staff, as they were changing out of their costumes behind the bar. She knew the wisest thing for her to do would be to calmly go back to them and call the police. But the anger of the insult was far greater than any wisdom. So was the frustration of having been independent for four years now, and this man, no older than she was, trying to intimidate her, here, where she was the one in charge.

"If you don't leave the premises right now, then I will be forced to call the police." Kitty's heart was pounding.

"Do you know who you are talking to?" The young man was no longer leaning and sat bolt upright.

From somewhere deep down, Kitty mustered all the inner strength she could. She was physically drained from her long shift, but mentally she was determined she would not be beaten.

With professionalism letting her down, Kitty called on good old-fashioned insult. "An ignorant shit, who's old enough to know better!"

The eldest of the group, a short man in his late forties and dressed in a shiny, grey suit, with his sleeves rolled up, leant forward on the table. The hierarchy of the group was immediately evident as the rest of the men sat back in their seats and remained quiet. The older man crossed his stumpy legs to reveal tanned, bare ankles and white canvas shoes.

Kitty's desperate hope for mature and sane intervention came in the form of, what she could only describe as, an extra from *Miami Vice*. But it was still very welcome.

"Now, let's all just take a breather a wee minute." The deep-cut wrinkles around the eyes on the man's sunburnt face made him look like he was on the verge of exploding into laughter. But he didn't and spoke with control and gravitas. This was unsettling.

"Please excuse the lad, but he's overtired." As he still leant forward, the older man pushed up the left sleeve of his jacket to stop it falling back down. Kitty's attention was drawn to the gold Rolex watch he was wearing. "We've had a busy day." And then the joviality that had been threatening detonated into a wide smile. "Just like you."

Kitty found the man's facial expression infectious, like a yawn, and she too found herself letting the tension in her shoulders dissolve and her arms fall back down to her sides.

"And as long as we just have a few moments to finish off our drinks . . ." the man continued without breaking the bright smile. ". . . then, nobody is going to get hurt."

# Chapter 32

The cleaning lady had sent word that she was sick, so at eight o'clock on the Sunday morning Kitty was scrubbing the urinals in the gents'. She was dressed only in rubber gloves, a mask and a leopard-print dressing-gown. To a germ-freak like Kitty, this was living hell. Armed with a bottle of bleach in one hand and a can of air-freshener in the other, she felt repelled, as well as exhausted. It had gone midnight, the previous night, before the four undesirable customers had eventually finished their drinks and left. As Kitty remembered how intimidated she had been, the sick feeling she now felt at the pit of her stomach was only exasperated by the acrid stench from the toilets. When she reluctantly moved on to the ladies' toilet, Kitty felt even more repugnance at the hygiene habits of her own sex. This was not what she expected from her 'wine-bar' clientele. The combed-out hair, blocking the plughole in the sink, began to make Kitty balk.

If only Matt would call and put everything right. But as

she tried to brighten her mood with thoughts of her boyfriend, Kitty's memory kept wrenching her back to last night – back to the disappointment she felt as she recalled the moment when she had been forced to back down and walk away. She caught a glimpse of herself in the toilet mirror, her spiky fringe now frizzy about her face and the once poker-straight tresses kinked and flattened on one side where she had been sleeping. Under her eyes was dark and her usual olive, glowing skin looked dull and grey.

In six days' time she would be on an aeroplane to New York, and in seven she would be Mrs Matt Edwards. Now she felt a little better. But then she remembered how at the mention of 'nobody is going to get hurt' she had stared down at her tired feet and scurried like a mouse back behind the bar. Her fleeting brightness faded again.

After half an hour of squirting cleaning fluids and the occasional poke with a brush, Kitty decided that the first shift would be starting soon and they could share the rest of the sanitising between them. This was the first, and the last, public-lavatory cleaning that Kitty was ever going to do. Still in her dressing-gown, splattered with soapy water, she sat with a mug of black coffee and scattered till receipts on the bar before her. The bottom line brought some relief to her mood. She then pulled her notebook out from under the bar and quickly scanned her wedding 'to-do' list. There were big red ticks next to most tasks, including the finger-buffet, the cake for the return party and the wedding list in Selfridges. The only major outstanding action was a collection she had to do this Thursday. A coffee-mug circle muddied her neatly written '*Wedding dress – to be picked up on the 7th*'. A new, young designer in Soho had been recommended to her by one of The Jolly Man's customers. Kitty was the guts of the price of a small car out of pocket and after four consultations and three re-fits, she was apprehensive. The coffee she was drinking now left a fresh stain against a huge red tick beside 'Wedding rings'.

Just as she was about to head back upstairs and get dressed before her staff arrived, the telephone behind the bar rang. She hoped it was Matt.

"Hello, The Jolly Man," Kitty answered enthusiastically.

"Picnic, Hampton Court at about three."

"Who is this?" She wasn't sure, but she could guess.

"Red or white? I'm a bit of a red man myself. You will be finished work by then, won't you? Can you come?"

"White. Yes, I will be finished. But no bloody way, Dermot O'Kane."

"Och, Kitty. Why not?"

"How did you get this number?"

"Extensive and detailed detective work. And then I asked directory enquiries for the number of The Jolly Man in Kingston." Dermot laughed with ease and familiarity.

"Where are you phoning from?" Kitty was far less amicable.

"Just down the road in Richmond. I had a bit of business here and was feeling lonely."

"Well, be lonely somewhere else. I'm not meeting you," she said sourly.

"Why not?"

"Just."

"Go on," Dermot pleaded.

"I'm getting married next week."

"I only want to share my flask."

"I've stuff to get organised."

"What stuff?" Dermot was relentless.

"Stuff. And, we had a bit of bother here last night. I'm not up to socialising today." Adding "OK?" with as plummy an accent as she could muster. "And I don't want to talk about it."

Dermot was silent. Kitty filled the void with a full detailed account of her confrontation with the men from Dublin; down to what they were wearing and which deodorant they didn't use. She was relieved, at last, to have someone she could share the nightmare with, even if it was only Dermot.

"Well, what do you make of that?" Kitty finished with an air of superiority.

"What about rosé?" was Dermot's reply.

"No."

"I'll be there, Kitty, just outside the maze at three o'clock on the dot. If you can make it, great – if not, well, you're missing a chance to get me back for the dinners I owe you."

Two-thirty came and Kitty had absolutely no intention of meeting Dermot for the picnic. Matt was bound to call that afternoon and she didn't want to miss him. She also had no ambition to re-kindle acquaintances from her past, especially those as unsavoury as Dermot O'Kane. Her future was going to be successful, romantic and glamorous. Her past was everything but.

"Kitty, the ladies' sinks are blocked again," one of the bar-staff shouted.

Kitty didn't reply and had her fake Versace jacket on and was heading out the door.

\* \* \*

She was mildly impressed – a huge wedge of crumbly white Wensleydale, a large rustic loaf already torn into lumps, strawberries, cherries and a bottle of ice-cold rosé. The paper Tweety-pie plates distracted a little, but the sight of Dermot in yet another sharp tailored suit made her smile. Almost.

"Were you at Mass?" Kitty asked, looking down at her companion.

"No, why?"

"Just asking."

Dermot flattened the rug down beside him and handed her a plastic cup as she knelt down.

"What made you change your mind?" he asked, pleased with himself.

"I was hungry." Kitty sipped out of the cup with her little finger bent and sticking straight out. Then she remembered what company she was keeping and stuck it back in again.

"Did you wash them?" Kitty pointed to the fruit.

"With my own fair hands, in my own fair toilet." When Kitty didn't see the funny side, Dermot quickly added, "Of course I did. What do you take me for?"

The afternoon was overcast, but warm. Kitty hadn't bothered to change out of her work clothes – a sombre chocolate-brown trouser suit, which she felt reflected her current mood after last night's unsettling drama. The only evidence of her usual style was a broad gold belt, which had been drawn tightly into an extra hole added with a screwdriver. Kneeling down she could hardly breathe.

Both hungrily gorged on the feast and within twenty minutes all that remained were a few crumbs, pips and a cork.

"I'm going to keep this." Dermot lifted the cork and slotted it into his top pocket.

"What for?"

"As a reminder of the day I had Kitty Farrell, on a rug, in Hampton Court Palace."

"That's a very liberal use of the word 'had'."

"OK, what do you want to keep as a memento then?" he asked as he licked his fingers and pressed them down on the last few crumbs of cheese.

"What on God's earth would I want one for?"

"To tell everyone, that after all these years of begging, you finally had Dermot O'Kane, on a rug, in a palace."

Dermot lay flat and stretched out his arms and legs. Kitty remained bolt upright.

"So?" Dermot said.

"So?" Kitty said back.

"So . . . is the wedding on or off?"

Kitty stood up and brushed the creases away, meticulously removing stray crumbs from the neat tucks in her trousers.

"Where are you off to?" Dermot lifted his head up from the rug.

"I'm going. What kind of bloody question is that?"

"Sorry." He leapt up beside her.

"So you should be."

"Well, is it on?"

"Of course it is. Why shouldn't it be? I'm less than a week away from a dream wedding in New York and you have the brass neck to ask if it's on or not. I've met you three times in seven years, always in highly suspicious circumstances, and you assume you can pry into my personal life. Well, you can't." Kitty briskly turned away and headed back towards the park exit. But then, just as abruptly, she turned back around and marched over to him, until her face was only inches away from his.

"No, I'm not going to let you get away with it this time. What are you up to, Dermot? What's going on in your little life? Why are you here?" Even with her stilettos sinking into the grass, Kitty was still able to look down with supremacy.

Dermot had remained dazed and motionless during Kitty's tantrum. He could sense tourists walking by and feeling sorry for him. His cropped, dull-blond hair was not as short as the last time Kitty had seen him in the airport. He also had a day's growth of whiskers, casting grey shadows on his already pale complexion.

"I'm here because I wanted to be with you, that's all," he answered, staring at her straight on. "Nothing mysterious or underhand." He spoke with a seriousness that Kitty had never seen before. "Whether I'm with you, or thinking about you, I feel like that spotty teenager again. Not a care in the world. In a place far away from the life I'm leading now." He reached out and Kitty thought that he was going to hold her hand. He held the bottom of her sleeve instead. "Please don't go, not yet. All my life, I've . . ." Dermot paused, distracted by the softness of Kitty's dark eyes and the bemused expression they now betrayed. "All my life, I've wanted to visit the maze at Hampton Court," he smiled with the familiar boyish grin that both felt more at ease with, "and I'm frightened I'll get lost by myself."

Kitty didn't know what to make of Dermot, or what she felt. Was it pity? Or empathy? Or just intrigue? As he still smirked at his own awkwardness, Kitty followed him into the hedge-maze. A few minutes later, they were both laughing – in an emotional territory they both felt comfortable with. Dermot now revealed another, previously hidden, side to his character. He was a dab hand at animal impressions. As a result, he had a team of gardeners frantically running in and out of the dense maze, trying to capture what they thought was a rogue dog.

"It went this way!" one of them shouted over the hedge.

"No, we've been here before," another answered, followed by the sound of scampering feet.

This time Dermot was about to miaow, but Kitty stopped him by knocking him with her elbow into the dense bushes. He bounced back as if on a trampoline.

"Stop it. You'll get us kicked out!" Kitty laughed, enjoying the childish fun.

He grabbed her by the shoulders and twisted her upper body as she tried to walk.

"Come on, walk straight!" he jokingly ordered her.

She tried, but her flaying arms and legs wouldn't let her. She managed to release herself with an expertly delivered Donkey-Rub to his head.

"After all these years, Dermot, you're still a big eejit," she teased as she ran ahead.

"Do you know what I remember most about you when we were wee?" he asked, unsuccessfully trying to recapture her.

Kitty looked down at her chest.

"Aye, apart from those."

"My charm?"

"No, something you and your sisters all had in common."

Kitty looked down at her chest again.

"Aye, but apart from those." He continued undeterred, "All three of you were so different from the rest of us. And

I don't mean the way you looked. But you were all so independent, as if all you needed was each other or something like that. I was dead jealous." He immediately sensed a dip in her mood. She blankly stared at him, but through him at something that wasn't there. He knew he had overstepped the mark and instantly regretted it. So he did the first thing that came into his head – he stuck out his left foot and tripped her up. Each time she attempted to regain her feet, he would do it again.

Kitty and Dermot never found the centre of the maze. Two hours later, they were right back where they had started. They had spent their time chatting about the people they knew back home and their favourite haunts as children. Nothing more.

By the time she reached Merlin in the carpark and said her goodbyes, Kitty was ten minutes late for opening up the bar.

The early evening was as warm as it had been in the day. Leaves and dead insects had become baked on Merlin's bonnet. Just as Kitty was about to start the engine, she shoved a crumbled piece of paper into her jacket pocket. Dermot had given it to her when they parted. This was the second time he had given her his telephone number – this time with the promise to 'call if she ever needed a friend'. But unlike the last time, she knew Matt Edward's number by heart, and Jack Sheehan's had long since been forgotten. How times have changed, she now thought, as she held tightly onto the steering wheel of her old car, the one constant in her life.

Charlie and Bill were waiting impatiently outside the front door, as expected, when Kitty ran up the front steps to The Jolly Man, clutching a giant bunch of keys. She plucked out the right key first time and stood holding the door open, while her most committed customers raced over to their seats. As she was about to walk in herself, a very polite "Excuse me," was heard behind her. She turned and was confronted with a massive bouquet of freshly cut red roses, tied up with a lavish, silk ribbon. Immediately her heart jumped at the thought of her fiancé, but it quickly fell with a thud when she saw the hand that was clasping the flowers had a gold Rolex watch on the tanned wrist.

"What do you want? I'm not alone. I've customers inside," Kitty blustered through her absolute terror.

"Please, please. Don't be afraid. Please, accept these as an apology for how my colleagues and myself behaved last night. It was disgraceful and you acted impeccably." The man was shaking and Kitty sensed by the flow of what he was saying that he was reciting well-rehearsed lines.

"You're a marvellous manager. Wonderful. And if there is anything myself or any of my colleagues can do, to make it up to you, you have only to say. Any favour at all."

"That won't be necessary," Kitty found herself replying, somehow stifling the lecture she could have delivered on manners and appropriate behaviour.

"So, you forgive us?" the man asked.

"Aye, I suppose so."

"Thank you. Seriously, thanks."

The Rolex and the man turned and walked down the steps and disappeared around the back of the bar. Kitty tentatively followed to check that he had gone. The only evidence she had that he had actually been there at all was the sound of a departing car and the gigantic bouquet draped in her arms.

241

"Looks like someone loves you, Kitty," Charlie called over as Kitty, still stunned, finally made her way into the bar.

"*They* weren't picked up in a garage forecourt! At least a fiver's worth there," said Bill, revealing how long it was since he last 'said it' with flowers.

Kitty plonked the roses on the bar and searched through the wrapping for a card. There was no message. How odd! He seemed frightened of me, she thought to herself. But she hadn't told a soul. She hadn't spoken to anyone about last night. Then she remembered her telephone call earlier that morning. The call that she had been so disappointed wasn't Matt. She had told one person.

# Chapter 33

Kitty half-expected a horse's head beside her when she woke the next morning. Thankfully, it was only the pillow she always had tucked in beside her, whenever Matt Edwards was away. Her mind raced. Was that it? An eye for an eye – she was now in the 'family'? 'A favour', that is what the man had said. If he did her a favour, what would she have to do in return? What was Dermot involved in? Was this paramilitary stuff? Was Dermot O'Kane 'connected'?

The only thing she was sure about was that she had to somehow get hold of Matt. She was due to meet him at the train station the next morning, but she couldn't wait until then to speak to him. Last night she had tried the barracks for a contact number, but they had been unable to help. She had tried speaking to a few of his mates there, but most didn't even know he was back over in Northern Ireland. They were also more than a little concerned to discover that he was. How could she possibly get to speak to him?

Kitty did the unthinkable: she raced down the stairs into

the bar, without a lick of mascara or a press of the straightening iron. The clock above the optics chimed eight o'clock just as she lifted the telephone. She dialled and waited and then waited some more. Eventually the receiver was lifted at the other end.

"Hello," a deep voice responded – the half-awake croak in the voice audible.

In her haste to telephone her youngest sister, Kitty had totally forgotten the other inhabitant of O'Hara Drive – the one she hadn't spoken to in seven years.

"Hello . . . Dad . . . it's Kitty. Is our Heather there?"

"No, she didn't come home last night," Roddy Farrell answered, more in shock than his daughter.

"Will she be back later?" Kitty continued with feigned composure and indifference. She really wanted to ask why he wasn't already at work? Was he sick? But she couldn't.

"I don't know. She hasn't been back the last few nights."

Kitty recognised the new tone in her father's voice. She was familiar with the finger of blame and saw it pointing directly at her, along with the inference 'and who did she learn that one from?'.

"Will you tell her I called?" Kitty coolly asked. There was no answer. "Will you?"

"If I see her. You might want to try one of her friends." Roddy forced the words out. "Maybe they'll have a number for that new boyfriend of hers – the English fella – Matt something or other . . . Hang on a minute, they've both just come in."

Roddy Farrell's hand attempted to muffle the telephone mouthpiece, but Kitty could still hear raised voices and quick-fire, heated discussion in the background. She wanted to vomit. She felt numb. Inside, her stomach wrenched and twisted. How could this happen to her – twice? The two men that she loved and the two sisters that she loved. Should she hang up? Should she throw the telephone against the wall? Kitty could do nothing, as she stood, frozen, with the telephone crushed painfully tight against her ear. The muffled panic on the other end of the line ceased.

"Kitty? Kitty? It's me, Matt."

"I haven't spoken to my father in seven years." Kitty closed her eyes as she spoke and each word reverberated around her. "I'm sure it gives him great pleasure to tell me that you're Heather's new boyfriend!"

"Kitty, you've got it all wrong. He's got it all wrong," Matt attempted to interject.

Kitty wasn't listening. "Just tell me this. Was saying you were visiting your friends over there a lie?"

"Yes, but –" Matt tried again.

"Were you with Heather last night?"

"No, Kitty. Well, yes, I was with her, but –" Matt wasn't allowed to finish.

"I knew it," she calmly interjected. "I knew it would happen with you. Did you have to pick my own sister?" Kitty ploughed on, driven by her anger, disappointment, hate, panic, fear . . . all the combined forces of betrayal.

"Hang on a minute!" Matt stopped Kitty's tirade with his sharp tone. "What do you mean by you 'knew it'?"

"I knew you would do this to me some day. You're just like all the rest – you're not that special at all."

"You've just put two and two together and got ninety-three. And if you'd calm down, I'd explain to you how wrong you are." He took a breather, before adding, "But to say I'm like all the rest! If that's the case, you're just like the rest – you won't listen and you throw unfounded accusations at me. Maybe you're not that special, Kitty. And before you go off on one –"

"Go off on one?" Kitty interrupted again, latching on to what she wanted to and disregarding the rest. "How can we get married if we can't trust each other?"

"Yes, how can we, Kitty?" Matt agreed, delivered with what Kitty perceived to be indifferent resignation.

Kitty hung up the telephone and then took it off the hook again and let it hang down, so that Matt couldn't call her back – or rather, so that she couldn't hear if he wasn't trying to. She reached behind her and poured two shots of Bacardi into a glass. The dishwasher hadn't been able to remove a stubborn lipstick stain, but even though Kitty saw the mark, she still swallowed the neat liquor from the glass, in one gulp. She poured a second, equally large measure, but this time could only manage half, before gagging as the tears now flowed freely. She slumped to the floor, which had been mopped from the night before and was still tacky. Her long, frizzy hair formed a shroud around her shoulders and face. How could this happen to her, again? What could Heather possibly offer that she couldn't? Since when had a dowdy, overweight copy been anything to match a stylish and sophisticated original? Where Kitty sat, she stared at the worn path on the duckboard where the bar staff had paced night after night. The wear and tear was heaviest beside the ale pumps. Kitty felt completely terrified and entirely alone. She pulled herself back up, until she was standing back beside the telephone. Without thought, almost automatically, she lifted off the crumpled piece of paper stuck down beside the till and dialled the number. When the receiver was answered at the other end of the line, Kitty, still in a catatonic haze, calmly asked for "Dermot . . . Dermot O'Kane, please."

Within thirty minutes, Dermot was applying a cool, damp flannel against Kitty's brow as she sat wrapped in her duvet, rocking in a chair by the open bedroom window. In between sobs, Dermot had got the gist of the situation. Lacking experience in dealing with women in this state, he called upon memories of his mother nursing him when he was sick as a boy. 'Keep warm', 'fresh air' and a 'wet flannel' were the usual 'fixes' applied by his mother, individually, depending on the illness. But Dermot threw the lot in for good measure. He also rocked the chair for Kitty, as he knelt in front of her, on the floor. All Kitty had to do was pour her heart out, which she did, sporadically.

"How could he do this to me? How could *they*?"

"I know."

"I'm supposed to be collecting my wedding dress in three days' time."

"I know." (He didn't.) But even with his limited experience, he knew to say nothing and agree with everything.

Kitty's eyes were red raw as she constantly soaked up the tears, saliva and mucus with the steady supply of toilet paper given to her in clumps by her companion.

"I feel like such a fool."

"I know – I mean, Kitty, that's not true," Dermot corrected himself.

Kitty squeezed a peek through a gap in the duvet and saw that even now, at only a quarter to nine in the morning, Dermot was still dressed in a navy pin-striped suit, a white cotton shirt and plain royal-blue tie. Unlike yesterday, he was cleanshaven – as the tiny nicks on his neck and dots of blood on his collar revealed. But yesterday she hadn't noticed the fine blond hairs that curled down the sides of his neck. Dermot could see her stealing a glance at him and perceived this to be a break-through.

"You're a strong, beautiful, intelligent woman, Kitty Farrell. You'll know what to do."

"How intelligent do you think I am?" she sniffled.

"A first-class degree is pretty smart in anyone's books."

"A third. I got a third." She hid back down in the duvet.

"But I thought . . ." Dermot stopped rocking the chair.

"I was the only one in my year to come away with a lousy, useless third. Even my best mates from Malaysia, who spent their entire final year serving tables in the Foo Kee, scraped two-twos."

"Well . . . what's a qualification but just bits of paper? I don't have an exam-pass to my name and look at me –" Dermot stopped himself abruptly, realising his argument had just backfired. "Sure, the brewery think the world of you," he added trying quickly to cover his tracks.

"They think the world of the bottom line! For the past three years, all my profits have soared compared to the others. But where did it get me?" A whining tone was starting to infiltrate Kitty's posh accent. "I'm still here, pulling pints. Why should they send me up to head-office when I can do what I do here?"

"You're just upset and because you're upset, your judgement's a wee bit cloudy."

"Cloudy? There's a bloody hurricane going on here and I'm that bitch Dorothy, clicking my heels and swirling around in the middle of it." She wiped her nose this time on the corner of the duvet.

"Even Dorothy wasn't alone, Kitty. She had her dog Toto –" Again Dermot had to stop himself, as he really wasn't doing himself any favours.

Kitty had now let the duvet fall away from her face altogether. Not quite a butterfly yet, but still beginning to leave her cocoon behind. Her usually well-groomed hair had been entirely engulfed by the heat of the duvet and now looked half its usual length, as it had sprung into deep ebony curls. Her chocolate eyes looked heavy and her eyelids had puffed up like a newborn baby's. With her fists clenched tight, as she pulled the edges of the duvet around her, the sense of rebirth was complete.

Dermot anticipated that the time was right to bring some order to the chaos.

"OK, let's sort some stuff out. When are you supposed to be picking this boy Matt up from the train station?" Dermot stumbled slightly when it came to saying 'Matt'. He was inwardly surprised that he managed to say the name at all.

"Tomorrow afternoon."

"That gives you a day to get your thoughts together, before you meet him."

"I'm not going to meet him." Kitty didn't notice that she had stuck out her bottom lip.

"You've got to talk to him face to face."

"No, I don't." Her petulance grew by the second.

"You're supposed to be flying off to marry the man on Saturday." Dermot now got up from his knees and balanced in front of Kitty on his haunches. "You should at least talk to him before you call it off."

"I've been humiliated enough, thank you very much," she said, sulking.

"Don't have a go at me!"

"Sorry. I'm sorry, Dermot." Kitty leant forward. She suddenly left the sulking version of herself behind in the chair. "But it's over, honestly."

Dermot also leaned ever so slightly forward. "Look, the fat lady's not singing yet." He could kick himself for some of the lines that inappropriately just poured out of him.

"Aye, she has. She's also taken two encores." A faint smile lit Kitty's face.

"Has she packed her bag?" Dermot breathed a sigh of relief that all was not lost.

Kitty's smile widened and a wrinkle cut across her nose. "She's in the back of the limo, smoking a Woodbine and heading for the airport."

They sat, with him rocking the chair again and her sniffling, for a further half-hour. The sniffles became less and the rocking, due to Dermot's tired arms and numb legs, far less vigorous.

"How much longer does Mrs O'Kane recommend the duvet?" Kitty eventually asked. "I'm sweating buckets in here."

Not that it was necessary, but Dermot helped Kitty remove the quilt. Its work was now done. A gold silk nightdress, with shoestring straps and a rose imprint, was all that remained on her body. Dermot looked away awkwardly, then stood and moved over beside the window. His legs were all pins and needles, but he didn't say. He tried not to look back as he could hear Kitty now rocking the chair herself.

"Do you know, Dermot, on the first day I met Matt Edwards, I made a promise to myself that I would marry him. Mind you, I didn't think it would take seven years."

Dermot turned to respond, but then swirled quickly away again and focused his answer on the Thames. "Aye?"

"But now, when I think back, the signs were all wrong. I really feel that I was just waiting for this to happen."

"What was wrong?" Dermot asked as he stared at a life-belt hanging on the far side of the river.

Kitty thought first of Matt's army career, but she didn't want to say this to Dermot. She opted for her second thought. "He was too good to be true."

"Oh." Dermot's shoulders fell slightly. "That one." He added. "Women say that to me all the time."

"If you go around hijacking them, what do you expect?"

Dermot turned fully around and walked back over to Kitty. He grabbed hold of the arms of the chair, forcing the rocking to stop.

"Kitty, that was my past. And best kept there. I'm sorry for what I did to you. It means so much to me that you believe that."

"I do. I do." Kitty was taken aback with the sudden transformation in Dermot's manner. His mild joviality that sometimes dipped into buffoonery was gone, replaced with something intense and raw. This was the side of Dermot that Kitty knew nothing about, the side she assumed belonged to his mysterious world of deceit and mystery.

And this was the dimension of Dermot that Kitty now found surprisingly irresistible and seductive. The same way she felt about Matt all those years ago. With the authority of a praying mantis as she decapitates her lover after mating,

Kitty slowly parted her legs and softly squeezed her thighs around Dermot. Her short nightdress pulled tight across her legs and creased up, allowing a mere inch to cover the nakedness of her lower body. She could feel his body immediately stiffen, as he continued to stare directly into her eyes. He dared not look elsewhere. Kitty knew exactly what she was doing. As she pulled her thighs gently closer together, she reached forward to undo his trouser belt. He closed his eyes and, letting his right arm free of the rocking chair, grabbed Kitty's hand to stop her.

"Dermot, look at me," she ordered.

"No, no. I can't." Dermot kept his eyes closed.

"But, why not?"

"Kitty, you don't know how much I want this!" Dermot was mistaken. "But, it's not right. The time's not right."

"Look at me!" Kitty ordered again with more force.

"Trust me. You'll only regret it."

"Regret what?"

"Whatever you're going to do."

"Why won't you look at me, Dermot? That's all." Her voice was firm.

Dermot opened his eyes again, with the same intense focus as before, directed at her eyes only and nowhere else.

"No, Dermot, look at all of me."

For the first time since Kitty had removed the duvet, Dermot allowed himself to take in the female form before him. He began with her lips, then her chin and then her neck – taking in each contour and curve as if devouring an ice-cool drink. She suddenly didn't feel quite so confident. He stared at her voluptuous breasts and her erect nipples, as they added dimension to the patterned roses on the silk nightdress. With the same ravenous thirst, his eyes moved down to the small indentation that was her belly button and the soft mound of her stomach pressed against the folds of the delicate fabric. Finally he stared at her naked thighs, brushed close against his own.

Kitty's confidence had been totally destroyed. She no longer felt like the predator. Dermot felt the loosening of her grip against his legs and once again diverted his focus to her eyes only.

"OK, Kitty. I've looked at you. And of course you are beautiful. Are you happy? You've had your fun and it's time I went."

But Dermot didn't move. Kitty now was unsure as to who was the victim.

"OK. If you want to go, go," she responded, without conviction.

Neither of them moved an inch. Both had their own reasons for staying. Kitty's heartache over Matt had been temporarily frozen and she was reluctant to begin the thawing process just yet. Dermot had ten years of desire and longing to hold him here. She had the sense of danger and the forbidden, he the sense of security and of being allowed.

Who was the prey and who the predator was indistinguishable.

Dermot bent forward, as if he was going to kiss Kitty, but stopped just close enough for their breath to meet. He then put his arms around her waist and lifted her out of the rocking-chair. The tiny distance between their lips remained. He turned her around and walked her backwards towards the unmade bed beside the wall, then gently let her fall into the mess of pillows and ruffled sheets. Against the ivory of her bedding, Kitty's dark features and the rich tones of her silk nightdress were illuminated. Dermot used his flexed arms to hold his own body above hers, but their lips were still close, without actually touching. His thighs interlocked with her bare ones and he looked down on her with a sense of control and power. Kitty then took the opportunity to reclaim her sense of authority and let herself slide down the bed, until her groin was first against and then rubbing gently along his leg. As she did so, her silk nightdress, statically charged, stayed clung to the cotton bedding and, as a result, she was naked from the waist down.

Dermot forcibly dragged her back up again by the wrists and this time she could feel his breathing was slow and deep. Hers was shallow.

She began to undress him, but he remained motionless, aside from a few helpful movements when his clothes were awkward to slide off and they both gave a wry smile. When he was completely naked, he lifted himself away from her and slowly down the bed. He then, for the first time, began to kiss Kitty – initially just above her pubic hair, and then up and down her stomach, tickling her ribcage with his tongue. He remained calm, delicate and soft. Kitty let her head fall back on the bed and closed her eyes. And then, with continued sensuality, Dermot used his tongue to lift her nightdress up and over her breasts. Kitty felt like she would explode and Dermot implode, as she cupped and squeezed each of her voluptuous breasts and he, in turn, began to lick and tenderly bite each one. Kitty was fully aroused by the idea, not only of what this man was doing to her, but the fact that it was she who was allowing it to happen. With his own hands, Dermot then covered and squeezed Kitty's hands over her own breasts.

He continued to kiss her, moving now to her throat, neck and finally, her lips. Having already been so intimate and yet only now reaching a level that is usually the initiation of foreplay, it heightened their emotions more than anything that had preceded it did. Now the serene intensity was totally transcended by frantic and passionate writhing and caressing. Dermot entered her with the same passion.

And all the time they were having sex, the lovers kissed, almost fearful that they would lose this intimacy. They continued to share their bodies, their very souls.

Satisfied smugness radiated from Kitty's face.

"Have you come?" Dermot panted.

"Yes."

"Thank God – I've got cramp in my right leg."

By six o'clock that evening Kitty had managed to get Matt Edwards' ticket changed to the name of Dermot O'Kane and, after a stand-by cancellation, both Kitty and Dermot were on the late-night shuttle to New York.

Three days later, standing outside a registry office in Brooklyn, Kitty and Dermot were now Mr and Mrs O'Kane.

*New York*
*1 September 1989*

*Emer and Heather,*

*Merlin is parked in Bay E 4 of the long-stay carpark at Heathrow Airport. The parking ticket is in the glove compartment and the key's on the wheel arch. He's been there for four weeks now. For no other reason than I don't want to see him neglected, whichever of you wants to pay the parking bill can have him. I won't be coming home.*

    *Kitty O'Kane*

Emer gave Heather enough money for the airfare and to cover the parking ticket. While Heather was over in England, she visited The Jolly Man in search of clues as to the exact whereabouts of her eldest sister. But her disappearance was a mystery to them also; especially Charlie and Bill, who, it appeared, had been in mourning and hadn't been able to drink Guinness since Kitty left. After a few futile days of investigation, Heather, none the wiser, returned with Merlin to Portstewart (via a few emergency calls to the AA en route). When she happily passed over the keys of the old car to her very enthusiastic sister, Heather realised that she hadn't even noticed Merlin had been renovated, or that he was now gold.

## Emer, 1992

## Chapter 34

"Put the kettle on!" Emer called out, but there was no answer from the kitchen. James sat tearing strips out of magazines on the pouffe cushion, while his mother perched herself on the edge of the sofa. Emer and her boss, Barbara, had become the best of friends since James came along and popping into each other's homes like this, unannounced, was commonplace and totally acceptable.

"Black, no sugar, please, Barbara! I'm trying Weight Watchers this week."

But there was still no reply, only the sound of slow footsteps on the stairs. Eventually, an elderly woman, carrying a basket of dirty clothes, entered the room and very calmly asked Emer, "Do I know you?"

Ten minutes later as they sat on the right sofa, in the right house and two doors down the road from the first, Barbara burst into fits of laughter at the thought of Emer and her son, totally content, sitting in the wrong house.

"For heaven's sake, Emer, I don't even have a pouffe

cushion!" Barbara struggled to speak though the convulsions.

Emer failed to see the funny side. "The poor woman must have thought I was barking."

"Don't worry, I'll go round later and explain how your brain has shrunk."

"But it has." Emer felt her scalp through her short curls, as if sizing it up. "I'm not joking. I went to collect James from the crèche last week and even that turned into a total farce. I kept forgetting what I had just said and the other mother I was talking to had forgotten what I'd said too. Between us, we didn't have a clue what we'd been rabbiting on about for the ten minutes before. Entering into a conversation these days is a waste of bloody time."

"It'll come back." Barbara placed a reassuring hand on her friend's knee. "Conversation is overrated anyway."

"What about peeing yourself on a trampoline down at Barry's?" Emer added.

"Look, I went on a date last week and wet myself in the fella's car – just as I was about to get out. I haven't been able to return his calls since. And I haven't had any children."

Emer loved spending her Monday day off with Barbara. No matter what problem she had, or what new discovery she found with her post-pregnant body, Barbara always managed to cheer her up.

James had successfully hunted out the box of toys Barbara kept for his visits. His mop of bright-red curls danced as he jiggled with excitement at re-discovering his favourite Matchbox cars. Emer had dressed him this morning, hence the brilliant-white shirt, electric-blue corduroys and spotless suede shoes. On a working day, when she was forced to allow William to have a hand in the morning preparations, she couldn't expect more than a sweatshirt and jogging bottoms for her son.

*"Who's coming into my wee house? There's nobody in today, but my wee . . ."* Before Barbara could add 'James' to her song, the toddler came running towards her at full pace, almost knocking her, with her wide-open arms, down to the floor. They hugged and kissed, before James scurried off back to his cars, tugging at the uncomfortable collar on his shirt as he went.

"How's the potty-training going?" Barbara asked as she rejoined Emer on the sofa.

Emer spent the next five minutes detailing every inconsistency in her son's toileting routine. Emer's love of the minutiae in life had found new territories since becoming a mum. "I reckon he'll still be wearing nappies when he goes to school."

"As long as he isn't when he brings his first girl home, he'll be all right," Barbara cheerfully advised.

"That's what William keeps saying, but all James's pals were out of nappies nearly a year ago now," Emer whispered, so that her son wouldn't hear. "I think it's because he's tugged and stretched the wee thing so much, he's lost all control."

"This is James, not William, we're talking about?"

"Both." Emer chuckled in response to her friend's contagious, laid-back approach to everything.

Barbara disappeared to the kitchen for a moment and returned with a pot of coffee and a plate of warm, home-made, fruit-soda slices. Dollops of butter had melted through the thick wedges.

"Have you any idea how many units there are in just one

slice of that stuff?" Emer held her hand out, so that she couldn't see the plate – as if just by looking she would gain two pounds.

"It's Weight Watchers now, is it?" Barbara was more than familiar with her friend's fads.

"If I were to eat that," Emer pointed to the plate as if there was something hideous on it, "that would be my units for the week gone. I'd have to starve myself."

"All right then, Emer, what's low in units?" Barbara began to head back to the kitchen as she waited for the answer. "I'll see if I have it."

"There's loads of 'No Point Foods'. You can eat heaps of the stuff: broccoli, mustard-cress, egg-white, onion."

Barbara turned. "Emer, who wants to live by numbers?"

"OK, give us a slice. But, no butter."

Emer had been struggling to return to a size ten since James was born. She managed once, the first week in February the previous year. But when she recovered from the bout of acute diarrhoea and sickness, it was only a matter of days before she was back to her present size fourteen. So determined was she to get her figure back, that she refused to spend a penny on anything above a size ten. But Emer being Emer could not resist the need to shop. The result was a wardrobe full of tiny outfits, just bursting to come out and be shown off. Which they were, as Emer squeezed herself into ill-fitting bras, knickers, blouses and skirts – all the height of fashion and all unflattering and uncomfortable. Even Barbara, her best friend, hadn't the heart to tell her. She had made a few constructive comments, but Emer had chosen not to hear them. And William, her boyfriend, although his opinion on such matters was rarely sought, thought she looked beautiful whatever she wore.

Her biggest admirer by far, however, was her son, who reassured himself every ten minutes by pottering over and giving his mother a big bear-hug, the buttons on Emer's tight blouse popping with each squeeze, and then returning to poke pencils into Action Man's eyes.

After a second slice of cake and a second helping of guilt, Emer got ready to leave.

"You're not going just yet, are you?" Barbara was about to make a fresh pot of coffee.

"Sorry, it has to be a flying visit today – I'm cooking tonight."

Barbara grimaced.

"Exactly. So, I need plenty of time to get my act together."

"Who are you cooking for?" Barbara's grimace hadn't entirely gone.

"Oh, it's only our Heather. I've got William parcelled away with my dad, for a pint, and we're having some sisterly bonding time." This time, Emer pulled a face.

"How's she getting on?"

"Heather's Heather. She's finished her masters and they've offered her a part-time lecturing job." Emer began to help James tidy the toys back in their box. "She starts next month."

"Say congratulations from me, will you?"

"Aye, I will, but, Barbara, she needs out of that house," Emer continued as she got on her knees and reached under the sofa for a few wayward cars. "I'm going to have a chat with her tonight and see if I can persuade her to move out."

"That'll be hard on her wage," said Barbara as she assisted in the search.

"I reckon that's why she's taken a part-time job – stops her from having to make that kind of decision . . . got you, you wee bugger!" Emer yanked out a fire engine. "Well, that's my theory anyway. So, must go, vegetables to buy, food to ruin."

Emer scooped up her son, said her farewells and was out of the front door before Barbara had chance to get up from the carpet.

When James was strapped in his car-seat in the back, it brought him up to the same eye level as his mother. Emer adored driving Merlin when her son was with her. She loved the endless chatter they entered into and James's enthusiasm for this or that in-colour, or the new season's hairstyles. In the back of Merlin, strapped in, was also the one place where James couldn't soil, wreck, pull or destroy.

Not that there was much damage her son could do to a car what three years of neglect hadn't done first. The maintenance and upkeep of Merlin were low on Emer's current list of priorities. The pristine golden shell was now badly scored from children's bikes and a few careless manoeuvres on Emer's part. The chrome was dull and pitted with rust. Damp had begun to seep in through a warped door and even with the vanilla-scented car-freshener that hung from the rear-view mirror, a fusty smell escaped. But the car got Emer and her son from A to B and that was all she cared about.

Today, A was Barbara's house which was on the outskirts of Coleraine and Emer had to drive through the town centre to get back on the road to Portstewart – B.

"Look, Mummy! Shops!" James poked his finger against the window.

Emer's son couldn't read or write yet, but he could spot a 'sale' sign at fifty paces.

'That's my boy.' Emer smiled to herself as she continued her journey home.

James had been tucked up in bed for half an hour before his Aunt Heather arrived.

"Och, Emer, couldn't you have kept him up for me?" She was very disappointed.

"You try cooking ratatouille over a hot stove, with a three-year-old asking to swing on your boobs."

From a very young age, James had succumbed to the wonders of a mother with a large chest. He was prone to squeeze, flick and pull, whenever Emer was least prepared.

"So how many units is this?" Heather stirred the pot of indistinguishable mush. She and Emer had jointly decided to try the Weight Watchers' diet and, for the first time in years, they were privately enjoying having something in common.

"None – it's all free stuff – tomatoes, broccoli, carrots, cauliflower, mushrooms and . . . stuff."

"There must be something for the oil alone." Heather continued to stir in search of something she recognised.

"No oil. It's all boiled."

As Emer took over the stirring, the two sisters casually chatted about the day's news; Heather was intrigued by Hillary Clinton being appointed as the head of the health commission in the White House. Emer chose the story of the manicurist Loretta Bobbitt, who sliced off two-thirds of her husband's penis. Heather stopped chopping a courgette at this point.

Emer carried the large pan over to the kitchen table. The apartment was small, but Emer had created a bistro ambience in her kitchen with a pine table lit by a lamp that hung low just above their eye-level. With all the other lights in the kitchen and adjoining living-room off, the table could have been in a restaurant anywhere in the world. Anywhere, that is, where boiled-to-a-pulp vegetables would be served on Denby plates, with silver-plated cutlery and Tyrone Crystal goblets. At only one unit per small glass, a South African red sat uncorked beside them. The fine things that Emer liked to have around her were courtesy of her boyfriend's overtime, when he was forced every Sunday to forgo church service.

Partially by way of delaying having to eat the meal, Heather lifted her full glass to her sister's and began a toast.

"Here's to fighting the flab."

The glasses chinked expensively.

The first mouthful of the meal didn't slide down quite as easily as the first mouthful of heady wine. Emer stared across her mountain of vegetables and thought to herself: I'm only doing this, Heather, to keep you company. Her sister, likewise, stared across her heap of mush and had exactly the same thoughts.

Heather was now a size eighteen and a 40EE bra size, but she hid her figure behind size twenty T-shirts and elasticated, tie-dyed trousers. Her frizzy hair was pulled away from her face, into a tortoiseshell slide. Badly in need of a cut, her hair resembled that of a Hell's Angel's in length and a WWF wrestler's in texture. Emer, now a size fourteen and a 38DD, by contrast accentuated her figure with a tight floral minidress. Her short-cropped hair was the same length all over and two gold chain-earrings reached down to her shoulders. The chocolate-coloured eyes and the 'Farrell' nose, however, made it impossible to say they were anything other than sisters.

Emer waited a minute or two for the first mouthful of stew to be swallowed and the after-taste to fade, before launching into her planned assault.

"So, what are you playing at, Heather? Isn't it time you lived a little? You've got to move out!" Emer was never one to beat about the bush.

"Here we go." Heather happily put down her fork. "And I've been here ten minutes already. You're getting a bit slack."

"Why don't you travel a bit?" Emer lifted her sister's fork and gave it back to her.

"Don't try and live your life through me!" Heather argued back

"Oh, my little apprentice, you've come prepared this time!"

"It is getting a little boring." Heather hid her fork under the folded napkin.

"When did I last have a go at you about it?"

"I'm not going to do this, Emer."

"OK, OK." Emer retrieved the fork and stuck it into Heather's dinner. "Did I tell you I got a postcard from Wee-Sarah yesterday?"

"No. And?" Heather was expecting the rest.

"She's got a manicurist job on a cruise ship." She added matter-of-factly, "Says she's met some six-foot-five Norwegian who owns a hot-tub." And then sensing she might be forced to cut short her story, she quickly concluded with, "All because she had the balls to leave home."

"That's enough!" Heather slammed down her fork. She was having no more of it – either the conversation or the food. Antagonised, she poured two large glasses of wine (three units apiece), right to the brim.

"Go steady," Emer interjected.

"I need something to take the bad taste away."

"The ratatouille's not that bad, Heather! Add some salt."

"I'm not talking about the food."

"OK, I get the hint." Emer sulkily dipped her finger into her glass and watched her fingertip stain deep burgundy.

"Hint? A sledge-hammer couldn't be less subtle."

"Please, Heather," Emer pitifully begged. "Just answer me one question and then I'll shut up. You're only twenty-two for heaven's sake – don't you have any dreams for the future?"

"You've enough for both of us." Heather was quietly pleased with her assertiveness. She'd bought a book on it. Chapter 3 was all about 'The Family'; Section 3.1 dealt with oppressive siblings and the second section discussed 'shifting the focus of attention'. "Been shopping lately?" she tried.

"The summer sales up in Belfast were fabulous. Gorgeous blouses . . ." Emer began to ramble and her sister notched up another success.

By the time Emer had exhausted her shopping account, a second bottle of red wine had been consumed. The women had eventually done justice to the meal and only a few dehydrated mushrooms lay drowning in tomato sauce on their plates.

"You know, I do have dreams," Heather inadvertently found herself announcing as the last glass of wine sent the self-help manual plunging into the dustbin.

Now Emer was getting somewhere. How she had got there she didn't have a clue, but she thought it best to say very little. This felt very peculiar.

"I have this recurring dream, Emer, that keeps bugging me. I had it again last night."

Oh, God, Emer thought to herself. Her second most hated thing was listening to people talk about their dreams, the sleeping kind that is. Her first was trying to analyse them.

"I'm sixteen and I've just finished my 'O' levels." Heather rested back in her chair. "The world's my oyster and I don't know where to turn. I just wander about the school, roaming from class to class."

Any semblance of metaphoric or Freudian significance was lost to Emer, as she stood up and noisily began to clear the table.

"And right bang in the middle of all this indecision, there's a boy."

Emer stopped wiping.

"A boy who used to be in my class and I haven't seen or thought about for years."

Emer sat back down again.

"And in my dream, Emer, I tell him how much I care about him and how much I want to be with him."

"Was he gorgeous?" Emer couldn't contain herself any longer.

"Cillian Harte? No, a wet blanket really."

"But, I bet he's gorgeous in your dreams," Emer said, grasping at straws.

Heather thought hard. "No, he's a wet blanket there too."

"And what happens next?" Emer eagerly leant forwards on the table, unaware that her elbows were in the damp cloth.

"Nothing. I usually wake up and have my Frosties."

"What?" Emer was flabbergasted. "There's no sex?"

"No."

"Not even a snog?"

"No." Heather repeated with a 'so what' attitude.

"You should take a wander through some of my dreams –"

"No, thank you," Heather interjected.

"Typical of you to have a horny dream, with no horn and a fella you didn't even fancy." Emer stood up again, with disappointment branded on her face.

"But that's my problem, Emer. I did fancy him. I was mad about him. But I was too self-conscious to even let myself know, never mind him." Chapter 5, 'Knowing Oneself' came to mind.

Emer lifted away the unused cotton napkins and the silver holders and disappeared into the blackness of the living-room. Heather could hear her sister fistling about, but couldn't see her.

"And that's it, the same dream I've been having every night for the past few months," Heather continued chatting towards the black void. "Isn't it strange? Emer? Isn't it odd?"

Her sister returned carrying a telephone directory, with her new cordless telephone balanced on top.

"Let's phone him!" Emer plonked the directory on the kitchen table

"What?"

"Ring him and have it over and done with. Let's get this God-awful dream out of the way and then you can replace it with some proper ones."

"Are you mad?"

"Hagan . . . Harris . . . Hart?" Emer flicked through the pages. "With or without an 'e'?"

"You can't do this." Heather protested. "With."

"There's a whole load of them here. What street did he live on?"

"I'm not going to let you do this! Garden Avenue."

"Here we go. I've found it." Emer dialled the number. "Hello, is there a Cillian Harte there? Oh, I see . . . you don't know where they moved to? OK, thanks anyway. What? Well, thank you. Aye, people do say I've a nice voice . . . I suppose I could . . ."

Heather stretched over, grabbed the telephone and pressed the disconnect button.

"What? He sounded nice," Emer moaned.

"How does a boyfriend and three-year-old son sound? Anyway, what did he say?"

"He said I sounded like I was a newsreader –"

"No, about the Hartes." Heather was losing patience.

"The family moved last year to somewhere in Scotland," Emer whined, like a child who'd just dropped her lollipop in the sand.

"I suppose he went to Manchester University long before that anyway." Heather had her own disappointment to deal with.

Emer grabbed the telephone back and dialled three digits.

"Hello . . . yes, Harte please, Manchester. No, I don't have a street name. How many? Even with an 'e'?"

Heather could hear the operator's laughter down the other end of the line. Emer hung up.

269

"Oh, well, you tried." Heather slumped back down again.

"Don't give up that easily. At your work, doesn't the Uni library have telephone directories and stuff like that?" The cogs in Emer's brain chugged along with determination.

Heather nodded.

"Get the one for Manchester and ring all the Hartes."

"That would be madness and for all I know, after he graduated, he probably moved. And if he didn't, maybe he's just renting somewhere. Or maybe he moved up to Scotland to be near his family, or to London or maybe abroad."

"Maybe." Emer agreed softly, revealing a blemish in her single-mindedness, before adding enthusiastically, "Or maybe, he's sitting in Manchester right now, dreaming of the lost opportunity with the girl from his school."

"Oh, Emer!"

"Oh, Heather!" Emer then leant forward, wiping away the very last splashes on the table. "It's romantic. Do it!" There was a sadness to Emer's voice that Heather hadn't heard for a long time. Emer had got caught up in her sister's dream and it no longer seemed foolish or boring, but had almost become her own. "Do it, for all us frustrated romantics!"

"How are you frustrated?" Heather laughed, but her sister didn't.

"Promise me when you leave here, that you'll try and find this fella of yours. Do it for me."

"Don't be daft, Emer! You've got all a woman could want: a son who adores you and a boyfriend who worships the red carpet you walk on. How much more do you want?"

Emer didn't get a chance to answer, before the boyfriend in question could be heard cursing as he fidgeted with his key in the door.

"What's that smell?" He had finally mastered the lock and as he stumbled through the front door and into the living-room, William's presence broke the bubble – which contained the stench of two women who had just eaten four pounds of vegetables. He sounded slightly the worse for wear and fumbled to find the light switch. When he eventually found it, they could see what he couldn't. He must have put his Aran sweater on as he was leaving the pub – it was inside out. His mop of red hair also had evidence of today's plastering job and on discovering his girlfriend and her sister at the kitchen table, he greeted them with, "It smells like a dog died in here."

*Emer, 1993*

# Chapter 35

As Emer took the side road off the main Coleraine-Limavady carriageway, Heather, in the passenger seat beside her, didn't have a clue where they were going. This was all part of her sister's 'adventure', which Heather guessed to be a euphemism for something much more serious.

It was early evening of July 11th and William had taken James to see the bonfires. He argued the case by suggesting that their son should be aware of both his parents' cultures and subsequently explained to the boy about the fires being a 'warm-up' to the main event the following day. The deal was sealed once he highlighted that 'the annual parades were in commemoration of the victory of William of Orange over Catholic King James at the Battle of the Boyne in 1690', or rather when he added 'and there'll be burgers and sparklers'. Emer hadn't put up much of a fight, especially once she had realised that she would have the evening to herself and, more importantly, would be able to accomplish something she had been thinking about, and planning, for the past few months.

"Where are we going now?" Heather was uneasy. She didn't like surprises.

"Just be patient. All will be revealed soon enough."

The sisters had changed little over the past ten months. They were still on Weight Watchers and had lost a combined total of 20lbs. Unfortunately, they had found it again when they weren't looking as both had got into a cycle of yo-yo dieting. The cycle was based on fluctuating moods between the guilt of eating one chocolate HobNob and the sainthood of Ryvita and tomatoes for a week. This evening, a half-eaten packet of James's Jammie Dodgers was wedged between the front seats and the contents were being nibbled away as each of the sisters secretly broke off corners when she thought the other wasn't looking.

"All I'm going to say is that what we are about to do is in everyone's best interests. Even if it is dangerous and, I'm not too sure, possibly illegal," Emer crudely attempted to reassure her sister.

They both reached for a biscuit at the same time.

"Hey, Heather, what are you doing?"

"What are you doing yourself?" A few crumbs spat out as Heather replied.

"I'm just checking that they're fresh."

"So am I."

"Well, I'm not sure they are."

"Neither am I."

They both took a whole biscuit each and stuffed them into their mouths without biting.

Merlin chugged along, slowly. He hadn't gone above third gear in three months, after developing a dodgy plug lead. William had tried to fix the bent door with brute force, buckling it even further. The stench of damp carpet and mildewed seat-covers was only marginally masked by the musky smell oozing out of the leather door pockets, where no one dared to go.

'How's the hunt going?" Emer asked as she ventured into fourth gear.

"It's not." Heather stared out of the window. "The student records department in Manchester eventually gave me a number for Cillian's digs. But it appears he moved out eighteen months ago. His ex-landlord gave me a number in Cardiff, but the woman there said he'd moved out earlier this year. She didn't have a clue where he was now."

"But what about his family in Scotland?" Emer and Merlin gave up on coming anywhere near the speed limit and went back down a gear.

"I've tried nearly all the Hartes in England, Scotland and Wales. Nothing. It's useless and even if I did find him, Emer, what would I say? And, if I did get to meet him again, it could be such a disappointment. He probably doesn't even remember me.

"He must be <u>some</u> fella."

"He's not." Heather shook her head. "He never wore clothes that fitted him. Never washed, let alone brushed, his hair. And he was always annoying me."

"So, are you just going to give up?" Emer was about to overtake a moped, but had second thoughts.

"I suppose I haven't tried the Outer Hebrides or the Orkneys. Maybe his family live there." Heather turned away from the window and smiled at her sister.

"That's my girl." Emer grinned back.

Off the side road, Emer now headed right, along a dirt

track that cut through farmland. The farm buildings looked deserted and the land barren through overuse. A circle of lush Irish oaks surrounded what looked like an ancient burial mound, about half a mile up the road. Ironically, it was the only thing in the desolate landscape that looked remotely alive. What had been a balmy evening was now suddenly transformed with a sheet of low cloud and a dull drizzle of rain.

"Bugger, that's just what we need right now," Emer said as she scrutinised the beads of water on the windscreen.

Ever since Heather could remember, they had prayed for rain on the eleventh night, so that it would dampen spirits at the bonfires. Things were not looking good if her sister was now mysteriously disappointed.

"I don't know what you're up to, Emer, but I reckon we should go back."

"How many more times do I have to tell you to start living a little. Trust me, you're going to thank me when all this is over." Emer turned on the windscreen-wipers, but they jammed after half a swipe.

When Merlin and the two sisters reached the burial mound, they came across an even smaller dirt track, that firstly went around the mound and then entered a gap in the tree circle, just wide enough for the car and no more. Twigs and leaves brushed over Merlin's body, as Emer slowly drove through the curtain of branches. She then stopped the car and yanked on the handbrake.

"What now?" Heather asked, but she got no immediate reply.

Emer got out of the car and pulled open the bonnet. It creaked and groaned.

Heather wound down the car window as far as it would go, which was about halfway. "I'm not getting out of here!" she shouted out. "Not until you tell me exactly what's going on."

"Come and see," Emer replied.

Heather reluctantly left the security of her car seat and joined her sister at the front of Merlin. Both peered into what felt like the heart of the old car. To Heather's horror, however, this heart contained a cardboard box, inside which was nestled securely a glass milk bottle, half-filled with yellow fluid and a fabric wick wedged into the top.

"Mother of God, Emer, a petrol-bomb?"

"That bottle is the answer to all our problems. Merlin's had it. I can't afford to run the old heap any more and you hate him."

"So?"

"So, Heather, if I were to try and sell it, I'd maybe get £25 for scrap. But, what if he was taken by joy-riders and burnt out after they had their fun? Admit it. Merlin's worth more dead than alive. I'll go half with you with the insurance payout and you can get a wee run-around – a Fiesta. And I can pay off some credit cards!"

"You've lost it." Heather was still in shock.

"Wouldn't you like to see the back of him?"

"Yes, Emer, but –"

"Couldn't you do with the cash?"

"You know I could, but –" Heather nervously slammed the bonnet closed.

"Well, think about me and think about your wee nephew. He starts school in September. How do you think he's going to feel arriving on his first day in that heap of junk?" Emer pleaded.

"Now, Emer, he loves this car."

"Well, yes . . . but it's not safe. You've smelt him. That can't be good for a wee boy's lungs."

Heather had no immediate answer and started to walk around and around the car. As she did so, in flashes, she remembered the countless times Merlin had let her down and the nights waiting in the pouring rain for a visit by the AA. She thought back to Matt Edwards and the time he kissed her hand and she remembered the feel of its bonnet against her back as Michael Sheehan took everything away from her. Returning to the front of the old car, where Emer hadn't moved, Heather yanked open the bonnet again.

"Joy-riders don't nick twenty-three-year-old cars." Heather was now more matter-of-fact. "They go for Golf GTIs and XR2s."

"It's the eleventh night – they'll nick anything if they think it'll burn." Emer sensed a glimmer of hope.

"How are you planning we get back home?"

"A mile across that field, " Emer pointed, "and we're back on the main road. There's a bus stop along it after a five-minute walk."

"But, what if we're caught as we're leaving?"

"Heather, who's going to report smoke on the eleventh night? And even if they could see the fire through these trees, there's no one around for miles. I've been here four or five times and I've all the permutations worked out."

"I didn't know you had it in you." Heather looked her sister up and down as if seeing her for the first time. "But you do know that, if we were caught, this would count as insurance fraud?"

"So?"

"And criminal damage."

"No one will ever know, Heather. Think of it as a kindness. He's like an old dog. Merlin's had his day and we're just applying a bit of euthanasia. So, we get some money out of it – but what the hell, we've been paying insurance premiums for years now. They owe us."

But Heather didn't see it in terms of euthanasia. With the burial mound, circle of trees and the planned funeral pyre, to her this was a sacrifice. "Emer, I can't do it." She sat down on the damp grass and let the light rain drizzle over her.

Her sister knelt down beside her and jiggled the car keys. Heather instantly thought back to four years ago and to the time she sat with Kitty like this, outside of the hospital on the day Emer gave birth to her son. That was the last time Heather had seen her eldest sister, the beginning of the fiasco with Matt Edwards that ended so badly.

"You're right. I mean what would Dad think?" Emer desperately tried another tack.

Heather crossed her legs and offered no reply.

"And you know how much Merlin means to Kitty?" Emer gave it her last shot.

Heather uncrossed her legs and stood back up again. "OK, let's do it," she said calmly.

Emer was quietly pleased with herself for perceiving that the anger Heather still felt at the rejection from her eldest sister was far stronger than any moral or legal arguments.

"But you can keep the money, Emer. I don't want it."

Even better, thought Emer. This time she didn't argue back. She was too busy thinking about shoes, handbags and a holiday in the sun.

"And I think we need to make this look as realistic as possible." Heather maintained her poise. "We need to ram it into one of these trees. Make it look like an accident and that then the car caught fire as a result." Merlin was no longer a 'he' and was now, with Heather, very definitely an 'it'.

"OK." Emer was taken aback by her sister's ignited enthusiasm.

"Take the petrol-bomb out and once we've crashed the car, we'll set it off."

The crudely made bomb was left on the grassy hill, with an empty supermarket bag over it, to protect it from the rain.

"I'll drive." Heather snatched the car keys from her sister's hand and the assorted key-rings dug into her palm.

"OK," Emer agreed, still overcome by her sister's assertiveness, as she opened the door to the passenger side.

"I'll reverse back out and then come in again and try and hit that tree on the left." Heather started the car up.

"Don't go too fast." Emer was already holding on to her seat.

"This car only does slow, very slow and stop. Just relax, will you?" Heather turned to look out the back window.

"All right. We're not going to get hurt, are we?"

"I'm just going to prang it a little, Emer. You'll know it's coming and you can brace yourself." Heather could see her sister's white knuckles. "Not yet. Just before we hit the tree."

But Emer didn't listen and grabbed hold of the handle above the glove compartment with her right hand and pressed her feet tight against the front bulkhead.

As Heather reversed the car, Merlin's wheel skidded

slightly on the damp grass. Out of the circle of trees, she reversed a further fifty metres or so down the track, to allow some distance for the car to gather speed. When she then changed from reverse gear to first, her hand slipped on the gear-stick and the car stalled. On the third attempt, the car's engine re-started. The rain had got heavier and the tiny window-wipers miraculously un-jammed themselves and dragged across the window which was splattered with dead flies.

The car idled in neutral, with Heather's feet still on the clutch and brake-pedals. It felt heavy and cumbersome, the driver thought, weighed down with stories from across the lives of all three Farrell sisters. And memories of a life before that, of the twelve years he had before Kitty was presented with him for her birthday. He had twenty-three years to recollect, the same as Heather now, as she prepared to drive him to his last and final story.

"Are you ready, Emer? Emer, are you ready?" Heather looked across at her sister.

"It's the right thing to do, isn't it?" Emer just peered out of the front window.

"Aye. Are you ready?"

"I'm ready," Emer stuttered back.

Heather lifted her foot off the clutch and put her right foot heavily down on the accelerator. Merlin noisily burst forward, scattering the eager-to-roost birds. Heather just about managed to change to second gear as they approached the entrance to the burial mound and were now a few yards away from the circle of trees. The car appeared to drift along in slow motion, but both sisters bounced along inside at double-speed. Heather saw the tree she was heading for to her right and turned the steering wheel, brushing it against her thighs. A few feet of gnarled tufts of grass, nettles, sprouts of dandelions and the thick bark of an Irish oak stood between them and Merlin's sacrificial end. The noise of the engine blanked out most other sounds, except for one mighty roar, when Merlin was only a short distance away from the tree, and someone inside the car shouted, *"Stop! Please stop!"*

# Chapter 36

Emer secretly watched the 12th of July marches on the portable television in her bedroom. She was magnetised by the faces as she tried to pick out William's father from the parading Orangemen from Ballymena. Like a sore tooth, it pained her to watch, but she couldn't help herself. William had given the parade a miss, in favour of triple pay to guard the building-site from vandals. Emer had also opted out of the annual Catholic exodus to Donegal with her father and Heather.

James burst into the room.

"Mummy, can you blow anything?".

Emer quickly flicked the television channel, stopping on a more inoffensive daytime televised confrontation between daughters and their lesbian mothers. But she knew herself there was little she could do to mask the half of her son that was 'Orange'. He marched around the bed, drumming his toy drum and tooting on his toy whistle.

Emer attempted to change the subject. "I can't blow a whistle very well, but I can blow up balloons."

"What else can you blow?"

Nothing that little boys should hear from their mothers, Emer thought to herself and then smiled when she remembered 'A Mussenden Temple', Jack Sheehan's nickname for her oral-sex expertise. William, in sharp contrast, had started to irritate Emer by calling her 'Electrolux'. "*After all, nothing sucks like an 'Electrolux'!*" he would chant, echoing the television advertisement. Emer stopped smiling when she recalled her father overhearing William calling her that one day and asking if it was because Emer was good at cleaning.

Thankfully, James's short attention span had quickly moved on.

"Mummy, my hair hurts!"

"Your hair can't be sore. Come on over here. You're just bored. What about practising those Irish dancing steps I taught you?" She gave her son a hug.

"Och, that stuff's for girls! Big boys don't dance about like that." He snuggled into her neck.

"Maybe, someday, it'll be very trendy."

"Muuuum!" James groaned, stretching out the vowel for as long as possible.

Even at only four years, James's mother had succeeded in embarrassing him. He disappeared under the duvet and continued to toot the Orange Order anthem, 'The Sash', on his whistle, dipping occasionally into 'The Wheels on the Bus'.

Emer guessed that her son was getting stir-crazy, being cooped up in the small apartment all day. He looked pale and in need of some fresh air. But she couldn't face going out today. Even Merlin's golden colour, to her, had taken on a sardonic orange sheen this morning, in apparent sympathy with the 12th. This only aggravated Emer's disappointment with herself for calling out 'Stop' the night before and causing Heather to swerve away from the tree and shudder to a halt, halfway up the burial mound. They had driven home in uncomfortable silence. When Emer had opened the living-room curtains this morning and looked down at Merlin's brazen orangeness, she felt nothing but anger at herself for not being able to go through with it.

James climbed out of the duvet and snuggled his head against Emer's pillow, deeply inhaling his mother's smell.

Emer flicked the channels on the remote again, in search of cartoons, but when she looked back down at her son, only seconds later, he was fast asleep. She turned off the television set and tiptoed out of her bedroom, closing the door to, but leaving a one-inch gap. She peeked through the gap to check that he hadn't woken with all her movement, but through the sliver of her view, she could see the long, red eyelashes closed tight and the mop of vibrant curls motionless against the pale blue of her bedding.

With the unexpected gift of a few minutes to herself, Emer didn't know what to do. Should she get on with the ironing, or maybe check the new *Next* catalogue, or even treat herself to a slow, peaceful bath? As she struggled to prioritise what she should do, she got angry with herself for the minutes that were passing away with her indecision. And then she got angry with herself for being angry with herself and eventually she forgot what it was she was thinking of doing in the first place.

A unit-free cup of tea, no milk and no sugar and a digestive biscuit, would help her decide. She prepared the brew, cleaning up as she went and leaving the kitchen surfaces as spotless as when she began. The tea towel was folded away again in its proper place and the milk carton turned around in the refrigerator, so that the label was facing squarely outwards. Everything in the kitchen was either peacock-blue or egg-yolk yellow and included sets of pans and collections of pottery, systematically stored and ordered.

She sat back down on her sofa which, after she had been eventually forced to remove the protective plastic, was now covered with two, large blue throws. The biscuit, dunked in her tea, tasted delicious and before she knew it, she had returned to the kitchen for another one – a further five times. When she stuffed the biscuits into her mouth and enjoyed a fleeting moment of bliss, guilt and remorse quickly followed – only to be momentarily stifled by devouring yet another one. After the five, she felt so bad that two bars of chocolate, from the tin she reserved for James, were needed to dull the pain, along with a crust of fresh bread, drenched in butter and honey.

Before she knew it, Emer had eaten so much that her jaws ached. The full-up feeling she used to get as a child just wasn't there any more. Her metabolism was shot. She huddled up on the sofa, laden with guilt and disappointment, as if her whole world had come to an end. She cried like she had never cried before.

"Mummy, my clothes hurt!" James weakly called out to her.

The sweating, pure-white child, barely able to stand and gazing out at Emer from the doorway, bore no resemblance to the boy she had left sleeping only half-an-hour ago. Emer raced over to her son and carried him back over to the sofa. She knew exactly where to find the thermometer and within seconds was watching the strip on his forehead ignite the forty-degree mark, which was as high as the scale went. Only a few more minutes later and she had him undressed, sipping cold water, with a cool flannel against his brow. He had no new marks or blemishes, but she ran an empty glass all over his body, to see if any old marks refused to disappear. She had read about the test for meningitis in the leaflets given out by the health visitor, thinking then that she would never remember a word. As she continued to do this with one hand, she telephoned the doctor on call with the other.

She gave the female doctor a description of James's symptoms.

"Bring him down to the hospital? Yes, I checked, with a glass. I didn't see anything. Can't you send an ambulance? You have none? 'Otherwise detained'? Yes, I do know what day it is! Do you know how sick my child is?" she fumed. "Too right you'll be waiting for us! Forget it. I'm on my way."

With James drifting in and out of sleep, loosely wrapped in a blanket in the back seat of Merlin, Emer turned the ignition with her eyes closed.

"Please God, start!" she prayed.

Merlin started first time.

As she drove, Emer told James how brave he was and that they'd be at the hospital in no time at all. Under her breath, however, she continued to pray that the old car would get them there. But once she was out of the town and onto the open road, in the direction of Coleraine, something very peculiar and startling began to happen. Suddenly, out of nowhere, the gear changes, which were usually clumsy and grating, started to run smooth and swift. The typical coughs from the exhaust were silent. Merlin drifted from forty, to fifty, to sixty miles an hour, like a new breath of life.

"Please, Merlin, keep going!" Emer pleaded.

As if on air, the twenty-three-year-old car glided through Coleraine town centre and out towards the hospital. Emer chanted 'thank you, thank you' each time she braked and Merlin didn't stall and when the traffic-lights miraculously stayed on green for the entire way. Emer didn't consider herself to have had much luck in her life, but somehow, on this journey, she had it all. Even the marches appeared to have moved on in different directions to her journey and all that was left was litter and crumpled plastic flags.

With Merlin driving like a dream, she found herself getting caught up in frustration at the drunks and vandals keeping William away at work and the ambulance 'otherwise detained'. By the time she arrived at the turn-off for the hospital, Emer's frustration had developed into hatred.

When she arrived at the entrance to the accident and emergency unit, a team of nurses and auxiliary staff was waiting for her and her son. As they carried the now lifeless James into the hospital, his mother prayed with all her heart.

An hour later, Emer left the hospital and returned to Merlin, where she had abandoned him at the entrance. She had left his door wide open. Her face looked drawn and pale, the skin under her eyes was black and her eyelids heavy. Back inside the car, she closed the door tight behind her. She reached her arms around the large black steering wheel and cried like she had never cried before.

"Thank you, Merlin! Thank you!" she sobbed as she hugged the steering wheel tight against her chest. The doctors had managed to stabilise James's temperature within ten minutes of their arrival and following extensive checks and a few x-rays, her son had just been given the all-clear. They reassured Emer that a virus must have hit James hard and they wanted to keep him in overnight, just for supervision. Emer would be allowed a camp bed beside him. Once she had telephoned William on the building-site, there was only one last important thing she had to do. And now as she touched, caressed and kissed Merlin's interior, she couldn't stop herself from chanting: "Thank you, thank you!". Merlin hadn't let her down. And more than that, he had forgiven her. If she had burnt him out, as had been her plan, she would have had no way of getting her son so quickly to the hospital. Merlin had saved her from a lifetime of guilt at the very least and God knows what else at the very most.

She turned the key in the engine, wanting to hear his voice and feel the life within him. But he didn't start. She tried a second time and he spluttered for a few seconds and then the engine stalled. Emer laughed out loud, then she cried and then she laughed again.

It was in this exaggerated mental state that William discovered her a few minutes later.

"Are you all right?" He opened Merlin's door.

"I dunno."

"Are you laughing or crying?"

"I dunno."

"You said the lad was OK – he is, isn't he?"

"Yes, yes."

"So, what's wrong?"

"I dunno."

William knelt down beside Emer, reached into the car and put his arms around her. He had obviously raced over from the site and was even more splattered in plaster and dust than usual. He had also built up a sweat in his rush to get over to the hospital and its fresh smell oozed into the small cabin of the car. But Emer didn't care. She needed this hug more than anything and for the first time since she had met William, she wasn't imagining it was from somebody else.

Emer sensed that something cataclysmic had happened to her that morning. She couldn't put her finger on it exactly, but the one thing she was sure of was that she had suddenly discovered perspective. Her four-year-old son and a twenty-three-year-old car had given her a lesson that was long overdue. Emer knew that her future had to be different. She had made a promise to herself, as she sat holding her son's hand in the hospital, that her life would never be the same again. Even so, she had no idea just how different it was going to be.

As Emer and William continued to embrace, neither noticed an ambulance pull up beside them. The back doors swung open and four men were ushered out, draped in bloodied bandages and splints. The smell of beer fought a battle with anaesthetic. William was reluctant to release Emer, but over his shoulder she caught a glimpse of the men, still arguing with each other, as they scurried towards the waiting nursing staff. To Emer, they were all responsible for stealing what should have been her son's ambulance from him. She picked out one in particular for her rage, the one who looked most likely to have started the fight in the first place. This was the one she would later target with her anger. He was shabbily dressed in an overstretched sweater, battered jeans saggy around his behind and lank unwashed hair.

Emer didn't recognise him, even from the description Heather had given her only the night before.

## *Heather 1996*

## Chapter 37

Over the next few years, Heather Farrell found herself unwittingly involved in a slow-burning relationship. Her new companion was the same age as herself and shared the same troubled history. What had begun as adversarial, developed over the years into tolerable companionship. The two twenty-four-year-olds became the sort of pals whose company they enjoyed, but who they would never share secrets with. And this was all thanks to Emer. After the drama surrounding James's hasty visit to casualty, William couldn't be persuaded that Merlin was a safe and reliable second car for his family. But Emer refused blankly to have the old car scrapped. The only way that she could ensure Merlin wouldn't be destroyed, therefore, had been to persuade someone else to take care of him.

"Trust me, it's karma. He just knows you don't like him. You give him love and he reciprocates. You have to fight through your differences," Emer had pleaded.

"Bollocks." Heather wasn't convinced.

"Please, Heather! He saved James's life."

Thus, Heather had been blackmailed into giving Merlin a second chance. Plus the exchange was sweetened by Emer's promise to contribute £20 per month to the car's maintenance and repair. After the first few months, therefore, Merlin was given two remould back tyres and, after saving the donations for the rest of the year, he was treated to a new exhaust. William and even their father got involved in minor repairs and services. When Merlin squeezed through his next few MOTs, there was a sense of joy throughout the family. In the test centre, Heather had even mastered sounding off the air-horn stashed under her seat, while pretending to push what should have been the horn on the steering wheel.

On this haphazard footing, Heather's relationship with Merlin was nurtured. They became inseparable as she drove the old car daily, in and out of the university, where she still had her part-time lecturing job. She ventured all around *The Golden Triangle* as she carried out her day-to-day business.

Their friendship, however, was never tested beyond a seven-mile radius.

Today's thirty-five mile drive to Toome, therefore, was approached with trepidation as their relationship faced its first major challenge. Heather's investigations into the whereabouts of Cillian Harte had run hot and cold over the past few years. But today she was planning on chasing up one lead that remained lukewarm: the discovery that an aunt of his still lived in County Antrim. She was the only family member who hadn't moved overseas and it appeared, from Heather's source, that she ran a fashion boutique in Toome. The small town was generally only known to

Heather as it flashed past on the main Belfast-Derry road but she recollected a *Madame Chic*. She only remembered the store because a cold winter's night was imprinted on her memory, when she had waited for roadside recovery, directly across from the shop.

As Heather cruised into the town, a bald mannequin, dressed in a pastel cardigan and A-line skirt, confirmed the image of the shop that she had previously conjured up from memory. Turning the bend into the main street, she looked down at her own drab, shapeless clothes and decided she was hardly dressed any better.

The bell above the shop door tinkled as she walked in. It was a good few minutes before the ruffled shopkeeper emerged from a door at the back.

"Beautiful day. Can I help or do you just want to browse?" the tall, elderly woman asked as she continued to fasten the top buttons on her Crimplene blouse. The sleeves, being way too short, extenuated her height.

There was very little stock on the hangers and Heather calculated that two minutes were all a 'browse' would take, if that was what she was there for.

"Excuse me, I was looking for a May Harte," she enquired politely.

"Are you from the Inland Revenue?" The tall woman was suddenly less friendly.

"No."

"Or is it the Social Security?"

"No!" Heather was taken aback by the inquisition.

The disgruntled shopkeeper then pulled out a walking-stick from behind the dusty counter and began to lean hard against it.

"If it's the disability driving allowance . . ." The woman feigned a none-too-convincing limp.

"No, Mrs Harte. Nothing like that," Heather interrupted, taking a stab that she had got the right person. "I'm a friend of the family, so to speak."

The old woman threw her stick back down, shuffled around to the front of the counter and began to inspect her mysterious visitor carefully.

"I see." She was much calmer now. "Are you looking for a new outfit? I can see you might be." The old woman beamed at the thought that her unexpected visitor might soon become an unexpected customer.

"No, thank you. But if I were, I'd certainly know where to shop." Heather was endeavouring, as usual, to be liked. "No, I'm trying to track down a relative of yours. We lost contact nearly seven years ago now. I've tried everywhere and finally I managed to speak to his old headmaster. He told me about you." She smiled.

"This relative of mine must be some boy to have you go to all that trouble." May Harte winked and relaxed fully for the first time since Heather had entered the shop.

"Well, he is and he isn't, if you know what I mean."

"Not really, love. I find it hard to keep up with young ones these days." May Harte loosened her top button again.

They both smiled at each other, for rather longer than was comfortable, as each waited for the other to speak next.

"Well?" said May Harte, staking her claim as the more assertive of the two women.

"Well, do you know where he is?" Heather nervously enquired.

"I may look like a fortune-teller, love, but you'd need to tell me who he is first."

"Sorry, sorry. Cillian – your nephew." Heather blushed.

"I don't have any nephews!" May Harte answered sharply. The defensive wall that was so evident when Heather first arrived was hastily built again and May Harte was back behind the counter in a flash.

"But the headmaster said it was you who used to run a newsagent's in Portstewart. You and your sister – Cillian's mum!"

"I don't have any sisters," May Harte briskly replied.

"He said you were a tall, elegant lady." Heather attempted flattery.

"I'm wearing heels."

"But you match his description perfectly."

"Seamus! Seamus!" The old woman called into the back room from which she had first emerged.

A small, pale man, who Heather guessed to be in his late forties, appeared. He wasn't wearing his shirt and his hair was tossed. For a moment Heather wondered what Seamus and May Harte had been up to in there. She guessed that there was no 'may' about her – Cillian's aunt apparently 'did'.

"Seamus, this young woman isn't looking to buy anything." May Harte assumed an air of authority. "Would you show her out?"

"You must be joking." Heather couldn't believe the change in attitude again. "What have I said?"

"Please, Miss. We're closing for staff training anyway." Seamus had a night-watchman's air about him, but he was missing the uniform. He stretched his spine as far as he could, but still failed to come anywhere near the height of the two women.

Heather had never needed to be escorted out of anywhere in her life. Here she was, in the middle of nowhere, being turfed out of a dusty shop by an old lady and a boyfriend who reminded Heather of why brothers and sisters shouldn't get married.

Heather stood outside the shop door in total disbelief. She wanted to go back inside and confront May Harte further, but she hadn't the courage. She felt indignant and hopeless and hurt – all the emotions the final chapter in her new self-help book had guarded her against.

Heather needed about an hour to drive back to the university. Still shaking from her encounter, she was only just in time for her one lecture on a Friday. There were usually only half of the second-year Theatre Studies students there anyway on the last day of the week and those that were there usually dozed off after the introduction. But this did not deter Heather, who always prepared well in advance and gave her best, no matter what time of day or day of the week it was. So, after her ordeal in Toome, Heather arrived flustered, but still armed with her photocopied notes, slides, spare pens for those without and a well-planned, thoroughly researched lecture.

The class was even less well attended than usual, with the students approaching the final week of the summer term. But Heather, as enthusiastic as she could be under the circumstances, did her best to appear knowledgeable and passionate about what she was talking about. She always used her hands to emphasise points and would add jokes here and there for light-relief. But she seldom got a laugh.

Heather's commitment, over and above what the university required of her, was partly to compensate for the fact that she felt a bit of a fraud. Teaching 'practical stagecraft skills', when she had never set foot on a professional stage, always made Heather feel uncomfortable.

Each time she looked up from her notes, all Heather saw were a few tanned, young faces, winking and giggling with each other in anticipation of romance, the summer holidays ahead and their future potential.

"As a stage-manager, when you're putting your notices up in the rehearsal room for the cast . . ." she lifted her head again and was unable to make eye contact with any of her students, "it's important to put a tack in each corner of your notice – this ensures it stays smart and is easily read." She thought she heard a giggle. "Especially if your notice says something along the lines of 'I'm twenty-four years old and have never been in love or been loved in return." Heather looked up and still nothing. Her heart was pounding. "My one hope is a man I haven't seen since I was eighteen who, it appears, has disappeared off the face of the planet." When she looked up this time, she saw a few heads turned in her direction and those who had been doodling on the desks earlier had put down their pens. "Now this man's aunt, who is my only clue to his whereabouts, threw me out of her shop today – in Toome!" She emphasised the town to signify the depth of the indignity. There was silence in the room. "You may all just look at me and wonder why I deserve a love-life at all." Heather stumbled on her words, but continued nonetheless. "I know – those who can, do, and those who can't, teach, but I'm capable of a great many things. Underneath all this . . ." She paused and looked down at her bloated hands, peeking out from a shroud of black sleeve. "Why should it be so bloody hard for me to do just one simple thing and find Cillian Harte? He's just a man." And that was, Heather knew now, what all her self-help books had failed to help her understand. She was pinning her entire future on being able to find an old school-friend. He wasn't even a friend, more like an old school acquaintance. How sad must I be? Heather pitifully asked herself as she watched her hands tremble. She dared not look up and could feel all the attention in the room squarely focused in her direction. Suddenly, the woman who had never wanted to be the focus of attention, who had never wanted to displease anyone and couldn't even make the chorus, was now, very definitely, centre stage. How on earth can I make my exit? Heather nervously asked herself.

"Miss Farrell? Miss?" a soft voice from the front row called out.

Heather wondered if she should ensure an exit by making herself faint.

"Miss Farrell, I know a Cillian Harte. He used to live near us in Portstewart. He's been living back in the North this past year."

When Heather bravely looked up again, it was as if the spotlight was now focused on the girl with the soft voice. Everyone else in the class was out of focus and hidden in the dark.

"Do you know where exactly?" Heather asked, still struggling with the words.

"The last I heard, Miss, he was in Magilligan."

For Heather, the spotlight had been turned off and the stage was a blackout. Magilligan was a thirty-minute drive away and a maximum-security prison.

*Heather, 1997*

# Chapter 38

"Name?"

"Heather Farrell."

"Vehicle Registration number?

"HFB 71G."

"Make and colour."

"Volkswagen Beetle and he's gold."

The prison officer momentarily paused the vetting procedure, stopped scratching his groin and glanced up from his clipboard at Heather. She had already been searched and had surrendered her car keys and personal effects. The moment she had walked through the tiny side-entrance, beside the massive, main gate, she knew that Magilligan encompassed all that she would have expected from a maximum-security prison. Still with her, as the prison officer returned to his note-taking, were her first impressions of the height of the wall surrounding it, topped with huge steel rollers and razor-wire. The greyness of the day and the watchtowers dotted around the parameter gave a heavy sense of black-and-white prisoner-of-war films from days long gone.

"Before we go in, there's a few important safety warnings I need to give you." The officer began to fidget between his legs again.

"OK." Heather had even more reason to be as compliant as ever.

"If someone – if an inmate, approaches you and asks you to take a letter out to his sick granny . . ." he took a moment before delivering his finale, "don't."

"OK." She nodded enthusiastically.

"Even if they ask you to read it and you read it and your heart bleeds for the poor old dear. Maybe you see nothing harmful in it and you take it. The next time you come in here, the same inmate asks you to take another letter, or maybe a map . . ." He winked. "And you refuse – the same charming fella will tell you that when you took the note last time, they had you followed. They'll know where you live, where you work, where your kiddies go to school. Get what I'm saying?"

"OK." Heather nodded again, with less spirit.

"I don't want to worry you," the officer rested the clipboard against his pot-belly, making himself more comfortable, "but these are things you need to look out for."

"Sure." Heather couldn't think of anything more to say and didn't want to encourage the officer to detain her any further.

"And don't answer any innocuous questions – you know what I'm saying? 'What kind of car do you drive?' and the inmate then says, 'Oh, yes, I used to have one of those – what colour?' Am I making my point?" The officer patted the clipboard against his stomach.

"Absolutely," Heather replied.

"And oranges. Maybe an inmate tells you he loves oranges, but he doesn't have a visitor's pass this week. Maybe, asks you if a mate of his could leave a few somewhere, for you to pick up and bring in." He winked again, before adding, "Not a good idea."

"No?" Heather sensed he wasn't going to continue unless she made some sort of reply.

"They inject them with mercury."

"Oh." Heather still didn't see his point.

"Bombs." As planned, the officer now had Heather's full attention. "They can make bombs with those balls of vitamin C. Do you get my drift?"

"Yes. Very much so." Heather pretended to look as shocked as possible. It obviously did the trick and the prison officer returned his focus to his clipboard and signed along a dotted line at the foot of the page.

"Right then, if you follow Tommy here, he'll take you to the classroom. Good luck."

After six weeks of thorough vetting and the completion of a mountain of paperwork, Heather had persuaded the prison authorities that a trial class in drama-therapy was just what they needed. She discovered they already had an art-therapy class and had immediately seen this as a positive indication of the prison's 'open-mindedness'. She hadn't been able to discover if Cillian Harte was an inmate for sure, but she decided that there was only one way to be certain.

The first prison officer had been dressed in black, with a stiff black peaked cap. Tommy, was fitted out differently – less structured, with an all-in-one, dark blue overall and a soft baseball cap. But there was nothing soft about the Alsatian dog that walked beside him.

"Is it your first time inside?" Tommy asked, turning down the volume on his crackling walkie-talkie as he spoke and turning it back up again when he had finished.

"Aye, it is."

"Don't worry." He smiled warmly, instilling Heather with a little confidence.

A step forward, she thought.

"Just don't have any visible weaknesses."

Two steps back.

As they walked along the prison corridors, Heather noticed how high the waistband on Tommy's overall was, positioned just below his ribcage. He had the gait of a man much older, but she guessed from his youthful face that he was in his mid-twenties, like herself. Heather was absorbing everything around her, imagining she was Cillian seeing it all for the first time. Her first impression of the inside of Magilligan was its emptiness. She couldn't see any inmates, which was highly disappointing considering her mission here in the first place. There looked to be an abundance of prison officers – all of whom were dressed like and looked like Tommy.

They came to the exercise yard, which appeared to Heather to resemble a cage within a cage. In the centre was a football pitch and, around it, chain-link fencing. Above the pitch were wires, with bright orange balls attached. Tommy caught Heather staring up at them.

"They prevent extraction by helicopter." He gave her a knowing wink, which somehow, was far friendlier than the first officer's.

Having then taken right turns down two corridors, Heather's second impression of the prison interior was its gloss finish. Highly polished grey floors reflected highly glossed, grey walls. Here she saw her first inmates, walking in single file from one area to another. The men were dressed casually, if in a slightly outdated style, in tank-tops and corduroys. They curiously stared at the new visitor as they passed, but made no comments. Heather curiously stared back, but she didn't recognise any of them.

"This is the art class." Tommy and his dog stopped walking. "I thought you might want to meet the art tutor before you take your own session." He opened a heavy-duty door onto a polished room dotted with small tables that were all muddied with clay.

Heather was introduced briefly to Shirley, the art therapist, who was a bubble of enthusiasm, joy and hippy frills. Heather paid little attention to what the tutor had to say, as she quickly scanned the faces of the inmates before her. Their curiosity appeared to be cut short by a cough from someone in the back row and they quickly put their heads back down and continued with their work. But it was long enough for Heather to realise that she didn't know anyone.

Guns modelled out of the clay were the most common artistic expression. A skinny young man at the front was just banging his lump of clay against the table, which he looked to have been doing for some time.

"Don't you let some of the officers worry you." Shirley smiled sweetly. "I've been coming here for three years and never had any problems. Call in when you're done and let me know how you got on."

Tommy laughed and escorted Heather out of the classroom.

"What was so funny?" Heather asked, when the door was closed, fearing the answer.

Tommy enjoyed explaining to Heather the procedure of weighing the clay out before the class and weighing it all in again at the end. The week Shirley forgot to weigh the clay back in was the week a clay gun was used to take an external contractor hostage.

"And here we are, your classroom." Tommy regally opened the door to a room across the corridor from Shirley's class. "They're all waiting for you."

The minute Heather stood in front of the fourteen inmates, sitting in two rows, waiting patiently with their arms crossed, was the first moment that she questioned what she was doing there. For once, she was thankful for the protective curtain her hair formed across her face, as it partially hid her reddening cheeks. This whole charade was so out of character for her – she couldn't imagine anyone who knew her ever thinking she would get this far. What was she doing here? What mess had she got herself into and how much worse could it get?

"You can leave me now. I'll be OK on my own," Heather told Tommy. She was shocking herself by each thing she said and each action she took. Tommy obliged by leaving the room.

"What are you doing here?"

"Why are you coming to talk to us?"

"Who sent you?"

Heather batted back the questions as quickly as they came. Promptly it became obvious that the men were here purely because the choice had been this or bricklaying out in the rain. She also quickly realised that Cillian was not amongst them.

Once Heather had explained herself, she tried to begin the session with a few ice-breaking exercises. But the men were having none of it and sat, unflinching, with their arms still crossed. She explained, again, what drama-therapy was all about, but her second attempt to gain their involvement failed too. Her determination to succeed and not to resort to calling Tommy back into the room made Heather equally stubborn. Again, she was experiencing qualities in her character that had, hitherto, been uncharted.

"We can just sit here, for the next two hours, if you want." She paused. "I've nothing better to do. I'm going nowhere."

There was silence for ten minutes, as Heather's resilience was tested. She didn't move.

"Right, lads," a broadly built man in his early fifties, from the end of the row, quietly, but firmly called out, "do as the wee woman says."

From that moment, all fourteen men did exactly what Heather asked. The 'commanding officer's' approval, it appeared, had been given.

The inmates' enthusiasm quickly led from ice-breakers into role-play exercises. And after the first hour, Heather had them improvising conversations between themselves and loved ones; the same two-chair exercise that she herself had done as a student. This, however, was her first practical experience away from the academic environment. By the end of the second hour, some of the inmates were opting for role-play situations of a different kind; that of rejecting approaches by the paramilitaries when they got out of prison.

To Heather's astonishment, the atmosphere of the group became friendly and relaxed, with banter between themselves, but absolute respect for their new tutor.

For the first time, in what Heather considered to be her 'stagnant' career, she felt a sense of achievement. She was right there on the coal-face and it didn't frighten her. She had pushed herself beyond her usual limits and, as she said her farewell, she felt impassioned and full of life. Her heartbeat raced and she thought it would never slow down.

Heather's gushiness almost matched Shirley's, as she recalled her successes afterwards to the art-therapist. Shirley listened intently while she carefully cleared up the now empty tables, careful to pick up every crumb of clay. A lot of 'wonderful's and 'fantastic's were exchanged. Tommy waited by the door with an expression as confused as his dog. Heather could see that both man and dog watched her carefully as she flitted around the room, helping to collect the fragments of clay. She felt conscious of her size and tried to bend over sideways, rather than directly in front. But when she felt her baggy T-shirt gape open, she stopped bending down altogether.

So caught up in her drama-therapy success was she, that she had momentarily forgotten why she set out to visit Magilligan in the first place. She saw how foolish she had been to expect to see Cillian Harte amongst hundreds of prisoners. She also doubted that he was there at all. Cillian, in prison? Not a chance, she decided.

Shirley discovered a lump of clay stuck to the bottom of a table, under the guise of a piece of chewing-gum. She was pleased with her detection of it. Heather was equally satisfied with the chunk she discovered in the bin.

"What about these?" On a table in the far corner, drying beside a piping hot radiator, Heather came across an assortment of clay heads. They were facing away from her.

"No, they can stay." Shirley took off her apron, given to her by one of the prison officers, which was printed with the torso of a body-builder in tight, Lycra shorts. "They're portraits done in this morning's class. I've already weighed them."

Still, Heather couldn't resist having a look, even having persuaded herself how foolish she was being. Maybe there was a one-in-a-million chance that Cillian's face would be there. She turned the dozen or so heads around, one by one, as if they were the contestants in a beauty parade. Heather's pulse, that still hadn't subsided, jumped a beat. None of the sculptures was of Cillian Harte but one, third from the end, was undeniably of her.

# Chapter 39

"Heather, love, when you come back next week . . ." Tommy paused. He had already completed the necessary paperwork for Heather's departure and begun to search for her car keys in the drawer.

"Aye?" responded Heather, still not sure if there was going to be any 'next week'.

"I wouldn't do any of that stuff again, you know, with the inmates acting out being approached by the paramilitaries when they get out."

"You were listening?" Heather asked, but didn't wait for an answer. "I thought it was beneficial for the prisoners."

"It's the ones on the outside you need to worry about – if you know what I mean." Tommy smiled, which had been a rare occurrence during Heather's visit and for a moment she felt that she could see beyond the uniform and the stature it gave him, to the nondescript, plain man inside.

"And one other thing . . ." Tommy, who was about to place Merlin's car keys in Heather's hand, pulled them away again, "when you come next week, don't drive the same way home afterwards. On your way out, take a different road to the one you take this week. If you would usually turn left to get home, turn right. OK?"

Heather nodded with her hand outstretched before her.

"And one last thing . . ." The prison officer finally placed the keys in Heather's open hand and closed her fingers tight around them without letting go for a few seconds longer than was appropriate. He then turned off the volume on his walkie-talkie completely. "Are you doing anything tonight?"

As Heather drove Merlin down the long straight road, away from Magilligan Prison, she was struck by the contrast of the wasteland either side of her and the beauty of the rich and lush landscape beyond. The prison was set in one of the most picturesque areas in the province. Through her rear-view mirror she could see the trail of smoke, from Merlin's faulty exhaust, that she was leaving behind. Her head ran over and over all that had happened to her during those past few hours. But as she rethought her bizarre experience, she couldn't place herself in the frame at all. Was that her taking the class? Did she do that all by herself? And then compounded with the sense of disbelief, was the confusion surrounding whether Cillian Harte was still an inmate there and why she was the subject of someone's clay sculpture. The woman who was ever fearful of playing the leading lady was now centre of her own drama.

At the end of the prison exit road, Heather didn't take the planned left turn, back towards Coleraine. She found herself turning right, driving along country roads, which took her exactly where she wanted to be: Toome.

"Seamus!" May Harte didn't waste any time.

"Mrs Harte, I know all about Cillian and the prison. And I'm not going until you tell me all that you know," Heather said, frightening away the shop's solitary customer, a frail old woman who was rifling through the 'all for 50p' box of large knickers. When Seamus didn't appear from the back room, Heather guessed that he wasn't there in the first place.

"OK, you know as much as I do." May Harte acknowledged that her bluff had been called. "Aye, Cillian is my nephew, but no one in the family has ever done what that boy has." Mrs Harte dabbed at her dry eyes with the corner of a handkerchief. "He has let us all down." She continued trying to force tears and earning Heather's respect as the actress she was.

"Is he still there?" Heather's tone was controlled and determined. Although she knew it in her heart, she needed formal confirmation that the sculpture belonged to Cillian.

"Aye, he's still there. But I haven't been to visit. My sister's been over from Scotland a few times. She's the only one in the family who has. The daft eejit just can't see her son for what he really is."

"And what is that, Mrs Harte?"

"A liar, a thug and a drunk."

Heather drove back home in an even more dense haze of confusion. May Harte's concluding Oscar-winning performance of a feigned angina attack had cut short their conversation. Heather was too preoccupied with her dilemma to even consider that the attack might have been genuine. There was no way that she could match Mrs Harte's description of her nephew with the boy she knew. Cillian was the popular class swot – dependable, reliable and an awful dancer. The only trouble he had ever got into in school was the time he handed in his art homework a day late – and even then, the oil painting of Dunluce Castle was so exceptional the headmaster hung it in the assembly hall. Could there be two Cillian Hartes, she wondered.

Heather felt that she was writing her script as she went along.

The plot for Act Two was finalised as she pulled up to the driveway of O'Hara Drive. She was home at last. Only then did Heather decide that she would open this scene with a woman, played by herself, searching for her lost love. This character's tale would begin with having dinner with her lover's jailer – cue Tommy, stage right.

311

# Chapter 40

At Emer's insistence, William, Heather, Tommy and herself arrived at The Blue Bistro, all uncomfortably squashed into Merlin. Emer was so caught up in Heather's dinner-date that she had booked the table for them, decided what Heather should wear and invited herself and William along too. Arriving in Merlin was a 'karma thing'. Heather hadn't put up much of a resistance to the extra company, as she felt more secure in numbers.

William and Emer entered the restaurant hand-in-hand, with their fingers interlocked. They had been going through a second honeymoon phase in their relationship ever since their son's illness, which was significant in that they never really had a first.

Tommy walked a few steps in front of Heather, so that he could open the doors for her.

Once inside the tiny restaurant, William sat down and began flicking through the menu. Tommy held out the chairs for both Emer and Heather to sit down, before taking his own. He then selected and ordered wine for everyone, while his date fidgeted with the neckline of her dress. She had worn trousers for as long as she could remember and felt highly self-conscious in the midnight-blue, velvet shift dress – picked out by Emer. Heather had also been treated to the full works in Pores for Thought, including what she vehemently argued was a huge assumption on Emer's part: a bikini and underarm waxing.

Even though Heather felt highly self-conscious, she couldn't deny the sensation of feeling the most attractive she had looked in a long time. Ever since she had telephoned Tommy and agreed to a date, she had hardly been able to eat with excitement. The call was only four days ago, but she had lost all her usual bread-induced, bloated feeling and the rings on her fingers felt much looser than usual. With the £40 she discovered in her handbag, which she didn't know she had, Heather also treated herself to a visit to a hairstylist's. This turned out to be a very different experience from the barber's she found so convenient and inexpensive for dead-end trims. The frizz had been controlled with conditioners and the length had been drastically snipped to just below her jaw-line. For the first time in her life, Heather had a hairstyle compared to just 'hair'.

As Tommy tasted the wine and then gave his nod of approval to the waiter, Heather was able to shift her focus from her own appearance to that of her date. He was exquisitely dressed – slightly old-fashioned in style, but pristine and spotless all the same. His neatly cropped, fair hair was difficult to date, but looking at a small kink of hair at his temple, Heather guessed that it was cut this short to destroy all evidence that he too had curls. His features were perfectly proportioned, if lacking distinction. But then Heather felt that she had enough distinction for both of them.

All things considered, Heather was quietly pleased with her catch.

"So, Tommy, tell us all about yourself." Emer felt that she had managed to restrain her curiosity for long enough and, as per her usual form, bulldozed away.

"Emer!" Heather interjected.

"What's your uniform like?" Emer asked, grabbing Tommy's arm.

"Emer!" Heather tried again.

"Heather's a wonderful girl. Isn't she gorgeous . . ." Emer wasn't listening to her sister.

"Emer!" This time William interrupted on Heather's behalf, but Tommy held his hand up, signifying he was prepared to answer.

When Tommy had everyone's attention, including that of another couple at the next table, he began to speak. "It's OK. Yes, Heather looks stunning. Absolutely stunning."

Emer blushed for her sister, who in turn blushed for Ireland. William saw neither as he was by then busy trying to work out which was the salt pot and which the pepper.

The starters of basil and tomato soup, for everyone except William, were accompanied by Emer's incessant ramblings on her sister's highly prized qualities. While they waited for their empty bowls to be cleared, Emer switched back to her interrogation of Tommy. By the time the goat's cheese tartlet arrived for everyone, except William who had chosen a T-bone steak, the facts were that: Tommy was twenty-four, had worked for the prison service since leaving

314

school (like his father before him), was from Castlerock (just down the coast from Magilligan) and still lived there with his parents. Emer knew where Tommy shopped for his clothes, that he drove a BMW 3 Series, but longed for a 5 Series and that his cufflinks were handmade by Steensons in Belfast.

"Emer! Let the man eat!" William interposed again, affording his girlfriend the opportunity to hint that he had a piece of meat caught between his teeth.

Heather had noticed that her sister and her boyfriend did things like this now, without either being conscious of doing it. William would pluck stray hairs from Emer's sweaters and she would flatten wayward tufts of his hair. Their relationship had reached a new level, where Emer, though often still embarrassed by William's 'lack of sophistication' as she would call it, found herself increasingly attracted to his simple ways. Pivotal to this transformation, Heather decided, was the fact that their son James was now six years old and Emer was getting her independence back. She appeared to no longer see her boyfriend as a chain around her neck. William and her sister were starting to bridge their differences.

Much to Heather's irritation, Emer had also packed in what little practising Catholicism she had and put her faith elsewhere.

"Do you believe in karma, Tommy?" Emer was relentless in her persistence.

"I believe in fate and predestination, if that's the same thing," Tommy answered, very sure of himself. "For example, I believe that I was meant to meet Heather."

Emer clapped her hands in excitement. Heather didn't

know what to think. William asked for the dessert menu.

"Exactly. It was karma that brought you two together," Emer gushed with self-satisfaction and jumped up out of her seat. "Excuse us, gentlemen, while us ladies powder our noses." Emer put Heather's fork down for her and escorted her to the toilets.

As she sat on the toilet, Emer kept the door open with her leg, so that she could continue to chat to her sister.

"Oh, Heather, he's gorgeous! A real gentleman." Emer flicked the toilet-roll around, trying to find the end. "You don't know how lucky you are!"

Heather leaned against the sink. "But I explained it all to you – I'm only interested in finding more out about Cillian."

"You've the choice between a drunk prisoner, who you haven't seen in years and a polite, obviously infatuated, tax-payer." Emer pulled up her knickers and tights together and, forgetting to flush, went over to the sink to wash her hands. "Are you crazy? Look at you!" Emer turned her sister to face the mirror above the sink. "I haven't seen you this radiant in God knows how long."

There was no denying that her younger sister exuded sensuality. And when Heather looked at the mirror and at her sister beside her, it was obvious that this radiance was echoed in Emer. Emer was back counting units and this time she had lost over a stone. More significantly, the stone had stayed lost for the past six months.

"And what about you?" Heather spoke to the reflection of her sister in the mirror. "I haven't seen you this happy for just as long."

"I am. With having more time for myself, I've started to

make more time for William. Even getting a baby-sitter and going out together tonight – that wouldn't have entered my head a while back." The soap dispenser was apparently blocked.

"And what about the management course?" Heather tried to force some pink gunk out for her sister.

"Two more assignments and that's me. Barbara's got plans for opening up a new salon in Portrush and . . ." Emer paused for dramatic effect, "she's got me down as the manager. Things couldn't be better." She rifled through her handbag but when she couldn't find what she was looking for, she tipped the contents out into the sink. "Here, I've got something for you." Tampons, mascara, crayons and a few Irish punts fell out, along with a crumpled sheet of paper. "James wanted me to give it to you."

Heather unfolded the paper and rejoiced in the rainbow of colours and shapes. In the centre of the artwork were three figures: James, his father and his mother. Around which was a solid circle of yellow.

"A content wee boy drew this," Heather said, tracing her own finger around the circle.

"I know," Emer gushed. She thumped her fist against the dispenser and a blob of heavily scented, liquid soap splattered the sink. She continued to talk to her sister through the mirror's reflection. "And you could be just as happy, Heather, if you started making sense. There's a great man out there and he's real. Stop and smell the daffodils." Both women burst into giggles. "That's a cliché, isn't it?" Emer asked.

"Nearly – and a good one." Heather barely managed to respond through her laughter.

When the sisters returned to the table, the conversation

between William and Tommy was all 'alloys and spoilers'. But Emer wasted no time in turning it around to relationships and love.

The meal was finished and the two couples sat nursing Irish coffees for an hour, until it was time to leave and Tommy insisted on paying the bill. William was quietly relieved because, even though he had enough money to cover his and Emer's share of the meal, the £40 he had secretly stuffed into Heather's handbag earlier that morning had left him a little short of cash.

Emer and William were dropped off at their apartment first, at Emer's insistence, and then Heather drove Tommy back to her house on O'Hara Drive, so that he could pick up his car.

"So, your wee car's really . . ." Tommy turned down the radio volume and appeared to scramble to find something complimentary to say.

"Really is a heap. He never starts, has bits falling off and I hate him," Heather rather too enthusiastically finished Tommy's sentence for him.

"Really golden, was what I was going to say," Tommy politely added.

They both smiled at each other and then he twisted the radio dial away from the local popular music channel and searched for something else. The distance between Emer's and Heather's home was only half a mile and she had parked beside Tommy's car, just as he found Radio 2.

"I'm so glad you phoned," Tommy said softly, as the engine stopped. "I hoped you would and I've had a terrific night."

"I'm glad I phoned too." Heather hoped that the goose-

318

pimples that had just sprung up on her arms weren't too noticeable.

"And to meet your family too, that was a real pleasure," Tommy added with sincerity and a gentle smile.

Heather decided not to mention the other two members of her family, just yet. Kitty was still nowhere to be seen – and, as she spotted the curtain flickering in his bedroom window, her father was seeing rather too much.

"And I meant what I said earlier – you look absolutely sensational," he said, respectfully keeping his distance, with his knees turned away from hers.

Heather indeed felt sensational. She had surprised herself more over the past month than at any time in her twenty-four years. There was no denying that she felt invigorated, sexy and alive.

Tommy jumped out of the car and had Heather's cardoor open before she had chance to work out where he was going. He then opened the gate and escorted her to her front door.

Heather's stomach apprehensively twisted and ached. It was a long time since she had been this close to a member of the opposite sex who was so blatantly attracted to her – rather than she to him.

"I don't think we've any coffee, but we've tea or Complan," Heather joked as she turned the key in the door.

"I would love to. But, no, I'd better be on my way." Tommy remained on the front step.

Heather was momentarily deflated.

"I wouldn't be able to trust myself," Tommy whispered as he leant forward and gave Heather a slow lingering kiss, on the cheek. "What are you doing tomorrow night?"

"Nothing," Heather answered without thinking, with her lips slightly trembling in the wintry chill.

"What about the next night?" he asked again as he turned and walked back down the path.

"I said 'nothing' to tomorrow!" Heather shouted back.

"And what about the next ten years?" Tommy called, as he was about to get into his car.

Heather felt giddy and silly. Maybe she could put all the nonsense about her recurring dreams behind her. Maybe Tommy was 'the one' after all and karma had led her to him and not Cillian.

Just as Tommy was about to close his car door, Heather surprised herself, again, when she called out:

"Before I forget, Tommy! Is there any chance I could come along in the morning as well as next week? I'd like to do some work with the art class."

# Chapter 41

There was one table empty in the morning art class in Magilligan Prison. A lump of clay sat untouched. Heather's heart sank. Tommy and his dog were waiting outside in the corridor, but she knew he would be listening. Over the past week she had churned the whole 'Act Two' over in her head. She'd had two more, lovely dates with Tommy, but still felt driven to see her quest through to its conclusion. The two bunches of mixed flowers from these outings were in vases on her bedroom windowsill, along with the bunch of pink carnations Tommy had given her on their first date. Their vibrant colours came to mind now as she stared at the unused ball of grey clay.

Shirley was as effervescent as the previous week – even more so with Heather alongside her. Heather had concocted a ruse that she wanted to study the inmates working on individual artistic projects, for a shared role-play exercise she had planned for the afternoon. Shirley was delighted with the idea. Once inside the classroom, Heather toyed with simply asking where the man from the empty desk was. But if Shirley hadn't already connected her with the clay portrait, Heather wasn't going to encourage it now, for fear of compromising herself and Cillian.

Heather moved around the group, asking questions about artistic motivation and inspiration. The young man bashing his lump of formless clay against the table at the front of the class mumbled an answer, which Heather chose not to ask him to repeat. The two hours passed incident-free and were two hours that Heather felt had been completely wasted. At the end of the class, as Shirley and herself weighed back in all the pieces of clay, the art tutor ranted on about the aesthetic qualities of a lump of clay that had been moulded into an ashtray. Heather gave up hope of ever contacting Cillian again. Perhaps this was karma saying 'give up' and 'move on'.

"See how this lump of clay, even though it lacks formal structure, still maintains form and magnitude," Shirley enthused, even louder than usual, as she held the ashtray up to the light. And then, under her breath she whispered, "You know, he really is an excellent artist – a wasted talent. The likeness is unnerving."

Heather was stopped in her tracks.

"And see, under that table there . . ." Shirley continued to mumble, barely audible, "there's a note left for you, from a young man who was released last night."

"What?" Heather hadn't a clue as to what was going on.

"Shush! I know we're not supposed to pass on letters to the outside world, but seeing that you're 'inside' and not 'outside' as such, I thought it was OK." Shirley attempted to wink like the prison officers, but both eyes ended up closed.

"The young man said that he heard you had been here last week and asked me to make sure you got it."

Heather nervously glanced from the wooden table to the door and back again. She leapt across the room and searched under the table. A small, grey folded sheet of heavy-duty card was wedged between the table's leg and the base. It took some twisting to free it. Once she had it secure in her fingers, the door to the classroom was thrown open by the hasty advance of Tommy's dog, followed by his master.

"OK ladies, are we all finished?" Tommy cheerfully enquired.

"Finished with what?" Heather thrust the card into the ball of clay scraps that she had already peeled off the tables.

"The clay. I have the delights of the prison canteen to treat you to, before your class this afternoon." Tommy pretended to puke. "Throw that in the bucket and I'll weigh it for you."

Heather threw the clay, along with the note, into the bucket and as it landed with a thud a nervous squeak escaped from Shirley's mouth. Tommy moved the weight along the scales as he attempted to get an accurate reading. First he moved it by tens of centimetres, then fractions of millimetres.

"Hang on a minute. Something's not right." Tommy twiddled with the weight. "This clay is heavier than it was this morning. How can that be?"

"Are you sure?" Shirley didn't lie very well and her serious disposition resulted in a twitching grimace. "You guys never do it right – you always have a problem with size. Isn't that right, Heather?"

"Yes," Heather nervously agreed, without really getting what Shirley was at. But when Shirley almost blinded herself with over-enthusiastic winking, she eventually got the message. "Yes, Tommy. Come here a minute, I want to tell you something." Heather thought on her feet for a moment. "It's private."

He followed her to the back of the classroom, with the same obedience as his dog following behind.

"You know that kiss last night. . ." Heather paused again, not really sure what she was going to say next.

She could see Tommy blush at the memory of their first proper kiss, after three dates.

"How about the same tonight?" she teased.

Tommy adjusted his waistband even higher than it was before. But before he could answer, Heather was relieved to see Shirley giving the thumbs up behind him.

"See, Tommy – same weight as it was when we got it this morning." Shirley was back to her bubbly self.

Of course, Tommy needed to see this with his own eyes, which allowed Shirley the opportunity to pass the letter, which she had removed from the clay and had hidden behind her, over to Heather. Heather, in turn, tucked it into her own trouser back-pocket.

The letter remained secure and unread all the way through the huge portions in the canteen with Tommy and two hours of regression, oppression and suppression with fourteen inmates.

At the end of the long exit road, Heather took the right turn, as opposed to the left she had taken the previous week. The note was still untouched.

At the first lay-by she came across, she pulled Merlin over and took out the folded piece of card. Her hands were trembling and her heart fluttered in her chest. She scanned

up and down the empty road and then even up to the skies.
She was safe.

Magilligan
29 January 1997

Dear Heather,

When Shirley told me you were in here last week, I didn't
know what to think. At first, I was gutted that I'd missed you,
but then relieved. Do you remember the time I found you in the
disco carpark? I didn't know what was wrong. I so wanted to
help you. But there was a fear in your eyes, a sense of loneliness –
I felt that there was nothing I could do. I was completely useless.
But you were strong, Heather, even then. At the time, I never
thought I would see the fear that I saw in your eyes, ever again. But
I was wrong. Now when I look in the mirror, I see it all the time.

I am weak, you see.

I'm relieved that you didn't get to see me this way. Please
remember me as I used to be. I hope you weren't offended by the wee
sculpture I did of you, but that's all to do with a recurring dream I've
been having. I won't even begin to bore you with that now.

When I'm released tomorrow, I'm going to disappear
oversees and try to make a new start for myself.

So good luck with your life and I trust this letter finds you
happy and well. I promise that when we do get to meet again, I'll
make everyone who knows me so proud – even you, Heather.

I promise.

Cillian

Back home, Heather lay on her bed, staring out at the cold

grey sky and the even colder, black ocean. She read the note over and over, tracing each word with her finger, trying to visualise the man who wrote them. Occasionally she was disturbed by the sound of her father, downstairs, coughing as yet again the winter months brought infection to his weakened chest. Cillian's handwriting had changed little from what she remembered from the spidery messages and brilliant sketches he would sneak onto her workbooks at school. It was obvious from the change in ink tone that his pen had run out, halfway through writing the note. The cardboard he had used had a light groove, which distorted some of the letters.

Heather now had a choice. She had never had choices before. Her life was a given and she followed the path loyally. As a child her life was school and home. As an adult she went from home to work and then home again. There were no complications and no distractions. Her life had lacked spontaneity. She had tried to be the family 'rock', but when it came to her own personal life, she fled at the first hint of confrontation. But over the past few months, she had found herself doing things and saying things that she would never have predicted. Had the search for Cillian brought about this transformation, or was it because she hadn't found him that she had changed? After all, by searching for Cillian, she had found out so much more about herself and what she was capable of. And she had found Tommy.

For the first time, Heather felt on the brink of fulfilling her potential as a woman. Tommy was a gentleman and because of this he hadn't pressurised her sexually in any way. In fact, Heather thought, she was the more eager of the two to succumb. She was beginning to believe in her possibilities as a sexual and attractive being. Only that morning she had rifled through her wardrobe, looking for something appropriate to wear and had thrown out more than half of what she had. She hadn't cared about her clothes before, as long as they were clean, and even that wasn't always essential. She had worn mascara today and tried, with limited success, to recreate what the stylists had done with her hair at the weekend.

And now, making animal shapes out of the dull clouds, she felt empowered as she remembered how confident she was taking the drama-therapy class. There was no comparison with her usual lectures, which were largely based on the theories of other academics. Her first taste of practical experience was exhilarating and, furthermore, she knew she was good at it.

Heather read the note one last time. Heaps of mottled pebbles and translucent shells were on her bedside table. They had been built up from her solitary strolls on the beach. The largest stone, pink and perfectly smooth, fitted perfectly in her palm. Heather then wrapped Cillian's note around the pebble. Opening her bedroom window was difficult, partly due to the frame's warp and also the gush of the January wind, but she managed. And then with a mighty, girlie throw, the pebble and the note were cast far out, bouncing on the rocks and into the raging surf.

The search for Cillian was over, Heather had decided. Her future lay with Tommy.

Even though the note had been swallowed up by the tide, having read the words over and over, every imprint, angle and full stop had been permanently absorbed.

# Chapter 42

The last time Heather Farrell visited the Giant's Causeway she was five and, not being able to find a toilet, she had left her own personal imprint between two of the geometric basalt columns. Tommy's choice for their first month anniversary, at the end of February, therefore, struck his girlfriend as odd. She had hoped, by now, that they would be taking their relationship to a more physical level and she had something more romantic in mind. The couple were battered by a gale raging across the Atlantic and the immense force of nature confronted them as they walked down the steep hill to the hexagonal-shaped rocks.

Heather had also hoped to show off her new beige, suede skirt and matching waistcoat, which she knew emphasised her slimmer curves perfectly. She was also proud of the results of three hours in the hairdresser's chair, getting her hair strangled into sleek tresses. The finished ensemble would have looked stunning, if it hadn't been for her father's duffel coat, Tommy's hat and her streaming nose.

*"Do you know the myth surrounding the Causeway?"*

Tommy shouted, forced to compete with the elements. He then linked Heather's arm through his own and placed his hands in his pockets.

"*Aye, I do!*" Heather roared back. But it appeared he hadn't heard her.

"Well . . ." Tommy proceeded to remind his girlfriend of the battle between the Scottish and the Irish giant.

Somehow, Heather guessed, from the manner in which he told the story, the landscape appealed to Tommy on an emotional and instinctive plane, rather than on the cerebral level that she felt.

The couple were now halfway down the hill and before them stretched the thousands of hexagonal-shaped rocks, wedged tightly together. The range in the rock heights reminded Heather of the weather charts in travel brochures: the places she looked at, but never visited. The streams of foreign tourists that she remembered from her childhood and who she assumed must have ignored these weather charts when they made their travel plans, were absent. They were replaced by small, huddled groups of bright red and blue cagools, and dotted with spouts of steam from welcome flasks of tea. A few braved hopping along the rocks at the edge of the ocean, but they were quickly forced back by crashing waves. The plovers soared above their heads, before folding their wings and crashing, bullet-like, into the sea in pursuit of the silvery glints beneath the surface.

"Isn't this place magical?" Tommy squeezed Heather's arm with his own.

His girlfriend's hand was freezing and she was desperate to warm it in her own pocket, but she didn't know how to without upsetting Tommy.

"Aye, it is." Heather could just about see the magic, somewhere between the straggles of damp hair stuck to her face.

"That there is the Giant's Organ." Tommy pointed up to a rock formation with the shape of organ pipes carved into the cliffs above them. They now approached the main bank of the Causeway. Heather tittered to herself and then tentatively approached the rocks near her. They looked harsh and stubborn, forcing their own space, like a huge mouthful of cramped teeth. Except for the ones that had mostly been walked on over the centuries, which were worn down to individually indented pools. Tommy stepped on one and then sprang up and began jumping across and then up and down on the rocks, as if playing a piano with his feet. Heather struggled slightly with the inappropriate patent boots she had worn and the heels that kept sticking in the cracks. But she was enjoying Tommy's playfulness, which was a side to his character that she had begun to fear might not exist. She also took the opportunity to stick her frozen hand into her own coat pocket for warmth.

"And over there is where the local giant, Finn MacCool, dressed himself in a nappy and sat in a pram. The Scottish giant, on his way over, thought 'If that's the bairn, what size is the Da?'" Tommy pointed again, getting very much into the spirit of the tour guide.

Heather knew the story better than he did, it being her father's favourite, but she wasn't about to tell. She had decided that her newly found confidence now meant that *she* could decide when, and when not, to assert herself. Right now she was happy to let Tommy take control. Heather wanted to feel controlled.

"And then Finn MacCool lifted a lump of earth and threw it. The hole that was left is now Lough Neagh and where it landed is the Isle of Man," Tommy continued, as he hopscotched down beside Heather, who hadn't advanced further than the second level of rocks.

"Give me your hand." Tommy reached out his own hand to Heather's and she held it. He then carefully steered her up, onto the third and fourth levels. His hand provided invaluable support on the two occasions that she almost slipped. Tommy also slightly pulled her hand in the right direction, whenever, it appeared to him, that she was climbing in the wrong one.

"I can't climb any higher, I'll fall!" Heather whined.

"No, you won't. I won't let you."

Tommy guided Heather up to the top of the stack and, by squeezing her knuckles gently, turned her to stand, like him, facing out to the Atlantic. The majesty of the battle-grey ocean, leading out to the mist that masked the Scottish coastline, was undeniable. Tommy peered through the dense mist, in search of Rathlin Island, which he knew was there somewhere. Heather, in contrast, hunted for the sight of the spray from a whale, which she also knew was out there somewhere. But both were disappointed.

"On a clear day, you can see the Scottish coast!" Tommy shouted into the gusty air.

"Can you?" Heather played along with the tour-guide scenario.

"Beautiful," Tommy added.

"Aye, it is," Heather agreed, as she still looked out in search of the break in the water's surface.

"No – you, Heather. You're beautiful."

331

Heather turned to face Tommy and the compliment. The blast-chill from the wind had improved Tommy's usually quite plain looks, by giving him a rugged quality. His cheeks were red and the dusting from the ocean spray made his skin moist and translucent. The wildness of the elements, for that instant, were reflected in the intensity of his gaze.

This time, Heather pulled her boyfriend's hand towards her and slowly but passionately began to kiss him. Tommy kissed her back, with the fervour that she had been hoping for. The sensation was heightened when their ice-cold cheeks brushed past one another, contrasting sharply with the moist warmth of their lips.

Heather then took Tommy's hand and fed it through a gap in her duffel coat. Like a baby given the first chance to feed, Heather could feel Tommy's hand frantically grab at her waistcoat and then begin to squeeze and knead her breasts. The frenzy beneath was discreetly hidden from the outside world by the thick, heavy-duty coat. By the shortness of his breath as they continued to kiss, Heather sensed that now Tommy was out of control and she was the one who knew exactly what she was doing. The exhilaration was electric.

"Hello, Auntie Heather," a soft voice drifted up from down by their legs.

The couple swiftly put an end to their amorous embrace. Heather's nephew was staring up at them with eyes almost as big as the lump of snot hanging from his freezing cold nose.

"Has that man lost something in your coat?" James asked, tugging at his aunt's sleeve.

"No, James. He's just warming up his hands." Heather took a tissue from her pocket and wiped the child's nose.

"Can I warm mine up too?" James added with a look that betrayed slightly less innocence than was appropriate for his age.

"Where's your mum and dad?" Heather quickly asked.

"Mummy's over there somewhere and Daddy's just behind me." James turned to point in the direction of his father, who had just begun to climb onto the Causeway.

*"James! James!"* William was turned away, facing the opposite direction.

"William, he's here!" Heather called over.

James looked like an exact replica of the man now hopping towards them. Their red curls squeezing out of their matching knitted caps and fluorescent orange cagools were identical, except for size and the *'I love the Tweenies'* badge on William's.

"Hi, folks!" William's usual cheerfulness was subdued, but he still forced a smile. "We didn't know you guys were coming here."

"Where's our Emer?" Heather asked, searching amongst the other few visitors.

William's attempt at a smile immediately dissipated and a cloud fell on his brow, almost as heavy as the ones above them.

"She's over there." He pointed over the ridge of the rocks.

"Is she all right?" Heather asked quietly.

"You tell me." He looked down at his boots. "James, see how many of the rocks you can count and come back when you get to fifty." He tugged at one of his son's curls.

"But my legs are out of breath," James moaned.

"And if you do, I'll let you change the gears when we drive home," William sealed the deal.

James skipped carefully along. He had long since tired of shopping with Emer. The mother had had him to herself for the first eight years of his life, now it was the father's turn. "Maybe, Heather, you can get into that head of hers," William desperately asked, once James was out of earshot. "The last week or so she's been as miserable as sin. She's even given up her management course."

Tommy stepped back a few paces, affording William and Heather privacy and allowing himself a break from what he felt to be an awkward situation.

"Was the studying getting too tough for her?" Heather's need to be the Farrell problem-solver was still there.

"She was top of the class." William shook his head and glanced back down at his muddy boots.

Knowing Emer's fickle temperament, Heather had anticipated that her honeymoon period wouldn't last, but she had prayed that she would be proven wrong.

"Tommy, why don't you stay here with William and I'll go and find her." Heather was enjoying taking charge, but she was half-fearful that she was leaving the two men with an opportunity to engage in a 'what's wrong with the Farrells' conversation. But, equally, Heather couldn't risk Tommy overhearing any of her family skeletons from Emer – if that was the true cause of her sister's problems this time.

Heather didn't have to go far before she found Emer perched on a stone commonly referred to as The Wishing Chair.

"What's up?" Heather sat on a damp rock beside Emer, which was rather too small.

"What are you doing here?" Emer appeared pleasantly surprised.

Heather was equally surprised to find her sister looking miserable, dressed in an Aran sweater that was far too big for her and their father's battered deerstalker hat.

"It's our first-month anniversary," Heather casually explained, trying to hide her concern.

"And he brought you here, in February?" Emer also wasn't impressed with the choice of location at this time of year.

"You're here, aren't you?" Heather felt a flash of protectiveness, which quickly faded. "So, what's up?"

"What did William say?" Now it was Emer's turn to be defensive.

Heather quickly sensed that Emer wasn't herself. Her sister's short questions gave it away.

"He didn't say a lot. Just that you were a miserable bitch," Heather said, in a tone set to provoke a reaction.

"Did he say that?" Emer pitifully asked as she gently rubbed her hands against the stone chair, as if trying to conjure up a genie.

"Well, not exactly. But that was the gist of it," Heather said, conscious of the possibility of getting stuck between the basalt rocks.

The two sisters remained in silence, both immobilised for different reasons.

"Did you get here in Merlin?" Emer eventually asked, never one to leave a gap in a conversation for too long. "Did he make it in one piece?"

"Tommy drove us here. He reckons that Merlin's a death trap and won't set foot in him." Heather sounded relieved to have a second opinion on the old car's failings. "You can hardly blame him. The last time we drove Merlin, Tommy's foot went through the floor pan."

"He could have raced along like the Anthill mob." Emer splashed her feet up and down in the puddle before her. "You might have gone faster."

"Very funny. Anyway, Emer, now that you mention it . . ." Heather paused. "I want you to have him back."

"What?"

"Tommy says if I get rid of him, he'll go halves on a wee car for me. I've got applications in for a few full-time jobs and it won't be long until I can afford the second half. Go on, you have him back! Tommy says I should get a Micra. And what about karma?"

"I haven't heard of that one. Is it a Vauxhall?" Emer brightened, momentarily, but then the melancholy seeped back. "I don't know about karma any more. It could be bullshit."

"Oh, Emer," Heather pleaded, with little time these days for her sister's fads, "you take him back. He only ever brought you luck anyway. He hates me."

"No, he doesn't," Emer replied, in an unconvincing tone.

"Don't you want your lucky charm back then?" Heather grasped at straws.

Emer glanced down at herself, obviously as disappointed with her appearance as her younger sister was.

"OK." Emer gave a big sigh. "I'll have to take him back. But I don't know what I'm going to do with him."

"Bury him in the garden." Heather was delighted with the result. "And maybe he'll grow into a new one."

"Don't push your luck, Heather! Anyway I don't have a garden," she added, as if she had seriously contemplated the suggestion for a moment.

The negotiation was complete, with one party overjoyed with the contract and the other sensing she might have been duped.

A small group of tourists had formed a queue, just ten metres down the rocks from the sisters, in anticipation of their turn to sit in The Wishing Chair. Heather managed to squeeze herself free from her seat. But Emer didn't look like she had any intention of moving.

"So, what *is* up?" Heather asked again, with a little more urgency.

"Everything."

"Why have you given up on the course?" Heather was now towering above her sister, like a teacher scolding a moody schoolgirl.

"There's no point." Emer fitted the sulking role perfectly.

"Has the new beauty salon fallen through?"

"Oh, no, that's going ahead all right." Emer's spirits lifted slightly. "They've got bookings for the first month already and it's not even open yet." The deflated spirits soon returned. "But I don't care about that now."

"What happened with the Weight Watchers? You were doing so well, Emer!" Heather tried some encouragement but inwardly guessed, from her sister's appearance, that the root of Emer's problems was more than just calorie-induced.

"It was all a waste of bloody time!" Emer dramatically flung her head down in her hands.

"For heaven's sake, Emer, just come out with it, will you?"

Emer lifted her head back up, as if it was too heavy for her neck. Heather was ready to give her marks for dramatic poise, until she saw the genuine look of despair in her sister's tearful eyes.

Emer stood up, now eye-level with her sister. She looked down at the stone chair with obvious disdain.

"I'm pregnant – again," she sobbed.

"But that's great news!" Heather enthusiastically hugged her sister. She was still confused as to why Emer should be so depressed about the prospect. While still rather too vigorously embracing her, she concluded that there was only one other possible cause for Emer's anxiety. "It is William's, isn't it?"

Emer punched her sister so hard, that she broke the 'Farrell' nose in two places.

# Kitty, 1997

# Chapter 43

The trainee doctor had difficulty hiding his inexperienced embarrassment. He aspired to diagnosing stress injuries for the national athletics team, not protein in the urine of pregnant women. He kept flicking balls of cotton-wool and glancing around the room with feigned interest in the posters. But the consultant obstetrician kept forcing the young man's attention back to the matter-in-hand.

"Now, you see this breast here. Look at the way the muscle flops and falls down under the arm. This is very usual with a woman of this age."

The consultant released the right breast and it collapsed to one side.

"But, they are perfect." The consultant now directed his observations to his patient. "There is absolutely nothing to worry about. What you are feeling is quite common with pregnant women at six months." He then turned his diagnosis again towards the ample breasts themselves, as if they were a third party. "They're just getting ready for their important job ahead." He pulled down his patient's gown and then made hurried comments on a chart.

"I'll see you again for your next check-up in three weeks. The nurse will be back to do the rest of your checks today. OK?"

"OK." Kitty O'Kane answered, not quite sure whether to be relieved that the tiny lumps in her breasts were nothing or feel distraught that, at thirty-three, her finest assets were heading south. She was also concerned that the trainee had yet to wash his hands after giving her the all-clear with the urine test. She sat up and scooped herself back into her large bra and maternity blouse.

As the consultant swept out of the examining room, with the trainee scuttling behind, Dermot was coming the other direction, carrying two scalding-hot cappuccinos.

"Did I miss anything?" he asked as he gave one of the cups to his wife, who was perched up on the examining table. "What did he have to say about the boobs?"

"He said they were perfect and there was nothing wrong with them." Kitty wasn't about to tell Dermot about the wasted muscle tissue. He would discover that himself.

"I could have told you that, for a lot less money. Maybe I should just have a feel – you know, a second opinion" Dermot was never one to waste an opportunity, especially since he'd hardly got near his favourite two buddies of late.

"Do you ever give up?" Kitty rolled her eyes.

"No."

"How long have you got, before you have to go to work?" she asked, while blowing on the coffee to cool it down.

"Fifteen minutes. So, Kitty, if you let me have a good

grope around, instead of the nurse, we could both be out in ten."

Dermot and Kitty both worked in an Irish bar in Manhattan. Without a working visa, it was the best they could do when they first arrived in the States. Initially the pay had been poor, but the tips had more than made up for it. They both quickly learned to play on the American idea of what being Irish was and, combined with their willingness to work hard, they had succeeded in earning quite a reasonable 'top o' the morning' living. Seven years later, they now jointly managed one of the most popular Irish bars in the City. Their wallets were nearly as big as their expanding waistlines – that is, until the unexpected happened and Kitty got pregnant. Then Kitty's waistline had very much taken the lead. But luckily for her, Macy's sold a range of leopard-skin maternity smocks and gold scrunchies to tie back her still long, ironed-straight, ebony hair – a further blow to their dwindling finances. Dermot, by contrast, spent little money on himself and a faded sweatshirt was all that he required to hide his growing beer-belly.

"Look, we can't afford for you to be late again, especially with me not working for the next few months," Kitty lectured, only now able to sip at her cooled coffee.

Without a visa, Kitty and Dermot had little rights with regards to maternity leave or health insurance. Their savings were shrinking rapidly.

"Don't worry, Kitty. Just you concentrate on your pelvic floor." Dermot sat down beside his wife. "It'll make a change from me doing it."

The nurse noisily entered the room, pushing a portable scanner on an aluminium table.

Both Kitty and Dermot saw nothing other than the size of the black nurse's huge backside, as she bent over to plug the machine in.

"How're we doing, Kitty?" the nurse drawled in a thick accent.

"We're doing fine. When The Bump hears 'Born to Run' he does back-summersaults." Kitty rubbed the side of her stomach.

"Well, there's no accounting for taste." The nurse gave a deep laugh, which shook her bottom (much to Dermot's delight). "Now, get ready, Kitty. You know this can be a little cold."

Dermot stood up and Kitty lay back again. The nurse pulled up Kitty's blouse and squeezed a lump of icy gel onto Kitty's round stomach. With the tip of the scanner, she spread the gel around and then turned on the monitor. Kitty wanted to ask if the machine was sterile, but she managed to stop herself. The monitor was a blur of fuzzy, white dots for a moment, until a baby's small, round bottom became very evident within the haze.

"The Bump's mooning at us," Dermot proudly announced. And then he moved closer to the screen in search of evidence as to what sex The Bump was going to be.

"Would you mind just scanning the top half of the baby, please." Kitty pushed her husband away. "We really don't want to know the sex."

"Sure, honey." The nurse twisted the scanner on Kitty's stomach.

Dermot groaned disappointedly.

"Look, he's sucking his thumb," the nurse gushed, with her face lighting up as if this was the first ultrasound scan of a baby she had ever seen.

It took a moment or two for Kitty and Dermot to decipher the fuzzy images before them, but together they solved the puzzle and the tiny face, with closed eyes and a plump nose, lay gently gnawing on his fingers before them. The Bump was a baby. Kitty wanted to cry, but held it back. Dermot just let it all out.

"Now, at the moment, your baby is lying breech." The nurse began to wipe the scanner clean, leaving the paused image of Kitty and Dermot's baby to flicker on the screen. "Which means absolutely nothing at this stage. But, let's just say, on the off-chance that he doesn't turn, we'll need to talk about caesarean. I'll go and get you a pamphlet."

"OK, thanks," Kitty said, pulling down her blouse and sitting back up.

As soon as the nurse had left the room, Kitty turned to Dermot. "We can't afford a caesarean!"

"Did she say 'he'?" Dermot was in a world of his own.

"Where will we get the money from?" Kitty's world was more pragmatic.

"Or do they all say 'he' because it's nicer than just 'it'?"

"I'm serious, Dermot. We can't afford a caesarean."

"Well, jump up and down a bit," Dermot joked as he sat back down on the bed and bounced up and down.

"Oh, Dermot." Kitty was tiring of her husband's humour. After seven years, she felt that he was starting to repeat himself, a lot.

Dermot shifted along the bed until he was beside his wife and put his hands on her bump.

"Kitty, you heard the nurse – The Bump will most likely turn way before he's due." His voice was now soft and sincere.

343

"But what if he doesn't?" Kitty pleaded.

"If we were worried about what-ifs and buts . . ." Dermot kissed Kitty's stomach, "we wouldn't be here now."

"That was all right when there was just the two of us. We could be carefree then. But it's different now. There's a baby. I don't want to bring a baby up here with no security and no future." Kitty stared at the frozen image on the scanner.

"The Bump's got us, what more does he need?" Dermot kissed his wife again, this time tenderly on the lips.

"What do you mean 'he' anyway?" Kitty relaxed slightly. "Did you see something you shouldn't have on the scanner?"

"No." This time it was Dermot who was serious. "He, she, what does it matter? The baby will be loved – that's what matters."

Kitty wished she could agree. Her view on what mattered was at odds with her husband's. "We'll have to cancel our weekend away. We're going to need the money."

Dermot nodded in agreement, worn down by Kitty's persistence. This would have been a trip of a lifetime to whale-watch off the coast of Cape Cod. Dermot was disappointed. Kitty was devastated.

The nurse returned.

"Hey, you guys are from Ireland, right?" The nurse waited for the nods, before continuing with, "Did you see the news this morning?" She threw a copy of *The New York Times* on to the end of the bed.

"No," Kitty answered for both of them, remembering that having lain in that morning, they had been forced to rush out of their rented apartment in Queen's.

"There – check the newspaper – it's in all of them." The

nurse then looked around her, appearing slightly confused "Now, what did I go out for? Oh, yeah, leaflets." She disappeared again, sashaying along with the rhythm of her laughter.

Dermot lifted *The New York Times* from the bed and read the headline out loud.

"Peace in Ireland." He then read the full details of the IRA's 'unequivocal' cease-fire declaration, announced only the day before – Sunday the 20th July. When Dermot had finished, the couple sat, speechless. Kitty grabbed the newspaper from her husband and read the article herself, as if she didn't trust Dermot to have read it properly. When she was reassured, Kitty swung her heavy bulk down off the bed.

"Dermot, this is it – the answer to all our problems." She began to look for her boots.

"What is?" Dermot felt that he had been left behind somewhere.

"We can go back home. We can have our baby back home." The patent black boots were awkward to zip and Dermot began to help her. "This cease-fire means it's safe for you to go back. All that nonsense will be over."

"What on earth are you talking about, Kitty?" Dermot really didn't have a clue.

"Your involvement with the paramilitaries. The Troubles are over. You can go back. We can go back as a family! Isn't that why you wanted to escape and come and live here in the first place?"

"I came here to be with you – not to escape from the IRA. Is that what you think?" Dermot didn't get around to zipping the second boot, leaving his wife balancing on one foot. "Is that what you've thought all these years?"

"Of course." Kitty had no sense of how ridiculous she looked or sounded to her husband.

"And that's why you've never asked me why I hijacked your car?" Dermot lay down on the hospital bed and covered his face with his hands.

"It was obvious. The same way you had your contacts in 'the boys' to frighten the Rolex-man off in Kingston. You were 'connected'." It was Kitty's turn to sit on the bed beside her partner. "Weren't you?" she quietly added, the sense of doubt beginning.

Dermot remained with his face covered by his hands and then he started to laugh.

"No, Kitty, no. I was connected all right, but not to the paramilitaries." He moved his arms and rested them behind his head as a cushion. He looked very relaxed. "I used to buy stuff off thieves and then sell them on. That's all. I was a kind of middleman."

"What kind of stuff?" Kitty's stiff back revealed that she was anything but relaxed.

"Benefit books, pension books, credit cards – that sort of thing – anything that can be forged and used by somebody else. I had nothing to do with the paramilitaries."

"But what about the hijack and the bomb scare?" Kitty interrogated further, the tension in her shoulders and brow also now visible.

"The bomb scare had nothing to do with me. I was just caught up in it like the rest of you." Dermot laughed again. "Only I had stuff in my pockets that I didn't want to have to explain if I had been searched."

"But the stuff I found in the pockets of that grubby mac of yours . . ." Kitty sounded desperate.

346

"What? Passports, birth certificates, driving licenses? All documents that can be forged." Dermot's laughter turned into a warm, confused smile. "Why, Kitty, what did you think they were for?"

"I thought they belonged to your other identities – your secret world as a terrorist. Like the man with the Rolex – the same man I'd seen you meet at Heathrow airport."

"He was just a petty thief, not a terrorist. Soupy Campbell fancied himself as a 'hard man', I'll give you that. He specialised in birth certificates and worked mostly overseas."

Kitty glanced away from her husband and back to the flickering image on the scanner. She imagined how she would feel if her baby's birth certificate was stolen and forged. She suddenly felt the need to hit out.

"So, why did he buy me flowers?" She angrily spat the words out.

"I told the fellas up the chain from me, about how he had treated you and said I couldn't work with him any more. They must have had a word with him – not me." Dermot's mood was also shifting, as he didn't appreciate having to explain himself. Kitty hadn't asked for answers when she thought he was a terrorist, but now it was the Spanish Inquisition.

"But why did you come to New York with me, if it wasn't to escape from the paramilitaries?" Kitty's questions were relentless, but her tone was more pitiful than angry.

"I told you, to be with you," Dermot answered matter-of-factly and this time without emotion.

"So, if I hadn't asked you to come with me?" Kitty turned her back away from Dermot and stared at the door. She was stunned rather than angry now.

347

"I would probably still be there now – doing the same thing."

Kitty and Dermot remained silent, drained of emotion. Both sensed that their relationship could now go any number of directions. Kitty still faced the door and Dermot looked up at the ceiling. The flicker of the scanner caught both of them in the corner of the eye. Dermot was the first to make his decision.

"But, Kitty, I'm so happy I'm not doing any of that stuff any more. You got me out of it and I will never, ever go back."

He began to rub the base of Kitty's spine; the part that ached in the evenings having carried the burden of his child all day.

The seedy, 'lowest of the low' nature of Dermot's prior life contrasted starkly with the dangerous, intriguing world that Kitty had naively created for herself. The danger that had sustained their relationship thousands of miles from her home was nothing more, she thought as she continued to stare at the door, than that of a 'grubby go-between'. Kitty was six months pregnant with the child of a man who was not what she thought. Dermot might have made his decision; hers would come later.

*Emer, 1997*

# Chapter 44

Emer's second pregnancy followed the same pattern as her first – miserably. Even down to wearing William's bottle-green, track-suit bottoms. She had totally given up on trying to control what she ate or what she looked like. Her boss, Barbara, had patiently tolerated her employee's bad timekeeping and promised to keep the management position in her new salon open, for when Emer was 'more herself'. But Emer didn't care. She had thrown herself totally into self-pity and the only person capable of bringing joy into her life right now was her son.

The school summer holidays were halfway through and Emer had brought James to the building site to have lunch with his father. She found she could no longer amuse her eight-year-old with trips to the shopping centres and could only content him with a regular fix of diggers, mud and dangerous tools.

But James still held on to some of his mother's traits and, before she had stopped the car, he had the car door open and was out, racing over to William. It took Emer a while to manoeuvre her bump from behind the steering wheel and then even longer for her to wipe away the splatters of mud on Merlin's bonnet. She still had some hope that the car would bring her good fortune again, but her patience, like her car, was more than frayed around the edges.

William and James had a sneaky kiss, before lunging into more open, masculine high-fives.

"Well, how did the meeting with the boss go?" was how Emer chose to greet her boyfriend.

"No pay-rise, I'm afraid," William responded flatly.

"Promotion to site foreman, but no extra money?" Emer didn't hide her irritation. "That's just not on."

"Only joking, Emer. I'm getting an extra ten per cent – plus use of the van." William beamed from ear to ear.

Emer rolled her eyes. After all these years, William still got her with softening mediocre news with a poor, pretend alternative. They had hoped for a twenty-per cent rise but now, compared to nothing, ten per cent didn't sound too bad.

"And look what else I get the use of!" William led his son and his girlfriend through the mud and over to a caravan in the middle of the site. "The site foreman gets somewhere private to do the wages and deal with the buyers. We can have our lunches in here now."

"Cool!" James gasped in awe.

Emer just gasped in amazement as she was shown into the tiny sitting-room, a credit to everything that was 1970. She didn't notice the vase of fresh wild flowers sitting on the table, which William had picked and arranged in preparation for her visit.

Emer had packed a flask of coffee for her and William, a carton of blackcurrant for her son and rounds of ham sandwiches for the three of them to share. The table was just about big enough to put them out, once Emer had thrown out the broken vase of what she thought were weeds.

"Daddy, can I go and sit on the digger?" James asked, still chewing on his sandwich.

"No," Emer answered, at the same time as William answered, "Yes".

"The lad will be careful. Won't you, son? Go on, Emer, let him have his fun," William argued the defence side of the case.

"Am I the only one who says 'no' around here?" Emer took up the prosecution.

William and James presented their next evidence in the form of miserable, large doe-eyes. They looked so alike.

"Go on then." Emer didn't call in the jury. "But don't turn on any switches."

James leapt up and ran out, clutching his carton of juice and the rest of his sandwich.

Now that Emer and William were alone, they regretted the absence of their son and his dilution of the atmosphere between them.

"How's the baby?" William tentatively asked, as he tore into a sandwich.

Emer was more interested in the thick, black grime under her boyfriend's nails. "Don't you ever wash your hands?"

"No need to ask what mood you're in, is there, Emer?" William threw down the half-eaten sandwich.

"How would you feel with a four-stone lump stuck to

*your* stomach?" She pushed her hair away from her face and behind her ears. She had recently given up the regular visits to have her tresses cropped short and stylish, in favour of a more respectable tightly curled bob. Though the curls were natural, the cut made her hair look like a do-it-yourself perm.

"True, Emer, I don't know what it would be like." William didn't usually answer her back when she was in these moods. "But I could always ask one of the trillions of other women who've got pregnant, without as big a fuss as you're making." Over the past few months, even William's mild and tolerant nature had been stretched to its limits by Emer's sulks and self-obsessions.

"Well, why don't you?" Emer threw her sandwich down on top of William's. "And while you're at it, get one of them pregnant. That way they'll have to put up with you, instead of me!"

Emer knew, each time she did it, exactly how cruel she was being. She wanted to stop and go over and put her arms around William's shoulders, but she couldn't stop. He was her nemesis and brought out all her frustrations and disappointments. Every night, when James was asleep, she found herself arguing with him. Fearful of waking their son, both fought via whispers and sign language. This only exacerbated the argument and the emotions.

The couple could now see James, oblivious to it all, jumping up and down on the truck and laughing with the builders as they teased and joked with him. The caravan walls contained his parents' anger and protected him from them, but not them from themselves.

"Is that what it's all about, Emer? You just want me to

go?" William stood up, turned his back against the window, blocking Emer's view of her son. "If so, for God's sake, just come out with it. Because all this bitching isn't doing James any good or the new baby and it sure as hell isn't doing me any favours." William's huge frame impeded the natural light.

"And what about me?" Emer haughtily asked, partially shaded by William's shadow.

"'And what about you?' Is that all you can think about?" The sense of William's frustration oozed out of every word.

'How dare you' was written right across Emer's face, as she now glanced down at her vulnerable form. 'How dare you talk to a pregnant woman like that?'

William turned back to see if his son was showing signs that he could hear them. It was obvious that he couldn't, as James was now proudly showing the roofers some of Merlin's unique features, including the dent in the bonnet where Emer had hit a rabbit. James's passion for Merlin more than compensated for the lack of it in his mother nowadays. And its current road-worthiness was only possible due to James's regular cleaning and polishing and begging his father and grandfather to give Merlin a service. He looked totally content with his little world.

"James deserves more than this." William turned back around. "Both our children deserve more. Do you remember, once upon a time, I said someday you were going to beg me to marry you? And I said I'd say 'yes'."

"So what?" Emer looked away.

"I'm only realising now that that is never going to happen," he said quietly.

"Too right it's never going to happen." Emer found

herself digging the knife in further, more out of stubborn pride than anything else. Her anger stifled the complex feelings she had for William, which she had never been able to qualify.

"In that case, Emer . . ." He leant forward and gently turned her face towards him. "I'm not going to hang around any more on the off-chance that you change your mind and realise just how much I love you and you love me."

Emer's relationship with William had never been simple. She had been drawn to him, when everything about him said he was not the one for her. If she had described her ideal man, William wouldn't have figured in any part. And yet, he had a hold on her that she fought daily. He gave her a security that she had never felt at home, but one that, at the same time, irritated and demented her. He wasn't, and never would be, Jack Sheehan.

"Oh, give us a break, William! Don't be so bloody melodramatic!" was Emer's parting response.

That night, while James was sleeping, cuddled next to the foam Volkswagen Beetle his father had bought him, William packed his things into one suitcase and returned to the caravan. Emer watched him leave in his white Hiace van and then, emotionally numb, stared out across the road and over to the expanse of ocean.

* * *

On the other side of the Atlantic, Emer's eldest sister lay in bed, unable to sleep. The past week had been difficult for her. Dermot and herself had argued a great deal, mostly about whether or not to return home. Combined with that, Kitty was anxious about her unborn baby. He hadn't done his usual somersault for the past twenty-four hours. She had played her Bruce Springsteen CD over and over all afternoon, but still no reaction.

Kitty hadn't shared her concern with Dermot, because throughout the pregnancy so far, she had been prone to paranoia. Before the lumps in her breasts, there had been scares that she'd eaten the wrong kind of food, or that the baby was lying too high or too low or that she'd exposed him to subway fumes.

And anyway, since his revelation about his past life, Kitty felt less inclined to share anything with Dermot. So, she lay in bed watching CNN, with the volume turned down, on the small portable television in the corner of the room. Her left hand rested on her stomach, wishing and praying for movement. But the baby remained still. Dermot lay beside her, equally motionless. He was not long in from his shift in the bar and while Kitty pretended to sleep, he had undressed, crept in beside her, kissed her stomach and then rolled over and fallen fast asleep. Kitty timed the whole thing by the alarm clock on her bedside cabinet – three minutes in total. But even in that short time, he had managed to irritate her somehow.

'Please, kick,' Kitty whispered to her baby and then carefully prodded where she guessed it would be. When she got no reaction, she poked harder and called louder 'Kick, will you?' but still nothing happened. She managed to disturb Dermot slightly and he groaned 'What's that? Who's that?' before falling back to sleep, not waiting for any answers.

Kitty glanced down at Dermot, then at her bump and finally around her tiny bedroom and the furniture they had bought second-hand. 'Was this it?' she thought to herself. 'Is this the best I can do?' She thought back to the hopes she had with Jack Sheehan, choosing to skip over how the relationship had ended. She then thought of the promising future she felt she had with Matt Edwards, also editing out how that relationship had ended. She realised that she had never taken the time to qualify her feelings for the man sleeping beside her. They had drifted into a partnership and that drift had lasted seven years. She had never, in all that time, asked herself the question: 'Do you love this man?' And even now, she gave it no further thought, deciding to save it for another time.

Right now, her focus was on the uncomfortable bump that made it impossible for her to lie on her front or her back. Moving from her left to her right side was a major manoeuvre and usually announced by Dermot making the beeping sound of a reversing juggernaut.

She turned her focus to the television in the corner of the room, in the hope of distracting herself from her chaotic thoughts. The news studio looked to be in turmoil and the heavily made-up newsreader appeared to be crying. At first Kitty found it difficult to pick up the pieces of the story that had obviously just broken. There were lots of shots of a shiny black car and a road tunnel. She struggled with the lip-reading for a further few minutes before turning up the volume. Dermot slept on.

"*News in from the hospital is that Princess Diana did not survive the car accident . . .*" The newsreader struggled to continue the announcement and paused for a moment, as did Kitty as she felt herself hover in the void of shock and disbelief. It was the middle of the night in New York and she felt that she was the only person, that side of the

Atlantic, hearing the awful news. The darkness of the room and the feeling of being all alone intensified her emotions.

While Kitty's outward facial expression was of disbelief, on the inside Kitty's baby kicked her. She instantly, with some essence of guilt, overflowed with joy and relief.

\* \* \*

Emer Farrell, who still had no interest in the world around her and had no notion of listening to the news, busily washed her bedding and cleared away any sign that William Todd had once been a part of her life.

# Chapter 45

Yet again, Emer was having difficulty with breast-feeding. 'How could I be built for anything but?' she thought, looking down at her huge, engorged breasts. At last she had a moment's peace and quiet and she was going to give the feeding another go. Her afternoon visitors were all away and the room was serene. Her father had paid for her to have a two-bed, private room. They couldn't quite stretch to a completely private room, but with the curtain around her, Emer felt relatively secluded. She had heard the nurses bring a new mum in to the bed beside her, but she guessed from the silence that the woman must now be sleeping.

Emer's son Luca was two days old and had so far only managed to feed whenever the midwife deftly manoeuvred Emer's nipple straight into his hungry mouth. But Emer was determined to do it by herself, this time. Her milk supply had only just fully come in and she felt that her breasts were on fire. She unbuttoned her Marks and Spencer's pink cotton pyjama top, which perfectly matched the dressing-gown, slippers, toilet-bag and towel on the chair beside her bed. She undid her maternity bra, that to her annoyance was already stained with milky patches, and lifted Luca to her nipple. He greedily sucked around and to the side, which was agony for his mother. Eventually, after several attempts to reposition him, Emer felt that her son had latched on correctly and she relaxed her shoulders and closed her eyes. But when she looked down again, she realised that Luca had worn himself out with the battle and had fallen back to sleep.

She waited for a moment, staring down at his tiny head, nestled into her exposed breast and ran her finger over his ebony curls. There was no way that William was going to get to name this child: he was very much the mirror image of his mother.

William and her father had taken James off to McDonald's for a celebratory treat and Heather had gone to stock up Emer's fridge for the baby and mother's impending arrival home the next day. Emer wasn't too enamoured of the thought of James staying with William in his caravan overnight, but she knew she would need the rest when she got home and James was delighted with the idea.

Emer lifted the sleeping baby up from her bed and gently placed him in his cot beside her. She had been worried that she could never love a child as much as James and with the stress of the pregnancy and with William moving out, she had even more reason for concern. But her worries had been for nothing. The moment the midwife placed her son, still attached by the umbilical cord, in her arms, she was in love.

William had been there at the birth, which initially she thought would be weird, but when it came to the delivery she was inwardly very grateful. For the few seconds when they both looked at their son for the first time, all the animosity and hatred that existed between them had gone. It didn't take too long to return, but Emer knew that she would savour the moment forever.

Emer lay back down on the bed, hopeful of grasping a few minutes' sleep, before her baby woke up even hungrier. She stared at her son through the transparent cot. Behind the curtains she could hear the new mother stir. They must have taken her baby to the nursery so that she could rest, Emer thought, with a hint of satisfaction that she was now experienced in all things maternity.

"Where's my baby?" the woman quietly groaned as she began to wake.

Emer immediately recognised the voice and, as quick as her stitches would allow, she hopped off her bed and pulled across the dividing curtain.

"Kitty?" Emer gasped.

"Emer?" Kitty was struggling to support herself with her arms. Her long, sleek hair was pushed to one side and a zebra-skin dressing-gown was tied in a knot above her still enlarged and bloated stomach. "Where's my daughter?"

"Don't worry – they'll just have taken the baby to the nursery." Emer helped her sister to sit up. "I'll buzz the nurses for you."

The midwife swiftly answered the call and reassured Kitty by saying she would go and fetch her daughter for her.

Emer sat down on the bed beside the sister she hadn't seen or spoken to in twelve years and reassured her that her baby would be fine.

"What's her name?" Emer asked tenderly.

"Niamh." The trace of anxiety was still evident in Kitty's slightly Americanised twang. "And where's your baby?"

Emer went and wheeled her tiny son over. Kitty burst into tears.

"What's his name?" Kitty was trembling.

"Luca." And then Emer followed suit and also began to weep.

The flooding hormones weren't the only influencing factor on the two sisters' uncontrollable sobbing.

The midwife did not know what to make of the situation, when she returned with Kitty's baby.

"Is everything OK?" she asked, passing a box of tissues around.

"Aye."

"Aye."

Both sisters blubbered.

Kitty was still numb from her caesarean and couldn't move her legs, so Emer wheeled the sleeping Niamh over beside her mother and then wheeled her own son over beside his cousin. The sobs reduced as the proud mothers stared down at their sleeping babies, who could have easily been mistaken for twins. Their mothers, however, looked very different. Emer's excess weight had aged her somehow, and her slightly old-fashioned bob and dabs of blue eye-shadow added ten more years to her thirty-one. Kitty, even after childbirth, was still heavily made-up, with pencil-thin eyebrows and long polished fingernails decorated with fake diamonds.

They hadn't seen each other in all those years and yet the silence they enjoyed while looking from cot to cot felt both comfortable and natural. They were in no hurry to speak, since at this moment neither had any interest in their pasts. How could they, when their futures lay right there, in front of them?

"Jesus, what a shock, Kitty! I thought you were still in New York." Emer eventually ventured the first shot across the bow, whispering as she spoke.

"We came back two months ago." Kitty lay back down. "We've been staying with Dermot's parents."

"And where's Dermot now?" Emer quietly asked, flicking through and inspecting the labels on her sister's pile of baby-clothes on the cabinet beside them.

"I sent him back home to get some sleep. I was in labour for ten hours before they decided to give me a caesarean. He looked more knackered than I did." Kitty gave a wry smile. "Where's your fella?"

"He's not my fella any more," Emer answered flatly.

"Aw, Emer!" Kitty was lost for words.

"But right now he's taking care of James." Emer diverted her attention to the assorted selection of disinfecting-wipes and bottles of sterilisation fluids on Kitty's bedside cupboard.

"And how is the wee lad, Emer? I bet he's as proud as punch with his new brother."

"Oh, Kitty, he's just so – so gorgeous!" Emer gushed and her eyes danced. "He's so grown-up! Wait until you see him!"

"I can't wait." Kitty smiled.

"And our Heather, what a change in her. And Dad . . ." Emer paused.

Suddenly, the carefree chit-chat felt false and contrived to both women. The happy-family act didn't wash any more. The surreal comfort zone of a few minutes ago had been transgressed as both sisters felt themselves being dragged into the real world. Their problems had to be addressed.

Emer's first thoughts were to return to her bed and yank the curtain closed behind her. Kitty's were much the same. But neither moved, frozen by the sense of their own personal injustices.

"How could you have had an affair with Jack?" Kitty felt her injustice had first priority.

"It wasn't an affair." Emer stood up and paced around Kitty's bed, almost flaunting the fact that her sister couldn't move. "Well, I suppose it was. He was married. But I didn't know about you and him."

"He never told you?" Kitty moved her head from side to side, as she followed her sister with her eyes.

"Never."

"You never discussed his previous relationships?" Kitty didn't sound too convinced.

"No. Did you?"

"No," Kitty answered under her breath.

"Well, then. I wasn't interested in his past." Emer's pacing now reflected that of the expectant fathers out in the corridor.

"Neither was I," Kitty said softly. "Will you stop moving?" She rubbed her sore neck.

"Come to think about it, Kitty, all that sneaking around and not telling anybody – I thought it was to do with protecting me. But it was his wife he was hiding from."

"I guess so." Kitty appeared subdued, but then abruptly lifted herself up from her pillow, supporting her upper body with her arms. "Why did you let Dad just cut me off like that? Why didn't you tell him that it was your own example you were following, and not mine?" Now Kitty was angry. "Why did I have to take the blame for the whole thing?"

Emer began to pace again, but caught her sister's annoyed look and stopped at the foot of the bed.

"I was happy to be the eldest sister, Dad's golden girl," she confessed. With an apologetic tone, she then added, "You were always the favourite and it was my turn." She paused and, when she saw Kitty was about to hit back, she rushed on with, "OK, I was jealous too. Jealous that everything I had, you had before me – even Jack. I did love him, you know, and it took me a long time to get over it. If I got over it at all." Emer glanced across at her new son. "I still haven't found a man who could come close to Jack . . ."

"Neither have I," Kitty interrupted angrily, eager to snatch back the high ground of the argument, even if physically she was stuck with the low, "and I couldn't even go to his funeral. At least you had that to yourself!"

"Aye, right – me and his wife remember? Can you imagine how I felt when she lectured me on what she discovered in Jack's coat pockets – in front of the priest?"

"What did she find?" Kitty calmed down, slightly. "I can't think what I may have given him. I never had any money. The only thing I ever gave him were . . . poems . . . we used to write each other poems." For a moment Kitty enjoyed a bubble of nostalgic, romantic recall and smiled to herself.

"So did we." Emer thrust a pin in the bubble.

"But ours were very passionate." Kitty defended the memory.

"So were ours. Quite pornographic really." Emer also

smiled at the memory, but hers was more hard-core than romantic.

"So, he kept the poems from both of us – in his pocket. Stupid bugger! He was just asking to be caught," Kitty concluded, sensing for the first time how petty and insignificant it could all have been to him.

"Kitty, it was all a game to Jack Sheehan. It was all just a titillating game. Maybe he was just bored. That's why he enjoyed playing two sisters off one another and that's why he was killed pretending to race the Northwest 200. He was bored and we were young and stupid."

But to the Farrell sisters, Jack's personal dissatisfaction had caused a rift that lasted twelve years. Emer walked back around the bed and sat back down beside her sister. She ran her fingers through the side of Kitty's flattened hair and loosened the strands.

"I'm sorry, Kitty," Emer said firmly, with uncharacteristic sincerity.

"So am I, Emer." Kitty was just as eager for the rift to be healed. "So what you're saying is that only one of my sisters really cheated on me." Kitty smiled, enjoying having her hair played with. "Well, that's a start."

"What are you talking about? Our Heather could never cheat on anybody –"

"No, I couldn't," interrupted Heather, feeling a fleeting awkwardness at having to break the intimacy before her. She just overheard the end of her sisters' conversation as she arrived at the door to the room, laden down with toiletries and a bunch of lilies for Emer. She had long since forgiven her sister for the broken nose, partly because she blamed the violent reaction on Emer's hormones and partly due to what she saw as an improvement in her profile. Which, when combined with her slimmer physique and careful attention to what clothes she now wore, resulted in a Heather oozing self-confidence as she swept into the room. "Do you have to bring a baby to this party, or can just any one join in?" She then rushed over and studied the two cots.

"She's Kitty's – 'Niamh'," Emer answered Heather's perplexed expression. "Isn't she just gorgeous?"

"They are both absolutely beautiful!" Heather was finding the situation hard to compute: first, Kitty, then the scene that greeted her of Emer de-tangling Kitty's hair and thirdly, the two babies lying beside each other.

"Where have you been, Kitty?" First things first, Heather decided. "I looked for you all over the place after we got your letter. You got it all wrong, you know."

"If I did, why was Matt Edwards with you?" First Jack and then Matt – Kitty began to feel swamped, but she was determined to sort things out. If only she could get up and move about! "Why did Dad say he was your boyfriend? Why the big secret?"

Emer made way on the side of Kitty's bed for Heather, who took up the position readily. This was one of the Two-Chair exercises that she had already rehearsed.

"The big secret was nothing more sinister than Matt and myself trying to reconcile you and Dad before your wedding. Matt was over to try and persuade the old bugger to come over to England." Heather took a breather. "He was trying to befriend Dad first – show Dad that he could be both a soldier and a nice bloke. Dad just got it all wrong about me and Matt – that's all. We never got a chance to explain it to

366

him. He never was very trusting of his daughters' relationships with men." There, she had said it all, exactly as it happened and word perfect with the rehearsed script.

Kitty was left speechless. She could see Emer over Heather's shoulder, nodding her head in agreement with all that their youngest sister had said.

"So," Kitty managed to say, "Matt wasn't cheating on me?"

"No," Emer interjected Heather's answer.

"He was just trying to patch things up between Dad and me?" Each word Kitty uttered distressed her.

"That's all," Emer interrupted again.

Niamh woke up. Obviously from the roar escaping from her lungs, she had recovered from the trauma of her birth and was ready to be fed. Kitty didn't hear her. Her thoughts were far away. She had married a man who not only was not what she had first suspected but also, she now painfully knew, had been a hurried substitute for another. And this other man had been mistakenly accused and rejected. Had she just given birth to the wrong man's child?

*Kitty, 1998*

# Chapter 46

After only one call to the AA, Emer and Heather made it to Belfast, in one piece. They were thankful, however, that later that night they would be getting a bus, rather than driving back to Portstewart. Kitty and Dermot's new home was in the university area of the city and when Emer and Heather eventually found the right house, they discovered three other clapped-out Volkswagen Beetles dotted along the street.

"Maybe this is like an elephant graveyard for Beetles," Emer joked.

For the first time, William was looking after both James and Luca for the weekend, as so far Emer hadn't been apart from her youngest son for more than a few hours. A full hour of the journey had gone before Heather managed to persuade her sister to talk about something other than new teeth, nappy rash and mushed-up banana. After the birth, Emer was becoming more like her old self, only with a hint of sadness around the edges.

As the two sisters pulled up in the car, Kitty greeted them at the door, with Niamh balanced against her hip.

The purpose of the visit was to return Merlin to his first owner within the Farrell family.

"Oh, girls, what have you done to him?" Kitty was disappointed. "He was never in that state when I gave him to you! He was pristine." She patrolled around the car, inspecting every badly welded patch and flash of rust.

"He was a pristine piece of shit!" Heather laughed as she rammed the car door shut, for what she hoped would be the last time.

The door didn't close properly and Heather had to slam it closed a second time. Emer was already in through the front door.

Once Niamh had been cuddled and passed around by her aunts, Emer then inspected Kitty's new house from top to bottom – giving decorating and storage advice as she went. She had a few tips on home energy and couldn't resist switching off Dermot's PC in the boxroom and the light in the bathroom.

"Where's Dermot?" Emer asked, this time checking if the freezer needed defrosting.

"He's at work." Kitty was busy making tea. "He'll be back later on. I've badgered him into taking Niamh up to the Botanic Park when he gets back."

"Does he still not travel too well?" Emer asked, hacking away at the packed ice in the freezer with a knife.

"Need you ask? I don't know what's got in to him. I can hardly get him out of the house these days. He goes to work and comes home again. That's it. It's as if he's frightened of it not being here when he gets back." Kitty dipped one teabag in and out of three mugs of hot water.

"And how's the new job working out?" Heather enquired, playing hobby-horses with her niece at the kitchen table.

"Great. I hardly ever get to see him." Kitty poured in the milk.

Emer and Heather laughed, but Kitty didn't. She put the three mugs on the table, along with a plate of peanut-butter sandwiches and, with Niamh still on Heather's knee, she began to play "Round and Round the Garden", on her daughter's palm.

Dermot had got a job managing the Queen's University bar. When he wasn't working, Kitty often worked a few hours there, while he took care of Niamh. The pay wasn't enough to afford a childminder, so Kitty squeezed in some extra hours whenever Dermot was at home. This suited her.

When Niamh went upstairs for her afternoon nap, Kitty got out a bottle of Pimms, some lemonade and a box of Pringles and took them out to her backyard. This was a small concrete yard but, being a sun-trap, she had managed to grow luscious pots of vibrant fuchsias, ferns and jasmine there. This was Kitty's little oasis, where she could imagine she was a mile down the road in the upper-class part of South Belfast. She had two sun-loungers, which were commandeered by Emer and herself. Heather made do with a row of upturned crates, with cushions along them. The August sun was trapped within the red-bricked yard and Emer and Heather gladly accepted the ice-cool drink, but declined the crisps.

"You two are desperate. What is it this week?" Kitty lay back on the lounger and rested her arms behind her head.

"The cabbage soup diet," Heather answered.

"Just don't stand downwind of us," Emer instructed.

Whatever diet they were on, it really suited Heather. For the first time, ever, the Farrell sisters were all the same dress-size, technically. But, practically, they each had their own interpretation of what that was. Heather was back down to a size fourteen, but, just in case her weight-loss was short-lived, she still would sometimes buy a size sixteen. Today, for the first time, she was wearing a pair of jeans and a tight, low-cut T-shirt, again for the first time. She had managed to keep up her regular hairdressing appointments and now had a few damson highlights.

Emer's weight loss was less dramatic than her sister's but she had lost the bulk of her pregnancy weight-gain and now was battling with the pre-pregnancy stuff. Her body frame slid between a size twelve and fourteen, but her clothes were always a size ten. She had moved away from the temporary 'mumsy-look' and was back with the short spiky hair and modern fashions – hence today's tight, khaki combat trousers, worn together with a matching, boob-crushing, sleeveless blouse.

Kitty's body shape had changed considerably since the birth of her daughter. She could still legitimately fit into a size fourteen, but her body distribution had undergone seismic shifts. There was now little difference between her hip and waist measurements and both were literally overshadowed by huge breasts. Animal-patterned prints were still her first choice in clothes and when not available, anything that looked more expensive than it actually was would do. As she now licked the salt from the crisps off her fingers, she was slightly envious of her sisters' far more slender proportions.

"OK, give us the recipe to the soup. But the ingredients will all have to be organic." Kitty thus joined the dieting treadmill. And as they exchanged low-calorie recipes, the three sisters lay down and bathed in the mid-afternoon sunshine – with their chests forming the peaked outline of the Pyrenees.

"Go on, tell her." Emer couldn't stay still for very long and was the first to sit up and break the contour of the mountain range.

"Tell me what?" Kitty was the next to sit back up.

"Kitty . . ." Heather remained motionless.

"Aye?"

"Are you in a good mood?"

"Why?" Kitty wasn't going to make it easy for her youngest sister.

"Are you?" Heather was still laid flat.

"Aye, considering." Now Kitty was finding Heather as irritating as when she was twelve.

"Considering what exactly?" Heather eventually sat upright, with the impression of the crate on her T-shirt and, no doubt, her skin.

"Considering you're doing my head in." Kitty threw the now empty crisp-tube over at her sister. "Why do you want me in a good mood?"

"I've got something for you." Heather teased. "You know I've got a full-time job now, as a drama-therapist with the local health board?"

"I don't need any therapy."

"No, nothing to do with that. It means I've got a bit more money than usual and –"

"And you want to give me some?" Kitty interrupted.

"And me?" Emer wasn't going to be left out.

"No. With Dad having to take early retirement with that bad chest of his, I bought him a wee computer." Heather mimed typing on a keyboard. "Nothing fancy, just your basic stuff. You know, give him something to do"

"So. What's that got to do with me?" Kitty asked moodily.

"Mother of God, Heather. Get on with it," Emer butted in, with her exasperation branded on her face. "Dad's got a computer. He's now on the internet and he wants your e-mail address so he can contact you. That's all. No great shakes. You give us your e-mail, we'll give it to him. End of story. Any more Pimms?" Emer tipped her glass upside down to emphasise that it was empty.

"Hang on a minute," Kitty said sharply. "What have you two been saying to him?"

"Nothing," replied Heather, hesitantly.

"We told him you were both daft eejits and he's got a granddaughter here who needs a doddering granda," Emer answered, already bored with a conversation that had nothing to do with her, or the shopping.

"Emer!" Kitty barked back. "Don't get me started on this."

"What?" Emer yawned. "So, he's a daft bugger. But you can't not talk to him forever!"

"Do you forget everything that he put me through? And us, what we all went through? Why we're outsiders and why we'll always be?" Kitty sat at the edge of her lounger, in order to stand up, but was almost crushed when the chair bent in two. The Farrells had yet to master dramatic exits.

"What's he done, Kitty?" Heather interrupted sharply. She felt that she could no longer tolerate her big sister's small-mindedness. "Aye, you've still stuff to sort out about Jack Sheehan, but surely you're not still embarrassed about Dad. Have you not grown out of that silly nonsense?"

"Of course I'm not embarrassed," Kitty answered sulkily. She was not used to being put in her place by Heather.

"We're different from everybody else because of what we have on the inside," Heather continued. "That's all. We're in our thirties, but we still haven't sorted out stuff from our teens. And you, Kitty, you're not that much different from the stubborn wee bitch who got a Volkswagen Beetle for her eighteenth birthday and didn't even say 'thank you'."

Kitty tried to argue back, but she couldn't. She eventually managed to stand and then occupied herself dead-heading her flowers. After a few seconds, with a handful of crushed petals in her hand, she had the courage to say what she honestly felt.

"He probably just wants to tell me what a disappointment I am to him – no money, no career, married to a dead-beat."

"Look, Kitty," Emer decided to take up the mantle, "if anyone's going to be a disappointment, it's going to be me – two kids and no boyfriend, let alone a husband." Now that she said it, Emer didn't like how it sounded.

"That's right," Heather agreed.

"And what about you, Heather?" Emer was none too pleased with her youngest sister's speedy agreement.

"Well, I know I had a shaky start, but I've got terrific career prospects," Heather enthused. "I'm saving up to move in with Tommy . . . What's the look for, Emer?"

"What look?" Emer joined Kitty by the plants, but began to remove the heads of the still healthy buds.

"I know the look. What's that all about?" Heather asked.

"Well . . . Tommy?" Emer shrugged her shoulders.

Kitty was happy to stay in the background for a while, steering Emer away from her most precious plants. She had a lot to think about.

"What?" Heather persisted.

"He's hardly something to shout about from the rooftops about, is he?" said Emer.

"I thought you liked him." Heather, for a rare moment, took her rightful position as the baby of the family and pouted her lips.

"I did, but then that was when my judgement was flawed. Sure, I even liked William then. There's something odd about that fella of yours."

"Aye, that's true," Kitty agreed and then instantly regretted involving herself again.

"He gets on great with your Dermot," Heather defended herself, as she sat up on the lounger, with Kitty and Emer buzzing around her like irritating wasps.

"And that's in his favour?" Kitty stopped buzzing.

"What's odd about a man who buys me flowers, who opens doors for me and who treats me with respect?"

"Nothing . . . but then should you trust a man whose belt is just below his boobs? That's all I'm saying on the matter." Kitty turned away and hid her smile.

"And a fine set they are too." Emer laughed openly. "And we should know."

"Look, Heather, for one thing, he was the one who got you to part with Merlin – bad karma!" Emer chuckled.

"But I gave him back to you and you didn't want him either." Heather now began to see the funny side of the farce.

"Because I don't believe in that new-age rubbish any more, that's why."

"So," Kitty interjected abruptly, "is that the only reason I'm getting Merlin back, because you two have had enough of him? I'm his last resort?"

The three sisters sat back down on their sun-beds, not knowing exactly who was in the wrong, but sure it wasn't them. The sun had travelled right across the sky above them and now only the far corner of the tiny yard was still bathed in sunlight. The three sisters began to clear away the lounges, glasses and dead flower-heads.

"Cillian – now he was the man for you, Heather." Emer's confrontational recess was over.

"Jesus, Mary and Joseph, Emer! You don't give up, do you? You never even met the guy!" Heather rolled her eyes.

"I know, but if I did, I would like him."

"Who's Cillian when he's at home?" Kitty asked, carrying the last empty glass inside.

Emer enjoyed going to great lengths to explain that the problem with Cillian was that he was never at home. In fact, he had vanished without a trace. While she told the story, Heather washed the dishes from lunch and Kitty cleared the table. Emer was about to dry the soapy dishes, but Kitty stopped her with something about 'rinsing' and 'germs on the tea-towel'.

"And when did you last try and find this guy?" Kitty asked, mildly amused by the mystery.

"I'm happy with Tommy." Heather was more serious.

"I bet you tried as recently as last week," Kitty joked.

"OK, I tried on the Internet last night," Heather confessed. "Just out of curiosity, nothing more. I went into a search engine and found out that there is a lovely C Harte who's a drag artist in Coventry. I'm not even going to tell you what the 'C' stands for."

"Could that be him?" Emer asked.

"I'm not even going to answer that one." Heather flicked suds in her sister's direction.

"You say this guy was in Magilligan, Heather? Does Tommy know what happened to him?" Kitty asked.

Heather didn't answer.

"You haven't mentioned this to Tommy, have you?" Kitty concluded.

"How could I?" Heather stared at her reflection in one of the soapy glasses.

"You could turn down his volume and get a word in edgeways for a change." Emer was never far from the action and always ready to light the fuse. The Farrells were never short of ammunition.

Heather took up the defence. "You've some need to talk, Emer! You never shut up talking about the biggest load of nothing."

"She has a point there," Kitty agreed.

"Talk about calling the pot black!" Emer looked gobsmacked. "You've been living in Belfast five months, Kitty, and you already have the accent of a middle-class, Proddy housewife."

"At least when I talk, it's about something more than the quality of a particular washing-up liquid!" Kitty took the offensive.

"Aye, how many types of germs there are," said Emer. "So much more intellectually stimulating!"

The bickering was flying from all sides, as the Farrell

sisters appeared to be making up for lost time. They each fought their own corner with passion and there was a sense that they were enjoying the emotion and, to a large extent, the honesty.

"And while we're at it . . ." Emer inhaled a quick gulp of air, before continuing with, "don't you come anywhere near my boys with those clippers of yours. Just look what you've done to poor old Dermot's hair!"

"And what does 'poor old Dermot' mean?"

"You tell me. You're the one who treats him like something yucky stuck to your shoe." Emer pretended to wipe something off the sole of her sandal.

"And you know how to treat a man, do you?"

"Jack Sheehan never had any complaints." Emer mimicked her sister's phoney accent.

"Why should he," answered Kitty, "with you throwing it at him?"

Heather pulled both her sisters by the ear, and sat them down at the kitchen table. The foam on her hands gave the ears Spock-like tips. She disliked always having to take the motherly role, but somebody had to. She had to drum some sense into them.

"Jack Sheehan's dead, finished, finito." She sat down beside them. "Move on, please. Both of you."

"What? Like you've done?" Emer sulked.

Emer, Kitty and now Heather fumed again, in silence – laden with their emotional heavy baggage (rucksacks and stuffed donkeys included).

"Here's Dad's e-mail address." Heather broke the stalemate by pulling out a crumpled piece of paper from her jeans' pocket and handing it over to Kitty. "If you want to use it, use it. If you don't . . ." Heather paused and searched for the right words. "He's made the first move, Kitty. Are you big enough to make the second?"

"Since when did you start writing scripts for soap operas?" Kitty smiled at her baby sister.

"Since you became an ass," Emer answered for Heather.

The cathartic abuse continued for the rest of the afternoon. The bottle of Pimms, followed by a couple of bottles of wine which Dermot brought back from the bar a little later, didn't help. He got back from work just as his daughter was waking up from her nap and agreed, for both their sakes, to escape to the park.

Half an hour later and, according to Emer, Kitty was 'still an ass', but now this was not just because of her stubbornness, but also the size of her backside. Her point was proven when they dusted chalk on the back of their trousers and then measured the residue when they each sat down on the kitchen floor. Heather had given up on trying to retrieve the situation, as more often than not her good intentions were thrown straight back at her.

"OK, if I were so stubborn, Emer, would I do this?" Kitty got up from the floor, dusted off the chalk and marched upstairs towards the boxroom on the first floor. Emer was two steps behind and Heather followed at the back.

Kitty spent a few minutes fiddling with buttons on Dermot's computer, trying to make it start. Emer, who hadn't handled the alcohol too well, pressed any button she could find. Eventually, Heather was the one to spot the problem and switched the mains on, where Emer had switched them off when they first arrived.

Kitty launched Outlook Express and from the scrap of

paper Heather had given her, typed in her father's e-mail address, followed by –

*Dad*

*I understand that u r trying to contact me. Why?*

She let her finger hover above the 'send' button, but Emer jumped in and pressed it for her.

"Emer!" Kitty shouted.

"What?" Emer couldn't see the problem.

"There was other stuff I was going to say." Kitty stared at the 'message sent' notice.

"Like what?" Heather asked, slamming closed a desk-drawer that Emer had begun to pry into.

But Kitty didn't have an answer. That was it, done. Suddenly she didn't feel quite so tipsy.

"I'll probably never hear back from him anyway. Good riddance!"

Then, as Kitty went to log off, the *'You Have Mail'* sign flashed. She opened the message.

*Hello Kitty*

*It is good to hear from you. How is Belfast? Is it a nice day? The weather here is beautiful. Too many wasps though.*

*Dad*

Kitty quickly typed in a one-line response.

*Fuck the wasps. What do you want?*

She pressed the send button, before either of her sisters could stop her.

"Kitty!" Both Emer and Heather shouted as they tried to grab their sister's hand.

"If he thinks I'm going to pretend like nothing has happened, he's got the wrong daughter."

"What's that supposed to mean?" Emer protested.

"Aye." Heather's protest was less vehement.

Before another fight could ensue, the *'You Have Mail'* icon flashed again.

But this time Kitty was slower to press the button. She was fearful of getting the answer that she sought. She took a deep breath and then eventually pressed the *'Read Mail'* button. The message was from a porn site, which she had been getting regular junk mail from, ever since she'd input "Brad Pitt + naked" into a search engine.

Initially, the three sisters were all relieved that it wasn't their father – but then they were each disappointed.

"Oh, Kitty, Dad's an old man. Maybe, it's just taking him a while to type," Heather consoled. "Wait a minute or two."

The sisters waited for half an hour, but no return message.

When Dermot drove Emer and Heather to the bus station later that night, Kitty went back upstairs and checked her messages. There was nothing. She read Niamh a bedtime story about princesses and when Dermot hastily returned from the station, he read a story about dragons and wizards. When Niamh was safely asleep and Dermot back out to work on his evening shift, Kitty checked her messages one last time. Nothing.

She sat down to watch the nine o'clock news with a cup of black coffee and a slice of dry toast. She was starving, as well as miserable, but determined not to be outdone by Emer and Heather. But the hunger and the self-pity immediately evaporated as she turned up the volume to hear the news headlines.

*"At 3.10 this afternoon there was a car-bomb explosion in Omagh town centre. The figures have not yet been confirmed, but 29 people, plus two unborn babies, are feared dead."*

Kitty watched the rest of the news in a trance. It had taken becoming a mother herself to finally gain some understanding of the reality of the world she lived in. Her romantic notions of what Dermot could have been suddenly made her feel immature and stupid. This was not what she had brought her family home for.

She raced back upstairs to Niamh's room to check that she was OK. Then her next thought was her e-mails. She quickly scrambled a message together.

*Dad*

*This is all so petty. There are mothers, fathers, grandparents and children out there right now, grieving over their brutal losses. And you can't bear to talk to me because I disappointed you once – and still disappoint you.*

But Kitty didn't get the chance to send her message, because before she could finish it, the 'You Have Mail' icon flashed. At the very same time, somebody else out there had a notion to contact her. She opened the message.

*Kitty*

*I'm sorry it's taken me this long to get back to you. You are right, Kitty – so what if there's too many wasps. Can you find it in your heart to let an old fool back into it? Life's too short and I've wasted too much of it already. Does your daughter like old wrecks? I hope so, because maybe she'll welcome me, as well as Merlin.*

*The Farrell Sisters, Present Day*

# Chapter 47

Unlike her sisters, Emer O'Kane wasn't surprised to see the unexpected visitor waiting at the front door. They each looked through the front window at the figure in the doorway and then one by one looked away from the man, to check down the footpath and out onto the road. Seeing the figure had brought very different, contrasting sensations to each of the three sisters.

Since Emer was the one who had made contact and persuaded the mysterious guest to visit today, she felt inwardly satisfied that her scheming had come to fruition. She hadn't, however, expected to recognise the man – but she did, though she couldn't quite work out where from. She went to open the door, while the other two remained at the window.

"Cillian Harte."

"I'm Emer," Emer greeted Cillian coolly. "I'm Heather's older sister. Well, not much older . . . her sister, anyway. Thank you for coming. Come on in."

Heather didn't move from the window. Her low-cut T-shirt and her exposed breasts, heaving and panting, more than made up for her facial lack of emotion. So, the figure she had seen crossing the road in the rain that day had been Cillian after all.

He was drenched. He was also unshaven, with his face hidden behind lank, long hair that made wet circles where it lay on his long, grey coat. His awkwardness was evident as he looked down at his feet, staring at worn desert boots with odd laces. The childish sounds of Dermot and Tommy competing against one another on the computer upstairs, were interrupted by a very polite and meek, "Hello."

Cillian went to shake hands with Emer but, before he could, Emer made the connection she was searching for.

"I do recognise you! How could I forget? You were the ringleader in that fight that kept me from getting my son to hospital in an ambulance." Emer left Cillian, with his hand still outstretched and marched over to the empty fireplace. "It's your fault my son nearly died. Why in God's name, Heather, were you so hung up about contacting a low-life like this?"

"Emer!" Kitty interrupted. "This is my home. Please be civil." She shook Cillian's hand. She had been expecting someone else from the past for quite some time now, but she was not too disappointed as she was pleased to meet the man she had heard so much about from Heather.

"I'm sorry about your son, Emer. But I really don't remember any ambulance," Cillian quietly apologised, still unable to look up from his feet.

"That's because you were so bloody pissed," Emer fumed.

"Emer!" Kitty interjected again.

"I am sorry." Cillian made a second attempt, this time lifting his eyes, with long curled eyelashes, up as far as their knee level.

"Come and take a seat, Cillian. I'm Kitty. I've heard a lot about you. Let me take your coat."

Cillian complied and Kitty lifted his coat and spread it out on the radiator. Heather had yet to move away from the window, let alone speak.

Kitty looked over to Heather in an attempt to encourage her to break the silent tension, but when her sister showed no signs, Kitty sat down on the sofa, beside their unexpected guest.

"How did you know we'd be here?" Kitty asked softly.

"Emer phoned my digs. She said she'd been trying to find me for ages – a surprise for Heather or something. But it wasn't until I enrolled on the Fine Art course at Queen's that she managed to track me down on the Internet. You see, Big Brother is watching – or should I say 'Big Sister'." At Cillian's dismally attempted humour, everyone visibly squirmed.

There was an awkward pause.

"Emer, don't you need to give me a hand in the kitchen?" Kitty jumped up from the sofa and made her way over towards the kitchen door.

"No." Emer still had a stony glare and her back to the fireplace.

"Yes, you do," Kitty asserted and manhandled Emer out of the living-room.

Cillian and Heather were alone.

Heather left her place by the window and sat in Kitty's imprint, left behind on the leather sofa. She was pleased that she fitted it exactly. Like her old school-friend, she too sat with her hands on each knee and staring down at the carpet.

"I had no idea Emer was trying to find you, Cillian," she said tenderly. This was not how she had rehearsed her lines for their meeting. She was being forced to improvise.

"Look, if I'm in the way, maybe it's best that I go." Cillian rushed his words.

"Of course you're not in the way."

"Your sister just phoned me last night and said that you'd be here today if . . ." He paused and began to rub his knees along a familiar worn path in the denim.

"If what?"

"If I wanted to catch up with an old acquaintance or something."

Cillian nervously rubbed his knees harder and Heather could see his severely bitten nails and cuticles.

"Maybe, Cillian, we should start this conversation again." She steadied his right hand with her left. But still, neither could bear to look directly at the other. "This is all a bit crazy for me. Let's start as if we've just met each other, walking along the promenade back home."

"OK." Cillian nodded.

"Hi, Cillian! Long time no see!" Heather affected a cheery voice.

"Hi, Heather! What have you been up to?"

"You know, this and that. What about you?"

"Same." Cillian struggled with his lines.

"Great." As did Heather.

But she wasn't content to let it end this way.

"By rights, now we should just say 'see you again some

time'." Heather now looked up and saw that Cillian was already staring across at her. He had that familiar broad smile, more like a boy of twelve than a man of thirty-two. "And then the script would suggest that we kiss on the cheek and wave goodbye."

"By rights, I suppose so." With his pupils fully dilated, Cillian's hazel eyes looked enormous.

"But then . . ." Heather was still holding his hand. "That wouldn't tell me why you didn't finish college and why you just disappeared, only to reappear again in Magilligan prison. And why were you making a clay sculpture of me – which was very good by the way. And now another mystery: why you were being taken to hospital in an ambulance."

"There's a lot of why's." Cillian used his other hand to clear a few damp strands of hair away from his face.

"There sure is," Heather agreed, as she too, subconsciously, twisted one of her own neatly trimmed curls.

"It's OK to feel cool and confident when you're in your home town, a small place like Portstewart." He looked to Heather for agreement. "But when you feel stupid and a complete loser when you're away, it can just spiral. And I guess that's what happened to me in Manchester. I was too stubborn to come home and too weak to stay and make a go of it."

"So, what did you do?" Heather asked, rubbing his knuckles reassuringly.

"Why does anyone go off the rails, get into drugs and drink, steal from people, including their family – just to buy cheap vodka or an ounce of dope?" He took a deep breath and added, grasping for a safety-net, "It's all because my parents made me wear a dress when I was a baby."

"Cillian! Be serious!" Heather nudged him with her shoulder. "Whatever you did, it must have been pretty bad for you to end up in Magilligan."

"I broke into a chemist's and stole prescription drugs. Not very well, I may add, and ended up in hospital with severe blood loss from the broken window. I got my prescription then all right. "

"I see."

"I think the last time I felt truly happy, Heather, was when you flashed your boobs at me in the swimming-pool. I thought I'd died and gone to heaven." Cillian beamed a smile, showing he was in much more confident territory.

Heather stared. "One, I didn't flash them at you, you just happened to be there. And two, if it was so good, why didn't you talk to me for months afterwards?"

"Heather, I waited for you in the café, like we said, and you never appeared. I thought you just weren't interested."

"And Siofra Bones was, was she?" Heather had nothing to lose.

"Who's she?"

"The one you dated for the second half of lower-sixth? The one who had her tongue tangled around your tonsils at the school disco?" Kitty laughed.

"Well, some impression she must have made, because all I remember about that disco was you in your very provocatively torn denims. And don't think I missed you sneaking off the dance floor with Mr All-America. Your first love, was he?"

Heather's smile abruptly vanished and she shook her head. She let go of Cillian's hand and crossed both her arms across her chest.

"Is that it? Did the bastard break your heart and that's why you were crying in your car?" This time he reached over and pulled her hand back.

"Something like that." Heather gave her best performance to date and smiled gently. She had never told anyone about her experience that night. It had never entered her head to tell Tommy. She sensed, however, that even though the time was not right now, here was a man, whom, someday, she would entrust with her secret.

"But life's been good to you since?" he asked in a tone that made her feel that he already knew.

"It has." She didn't have to act the good humour now. "I manage a organisation here in Belfast that brings the arts as a therapy to institutions. You know – like hospitals, prisons, old people's homes, that sort of thing. We do drama, music and art." Heather loved to talk about her work and the passion she felt for it lit up her entire face. "Shirley's even on my team now. Remember her from Magilligan? She's great to work with."

"Are you married?" Cillian searched for the wedding band on the hand he was holding.

"No, but I live with my boyfriend, Tommy." She didn't add that they were going through a rough patch, or more precisely, only half an hour ago she had told him their relationship was over. She preferred the image of herself as the 'confident' and 'successful' Heather and not the one on the periphery of life.

"Good for you." Cillian was once again conscious of his shabby appearance and looked away and back down at his feet. "So, I've come a wee bit late to sweep you off your feet?" he added with a smile of resignation.

"About five years." Now Heather felt nervous too.

Cillian stood up from the sofa and sauntered over to the radiator. He ran his fingers along the white stripes of salt that had formed across the shoulder of his coat, where it was beginning to dry out.

"Do you remember the note I wrote you, Heather? In Magilligan? I said the next time you would see me, I would make everyone around me proud? Well, I'm back at college, I haven't had a drink in four months and I change my underwear at least three times a week. But, I've still a long way to go and I need time to get there." He pulled the damp coat on, then squeezed the buttons down the front closed. "Maybe, the next time you see me, I'll make you proud. I'll be wearing a shirt and tie and driving a BMW." He gave her a playful wink. "But then, don't trust me. I'm a liar."

Heather immediately thought of Tommy's BMW parked outside. He had bought his dream-car with his redundancy money, since there were no prisoners left in Magilligan for him to guard. She thought of his crisp shirts and smart ties. She stood up and followed Cillian to the door.

"You should be proud of yourself, Cillian." She leant forward and kissed him on the cheek. "Isn't this how we said we should part?"

"And we wave goodbye, I get in the car and then you chase after it, begging me to stay," he said, sweeping all of his lank hair away from his face with one hand and turning to leave.

The living-room door opened a few inches with a squeak and then burst open fully.

"Cillian Harte?" Tommy asked haughtily. He stood with his legs as wide apart as possible, in order to take up more space.

"Tommy the Dog-man? This is your Tommy, Heather?" Cillian stepped away from the front door.

"You guys know each other? Of course – Magilligan." Heather opted for the role of the innocent this time.

"Oh, I know Tommy all right." Cillian crossed the room in two huge strides, until he was only a foot away from his ex-guard. "I've the five-inch scar on my leg to show how well I know Tommy, or rather, how well I know his dog."

"You got what you deserved." Tommy backed away slightly.

"I painted your portrait."

"Without my approval." Tommy raced through his words.

"It was art." Cillian pronounced each letter.

"It was insulting," Tommy replied, running each word into one.

"And the guy in the next cell to me, when he wet his bed, was that insulting? Or was letting your dog take a chunk out of him therapy?" The tip of Cillian's nose brushed Tommy's.

Tommy moved away and took up position by the window.

"Don't listen to him, Heather. He's just a drunk and a liar, who wouldn't know what day it was even though it's printed on his dole cheque." He appeared empowered by his new position – a potential escape route – or he was until Cillian followed him and with his left hand squashed his face against the glass. Tommy didn't resist.

"You are right, Tommy," Cillian spat with the finesse of a Shakespearean actor. "I am a drunk and a liar. But at least I fight my own battles. Where's your dog now?"

Tommy involuntarily gave out a tiny yelp.

Cillian let go of Tommy's face and pulled away. He appeared satisfied that Tommy had been punished enough but, as he turned to walk away towards the front door, Tommy hurled one of Kitty's pots of nibbles at the back of his head. The force of the blow sent his victim crashing over the coffee table, sending carrots and Brazil nuts flying around the room.

Emer and Kitty in the kitchen heard the racket and hurried into the living-room. Dermot followed a few steps behind. Everyone, except Tommy (still seeking refuge by the window), helped lift Cillian onto the sofa. He was dazed, but not too badly hurt.

Heather fetched some ice and searched for a wound to apply it to, but Cillian's skull was a maze of old and recent scars. Dermot tried to find out what had happened from Tommy, but he wasn't forthcoming. Kitty was trying to contain Emer who was all set to start vacuuming.

Heather encouraged Cillian to lie back and close his eyes while she applied the ice, wrapped in a tea-towel, to his forehead. She could physically feel Cillian struggle to restrain himself from continuing the fight, as he clenched his knuckles. But this was one place where Cillian didn't want to resort to his old ways.

Heather didn't know what to do. What should she think of Tommy? Ever since she had met him, she had become everything she wanted to be. She was successful with her career, she had become reconciled with her family and was content with the way she looked. But was this because of Tommy, or in spite of him? Even without Cillian's appearance today, she had been asking herself these questions for some time now. Did she truly have control over her life or was she just afforded permission? Did she want to make her own mistakes? Or should Tommy protect her from making a fool of herself, the same way that he protected himself? As the ice-cold water trickled down Cillian's cheek, Heather realised that these were brand-new questions. But above all, did she want to turn the volume up when *she* spoke? There was only one way to find out.

"Tommy, you heard what I said on the way here." She glared at him. "Well, get out! I don't ever want to see you again."

"Heather, sweetheart," Tommy moved towards his girlfriend, adjusting his tie and pulling up his trousers as he did, "see sense."

"Get out! I'll be over to get my things in the morning."

Tommy looked for reinforcements from around the room. There were no signs from any of the Farrell sisters. Dermot was left to escort the dejected shell of the man to the door, comforting him with 'leave it for now' and 'it'll be fine tomorrow'. Tommy didn't look back as he closed the front door behind him.

"I should go." Cillian was a little unsteady on his feet. "I didn't come here to create havoc. I've done that in enough places over the past few years." He turned to Kitty and Emer and added, "I'm sorry" and then to Heather, "Please forgive me."

As he reached for the door handle, Heather jumped up from the sofa and pushed between him and the door. She had to suck in her chest to squeeze past.

"Cillian, you just saved me from a long-drawn-out ending that was on the cards anyway." She smiled. "I always like to get my endings right. It's a drama thing."

"This is where our ending should be the wave goodbye, isn't it?"

Looking over Cillian's shoulder, Heather saw three very puzzled faces staring back.

"I get in the car and then you run after it," Cillian continued, then added with slight embarrassment, "But, I've no car."

"I haven't run in years," said Heather with her own hint of self-consciousness, as she peeked down at her chest, hinting at the reason why running wasn't an option for someone built like she was.

"I'll be back with a set of wheels." He smiled. "Maybe no car, but a set of wheels all the same."

Heather stepped aside from the door and twisted the handle open.

"But, Cillian, you said, 'Don't trust me. I'm a liar'."

Cillian opened the front door wide.

"OK, if a liar says that he won't come back, that means that he will." He waved goodbye to Kitty and Dermot and nodded his head to Emer.

"OK." Heather grinned.

"Then I won't come back." Cillian jumped over the step and darted along the path and out through the front gate. A light rain shower had begun. He appeared determined not to get wet this time. His long, grey coat flapped behind him like wings.

Heather closed the door and rested her back against the dimpled glass.

"I could always take up jogging," she said, beaming at the disbelieving faces of her family.

"By the time that one comes back, you'll be ready for a marathon." As expected, Emer was the first to vent her opinion. Her low expectation was shared by everyone, except Heather.

# Chapter 48

No sooner had Emer volunteered her lack of confidence in Cillian's intentions, than the doorbell rang for a second time. All three sisters were quietly relieved that their father had arrived to bring some order into what was rapidly turning into chaos. The irony that it was their father of all people who would hopefully bring calm was lost on Emer but not on the other two. When Kitty opened the front door this time, yet again their visitor – who was not in fact Roddy Farrell – staggered both Emer and Heather. Kitty wasn't as dumbstruck. This time their visitor was one that she had been responsible for contacting. She was astonished to see him on her doorstep, but nonetheless, she had been expecting him for some time.

Ever since she heard, five years previously, that Matt Edwards had not cheated on her, Kitty had thought of little else. Her relationship with Dermot was loosely tied together with the love for their five-year-old daughter and what shreds she had left of her Catholic faith. But she couldn't escape from the feeling of regret. She had written several letters to Matt's parents and made countless telephone calls, explaining to them how foolish and hotheaded she had been. There was unfinished business there, but now, as Matt stood before her, she didn't know how it was going to end. Right now, she couldn't be sure as to why he had travelled from England to her doorstep. What was Matt's agenda?

"Hello, Kitty."

"Hello, Matt."

He was even more handsome than she remembered. His speckled, turquoise eyes were illuminated by a caramel tan and his black-tar crew cut showed none of the grey splinters that both Kitty and Dermot had. He had also matured from his drainpipe jeans and T-shirt into a casual black suit and white open-necked shirt. Kitty suddenly felt very inadequate.

"What a pleasant surprise, Matt." Even though she was out of practice, Kitty gave her best seductive smile. "Oh, how rude of me. Come in! You know our Heather."

"Hi, Heather." He gave her his obviously very well-practised firm handshake.

Heather nodded and, stuck for words, retreated back over to the sofa, hiding her stomach with a puffed-up cushion.

"This is my other sister, Emer," Kitty continued the introductions.

"We've also met, briefly." Matt stood back and admired the slimmer version of the famous Farrell sisters' physique.

"Aye, briefly in O'Hara Drive." Emer blushed, before she too back-stepped over to the sofa and sat with a folded newspaper over her midriff. "Too brief for my liking," she added flirtatiously, once secure behind Dermot's *Daily Star*.

"And I'm Dermot, Kitty's husband," Dermot interrupted, staking his claim from the fire-place.

"How do you do." Matt was forced to walk across the room, holding out his hand to greet him.

They shook hands. The physical differences between the two men were vast. As were the other differences: the man whose final destination was always home, against the man who wanted to travel the world. Kitty was forced to remember how her immaturity had sent her off for New York, thinking that she was playing a soldier off against a terrorist. How wrong had she been!

She pictured herself now as the heroine in the movies, when the hero returns to claim what once was his. Since leaving Portstewart and going to university, her life had been a catalogue of disasters. She had aspired to make something of herself, but had faltered at every hurdle. Now she had the opportunity to take that leap and to escape from her life — a life that was only an hour away from being that of a camper-van owner. Could this be the chance to start anew and make a different life for her and her daughter?

"We've already had one fight here this afternoon," said Emer by way of providing the catalyst for further drama.

"Emer!" Heather walloped her sister with the cushion.

"What?" Emer fixed her hair again. "Sure, she'd hardly changed her sheets and she was off marrying Dermot." She was determined that if she couldn't sustain a relationship, she would surely cast doubt on all those around her.

"I'm sorry about this," Kitty apologised as she cleared herself a space to sit on the coffee table.

But Kitty wasn't sorry. She was revelling in the situation. There was something empowering about having two men fighting for her. She was again feeling some of the magnetism that she delighted in as a teenager. She was relishing the game.

"Take a seat." Kitty cleared another space besides her. "Can I get you anything to drink?"

"Thanks, but no thanks. I shan't be staying." Matt remained a few steps away from Dermot.

Dermot maintained his position at the point of focus in the room, with his legs straddling the fireplace, as if marking this three foot square as a symbol of his home.

"I just came here so that I could respond to the letters you've been sending to my family, Kitty. I wanted to do it in person." He turned his back on Dermot and faced Kitty directly. "After all – it's been a long time."

"What letters?" Emer began to ask Heather, but she was too busy observing Dermot, who didn't say anything.

"That's very kind of you," Kitty responded to her ex-boyfriend, also very conscious of her husband's stony face behind him.

"Merlin's not in quite the same shape as the last time I saw him." Matt tipped his head towards the window and the view of Merlin's dented roof.

"Are any of us?" Heather offered in an attempt to defuse the tension.

"Speak for yourself. I used to be three stone heavier than I am now, Matt –" Emer's attempt was more an effort to include herself in the conversation.

"Emer! I'm sure Matt hasn't come all this way to hear you rabbit on about yourself," Kitty said sharply.

"Aye, Matt, what have you come here for?" Dermot spoke in a tone that needed little interpretation.

"You have a right to ask." Matt turned so that he could address both Mr and Mrs O'Kane together. "I agree with what Kitty wrote in her letters – there's unfinished business here."

"Look, fella, as far as I'm concerned, it was finished a long time ago." Dermot raised his height and his posture by balancing on his toes. But the harshness in his voice elevated him even higher. "Kitty and you were well finished when I came along. Aye, the marriage was hasty by anyone's standards, but we've twelve years under our belt now – and a daughter to prove it."

The under 'our belt' analogy made Kitty grimace. She wished he could have chosen a more romantic expression.

"I have no beef with you, Dermot." Matt held up his hands, as if he was a cowboy showing that he was unarmed. "This is between Kitty and myself."

"Oh, and you'd like us all to leave the room and let you get on with it, would you?" Dermot appeared poised to pounce as he precariously balanced in front of the fireplace.

Now Kitty was surprised. She had rarely seen Dermot betray any hint of jealousy and, as he now stood as if defending all that he had, she was slightly taken aback.

"No, no," Matt insisted. "No one has to leave. As I said, I'm not staying. What I have to say can be said in front of you all."

Kitty instantly swapped her feelings of confidence and excitement for those of insecurity and apprehension.

"Kitty, you asked me in your letter if I still felt for you the way you still felt for me." Matt stayed positioned between the couple, but turned his head towards Kitty. He appeared relaxed and sure of himself.

"What the fuck?" Dermot roared, himself now glaring in his wife's direction.

"Did you mean that?" Matt asked Kitty, softly.

"Kitty, what are you playing at? Of course she didn't!" Heather interjected, standing up and holding on to Kitty's shoulder, as if nominating herself as her sister's voice of reason.

"I bet she did. Didn't you, Kitty?" Emer stirred from the security of the sofa.

Kitty pulled Heather's hand away, signifying that she could speak for herself. By pulling her long poker-straight tresses down around her, forming a frame around her face, she bought herself some more time to think. She wished that she had put that third coat of mascara on that morning and that she had chosen a skirt rather than leggings.

"Yes, I did," Kitty quietly answered back when she was ready.

She felt invincible.

"That's what I thought," Matt replied with equal gentleness. "So, I've come here today to put an end to this charade you're living." The softness was immediately replaced with what sounded like the start of a shopping list. "First point, Kitty, is get on with your life – and second, leave me to get on with mine."

Dermot retreated back onto the balls of his feet and hung his head down. Heather and Emer mouthed inaudible words, like fish. Kitty too looked like a fish, one gasping for air on the riverbank.

"What are you saying?" Kitty struggled to say. "Don't you see? It was a big mistake all those years ago! If it hadn't been for my stupidity then, we would still be together today."

"No, we wouldn't." Matt was totally restrained.

"Yes, we would," Kitty pleaded.

400

"No, we wouldn't, Kitty. I only agreed to marry you in the first place to stop you nagging me about it. We wanted different things, but we always ended up with what you wanted." His composure was unfaltering as he pointed directly at Kitty's stunned face. "You, Kitty, not me."

"But we were so happy together," she faltered.

"Yes, Kitty, I thought we were. But it wasn't until we split that I realised how much more to life there was." He leaned forward and whispered so that only Kitty could hear. "I was just along for the ride." He then marched across the room, as if on one of his army drills and yanked the front-door open. But before he left, he had one other item on his shopping list. "So, Dermot, you're welcome to her. But do me a favour and stop her pestering my family, will you? Otherwise, I'll have to get a court order."

The door slammed to, and the front-door key in the keyhole (attached to Merlin's ignition keys and three key-rings) slid out and crashed down onto the floor.

# Chapter 49

When Matt Edwards slammed the door on his way out, Kitty didn't move. She couldn't. She looked down at herself from the ceiling, a pitiful, pathetic figure. Her false hopes for Matt had kept her going over the years and now they lay in tatters around her. She had never, ever contemplated that the 'unfinished business' she wrote about would end this way. Even her relationship with Matt had been a lie. Was there anything honest about her left? Kitty looked across at Dermot, who had yet to leave his pivotal position in front of the fireplace. She could feel his pain. He stared down at his feet, his head appearing too heavy for his shoulders. Only now that she felt as desperate as he looked, did Kitty study Dermot as a man and not as her second or even third choice. Only now she realised that as a father and as a husband, he was faultless. Kitty had felt that their relationship had been built on disappointment and false assumptions, but now she could see that it had been built on the bedrock of truth.

"Dermot, I'm sorry," Kitty murmured with the gravity of

knowing her apology was both long overdue and pointless. "Please forgive me. I'm such a fool."

"An ass, actually," Emer squeezed in her contribution from the sofa.

"Emer!" Heather came to the defence. "Maybe it's time we left these two alone."

Emer didn't move, so Heather dragged her to the kitchen by her skinny wrist and closed the kitchen door behind them. Emer pushed a tiny gap back open.

"Come away from there!" Heather ordered, as she looked for something highly calorific in the refrigerator.

"Our Kitty's doing a lot of talking." Emer sat on the tiled floor and peeped through the gap she had left.

"Stop it . . ." She couldn't resist. "What's Dermot doing?"

"He's not doing a lot. Just standing there," Emer whispered, with her nose squished against the door. "He doesn't look very happy."

"Would you?" Heather discovered a box of cheese triangles and began the painstaking process of peeling the silver paper off each one.

"I suppose not."

"What's happening now?"

"Nothing. Hang on a minute. He's moving." Emer moved her eye up and down the gap in an attempt to improve her view. "He's going over to the coffee table . . . and he's sitting on it."

"Beside Kitty?" Heather mouthed the words as she joined her sister on the floor and began to feed her mashed-up chunks of processed cheese.

"Not exactly. He's about as far away from her as you can get. It's a wonder he doesn't fall off." Emer chuckled.

"Shush!"

"Go on, Kitty, turn on the waterworks!" Emer scrunched her face as if she was seriously considering telepathy.

"Is she crying?"

"Not yet. She looks very apologetic . . . oh, she's on her knees. Isn't that a bit too needy? Any more squidgy stuff to eat?"

"Emer! She's trying to save a marriage!"

"Fair point." Emer softened. "But she'd need to start crying soon, or even I'm going to lose interest. Oh, there we go!"

"What now?" Heather tried to see for herself, but Emer wasn't giving up her prime position.

"Wow, our Kitty knows how to lose it!" Emer quietly cheered her eldest sister on. "There's snot and everything going on there. I can't look any more." She abandoned her peepshow and made her way to the kitchen cupboards. "What was that stuff you were feeding me anyway? I hope you didn't find it in Dermot's socks. Is there any more?"

"Emer, have you any idea how serious this is?" Heather gently closed the door shut. She could forgive herself for being an accomplice, but she couldn't spy on her own. "You might be OK, Emer, but I can't see our Kitty as a single parent somehow."

Emer joined the search for anything non-organic and carcinogenic in the cupboards. Today was not one to be calmed with cabbage soup

"Who said anything about being OK?" Emer stopped turning the tins on the shelves so that they faced outwards.

"Well, Emer, you carry on as if nothing's wrong. You're just merry in your own little world."

"Heather, stick to what you know best and leave the advice to others more qualified." Emer slammed the cupboard door. "I don't need any of your therapy." The door bounced open and she slammed it again

"Where the hell did that come from?" Heather asked in disbelief.

"Do you think I don't have problems? The organ-grinders have all had their dramas today and the monkey can just dance, is that it? Do you think I don't think about the bigger picture?"

"Well, if you do, Emer, you hide it well. What have you ever thought of that was any bigger than the big toe of one your pedicure appointments?"

Emer sat down at the kitchen table and stared at the dregs of cold coffee as it began to stain one of Kitty's bleached-white mugs. She leaned her face against her hand and, with the other hand, stabbed her fingers through her mass of short spirals, with each curl remaining upright, defying gravity. The ritual was precise and deliberate and one that Emer had obviously repeated over and over before. The stress in each curl, as it was tugged, was matched only with the stress glaring from her distant gaze.

"The future of my sons?" Emer squashed down one of the curls. "How much I messed up with William?" She pressed down another. "How close we came to being a normal family?" And another. "How much being here today has made me question what I just threw away? And that's just for starters. Why should I need to know about wars in the Middle East, when I've my own bloody battles going on?"

"I'm sorry, I just never . . ." Heather sat down on the table beside her sister and squashed down the few remaining strands of hair herself. She was reminded of her discovery of Kitty and Emer in the maternity hospital and that brief moment when Emer was grooming Kitty's hair. She had envied that intimacy at the time.

"When I woke up this morning, I thought my family would be better off without me," Emer continued, still mesmerised by the abandoned mug of coffee. "I bought a one-way ticket, without a clue as to where I would go next."

"You were planning not to go back to your boys?" Heather tried not to sound too alarmed.

"They're at the age now when their dad's all they want. I came here thinking William would do a better job from now on." Emer bit her lip in an attempt to stop it from trembling. "But, of course, I would never leave them. It was a notion that passed the minute I set out in the bus. It passed as quickly as the hundreds of times I rehearse saying 'Will you marry me?', to William in my bathroom mirror.

"I know you don't have much faith, Emer, but don't give up hope. I know that I will see Cillian again. Dermot and Kitty are going to patch things up and you'll work something out, I'm sure." She put her arms around Emer's shoulders, which had the required calming affect. "Trust me, Emer. I'm a drama therapist." Heather smiled. She was back in her role as the family problem-solver and example of sanity. But now, rather than being thrust upon, she was ready and equipped.

"What do you think they're doing now? It's all gone very quiet." Emer smirked mischievously.

"I dunno. I hope it's not 'making-up sex'." Heather pulled a face.

"Will I look?"

"Go on then. But, if Dermot's naked, I don't want to know."

Emer stood up and tiptoed back over to the door and peered through the gap.

"They're both still sitting on the coffee table. Dermot's got his arms around Kitty's shoulders, but, thank God, they're both still wearing their clothes." Emer gave the thumbs-up signal.

"Is she still crying?"

"I don't think so."

"See. I told you everything would end happily." Heather spoke louder than she intended.

The two sisters then heard the front door open and close.

"That'll be Dad at last," Emer gushed as she yanked open the kitchen door. "Thank fuck! I couldn't take any more."

Emer and Heather barged past each other in order to get back into the living-room first. Kitty was by herself.

"Was that Dad coming in?" Heather asked, scanning the room.

"No – Dermot going out," Kitty answered abruptly.

"Where's he gone?" Emer ran over to the window to see if she could see him. The gate had been left open, allowing a glimpse of Merlin's rusty bumper and bedraggled, pockmarked bonnet.

"He's left me," Kitty answered, staring at an empty bowl besides her.

# Chapter 50

The sound of a key tapping on the front door was ignored for a while. Heather eventually opened it, relieved that this time, at last, it was their father. The journey had left Roddy Farrell slightly out of breath and he had to take a few big gulps of air before shuffling up the front step and into the house.

"How long were you going to leave me waiting out there? I was about to leave." His strong cockney accent had lost little of its richness in the thirty-four years he'd been living in Ireland. But his once native Jamaican twang, which he brought to his adoptive family as a ten-year-old, had long since disappeared. He stepped into the living-room and onto the bunch of keys on the floor, which he then lifted.

He was more than adequately protected from the chill of the April shower with layer upon layer of cotton, wool and waterproof fabrics. His pure white Afro was clipped short, but a pencil-thin moustache still had splashes of ebony. Roddy took off his overcoat and shook it before coming in.

He then folded it inside out and gave it to his eldest daughter, along with the keys. She put the keys back in the keyhole. But he held tightly onto the A4 sized parcel he was carrying, which was wrapped up in a supermarket plastic bag and tied securely with string.

Roddy Farrell could sense the tension in the air, as his daughters fussed around the living-room without really doing anything. But he was slowly learning the lesson not to interfere with any of his daughters' lives.

Heather rallied everyone together, ordering Kitty to put the kettle on and Emer to make more sandwiches. She herself led her father into the kitchen, bombarding him with information about nothing in particular. Kitty and Emer's tasks eased the tension slightly. As Roddy Farrell stretched his back against the kitchen chair, his three daughters buzzed around him, occasionally tripping over each other.

He couldn't remember the last time the four of them had been together, alone. There had been his grandchildren's birthdays and festival holidays, but there were always other people around, including Dermot and Tommy.

"Where's the menfolk?" he asked, puffing slightly.

Kitty checked that the kettle was boiling and Emer provided a second opinion.

"I don't think they're too interested in giving Merlin his big send-off." Heather decided that this half-truth would postpone any indelicate explanations. "He doesn't mean as much to them as he does to us."

Roddy took out an inhaler from his back pocket and sucked on it greedily.

"So, you do like the old banger after all?" Roddy asked, his usual, languid delivery returning.

"Oh, we've a love-hate thing going on." Heather smirked. "We're the same age for one thing. Seeing him sent to the scrapyard makes me think about my own future."

"Don't worry, Heather, we've no plans to put you out of your misery just yet," Emer chipped in, as she dolloped lumps of cottage cheese onto thick wedges of bread.

"And Kitty, how do you feel about getting rid of him?" Roddy asked, slightly more tentatively.

"Getting rid of what?" Kitty's thoughts were elsewhere.

"Will you miss him?" Roddy tried again.

Kitty stared at the kettle as the steam poured out.

"Kitty!" Heather switched the 'off' button. "Dad's talking about the car."

"Yes. Yes, I will." Kitty turned around and the earlier look of resignation had gone. "I just regret not having the money to do him up again, the way I did before."

"Well, there's no time for regrets now, when he's all but been squished and recycled into a Fiesta," Emer volunteered as she sneakily chewed on chunks of Swiss Roll.

"And you have no regrets, Emer?" Roddy asked, drawing a fingertip along the line of his moustache. "You don't want to keep him this time?" He had a commanding presence.

"I can't afford to run him, any more than Kitty can. And I don't believe in karma any more. If you give out good karma, you're not guaranteed to get the good stuff back again. If anyone should keep him, it's our Heather. She's got the money –" Emer was happy to keep going, but Heather interrupted her.

"But not the inclination, I'm afraid. Too many bad experiences, bad dreams and too many roadside recoveries for my liking."

"So, you're all agreed then? You want me to take him to the scrapyard. Well, I brought him into this family and I can easily take him out!" Roddy slapped his hand against the kitchen table, to emphasise the finality of the decision.

The three sisters jumped with the suddenness of the thud, but said nothing.

Heather then disappeared into the living-room and reappeared seconds later, carrying the bunch of keys and key-rings. She pulled off the front-door key and threw the bunch onto the kitchen table.

"Look, the scrapyard closes in an hour," she said. "Take him and have done with him!" The others just nodded their heads in agreement.

"OK, then." Roddy lifted the keys and inspected each of the key-rings that belonged to each of the sisters. His eyesight wasn't as good as it used to be and without his reading-glasses and even holding them out at arm's length, he couldn't really make out which belonged to which daughter.

Roddy supported himself against the table as he began to stand again. Kitty put her hand on his arm to assist him. She expected him to push it away, in his usual obstinate manner. But he didn't.

"Hang on a minute, Dad." Kitty sat down beside him. "What about the package you said you had for us all to see?"

"Maybe there isn't time to show you." Roddy tried to stand again. "We could do it another –"

"Yes, there is." Kitty was determined. There were going to be no more outstanding surprises after today was over. "What is it?"

Roddy lifted the wrapped package from his knee and

began to untie the string knot. His mahogany hands were rough and dry and his white palms etched with scars from years of outdoor work. The knots were awkward, but the sisters expected an offer of help would have been rejected.

"It's just some things I've been gathering together over the past couple of years." He struggled with the string. "You know, to stop myself going mad with boredom after I retired. I've been hunting out old photographs. Some belonged to us and I found them stuffed up in the attic. Others, well, I had to do a bit more research. I was up at the Central Library getting one of them today."

Roddy eventually loosened the knot, as Emer and Heather also took seats around the table. Once it was open, Roddy took some envelopes out of the plastic bag and laid them on the kitchen table, in a line. There were three in total. He lifted the first one, which was the oldest, most battered envelope and had childlike crayon scribbles all over it.

"I don't know what possessed me to bury these away. I guess, I must have decided that they would upset you three, if I had them lying around." He paused. "No, that's not true. I knew that they would upset me."

The sisters looked at each other in disbelief at their father's acknowledgement of something which he would have seen as a weakness.

"These are for you, Emer." He passed the envelope over to his middle daughter.

The photos were more brown and beige than black and white and were mostly group photographs of the three Farrell sisters, with their mother and father.

"I've never seen these before!" Emer stared at the images with astonishment. "I thought we only had a couple of photographs of her on her own." In particular, she was drawn to the youthful image of their mother, whose face was so like her own. "If I remember rightly, your line has always been 'we didn't have money for photographs in those days'. She looks gorgeous!" Emer drooled.

"She's beautiful," Kitty added, softly. "And look at Dad."

Kitty was the first to realise that, even though they had seen very few images of their mother in her prime, they had seen none of their father. He was a strikingly handsome man. And the contrast of his blackness and strong presence, against the pale smallness of their mother was even more remarkable.

"What an odd couple you must have been in those days!" said Kitty, placing a hand back on her father's arm. Only this time, she wasn't merely trying to offer a steadying hand.

"That's one way of putting it," Roddy smiled.

"You must have been such a novelty when you first came to Northern Ireland." Emer laughed, studying the images of herself as a skinny youngster, with everything she wore matching, including the bows on her socks.

"I didn't mind the kids coming up to me in the streets, just wanting to touch my skin." Roddy squeezed the skin on the back of his hand, which stayed pinched for longer than even he expected. "That was kind of nice. But . . . your mother was the one who always felt like an outsider."

"So, why did you stay here – especially after Mum died?" Kitty asked nervously. "Why didn't you just move the whole family back to England or to the Caribbean? Why stay here, of all places?" She sounded desperate.

"Because this was your home." Roddy beamed. "And my home was wherever you three were." He looked slightly embarrassed and then added, "And I was stubborn. It's a

413

genetic condition." He self-consciously chuckled, which caused him to cough.

Heather fetched him a glass of water.

The Farrell sisters' own feelings of isolation, of being unusual and never quite fitting in, only now seemed real as they stared at the sepia images of their parents. The family had rarely spoken about their past, as if they didn't have one. It had always embarrassed the daughters and had pained the father.

Emer, in particular, was disturbed by what she saw in the photographs that had been given to her. She had begun to think that she hadn't a chance at a functional relationship, having come from what she always perceived to be such a dysfunctional family. But on every photograph before her, whether on the beach, formally posed, or larking about in the garden, their father always held their mother's hand, not in the conventional way, but always with the fingers interlocked, the way William held hers. Her father and her mother were physically as odd a couple as Emer felt that William and herself were. But there was no denying from the photographs – they fitted perfectly.

Roddy unsealed the second envelope, which was covered in brightly covered stamps.

"And, since I was looking at the past, I thought, why not go back even further? This is for you, Heather." He poured out one, A5 photograph, turned downwards. "I got in contact with an agency on the Internet that helps people trace their families. It appears that when I was brought over for adoption all those years ago, I left a half-sister behind." He turned the colour photograph over. "And this, girls, is her: your Aunt Felicia."

The three sisters stared down at the grey-haired old lady, beaming broadly as she sat on the front porch of a massive colonial mansion. She had a cheeky smile, as if she'd just been allowed that moment's indulgence, before she was ushered back to her chores in the kitchen. Her dress was an avalanche of brightly coloured flowers and there was no mistaking the distinctive 'Farrell' nose.

"I can't believe it. Look at the house – does she work there?" Emer's interest lay in the bricks and mortar and the hope of tracing her own obsession with domestic duties to that of her aunt. Emer now had a preoccupation with her past, as well as her future.

"Kind of," Roddy nodded. "I think she keeps an office there. She's the ex-Chief of Police. That's her home." He sat back in his chair, proud. "She's retired now."

This one photograph conjured up a thousand images to the sisters, of an aspect of their heritage and their culture long since denied to them. They each often felt disadvantaged by the bi-cultural divisions in Ireland and now they could see they had their own culture to be proud of.

Heather was the only one of the Farrell sisters to see in the eyes of the old lady a woman who was confident, independent and strong.

"But why now, Dad, after all these years?" Kitty asked.

"I don't know really." Roddy tossed the remaining package from hand to hand. "I suppose you've all gone and got on with your lives. And done a grand job – despite me." He swallowed hard. "I felt lonely."

No one chose to ask Roddy to define 'grand job'. They could disappoint him later.

"Let me guess what the last envelope contains – pictures

of cousins, second cousins, nieces, that sort of thing?" Emer asked cheerfully. Her face was beaming as if she had been given a new store-card.

"No, your aunt never married. I've no other photos from Jamaica." Roddy began to peel back the seal on the unmarked, plain white envelope. "No, this is a photograph I took way back in the early seventies. Well, it's not a photograph as such – it's a newspaper article that includes the photograph I sent them. I never kept the negative, so I thought the photo had long since been lost. But I found the article today, in the library. It's got nothing to do with the other photographs I've shown you, but I thought you girls would like to see it." Roddy emptied the envelope out onto the table and a folded sheet of white paper fell out. He unfolded it and lay it out for all to see.

Kitty read the headline:

*"Dopey Dick is Free."*

The photograph Roddy had taken all those years ago was of the Craigavon Bridge in Derry with, just underneath it, the dorsal fin of a Killer Whale.

"When was this taken?" Emer asked, too impatient to read the text.

"In the seventies. I was doing some building work there and I used to take my camera everywhere in those days. One day, I was just about to cross the army checkpoint at the centre of the bridge, when this bloody great whale appeared on the surface of the river." Roddy graphically imitated the movement of the creature with his hand. "I thought I was seeing things at first, but then a whole gang of folks saw it too and we crammed the bridge trying to get a second look." Their father was as excited in re-telling the story, as he had been in being there nearly three decades ago. "He was absolutely amazing. The Orca had followed a shoal of salmon right up the River Foyle. The army at the time had booms across the river, either side of the bridge, to stop bombs being floated on it towards the bridge. With his sonar, the whale couldn't see a way past them and he got trapped in the stretch of river between them. The locals called him Dopey Dick. But I didn't – I called him a miracle." Roddy looked up towards the heavens. "He was there for weeks." Roddy's exuberance calmed. "His dorsal fin, that had been so proud when I first took this picture, eventually began to droop. He began to look very depressed."

"How did he get out?" Heather asked, transfixed by the faded image.

"The army gave permission to open the seaward boom and they got a boat loaded with salmon and guided him out." Roddy used his hand again, to imitate the motion of the whale as it swam away.

"And he was free?" Kitty nodded vigorously.

"Well, a whale was found beached on the shore shortly after." Roddy's hand stopped moving.

"Oh, no!" All three sisters groaned.

"But that wasn't him." Roddy smiled. "I'm sure of it. There was a story later of a fishing boat almost being turned over by what they thought was a big shark. I'm sure that was Dopey. There were loads of sightings afterwards of an Orca out there. He was still alive all right." Roddy added with utmost confidence, "He most likely hunted off the Antrim coast before heading further north."

"So, there are whales out there?" Kitty gasped.

The sense of hope, even against the highest probabilities,

instilled the hearts of Kitty, Emer and Heather. While no one was looking, Kitty took the sheet of paper and folded it, until it was the right size to fit into the cup of her bra.

Emer was the first to notice the time.

"Shit, it's only ten minutes before the scrap-yard closes! You'd better get a move on, Dad!"

Roddy collected his coat and led the way out of the front door and down to the gate. His daughters followed like ducklings. There was a break in the shower and Merlin had a shield of freshly fallen raindrops, caught in each of the dents in his bodywork. The pearlescent sheen from the gold paint had long since faded.

"I didn't think it was fair to leave Merlin out. After all, he's been part of the family for some time." Roddy tapped the old car's roof, gently, with his daughters' bunch of keys. "So, I kept a photograph for him too."

From out of his damp coat pocket, Roddy pulled out a small photograph, taken when he was restoring Merlin for Kitty's eighteenth birthday. The car's engine lay on the ground and his door panels were missing. The bonnet was open and the straw bed, where the litter of kittens had been, was still there, but empty. Roddy passed the photograph around, for all his daughters to see, but they didn't appear interested. They were each far too pre-occupied with their own thoughts for the future right now, to be bothered with a heap of junk that belonged to their past.

"I was just thinking," Roddy ventured, not sure if anyone was listening. "Would anyone mind if I held onto Merlin? He would give me something to do, now that I've got time on my hands. You know, do him up a bit – spend some time on him." He rubbed his hands together, partly to keep them warm. "This old man," he patted the roof and then his own chest, "could be this old man's retirement project."

There were no objections.

As Roddy bent over, to look inside, he could see the reflection of himself and his daughters behind him, in the scratched side window. The rusting door panel surrounded their blurred images. The Farrell family fitted the frame, perfectly.

"Then, you never know, maybe my grandchildren can have their own adventures in him when they're older." Roddy breathed on the window and polished it with his coat sleeve. "Hello again, Merlin," he smiled.

There were no objections.

## THE END

THE END